Lunar Dust, Martian Sands

by
Tom Chmielewski

TEC Publishing
Kalamazoo, Michigan, USA

Lunar Dust, Martian Sands
Copyright 2014 by Tom Chmielewski
ISBN 978-0-9815338-3-4

Published July 2014

Cover and book design: TEC Publishing
Cover Illustration: (c) 1971yes | Dreamstime.com

Also by Tom Chmielewski

Audio Drama
    Shalbatana Solstice (prequel to *Lunar Dust, Martian Sands*)

Non-fiction
    The Complete Idiot's Guide to Barter and Trade Exchanges, with Jerry Howell

About the Author

A long-term journalist who grew up in Detroit, Tom Chmielewski has worked in newspapers, magazines, publishing and online content. He is also a life-long fan of science fiction. He attended the Clarion Writers' Workshop, the oldest workshop of its kind for writers of fantasy and science fiction. *Lunar Dust, Martian Sands*, is his first novel.

You can read more of his musings about Sci-Fi, science, space exploration and other topics at *MartianSands.com*.

Acknowledgments

This novel began in northern Michigan near the Lake Huron shore during a rare time when all I had to do was write for myself. But a book is not created by just oneself. I must give a special thanks to Gina C. Pecora, an editor and friend who I've worked with periodically for many years. I would send her copies of chapters, and she would call me from Denver to read out loud, with dramatic impact, sections she liked, and ripped sections that needed work. Gina has been a driving force to bring the novel to publication.

Many more colleagues and friends have read and critiqued the work, and offered much encouragement and direction. To all of them, I say thank you.

Contents

CHAPTER I

The Colors of Earth

Colors always got to Ed after lunar landing. Not on approach, mind you. Arcing in from orbit, the moon below was as breathtakingly gray as ever, blinding in sunshine, deceiving in shadow.

The human outcroppings of Tranquility Center – the white surface hangars, landing pads, power grids – nearly all the visible hints of the mostly underground settlement clashed as alien rectangles against the circular lunarscape. The robot miners plowed straight but shallow strips across the Sea of Tranquility, stripping the lunar dust of the precious helium-3 that fueled the fusion drives to Mars and beyond, left there by the solar wind over billions of years. Humans had trod in that dust for only a little more than a hundred years, but the news from Earth said a growing number of people thought that century of dusty Moon boots was enough. As for Mars, Ed and other Martians feared they could end up abandoned, or worse, forced to return to Earth.

Enjoy the view while you can, Ed thought, the cockpit's wraparound view-screens screens showing the rapid approach of the lunar surface beneath him.

"*Cydonia Zach*, Tranquility Center. We read you on the mark, Ed."

"Roger, Tranquility," Ed answered and clicked off. "Now all I have to do is ride this tug down and find out what cargo is so vital it deserves a special run – and why no one will tell me what it is." The bigger questions would have to wait.

That color thing – it didn't hit Ed immediately after landing, either. As Ed's tug sank into the airlock on the elevator pad, and the doors above the ship slid into place, there were the sounds that struck Ed first, sounds that for the first time since he left Mars came from outside the ship. They began muted but urgent: air rushing against the hull in a barely audible hiss, growing to a raspy roar as the pumped-in atmosphere replaced the sound deadening vacuum. Quickly the rush of air shut off, replaced by the harsh, unnerving clangs of metal against metal as the lower bay doors unlocked and opened to the loading docks beyond. The squat ground transport below the tug, silent on the surface except for vibrations through the hull when it slipped into place, now kicked into a loud whine as it carried the tug and its cargo module toward the docks.

A few colors slipped into view: flashing yellow lights from the transport, olive green coveralls and bright orange vests of the dock workers, signals that flashed red or shone a solid green over doors, cranes and other gear.

Ed stepped out of the *Zach* after it reached the loading bay, and the industrial colors mingled with the whirs and groans of equipment, the warning siren of the overhead crane as it moved above the cargo module, and the echoing calls of workers. But they were only different in degree from similar scenes on Mars, Ceres, even the moons of Jupiter. The smell of machines, graphite, sweat, was only a bolder extension of the tainted recycled air of the tug. It was technology and industry in combat against vacuum and radiation, fought out across the solar system.

Ed checked in with customs, signing and thumb printing electronic forms on screens recessed in the gray counter-top, while just beyond the office window the crane lifted off the cylindrical cargo module he just signed for.

It really hit him after the customs procedures and security checks, when he walked down the tunnel and into the Commons to face a rising curtain of color, sound, and motion.

In a wave, the colors of Earth washed over him, worn on the backs of tourists, students, researchers, greeting them all on the walls of shops that sold gear, photos, art, and dreams of space. There were the greens – the neon greens of dyed hair on the young, the dark greens of pullover shirts worn by nervous administrators.

There were the reds and purples on the jackets of Asian tour groups, the light sepia checks and burnt orange stripes on the shirts of European scientists.

There were the blues – the dark blue, the light blue, the sky blue, the ocean blue, reproduced on posters, painted walls, shirts and ID badges, neckties, scarves and bracelets. And hanging in permanent display in the sky beyond the transparent Grand Arch of the Commons, blue Earth.

Ed always stopped for a split second, letting the color receptors of his eyes recalibrate as he took in the three floors of the Market Commons. The noise, on the other hand, wouldn't wait. After the gentle but constant buzz and clicks on the *Zach*, the voices of too many conversations to distinguish, too many languages to decipher, overwhelmed him. Only bits of conversation slipped through as he walked into the crowd.

"The hydroponic vegetables are so bland ...."

"She didn't want to take the flight at first. Now she wants to come back when she's in college and ...."

"You know, Sen. Decker says we should chuck all this. Nobody knows him yet, but I may vote for him. I'm just glad I got here before...."

"That ore strike was a bust. The deposit lay only on the surface, left there by another asteroid, I suppose ...."

"Mars is overrated. The restaurants are great, but the hotels ...."

"... sucked all the air out of the cabin. Some idiot ...."

Ed was curious about the idiot, and angry at the tourist who went to Mars for the hotels. What do you expect for a tourist season that lasts for four months every two Earth years? But he continued on through the congestion and confusion. Signs – lighted, animated, bold, multi-lingual – pleaded in audio for anyone's attention.

"Surface tours twice a day. Take your own giant leap. AAA discount."

"Lunar Liquor – Best prices, local distillery."

"For your safety, jumping between floors is prohibited."

Ed had to pick his way through the crowd across the commons. The smell of spices, faux coffee, lush plants and all those people turned his senses as much as the bodies blocked his path.

"Martian leather?" A female voice, young, clear against the background.

"That's for me," Ed thought. He started to turn, remembered to smile, and faced her. Young indeed; blond, slight build, a college student on a study grant most likely. Her face shone in the heavily filtered beam of the setting sun slipping through the ceiling panels, a sun that wouldn't reach the horizon for another two days.

"Where did you get your jacket?" she asked, a bit too eager to have been on the Moon long.

"I got mine on Mars." Ed tried not to sound too rehearsed. The jacket was a light, casual design, with a small 4th Orbit logo, the numeral next to the circle and arrow symbol for Mars, stamped over the breast pocket. "But I just landed with a new shipment for the Mars Emporium," nodding to the storefront across the way. "I bring in most of their stuff from Mars and the Belt."

"You're a pilot?"

What could he say? It's a job. He wouldn't want to do anything else, but mostly Ed saw it as getting paid to push buttons and watch readouts – and to be an interplanetary pitchman on those few days between weeks of spaceflight. "Yeah, I run a tug, the *Cydonia Zach*, mostly on the inner orbit routes from Mars to the Asteroid Belt and here. The Emporium gets the pick of my cargo. You should check it out."

"Are you going there?"

"I'll be there in a few minutes. Go ahead."

She turned and darted through the crowd, a bit too fast. She didn't have her lunar legs yet, and an older woman, a staffer, had to catch her from tumbling. She made a quick glance back to see if the pilot had seen her gaffe, but Ed turned his head and pretended not to notice.

"And another hero worshiper is born, or at least made," said a new voice with a French accent, one that made Ed smile without having to think about it.

"Paul! I was hoping to run into you down here."

"Not in the same way that girl runs into people, I hope," Paul answered, smiling broadly as he extended a hand which Ed warmly grasped.

Paul and Ed had been friends since they roomed together on a Jupiter education-research expedition a decade earlier. Paul Cherault, then 22, had just come up from France on an EU grant. Ed was two years older as counted on Earth. He was born in Canada, and even though Ed spent his teen years on Mars when his parents moved there, he still spoke enough French to strike up a bond with Paul.

They remained friends even after their paths diverged. Paul looked his part as the corporate tech. He wore standard, sharply creased, deep blue coveralls with an Asteroid Technologies patch over the left breast pocket. He was thin, hair closely trimmed, clean shaven.

"Your uncle still wants you to have that rugged, space pilot look, I see," Paul said.

"Hey, I would have shaved before I landed, but my uncle thinks the look reinforces the romance of space."

"In order to lure unsuspecting young girls to the Emporium to buy exotic goods?"

"You can't get more exotic than Mars."

"Do Martian cows really make that much of a difference in the leather?" Paul chided. "The lighter gravity makes it more supple, I suppose?"

"A cow's a cow. But you don't see anyone spending their weight allowance shipping leather jackets up from Earth, do you?"

"You do not see many people wearing jackets up here. The enclosed environment never changes more than a degree."

"It's all marketing. But hey, you saved me a trip to your lab. Here's the sample you ordered," Ed said, handing over a small sealed box.

"I am sorry if it is my fault you came so late in the window. I did not know it was you who would take the ore shipment contract."

"Astech's paying a good premium for a rush order. Somebody on Earth wants this really bad."

"This ore, it is impossible to find down there. Our customer has some process where only this will do, if the grade is as good as the miners say it is. It will not take me long to certify this sample. Meet you for dinner?"

"Sure, but it can't be a long night. I take off tomorrow."

"So soon?"

"I wish it wasn't. Spent so much time on that damn tug this trip, I wish I could have at least a couple of days layover. But I'm pairing with a passenger run, the last transit on the schedule this window."

"Of course. But Marta is cutting your schedule a little thin, no?"

"More so than usual. I'm going to the Emporium now to find out why."

"You think she will deign to tell you? She runs quite a shipping empire for your uncle from behind that art shop. I suspect even he doesn't know how she does it."

"He doesn't want to know. He has too much else going on. Let's meet at the Apollo at 7. I have some wine my uncle wants the chef to try."

"Better than the last batch, I hope."

"It's getting better," Ed said, not to convincingly, "but we won't be shipping to Earth anytime soon."

Paul laughed. "My parents will be relieved. *Ce soir, doc.*"

Paul headed off for his lab, and Ed turned back for the Emporium, his jacket drawing a few more stares as he went.

All the stores at that end of the Commons targeted the tourists and short-timers, but the Emporium specialized in Mars and the Asteroid Belt, selling a classier, higher-priced slice of romance that attracted long-term lunar staffers as well.

Marta kept the store a little dark to force shoppers to slow down when they entered to let their eyes adjust. She arranged her display shelves and half-walls in an irregular maze, making a shopper explore the space rather than just casually look. Sculptures proved the most popular among the artwork, carved and polished stone that once lay half buried in Martian sand or drifted free amid a ruin of rocks halfway to Jupiter. Many were in a sharp-edged modern style dubbed Post Earth. Others were naturalistic, and Ed saw that the *Zach*'s sister ship, Wayfarer, had delivered a new line of religious icons from the Franciscan mission on Mars. They sold surprisingly well in an engineering and science community.

"Is Marta here?" Ed asked the clerk behind the counter.

"Out back," she answered. "She's waiting for you." The clerk turned her attention back to the girl asking about the jackets as he stepped around to the stock room.

Marta's a short, thin woman in her early 60s, or so most people thought. She wasn't born on the Moon, but no one could remember a time when she wasn't there. The story is she married a researcher, researching what is unclear, but when he went back to Earth, she stayed. Marta held a variety of jobs, but had a knack for arranging things that others couldn't. She had been arranging shipments between Mars and the Moon for years when Ed's uncle set her up as a subsidiary of his expanding 4th Orbit Enterprises, with the Mars Emporium its most public face in Earth orbit.

Ed found her on a stool, scowling at a computer panel. The shop's back area opened onto the cargo tunnels that led to the docks. The rear overhead door was open, and part of the shipment Ed just brought in for the Emporium was already sitting in front of Marta, waiting to be uncrated. Ed was relieved to see her scowl soften when she saw him.

"Ed, nice job on the ore shipment. They just docked the module at L-1, and only need the certification before sending it to Earth."

"I just gave the test sample to Paul," Ed said, resting against a counter and leaning back to steal another glimpse at the girl out front.

"Sorry I had to bounce you around so much in the Belt to make the trip pay off."

"Hmm? Oh, yeah. You know, if I had just sat at that asteroid while they dug the stuff out, it would have paid off for the price Astech put on it."

"Just sitting around on your butt never pays off. The extra deliveries in the Belt while Astech was digging was pure profit for all of us."

Ed put up his hands in surrender. "OK, OK. So what's the special delivery you have for me to take back to Mars?"

Marta jabbed her thumb to her right and behind. "Her."

A woman sat at a small table, mostly blocked from view by an over-flowing, free-standing shelf until Ed took a couple steps back. She wore a loose, tan suit that showed off her figure without bragging about it. Her hair was dark, short. Ed took her to be in her mid-30s, maybe a touch older. He turned back to Marta.

"You're having me haul a passenger module back?"

Marta didn't look up from the screen. "You're not. Just her."

"But where am I'm going to put her?"

"You've got an extra bunk in the *Zach*. That'll do. Hey Frank! What's the deal with the S-47 drill?"

A beleaguered voice came from around the corner. "They said it will be here this afternoon."

"They've been saying that for three days now. Call them back and tell them I'm locking up the module by six. If that drill isn't here in two hours, I'm selling the space to another shipment, and they lose their deposit."

"All right, I'll take care of it."

Ed leaned over her screen. "Marta, that passenger run I'm pair-ing with tomorrow isn't full. Why doesn't she just buy a ticket on that?"

"Actually, I did have a reservation with that run," came a voice from behind him with a trace of a British accent. Ed turned to face the woman. She held out her hand. "Faizah Westerhof."

"Oh, um, sorry. I didn't hear you walk up," Ed answered, returning the handshake. "So – why aren't you taking the passenger run?"

"It's best I not publicize my departure from the Moon."

"Really? Why?"

Faizah said nothing.

Ed stared back and waited for an agonizingly slow moment until Marta finally spoke up. "Ed, on this one, don't tell anyone you're carrying a passenger, and don't ask her why she's going with you. If your uncle wants you to know, he'll tell you when you get to Mars."

"That's right, Carl Chubeck is your uncle." Faizah said, then turned to Marta. "Is that why you juggled schedules, Marta, so Mr. Ferald here would take me? Family keeps better secrets." She turned back to Ed, her green eyes sharp and cold. "At least, you'd better."

"Not much of a secret to keep if no one lets me in on it. Do you know when we take off tomorrow?"

"Marta and I agreed to meet here at 4:30 in the morning."

"Four-thirty!? Marta, We don't launch until 11."

"Nobody launches until 11, and the last launch overnight is at 2," Marta said. "No one will be in the docks at that hour, so no one will see her get on board. Technically, she's crew and certified by 4-O, so she clears security – as soon as we get around to forwarding the forms."

"What about Mars customs?"

"By then it's too late," Faizah said. "If we can keep the deception going longer, fine. If not, there won't be another Mars trip for two years."

"Can you tell me what it's too late for?"

"No." Faizah turned and headed for the back door without waiting for a reply. "I will see you tomorrow morning."

"Friendly, isn't she?" Ed said.

"You have a month to get acquainted," Marta said, "but I wouldn't get your hopes up. She's all business."

"And I'm not?"

"I'm busy," she said, brusquely. "Get out of here, and don't be late in the morning."

Ed shrugged, and headed back into the storefront on his way to leave. But he didn't quite make the door.

"Are you leaving already?" said the girl from the commons, rushing up to intercept him. "I was hoping you'd help me out on picking a jacket."

"All business," Ed muttered to himself.

○○○○○○○○○○

As Faizah left the Emporium, she decided Ed Ferald seemed competent enough. Of course she knew he was Chubeck's nephew as soon as he spotted him and her face recognition program displayed his I.D. on her contacts. Marta assured her earlier that the pilot represented the good side of nepotism and he would keep quiet about her passage on the *Zach*.

Faizah hoped her regular stops at the Emporium since she'd been back on the Moon the past month would prevent anyone interested in her travel plans from connecting them to her latest visit. A slim hope. As she left the shop, someone grabbed her arm.

"So, you are launching on the *Zach*."

"Alan!" She was more angry than surprised. "Should we be discussing this in the Commons?"

"Why not?" Alan said. Tall, medium build, black hair, thin mustache. He kept hold of her arm and leaned in close. "Everyone in here's talking. No one's listening."

"Someone may be."

"Let's walk, Faizah. No one will pick us up in this noise. I was expecting to hear from you sooner."

"I didn't want to call. Encryptions can be broken, even ours."

"Not a chance," he said. "You took more of a risk going to the Emporium."

"The owner's my client," Faizah said, not even trying to hide her annoyance. "Avoiding the place would raise more suspicion. Besides, Marta only has to tighten security on the tug and the remaining cargo module we lift off with tomorrow. It'll be all right."

"I hope so. The politics behind this are taking much too nasty a turn. Did you see the latest from Sen. Decker?"

"You mean the new accusations he's been throwing at anyone connected with space? That's to be expected as part of his run up."

"The pollsters are starting to take notice."

"It's about time, but they're still not asking the right questions."

"My client is, and I imagine so is yours."

Faizah angrily pulled her arm out of his grasp. "I'll worry about my client. You worry about yours."

"But you have a plan to stop Decker?"

"It's not my plan, and as for what it is, you know the rules."

"All right," Alan, raising his hands slightly in resignation. "We don't need that discussion again. But you will deliver the package I sent you? You can do that much for my client?"

"I said I'd do it, and I will."

"You know, Faizah, we really would make a great team."

"Goodbye, Alan"

ᴑᴑᴑᴑᴑᴑᴑᴑᴑᴑ

The chef at the Apollo swirled the red wine, then stuck his nose into the glass. Finally, he took a sip, swished the wine some more in his mouth, and since he couldn't spit it out in the middle of the restaurant, swallowed, then shook his head. "Your vintner is getting better, Ed. The grapes are improving. The white is quite good, and the red is passable. But I would never serve this at my New York restaurant."

"Your New York restaurant has its pick of any wine of Earth, but you're not paying to ship those cases up here," Ed said.

"But we do have a good brewer on Luna, and the beer you send us from Mars is excellent," the chef answered. "I can't believe I'm defending beer with my meals, but an excellent beer is better than a passable wine."

Ed put down his own glass. "Perhaps, but your customers expect wine, at least the tourists do. How can they resist the panache of a "Martian wine"? I brought you two cases to try out, no charge. See if your customers like it. If they do, place an order. We'll have a full run ready for next window."

"All right, I will take your wine." The chef drained the remnants and set the glass down on the table. "But I won't recommend it to my best customers." He turned toward a nearby waiter and snapped his finger. "Ramone, the glass."

Paul laughed as the chef walked away, and the waiter hurriedly removed his glass. "Ed, you're getting better at this every trip – a wine dealer tonight, a model for your uncle's tailor this afternoon."

"It's part of the job these days."

"Since when? You used to want to be a pilot."

"I'm also an agent for 4th Orbit. If 4-O doesn't sell stuff, I have nothing to pilot."

Paul finished the rest of his wine and grimaced. "4-O Transit handles more than its own product. Anyway, other companies would want to hire you for more pay."

Ed began to raise his glass to finish it off, then thought better of it. "You know something the rest of the solar system doesn't? Pilot seats are getting pretty limited."

"There's a new seat opening up at Astech."

That surprised him. "Is that an offer?"

"Not my department. But it is, let us say, an official feeler. I was supposed to ask if you were interested. It would be quite a bit more money."

"I thought Astech was committed to slow robot haulers for most of its shipping."

"It still is, but things like that rush ore shipment you made for us keep popping up all the time: equipment replacements, staff changes, science surveys. The company is building a new tug, and a dedicated constant-g drive for it so we don't have to depend on the leasing pool. You can take a look at it on your way out when you pick up your drive at L-1."

"I think I saw it when I dropped your ore shipment up there. Nice ship. Looks roomier than the *Zach*."

"It could be yours."

"Except it never would be mine, or even a piece of it. I'm really part of something with 4th Orbit, and it's more than just family."

"But with the bonuses Astech pays, you could invest in your uncle's business and still be a part of it, while drawing your paycheck from Earth."

"Not the same. Besides, I might complain about it, but actually I'm starting to like the sales part of this job. I'm part of the business rather than just pushing buttons and driving my ship to where I'm told – at least usually."

Paul paused a beat before responding. "Usually?"

"Never mind. It's a long story no one's told me yet."

"Ah, maybe not as much a part of the business as you wish?"

"It's still better than what I would have at Astech."

"Perhaps. But things are changing, exciting things. Worlds could open up for you if you're in a position to take advantage of it."

"From what I hear in the news, worlds will be closing down."

"Decker's not likely to get elected, and even if he does, Astech's protected. It's companies like 4th Orbit that would be at risk. Think about it, Ed, will you?"

"I will, but you'd have to tell me more."

"When I can. You'll hear from me. Now, let's get out of here and find a place that sells some of that 'excellent' Martian beer you just brought in, but at better prices than they sell it here."

"Not this trip, Paul." Ed pushed away from the table and stood up. Paul did the same. "I have to be at my ship at half past gawd-awful early tomorrow."

"I thought you said you were pairing with that passenger run. The *New Brunswick* doesn't launch until late morning."

"Neither do I. I have to get there early to secure some late cargo."

"Oh, it must be that last-minute shipment Marta was trying to arrange."

Ed tried not to show his surprise. "You heard of that?"

Paul seemed to brush it off as trivial. "Yes, I got a note from her this afternoon. She was trying to fill a spot on standby because somebody didn't get a shipment to her on time. Marta knew I was trying to send a last-minute shipment of my own. But I was able to get it aboard the *New Brunswick*. Somebody else must have filled your spot."

"Must have," Ed said, somewhat relieved, though he wished he had a better idea of why he should be. "I don't know the details. Marta only told me to be there early and make sure her last-minute cargo got on board."

CHAPTER 2
The Color of Money

"So what do we do, Marta – stuff her in a box and sneak her on board?"

"Ed, Don't be a smart ass at half past gawd-awful early," Marta said.

A cart was already loaded in the Emporium's back shop and waiting by the entrance to the loading dock. "The four of us will ride on the motor cart to the tug, go in and out loading a few small crates, Frank and I will go back and forth from here a few times, and Faizah goes on board and stays there. A careful look at the security cameras will show she stayed aboard, but no one's looking carefully this early."

Marta and Ed both had clearance to the loading dock, and no one would question them bringing in extra staff. As Marta entered her clearance code, everything looked normal. Security was high for people leaving Earth, but in space much of the responsibility was delegated to the shipping companies.

"You know, Marta, it's not against the law to bring along an extra crew member," Ed said, climbing onto the rear of the cart. Marta slipped behind the wheel.

"It's not the law we're worried about," Marta said. "We just don't want her trip to Mars to be common knowledge, at least not right away."

"Yeah, sure. It's just that of all the things my uncle and you have had me do, I've never smuggled people aboard the *Zach* before."

"We're expanding your horizons. Now shut up about it."

Faizah didn't say much. She didn't say anything. Her head moved casually, but Ed noticed her eyes shifted constantly in all directions, scanning to see if anyone spotted her. When the cart reached the tug, she got out quickly, grabbed a small box, and headed for the hatch.

"Frank, you and Ed grab that blue crate," Marta said as she took a dark brown duffel.

Frank and Ed each took an end and lifted, but even in Lunar gravity, it was heavy. "Geez, what's in here?" Ed said. "I thought we were doing this just for show."

Marta wheeled and looked ready to slug Ed with the duffel. She struggled to keep her rebuke to a whisper.

"Should we just get on the P.A. and wake up anyone who's dozing off down here to show off your secret passenger?"

Ed began to raise his arm to make an exaggerated show of warding off the duffel, but stopped when he saw the anger and fear in Marta's eyes.

"It's the new shipment that came in last night to replace that missing drill," she went on, a little calmer. "The dock crew was already done by the time it got here. They secured the outer door, so you and Frank need to haul it up through the *Zach* into the cargo module."

Ed didn't answer, but took the lead up the ladder into the tug's hatch. Once inside, the two men worked the crate up into the cargo module. Marta had left a space for it at the bottom of the module, and it slid in without much room to spare. But Ed stopped Frank from strapping it down. "I need to inspect that. I'll strap it down in a few minutes."

By the time they came back to the command deck, Marta had dumped the duffel on the tug's spare bunk. "Faizah, stay here," she said. "Frank and I will go back to the Emporium for some supplies we normally would have put on board last night." She turned to leave through the hatch, but Ed put a hand on her shoulder to stop her.

"Marta, you stay, too," he said, with no trace of the smart ass. "Frank, you go, and wait until Marta steps outside before you return."

Marta didn't protest and stepped away from the hatch. Frank shrugged and left. Ed closed the hatch behind him, then turned to face the two women. "Now, somebody had better tell me what's really going on."

Faizah looked annoyed. "I think Marta had it right last night. If your uncle wants you to know, he'll tell you when you get to Mars."

"No, that won't do," Ed said firmly and leaned against the hatch. "Marta's too uptight for this to be a simple business arrangement. As captain of the *Zach*, I have the right to know what I'm carrying and what risks are involved. I don't know who you are, but there are risks you aren't telling me about."

"You don't need to know who I am, and the risks are mine."

"Not the way I see it. As long as you're aboard, any risk to you may be a risk to me and my ship. I need to assess that risk."

"I'm afraid I'm not at liberty to tell you anything."

Ed stepped back and glanced at Marta, wondering how she would play it. Then he turned back to Faizah. "Then you'll have to find another way to Mars."

That caught Faizah by surprise. "You can't do that. My contract, my passage is with 4th Orbit. As a 4-O pilot, you have to follow orders. Even if he is your uncle, Chubeck would never let you get away with that."

"He can do it, and he would get away with it," Marta said quietly. "His uncle would be hopping mad, but he would back Ed up. It's his right as a ship's captain."

Faizah glared at Ed for a few seconds, her green eyes now hot with anger. Then she turned her head aside and slightly up toward the ceiling, thinking over her answer. When she spoke again, it was in a crisp, matter-of-fact tone. "I work with the firm InterCorporate Resources under contract with several space interests, including 4th Orbit. It's a private intelligence service, primarily for corporations. There are issues in play on Earth that will have a major impact out here, and they're coming to a head in next year's U.S. presidential election."

"Under contract as what, a political consultant?"

"Let's just leave it at consultant. But face it, there isn't much that gets people riled up more than politics, particularly when you throw new technology, budgets and space into the mix on a planet still trying to deal with poverty, wars and pollution. We spotted a trend no one else is onto yet, at least the so-called experts. The public's ahead of them, but even the pollsters read it as just noise."

"You mean Decker and next year's U.S. election, don't you?" Ed said.

"Yes. People up here are taking notice, but the smart money down on Earth hasn't moved, yet. The trends we read say it will. If those trends hold up, the results could be drastic for continued space operations. It could ruin what your uncle is trying to accomplish on Mars."

"So why is it so important for you to see my uncle?"

"Your uncle is key. He wields a great deal of back-channel influence in space and back on Earth. He's shown an amazing talent to use the system when it suits him, and to bypass the system when necessary to get things done his way. Many people respect him for it. Many fear him for it. And they aren't always different people. There are many parts of this crisis forming on Earth, but Chubeck will be at the center of that part which effects the Moon, Mars, the Belt, anything in space."

"Even so, why see him?"

"It's the timing. I could just send him a report, but there's a limit to how much you can trust the InterPlanet. The information would get out."

"So just give me a disk and I'll hand deliver it."

Faizah shook her head and sat down on the bunk. "It's not just the information. To act effectively, Chubeck feels he needs an ongoing discussion, not just with his cohorts and partners on Mars, but with someone who knows and has dealt with the situation daily on Earth. Someone to protect him, if it comes to that."

"And that would be you."

"That would be me. We thought it was too early for anyone to get wise to what we were doing. But someone found out I booked passage on the *New Brunswick*, and sent a message that" – she paused to give emphasis to her next words – "it would be dangerous if I took that ship to Mars. Don't ask who's behind the threat, because we don't know. It was forwarded to me by the people I work for on Earth. But if I don't go to Mars today, the regular passenger runs don't resume until the next launch window two years from now. Chubeck's effectiveness to act would be diminished, and other power brokers would have an advantage."

Marta had kept quiet, finding her own seat on the command deck. But now she joined in. "Could the threat be just a bluff?"

"We don't know," Faizah answered. "Since we don't know who's behind it, we don't know their capabilities, or their will to carry it out."

Ed was trying to take it all in, but with questionable success. "This is what I don't understand. If my uncle is one of the good guys, and I assume he is, who are the bad guys? Ultimately don't all of us out here want to keep things going and expanding in space?"

"I can't give you details yet, but understand it's not just us vs. them. There are many sides coming at this from many angles. It's not just a question of do we stay in space, but do we expand or cut back, who gets subsidized, who gets to turn a profit, who gets to benefit, who has to sacrifice? There are winners and losers no matter how this turns out, and everyone will be trying to cut themselves in on the winning hand. It may be a way of life for you, but it's also a matter of money, big money."

"And when it's a matter of money," Ed finished for her, "it becomes a matter of life and death."

"So, are we going to Mars?"

"As soon as I inspect that last minute cargo we loaded. And is that duffel your only luggage?"

"No. Marta had the rest loaded in the cargo module."

"You're not going to go through her luggage?" Marta protested.

"It's all right," Faizah assured here. For the first time Ed saw a touch of a smile. "Captain's prerogative, and probably a good one."

Faizah wasn't anxious for the tug pilot to go through her luggage, but he was professional and circumspect, looking only for anything explosive, leaving her clothes mostly undisturbed. Not that some of the lingerie in there couldn't throw some sparks, but Faizah let the thought drop – for the moment.

Ed was proving to be competent. She appreciated him taking the threat seriously. Faizah wanted to believe the threat was a bluff, but her colleagues seemed to think it could be real, particularly Alan. But then, he would.

Ed finished with her luggage without finding anything. Faizah was very careful about her luggage. The pilot didn't find any of her secrets either. The good ones were on coded disks. The best ones were in her head.

The late shipment turned out to be harmless as well, and Ed strapped everything back in.

"Are you sure you didn't tip anyone off about your plans?" Ed asked as the two climbed back down to the flight deck.

"Am I certain? No," Faizah answered. "But I took reasonable, even extraordinary precautions. To keep the ruse going, I have appointments at Tranquility Center for this afternoon and tomorrow, appointments the other parties will have to break because of emergencies I've arranged for them to have."

"I don't want to know how you did that, right?"

"No, you don't. There are a few people at InterCorporate who know my plans, of course. But to keep anyone who was interested guessing, I also booked a return flight to Earth in two weeks. We'll be well on the way to Mars by then."

Ed seemed satisfied, and Marta reassured as she wished them both a good trip. Ed settled into in his pilot's seat and dozed off until it was time to prep for lift-off. Faizah didn't doze. She patched into a couple of the loading docks' security cameras showing the *Zach's* exterior, but no one approached the *Zach* until the fueling crew arrived.

Neither flight control nor customs had any embarrassing questions about early morning activities as the time came to lock the ship down. The *New Brunswick* cycled through the airlock ahead of the *Zach*, and was waiting on Pad 3 by the time the *Zach* reached the surface. The ground transport moved the tug off the elevator platform and onto launch Pad 7 while Ed ran through pre-flight.

"How far ahead will the *New Brunswick* be by the time we leave orbit?" Faizah asked. She had taken the co-pilot's seat, but said little while Ed prepared for launch.

"We'll leave L-1 an hour apart. We both have extra cargo modules to pick up there, along with our fusion drives." Just then a small vid screen on the control panel brightened as a flash of light flooded the launch site from Pad 3, and the *New Brunswick* jumped silently off the moon's surface, the tug and the cylindrical passenger module above it speeding smoothly away toward the horizon.

"Roger, Tranquility." Ed switched off his mike and switched on the external screens. The cockpit's walls seemingly disappeared into a global view of the spaceport, the landing pad beneath the *Zach*, and the stars above them. The displays created the illusion of the two of them sitting in mid-air. No, that's not right, Faizah thought, but suspended above the surface except for deck's narrow gridwork. Ed pointed to a small ear set attached to the control display panel in front of Faizah. "Put this on so you can hear what's happening."

"Thanks," she said, "though I doubt I'll know what you're talking about. This is the first time I've been in a cockpit during launch."

"If something goes wrong, you'll know."

Nothing went wrong. Faizah listened to Ed and Tranquility Control run through a litany of switch positions and readouts that would appear on the opaque-glass control panel and clear heads-up display that partly wrapped around them. Faizah knew more than she let on, and could access the rest, but much of it was still baffling.

Yet everything was "nominal." It was mostly automated, but she knew pilots didn't leave it to computers or Tranquility Control to assure their safety. Launches were still tense. Not terrifying like the old days from Kennedy, but pilots never took them for granted. Ed concentrated on his readouts and his list as the clock ran down.

Faizah concentrated on her own list, her eyes by habit scanning the outside, though the threat wouldn't be from there. Had she avoided detection? Had someone figured it out and got to the ship ahead of her? Would her secret departure hold long enough to give them a real advantage; was the threat real or overblown? Blown, not a good word to think about right now.

The countdown reached 20 seconds. No one announces the passing seconds anymore, Faizah thought, but everyone always watches the clock. A steady tone went off at 10 seconds, but Faizah saw Ed didn't react. It must be normal. At five seconds the tone began to alternate with the changing digits on the display. At zero, a bright flash from below, a sudden pressure from above, and the lunar surface slipped away.

Not silently this time. The vibrations of the rocket motor echoed through the tug. The ship angled over on its arc, and the craters raced below them, shrinking as the *Zach* left the surface behind.

New numbers flashed on the displays. Velocity, altitude, fuel pressure. She glanced at Ed's face. It read nominal. She relaxed as the *Zach* gained altitude, and the Moon seemed safely far enough away. The engine cut out. No noise, no force pushing her into her seat. No lunch. Good thing, she thought as she swallowed hard, pushing the orange juice from that morning back down into her stomach. The com came alive.

"*Cydonia Zach*, Tranquility control. We show you in orbit. We're handing you over to L-1. Have a good trip to Mars, Ed. See ya' next window."

◇◇◇◇◇◇◇◇◇◇

The first space station built as a wheel to create artificial gravity was located at the nearly stable gravitation point at Lagrange 1 between the moon and the Earth. But it wasn't the grand space colony predicted by early visionaries of space exploration for the even more stable point at L5. The way station at L1 was big enough for about 100 workers and station staff, though the actual number present varied and was often much less, depending on ship building and maintenance activity scheduled. Extending from the hub of the wheel was a non-rotating gridwork of industrial modules and docking facilities that housed new vehicle construction and interplanetary shipping docks.

It was in the latter where the tugs refueled, took on their extra cargo modules, and docked with the fusion reactor drives. The drives, fueled by the Moon's Helium-3, provided the constant acceleration that shortened the trip to the planets from many months to a few weeks.

At its closest approach, with a light load, the trip to Mars could take about a month. At the back end of the launch window, it was a little longer, about half the trip acceleration, the other half deceleration, with some extra time for maneuvers to match orbits with the planet. The launch window occurred only every two Earth years. The extra distance outside the window required extra supplies and fuel for the trip, meaning extra weight that decreased acceleration, quickly lengthening the time it took to go to Mars, making it impractical and unprofitable for most traffic outside of slow robot haulers.

"Is that the *New Brunswick*?" Faizah asked, pointing to a tug-module configuration that was longer than she saw on Luna. It lay along the axis of one of the docking grids, with spindly clamps holding it in place.

"Yeah, that's her. They're hooking up her fusion drive now." The nozzles and fusion reactor were at one end of a long column that held an assembly of fuel tanks, thrusters, long-range communication/navigation gear, and a radiation shield.

Faizah didn't have long to look at it. Ed triggered a command and the *Zach*'s thrusters fired, swiveling the ship around until it was parallel with the docking grid. Another burn and the *Zach* lay motionless to the station. Ed switched on his mike.

"L-5 control, *Cydonia Zach*. On station."

"Roger *Zach*. Relax and we'll bring you in." Four small orbital tugs, each just big enough for a cockpit, grappling gear and thrusters, left the grid for the *Zach* to guide it into the dock.

"Do you really have time to relax?" Faizah herself felt more relieved now they were away from the Moon.

"I have to keep watch to make sure they don't dent up my ship, but yeah, I don't have anything to do at the moment."

"Then tell me something. Why the name *Cydonia Zach*?"

Ed laughed. "Have you heard of the Jackolope of the American West?"

"Somebody told me about it once when I was in New Mexico. Isn't that a mythical creature?"

"More like a tall tale, what old timers used to tell tenderfoots – newcomers to the West. It doesn't exist but it kept the newcomers going for a while and gave everyone else a laugh. *Cydonia Zach* is our version of that tall tale. *Zach* is the name Martians came up with years back for that face early pictures seemed to show in the Cydonia region of Mars. I'm sure my uncle was in on the start of it, making *Cydonia Zach* some kind of alien gremlin to blame for equipment breakdowns and mishaps, and to freak out rookies to Mars. Someone tagged the name on this tug when he bought it, and it stuck. As long as we're talking names, where does your name come from, and what does it mean?"

"It's Swahili for 'She who is victorious.' I grew up in South Africa."

"That must explain your last name as well – Westerhof."

"My grandfather was British," she said. Her family was safe to talk about. "There's some Italian in me too. When I visited relatives in Italy, I learned to make a mean lasagna."

"Maybe you'll have some time on Mars to make us some. Between 4-O Agriculture and Mars Co-op, we must have all the ingredients."

Faizah good-naturedly shook her had. "You need a really good wine to go with lasagna, and from what I heard at the Lunar restaurants, a good wine is hard to find on your planet."

Ed grimaced. "It's getting better," he said, not too convincingly. "Your parents must have been pretty confident of your future to name you 'She who is victorious.'"

"More like a hope, but they hedged their bets. Faizah is my middle name. Karen is my first name. But that sounded too mundane, so I switched it after college. You've been on Mars most of your life, right?"

"If you don't count my time on this tug. I'm a naturalized Martian. I was born in Canada, but I grew up on my uncle's farm."

"Which would be very mundane if his farm wasn't located on Mars. Have you been back to Earth?"

"No." Ed stopped for a minute to check the screen as the ship jostled from contact with the orbital tugs. "It's not hard to go down to

Earth, but it's pretty expensive to come back up. And these days, I'm in the vicinity only during the window to Mars, and that's too busy of a time for me to take a vacation."

"Do you miss it?"

"I miss the beach. We have artificial ponds and streams on Mars, particularly in the agridomes, but I remember as a kid my parents taking me to Lake Huron. I never saw the ocean, except from Earth orbit. I would love to stand on the edge of that much water. That would be amazing."

Faizah leaned over the control panel, trying to rest her chin on her hand, but her elbow kept floating off the panel and she quickly gave it up. "When I was young," she said, "I surfed in the ocean waves near Capetown. It seems a shame you never had a chance to even stand on an ocean beach."

Ed shook his head. "Not really. Have you ever looked out a window and watched the storms of Jupiter? Or slid on the ice of Europa? It may be too much to expect that I should also soak my feet on the edge of an ocean, or look up and again see a sky without a barrier of glass and metal."

"I always thought your uncle was a romantic, but it sounds like he passed that on to you."

"It's a defense against computers, orbital physics and recycled everything. Look, there goes the *New Brunswick*."

Ahead of them, the orbital tugs rushed back to the dock as the *New Brunswick*'s thrusters, now slaved with thrusters on the modules and drive unit, majestically swung the long line of the assembled configuration away from the dock. It continued to drift away, with cloud bursts from the thrusters keeping it on course.

Zach had already docked, and the orbital tugs were nudging two cargo modules toward it when the *New Brunswick*, more than a kilometer away, fired up its main drive, the blue glow obscuring the line of the ship as it began its long arc to Mars.

Chapter 3

Dancing Between Orbits

On their 19th day out, the Earth-Moon system was far behind them. Ed noticed the acceleration of .01g seemed more of a nuisance to Faizah than zero g. It was just enough gravity to give her a sense of down, making her forget how easy it was to go back up. Ed lost count of how many times she bumped her head when she stood up too quickly.

The radio speaker came to life with a quick beep.

"Cydonia Zach, New Brunswick."

Ed, sitting at the galley table, reached behind him and switched on the intercom mike. "This is *Zach*. Go ahead *New B*."

"All systems running nominal. Flip over and deceleration set to begin in four hours."

"We're right behind you, John. Everything's running hot and true here. Make sure this time all your passengers are tucked away for the zero-g flip."

"This is a well behaved group, Ed. No tourists. Hey, you've got a layover on Mars, don't you?"

"Two weeks. Then I've got a Belt run. You want to get in some racquetball?"

"Yeah, and some things I want to talk to you about. I'll give you a call a day or two after we land."

"Sure thing."

Faizah gave Ed an amused look. "Racquetball, in Mars light gravity?"

"You use the ceiling more than on Earth, and there are some special rules," Ed said. "You wear a lot more padding. It's better than basketball, which is just ridiculous on Mars."

Faizah's laugh, soft and reserved just after leaving Luna, had developed into a full-bodied delight.

"You've lightened up since we left the Moon," Ed said. "I still don't know who you are, not really, but at least you're making me a little less nervous now."

Faizah pulled back the curtain on her bunk cubicle and sat down, gently so she wouldn't bounce back up. "I think there's less to be nervous about. I keep going over the threat and what we know, but it doesn't add up. I deal primarily in corporate intelligence, but it's not usually cloak and dagger."

"Usually?"

"Relax. The information on the threat came from indirect sources. It may never have been real. The home office could have misinterpreted the message. Since we left, they haven't given me any more to go on. And you and Marta checked your cargo thoroughly. I don't think anything could have made it aboard."

"There are the two modules we picked up at L-1. Somebody might have slipped something there ahead of time."

"That doesn't track. It would have been tough to plant something up there, and even harder for anything coming directly from Earth. And if there is a bomb up there, according to the security manuals, it's likely not to do much more than destroy the module while leaving the tug down here intact. No, it would have been too difficult, too risky, and too little return. I'm still worried about who would be willing to use such drastic measures and why, as well as what they may try next. But there's too little to go on."

She may have seemed more at ease, but Ed sensed she knew a short list of people who would be willing and able to threaten her, and she indeed knew why. Ed still saw a cool efficiency about her. For the moment, that seemed to work in their favor.

The two spent time making sure the remnants of dinner and their own gear was secure for the few minutes of zero g when Ed flipped the *Zach* over and restarted the fusion reactor drive for deceleration. Time slipped to two hours to go – two more hours of acceleration that if not checked would send them out of the solar system.

All readouts were nominal – until a warning horn blared throughout the tug, jarring Ed out of his checklist.

Ed shoved Faizah aside as he dove into the control cockpit, banging his knee hard against the co-pilot's seat. He didn't take the time to notice. The warning lights flashed over the radar.

"*Zach*, cut warning. Switch radar to main display." The radar's graphic switched to the clear panel before the pilot's seat. Ed touched a spot on the screen, and the display zoomed in on an arc of reflections showing bright red, indicating high velocity in *Zach*'s direction.

"Faizah," Ed yelled, "get into an emergency suit."

She stuck her head through the cockpit hatch. "What happened?" Her face was grim, but no panic. She already had the suit bag in hand.

"There's a ring of debris heading our way."

"From where?"

"The *New Brunswick*. She blew up."

Faizah's grim determination set for facing an emergency changed swiftly to horror, freezing her. Ed saw, but there was no time. "We'll figure out what happened and why later. Now move."

Faizah steeled herself, then stepped back into the center of the cabin and unpacked the suit. "How long do we have?"

"Ten minutes, maybe less."

"But the *New Brunswick* was an hour away."

"That was at point-oh-one-one-g acceleration. This stuff's coming at us a lot faster than that."

Faizah quickly had the suit on and checked the small air tank. She left the headpiece unsealed. "Should I go into the airlock?"

"No. It sticks out beyond the cargo modules. Hold tight. I'm cutting the drive." Ed gave her a few seconds to grab onto something, strapped himself in, then shut down the fusion drive. As soon as it was off, he set all the reactor controls into a safe position, then fired thrusters to aim the cargo modules above the tug directly at the coming debris.

"Doesn't the cockpit stick out more than the airlock?" Faizah called out, gripping a handhold and trying to get her feet into a stable position.

"I'll be in there in a minute." He set the thrusters to auto pilot, and linked the com to his space suit. All lights green, all systems on safe, Ed unstrapped from the seat and launched himself into the crew cabin, closing the cockpit hatch behind him.

Faizah didn't say anything while Ed opened a locker and smoothly swam into his own suit in the zero g. She braced her feet against the galley table, sealed her headpiece, started the air recycler, and switched on her suit radio.

Ed sealed his helmet, then switched his radio to the shipping general broadcast channel.

"Mayday, mayday, mayday. This is the *Cydonia Zach* relaying a mayday for the *New Brunswick* on a high velocity Earth-Mars route. There has been an explosion aboard the *New Brunswick*. *Cydonia Zach* is trailing by one hour. Radar shows a sphere of debris, too much interference to make out the condition of the Brunswick. The leading edge of the debris field should hit us any minute. My emergency transponder is on continuous signal. I will continue to receive this channel and transmit when the debris passes."

Faizah found some Velcro straps and secured herself to the center of the passenger cabin. She handed some other straps to Ed, and he strapped into another handhold.

"We won't have long to wait," he said. "I turned the ship so the top cargo hold takes the brunt of the hits. At this distance, the debris may be too spread out to do much damage. We'll be all right."

"That last sounds more like a hope," Faizah said.

"I put us into a position where hope has a chance. But that's why when we pair up on a trip, we leave an hour apart, so if something goes wrong with one ship, it doesn't take out the other one."

"Is there…" Faizah hesitated. Ed didn't let her hang.

"I couldn't tell if there was anything left of the New B. There was too much interference. The radar will give us a better signal after the debris wave passes."

He was going to say more, but a dull thud cut him off, and both of their bodies jumped from the floor and tugged at the straps.

"That was a hit, dead on," Ed said. "Good thing the top module is depressurized. We won't have to worry about venting throwing us off."

Another thud, and an alarm horn triggered. A warning message flashed on a cabin wall screen. Ed cut the horn. "A communication dish. There's backup." A sharp clunk on the airlock startled them both. No new horn. The pressure readout in the lock was steady.

He felt his body pull sideways as thrusters corrected the ship's angle. There followed a cascade of soft hits, like a Martian dust devil blowing sand against a surface rover. Minutes passed. Nothing more.

Ed undid his straps. "We're through, but stay put and keep your suit sealed until I check the radar." He opened the cockpit hatch and floated in. Faizah waited impatiently until Ed called back, "It's clear."

Faizah unsealed the head piece and pulled it back, but she kept the rest of the suit on. Ed took his helmet off, stuffed his gloves in it and lodged it by his seat. But he, too, kept his suit on. "It's a good thing we weren't trailing right behind the New B.," Ed said, pointing to a rotating line on the console's main screen. "That radar image looks like the fusion reactor drive. It blew straight back. It won't pass us by much, but we're clear."

"What about the crew and passenger modules?"

Ed changed the display zoom and closed in on a fatter rotating line. "The passenger module looks mostly intact, but I can't tell if it's holding atmosphere. I think it was the tug that blew, splitting it apart in the middle." He punched up ship-to-ship. "*New Brunswick*, this is *Cydonia Zach*. We are trailing an hour behind and will attempt a rescue. Can anyone read me?"

"Are you just extending hope, or do you really have a way to rescue them?" Faizah's eyes were back to being cold, determined, studying the radar image and console controls intently.

"Extending hope is the first thing. Put us in a position to try something. But the *Zach* has grappling arms. We may be able to grab onto those modules at its center point and stop its spin."

Faizah looked doubtful. "Can the grappling arms handle that much spinning mass?"

"One thing at a time," Ed said, rapidly keying in commands. "I'm firing up the fusion drive again. The New B. is slipping farther away as long as we're just coasting." The drive kicked in and gravity returned. "Get on the ship-to-ship and keep trying to raise somebody. The tug may be gone, but the passenger module has communication gear." He was going to show Faizah how to key up the right channel, but her hands quickly punched up the correct numbers. Ed was surprised, but too busy to give it more than a moment's thought. Faizah slipped the receiver and microphone set over her ear.

"*New Brunswick*, this is *Cydonia Zach* closing in on your position." Good, Ed thought, keep adding on the positive. "If anyone can hear me, please respond."

Faizah kept repeating her message. Ed fine tuned the auto pilot. He was going to bring the *Zach* to about half a kilometer from the New B. and far off its rotational plane. He didn't want something breaking off and heading for his fusion reactor or his tug's fuel tanks. Many minutes passed before the main com channel crackled to life.

"*Cydonia Zach*, Mars Control. We received your mayday and are monitoring all channels. Be advised, there are no rescue cutters in position to attempt an intercept. The *Grissom* went down for refit two days ago. *White* and *Chaffee* are too far away in the Belt. We've sent a general call to all commercial craft, but it looks like you're the only one in a position to give *New Brunswick* any help."

Ed pounded his fist on his seat's arm. "Damn it! Why did they take the Grissom down early?" Faizah stopped her transmitting and gave him a questioning look. Ed calmed his exasperation and explained. "They were supposed to have five cutters spread out in orbits around Mars and the asteroid belt: three stationed around the Belt, one on call around Mars, and one free for maintenance at Phobos. But they never built the final two. Budget cuts, for five years now, so there are big gaps."

Faizah had cut her mike as soon as Ed pounded his fist. "That I knew, but shouldn't a cutter at Mars have remained active while there are ships still in transit from Earth?"

"It should. But they're always juggling schedules so they can swap out with the next cutter in line in the Belt. It's just a crap shoot if they're in position to do any good." He keyed in his own mike.

"Mars, *Cydonia Zach*. We're 23 minutes from rendezvous with the *New Brunswick*. Will attempt to grapple the passenger module and stop its rotation. We have not had any communication with the New ..." Faizah reached out to his arm to stop him.

"I'm receiving you, say again," she said.

"Check that Mars," Ed said. "We've got a signal now," then switched over to ship-to-ship.

"... no contact with the crew module – or command deck." The voice was female, halting, scared, obscured by static. "We have many injuries aboard, everything's a ... Can you help us?"

Faizah switched her mike off. "Her name is Jessica," she said softly. "I think she's a steward."

Ed switched on his mike, and tried to keep his voice calm. "Jessica, my name is Ed. I'm the pilot of the tug trailing behind you. We should rendezvous with your position in less than an hour. Are you the only crew member in the passenger module?"

There was a moment's delay. "George should be in here somewhere. I'm not sure what floor ... deck he's on."

"George is another steward?"

"Yes, there were two of us."

"None of the tug crew are with you?"

Silence, longer than a heartbeat, longer than a deep breath.

"I haven't seen them. I don't know why they don't send anyone up to check on us. But they must have got the ship back under control. We still have gravity. We must be accelerating.... Can't you get hold of them?"

Silence in return. Ed and Faizah's eyes locked, wordlessly trying to decide what to tell the frightened young woman in the battered remnants of the ship.

Ed keyed his mike. "Jessica, listen to me. There was an explosion on your ship. I think it destroyed the tug. The crew module above the tug may have also been badly damaged. The gravity you're feeling is from the passenger and cargo modules spinning end-to-end. Do you understand me?"

More silence.

"Oh god." Softly. An expression of horror. A prayer.

"Jessica?"

"We have injuries. Broken bones, mostly. I ... I don't know the bottom floors. George was down there before – before the explosion.... You can get to us?"

"Yes."

"What do you want me to do?" The voice was firmer, still scared, but taking the next step. "The screen is flashing 'Loss of central control,' and asking if I should turn on ... enable stability thrusters. Would that help?"

"No," Ed said quickly. "You don't have enough fuel in your module thrusters to stop your spin. I'll need those thrusters later. I can stop your spin when I reach you."

"Then I'll see to my passengers, and find George," Jessica said. "I'll have a portable with me if you need to call.... *New Brunswick* out."

Ed switched off his mike, and motioned Faizah to do the same. Until the *Zach* reached rendezvous, they could only wait. Ed studied Faizah's eyes, her face, not knowing if he could see the truth in her. "Did you cancel your booking on the *New Brunswick*, or was that part of the ruse to keep whoever they are from knowing you were on the *Zach* instead?"

Her face showed anger. Her eyes showed doubt. "If you knew me better, you wouldn't even think of asking me that, and I'd slap your face if you did."

"That is the problem, isn't it? Knowing you." Ed tried to keep his voice steady, calm.

Faizah turned away. "I canceled two days before you arrived, but I did cancel. I even argued in the port office about trying to get my deposit back, claiming I had an emergency that wouldn't allow me to be on Mars for two years. I made a public show of it. Marta will confirm that."

"Maybe not public enough. And you canceled only two days before?"

Now her face and eyes matched. Anger. "Yes, two days. I wanted to keep whoever was behind the threat guessing. Frankly, I wasn't sure if I was going to Mars, but you were always my backup. We thought we had a good enough ruse that I was staying on the Moon, and good enough security with your ship in case somebody didn't believe it."

"We'll have to figure out later what was good enough and what somebody didn't believe." Ed tried to soften his tone. He may need her in the next couple of hours, and the *Zach* was rapidly gaining on the remains of the *New Brunswick*. "Hell, we don't really know that it wasn't a coincidence and something just blew on that tug."

"Now that, I don't believe," Faizah said. She turned her face away again before Ed could read it. He turned back to the display, checking the closing rate. The com signal flashed, and he switched to the commercial channel.

"*Cydonia Zach*, this is the *Umi Explorer*. Can you observe the condition of the *New Brunswick*'s reactor and drive unit? We are in position to attempt salvage. We could rendezvous with the passenger module instead if something goes wrong in your efforts, but it would be beyond the Belt before we could reach it."

"Great," Ed said, far from meaning it. "Translate that as 'We could help, but it would take a long time and doesn't pay as well as getting the drive unit.'"

"So you just going to tell them to go to hell?"

Ed shook his head, and keyed the radar to get a close up image of the spinning drive unit. "I'll tell him the drive unit may be salvageable and send him a radar image so he can see for himself. If something goes wrong when I'm trying to hook onto that passenger module, we may need him to adjust his course and come to our rescue."

"You said the blast sent the drive back our way."

"Relative to us, but it's still going at a pretty clip through the Belt. It'll probably take a couple of weeks for the *Umi* to catch up to it."

As the *Zach* closed in on the *New Brunswick*, Mars Control reported they did some figuring and decided Ed's tug did have enough fuel to add the passenger module to its current load and still reach Mars, or at least come close.

"Don't worry. If you can get into any type of orbit around Mars, no matter how elliptical or unstable, our short-range tugs at Phobos can bring you in. But forget about adding the New B.'s two cargo modules. There'd be too much mass to slow down. You'd never make it. You wouldn't even come close."

"Mars Control, *Cydonia Zach*. Roger on your last," Ed answered. "That's pretty much what I figured. Will keep you advised. *Zach* out."

"Ed, Jessica's back on ship-to-ship," Faizah said. "Go ahead, Jessica"

Ed switched over. Jessica's voice was still halting, but no panic.

"... found one passenger – one man died. Many are injured, mostly broken bones, concussions maybe. Some look pretty bad. I don't know what I can do to help them. I – I haven't accounted for all 39 passengers yet."

Faizah responded "Jessica, have you found the other steward yet, George?"

"George? Yes. I found him on a lower deck, near where I found ... where the other man died. He was unconscious, but he was coming around. I don't, I don't really know how bad he is."

"Hold on, Jessica. We can see your ship now. We'll get to you shortly."

Ed and Faizah could spot the spinning modules slipping in and out of darkness as the *Zach* auto pilot brought them abreast. The drive cut off, and thrusters braked to hold the *Zach*'s position a half kilometer away. Ed undocked from the fusion drive, then fired thrusters to move the tug and cargo modules away from the drive unit before setting the tug free.

Faizah kept Jessica informed of their progress and made sure she and George were getting all the passengers strapped in. Faizah wasn't sure if Jessica was the senior steward, but George was still too incoherent for it to matter. It seemed lucky that George was able to function at all.

Ed piloted the tug to a position above the center point of the three rotating modules, then fired his thrusters to match the rotation. As he began to close, the commercial channel flashed again.

"*Cydonia Zach*, this is Polaris Enterprises, lunar based. We are prepared to offer you twice the normal shipping fee for recovering the Baker cargo module of the *New Brunswick*, plus pay any claims made against you or 4th Orbit if, in order to effect the recovery, you need to leave one of your current cargo modules behind. I am sending you a certified salvage contract via the InterPlanet. Additional fees and expenses are negotiable."

Ed sat back, stunned.

"Is that for real?" Faizah asked.

Ed punched up the message I.D. "It's from Polaris, all right, whoever they are. That one I can tell to go to hell."

"No," Faizah said. "I'll do it. You drive."

Ed adjusted the rate of approach and tried to correct for some wobble in the modules ahead. As they closed, the damage from the explosion became clearer. "The tug, it's just gone," Faizah said.

"That's what I figured. The crew module is just a mangled mess."

For runs needing additional crew, interplanetary tugs carried an extra crew module above it. It's a squat module, only two decks for cabins and storage. All that was left of this one was a ring of squashed and torn metal.

"How many were in the *New Brunswick*'s crew?" Faizah asked.

"Five. Rules for passenger runs require a pilot be at the controls round the clock, and they had a couple of system engineers for the passenger module. That's not counting the two stewards who stayed with the passengers."

The modules grew larger until they filled the view of the forward screens, motionless relative to the tug, the stars swirling behind them.

Ed activated the grappling arms, extending them into position. He had lined up the modules vertically to his perspective, and aimed the arms to grab holds set within the side of the cylindrical modules. He triggered the grapples. The left took hold, but an imbalance in the rotation forced the right to miss. The tug shuddered. Grimly, Ed reached with the right again. It held.

"Jessica, we have hold of your modules," Faizah said. "Hold tight while we try... while we stop the rotation."

"I warned the passengers," Jessica answered. "Go ahead."

Ed fired the thrusters in short bursts, shoving their bodies to the side. Sensor readouts glowed yellow to pink, showing the strain on the grappling arms. As they approached critical, Ed cut thrust, then fired again. In an interminable dance, the swirling stars slowed.

"Jessica, this is Ed. We've stopped your rotation. Can you get to a control panel?"

"I'm right by one. Go ahead."

"Is there a selection on the screen there for remote input?"

"No, I don't... wait, here it is. Press it?"

"Yes, and when a new screen opens up, read me the remote address."

It took a few minutes, but Ed had remote control of the module thrusters and set them on auto stabilizer. The grappling arms released their hold, and Ed guided the tug to the rear and the remains of the crew module.

"Can you still dock with the mess back there?" Faizah asked.

"Not with the crew module. I'm hoping the top docking ring survived well enough so I can trigger it to undock from the passenger module and the *Zach* can just pull it away. We'll just have to try." Ed stopped the tug next to the crew module. They could see through the twisted metal to a compressed, Picasso-like version of the interior. Jagged lines, blackened metal, part of a bunk, hanging wires, a flattened table. Ed decided not to shine a light inside.

He found a hold for the grappling arms and secured them. Then he called up the docking control on the passenger module and set the rear ring to release. The arm pulled at the wreckage. Nothing.

Faizah knew the answer, but asked anyway. "It's jammed, isn't it?"

Ed reached for his helmet and gloves. "I'm going to have to go outside and try to clear it."

"And what happens to me, Jessica and everyone else if you get caught up in that wreckage and can't make it back in?"

Ed floated through the hatch and headed for the airlock. "Just call the Umi Explorer and tell the pilot to come get you, however long it takes."

The combination air and thruster pack gave him some control as he went out, but it was awkward. Even with the pack's control arms folded up, they got in the way as he tried to free the docking gear. But if he used a tether, it could tangle in the wreckage and cut. If he floated free, he doubted Faizah had studied the controls enough to fly the *Zach* and come get him.

The passenger module was in a soft dock with the crew module. The four outer latches had partially opened, but the twisted metal on the crew module fouled the mechanism. If Ed couldn't free it, he would have had to give it up and dock at the other end. That would mean giving up his own cargo, which he was willing to do, and flying the passenger module back to Mars in an upside down position, which he wasn't anxious to try. These things were meant to have gravity in only one direction, and with a load of injured passengers, he didn't want to put their beds on the ceiling, even at .01g.

The two docking clamps on his far side looked in decent shape, and he was able to clear a third. But the fourth was so twisted, he was having to cut it off. Time was slipping away as the welder cut through the metal. If he didn't start the deceleration burn soon, he wouldn't make Mars. He wouldn't even get close enough. They'd be a long way toward Jupiter before the *UMI Explorer* caught up with them.

The radio beeped on. "Ed, can you read me?" A male voice he didn't recognize.

"Who's this?"

"Juarez, one of the passengers. Jessica just told me what you are doing out there. Do you need help?"

"Are you experienced in EVA?" Must be, Ed thought. Why else would he ask?

"Years. And I have my suit with me."

"OK, Juarez. I think I'm good on the outer clamps. I'm cutting away the last one now. But I haven't reached the center docking ring at the module's hatch. Can you get down there and check its condition, and if it's jammed, free it?"

"I'm getting my suit on now and I'll be on my way."

That was going to save some time, and Ed wasn't even sure he could get to the hatch from outside through the wreckage. The radio beeped again. This time, it was Faizah.

"Ed, Mars Control just sent a message. They say we'll need to get underway in an hour if they're to have a chance of pulling us into orbit."

"Roger. It'll be close."

"Oh, and Polaris Enterprises called again. They doubled their offer."

"Ignore them. They don't need a second round of your advice on what they can do with their cargo, as creative as it was." An insane message, but he had to chuckle over its absurdity. That's why Faizah relayed it, he thought.

Ed shifted the welder and lit it again. The wreckage took on more jagged, sinister shapes under the arcing light of the welder. The dark tint of his helmet's welding shield and the blinding spark blotted out the stars. He didn't see light and shadow now. It was reflective blue light, or nothing. What was the time? Finally, the strut snapped free and the docking mechanism was clear.

"Juarez, I'm done out here. How's the hatch?"

"I had to go through to the other side to clear it, but I think I have it now. But ...."

"Juarez, what's the problem?"

"There are two... I think there are two bodies in here. Should I bring them in?"

"Oh god," Ed whispered. A requiem. "Bring them in if you can, but hurry. We don't have much time. Faizah?"

"You have 38 minutes, actually," she said. "That is, we have 38 minutes."

"I'm coming in now. Juarez, tell me when you're ready."

That wasn't much time to retrieve the passenger module, dock with his own cargo and drive units, and get underway. Once inside, he shed his backpack but left his suit on as the air cycled in.

"Mars sent navigation info to match the times we might get away," Faizah said, grabbing Ed's helmet as he flowed into the pilot's seat.

"Juarez, are you ready?" tossing his gloves to Faizah as well.

"Closing the hatch now, go ahead."

"27 minutes," Faizah said.

Ed keyed the passenger module to undock from the wreckage, then punched the *Zach*'s thrusters to pull the wreckage free. It held. The passenger module turned, it's thrusters fired to correct. The wreckage shuddered.

"Damn!" Ed released the clamps.

"What are you doing?" Faizah said. "Keep trying."

"I am, but not on this side. I think the thrust is pushing the gear into another jam. I'll get on the other side and try pulling it from a different angle."

It was a desperate race, and time was winning. They had backup with the *Umi Explorer*, but not all of them. He feared at least some of the passengers would not survive the delay.

Ed hopped the *Zach* over to the other side and grabbed the wreckage again. He re-keyed the clamps, then fired the thrusters. A shudder, correcting thruster fire, a groan echoing through the arms and hull, a crack, and suddenly the *Zach* and the remains of the wreck of the *New Brunswick* tumbled away from the survivors.

Ed fired his thrusters and stopped the tumble. He released the wreckage, and without a second look turned the tug back toward the passenger module.

"19 minutes," Faizah said.

Ed lined up the *Zach* then fired again for docking.

Faizah leaned back, her head tilted up so she could focus through the top panels on the approaching ring above them. "What if the module's docking gear is damaged and won't hold?"

"Hope that it does."

They hit. Not gently. Their bodies tugged against their straps. Four lights turned green for the central hatch clamp and three for the clamps on the outer ring. One light on the ring remained red.

Faizah saw the red light too. "What now?"

"No time," Ed said grimly.

"Wouldn't it save more time to keep the New B's cargo modules and forget your own?"

"What, you want to collect on Polaris' offer?"

"No, it's just...."

Ed keyed in more commands and undocked from the New B's cargo modules. "It could make things worse. I don't know how heavy their cargo is. We could save time but gain too much mass to make it to Mars."

He set the passenger module thrusters to slave with the *Zach*'s, then shifted laterally to reach his own modules and drive. He had 13 minutes to put his ship back together and get underway.

But no more wrecked modules or jammed clamps. Ed wasn't giving the passengers a smooth ride, but he wasn't wasting time. The *Zach* banged into the two drifting cargo modules. Ed could have bought more time by leaving those modules behind as well, but he had six minutes left. Besides, that last jarring turned the last red docking lamp to green. He lined up with the drive unit, punched his forward thrusters, and slid into the docking clamps. The jarring wasn't as hard, but more satisfying.

Another thruster burn, and the ship swiveled to put the drive unit in front for deceleration. Ed checked the time. Four minutes. He triggered the drive, building up deceleration slowly to a force of .01g. Their bodies sank lightly into their seats. Ed's helmet clunked to the floor, bounced, then stayed there. Passengers had a sense of up and down again, and shifted their bodies to ease the pain their regained weight, however slight, caused them.

"Mars control, *Cydonia Zach*. We're underway."

As Ed switched off, Faizah jumped off her seat and rushed for the upper hatch. Ed grimaced as Faizah's head banged against the ceiling, but she barely noticed. "Jessica's going to need some help up there."

Chapter 4
Colors of Mars

Trees and grass glistened from the early morning rain, and condensation still dripped from the dome's hexagon panels that arched across the valley. The droplets refracted the sky's rose hue, deepening the sandy red of the canyon walls, adding a lush tone to the farmland that snaked between them.

Viking Glen, an agricultural settlement, had utilized the natural slope of the canyon floor for its drainage and irrigation, and a small stream bed that ran down its middle from south to north now gurgled with the fresh intake of water as it emptied into a pond and the community's recycling system. Mirrors on the western side of the dome sparkled as a computer adjusted their angles to throw the morning sun against the shadow cast by the canyon wall. A matching set of mirrors on the east side of the dome would do the same in the late afternoon, extending the hours of sunlight for the crops.

The gentle rainfall on the flat roof lulled Ed to sleep in, not that he needed much convincing. The moist freshness in the air was a welcome change from the *Zach*. This was only Ed's second sol back on Mars, but he was lucky he was back here at all. He had cut it pretty fine, using up all his fuel in the fusion drive to reach an extreme elliptical orbit around Mars. It was unstable, but it brought him close enough for the Phobos tugs to reach the *Zach* and bring it in. If he had started up his drive a couple minutes later, he couldn't have reached orbit.

Between that harrowing Luna-Mars run and the weeks prior in the Belt, Ed was relieved to be back in his home again, a small two-bedroom adobe on the northwestern edge of his uncle's farm. The farm was part of the agricultural settlement set in a canyon branch of Tiu Vallis. His parents had rented a house in the small village just down the road when they moved to Mars more than 20 Earth years before, but they spent much of their time off planet. So Ed spent much of his time at his uncle's place, learning a little about farming and a lot about his uncle. When his parents planned to move back to Earth, Chubeck convinced them to let Ed stay. He was only 17, but after eight years on Mars and in his uncle's company, he couldn't imagine finding a life on Earth. His uncle gave him a plot of land when he graduated from college, and as his skills and income as a pilot grew, he was able to build the small adobe as a place to return to after flights. He might add onto it someday, Ed thought, but it was enough for now.

Ed, in a Toronto Maple Leafs sweater, gray gym pants and sandals, stepped out the front door and onto the partly covered patio, sipping a cup of what passed for coffee on Mars. A black and white dog, an Aussie shepherd, was laying on the flagstone floor, but lifted her head to see if he brought out anything for her.

"Are you still here, Ariel? Don't you have to work today?" But Ed could see Roger, one of his uncle's farm workers, tinkering on an electric tractor by the barn, giving the dog some extra time to goof off. Ed reached back inside the door to grab a biscuit from a jar and tossed it to her. His uncle had several herding dogs on his farm. They were common on the Viking Valley farms. For some reason, Ariel had taken to Ed, and often stayed with him when he was back from a flight. Ed always welcomed her company.

Ariel put her head on his lap to be scratched, but she jerked to attention when a whistle came from across the road. Ed saw Roger wave his arm for the dog to join him, and Ariel bounded over the half wall that separated the patio from the small plot of shrub grass, sand and rock that was Ed's front yard. The dog took an extra boost against the top of the wall and sailed 10 meters before hitting the ground without breaking stride, apparently ecstatic at finally getting started on the day's job.

As Ed watched her go, he heard laughter from a two-seater commuter cart that pulled up in front. "You know, I think those dogs are the best adapted Martians up here," said a man just stepping out. He was short, in his early 20s, early 40s in Earth years, with trimmed black hair and wearing a tan uniform from Orbital Search And Rescue. His accent was Eastern European.

"Capt. Lenowitz, good morning," greeted Ed. Peter Lenowitz was the head of OSAR's law enforcement division on Mars. "Would you like some coffee?"

The captain shook his head as he walked up to the patio. "I think I'll wait until they finish the coffee plantation and can start using real beans."

"They just finished the dome and haven't begun soil generation yet." Ed said. "It could be a long wait."

"It will be worth it," Lenowitz answered, and slid out a chair to sit down. Ed tried to stop him, but too late. Lenowitz quickly stood up again.

"Sorry. It just stopped raining an hour ago." Ed reached back and grabbed a chair that had been under the roof. "Here, this one's dry."

Lenowitz took the offered chair and slid it around a white metal mesh table. "My fault. Your weather randomization always gets me when I come out to the agridomes. You know, the city's thinking of adopting a randomizing program for its weather as well, though somewhat less random than yours. Most of the rain would still fall between 2 and 3 a.m., but an occasional mid-morning rain or afternoon shower would be allowed – with two days notice. Of course we'd ban rain entirely from dawn to midnight during the tourist season."

"Of course." Ed sat on the banco, the bench that protruded from the house wall, and leaned back. "But you didn't come here to talk about the weather. So what's the news?"

"Tests show it was a bomb."

"So much for small talk," Ed said. "I guess I'm not surprised."

"Oh?"

"I mean, is anybody surprised? The tug's rocket motor wasn't running. What could have set it off? If the fusion drive had blown, that would have been different."

Lenowitz raised an open hand in caution. "The lab techs warned me not to rush to judgment, that something accidental could have sparked that explosion. But you're right, no one was surprised."

"How did you prove it? Was there residue on the bodies?"

"There was some, but not definitive. It was that chunk of hull that slammed into your top cargo module. An explosive chemical was embedded throughout its interior side, an explosive common for mining and geologic work."

Ed sipped his coffee, hoping he wasn't giving away anything, and wondering if maybe he should. "It must have been a pretty powerful explosive."

"It didn't have to be too powerful to set off the tug's fuel. In fact, as much as they found on that hull plate, the lab tech figures the bomb was bigger than it had to be."

Not for the first time Ed wondered how close he came to having that bomb aboard his tug.

"So what's next?"

"The FBI and Interpol are already on the case on Earth and the Moon."

"FBI? Why them?"

"They still have jurisdiction at Tranquility Center, where the bomb was presumably planted. A North American consortium owned the *New Brunswick*, and it carried a U.S. registry, despite the name. In fact, FBI agents are hopping mad they're outside the window and can't get to Mars."

"A low-mass tug-only run could make it, if Washington wanted to pay the price."

"Apparently Washington isn't keen on paying much of anything out here these days, and any tug operator in Lunar orbit is booked solid for the Belt."

"Why do they want to come here anyway? If the bomb was planted on the Moon, all their suspects must be there, too."

Lenowitz leaned forward on the table. "Actually, their chief suspect is here."

That surprised Ed. "Who?"

The captain looked him straight in the eyes. "You."

That shocked Ed even more. "What? Where in hell did they get that idea?"

Lenowitz shrugged his shoulders. "Apparently it's been standard FBI policy for more than a century now that in a bombing investigation, the first one on the scene is always the prime suspect until proven otherwise. But my OSAR counterpart on the Moon is trying to dissuade them from that theory."

"Thank you, but why?"

"I was supposed to interview you and account for your actions and alibis, if any, when you were there." Lenowitz pulled out a pocket tablet and turned it on. "But it turns out you were on the Moon for such a short stay, and so active in public places, that we can already account for all your time." He scanned a list that came up, and started reading. "1:13 p.m., landed at Tranquility Center. 2:30, cleared customs. Shortly thereafter you enter the Mars Emporium." He looked up from the list. "Apparently you always go there first when you land on Luna, and several witnesses verified your presence that day." His eyes shifted back down. "From there, a debit transaction has you at Crater Cuts for a haircut from 4 to 4:30, a badly needed haircut according to the stylist. By 4:45 you're at a bar buying drinks for an underage student."

"Hey, I didn't touch her."

Lenowitz looked up from his tablet. "We know."

"You know!?" Ed buried his head in his right hand.

"Anyway, she was under the drinking age, not the other thing," the captain went on. "We gave the bartender a warning."

Lenowitz shut off the tablet. "There's more, something about wine tasting. We know where you were during the time the *New Brunswick* could have been approached. And those hours when you were back at your hotel, presumably sleeping " – Ed gave him a scowl – "security cameras show the loading docks were mostly deserted and no one approached the tug."

OK, Ed thought, here it comes.

"In fact, no one was in the loading dock early that morning until 4:45 a.m. when you boarded the *Cydonia Zach*, a rather ungodly hour to be there considering you did not launch until 11."

"Yeah, that's what I thought."

Lenowitz was boring in now, though Ed had been expecting this since they landed. "Yes, you were there with two 4th Orbit Transit employees, and an unannounced passenger."

"Wait a minute, you interviewed her yesterday."

"Briefly," the captain agreed. "Her arrival on Mars was no secret. In fact the steward, Jessica, spoke quite highly of her. By the way, Jessica also spoke highly of you. She gets out of the hospital today and is going to be on Mars for a while. Provided there are no legal entanglements, you might ...."

"Can we get on with this?"

"If you mean your involvement with Karen Faizah Westerhof, yes we should."

"My involvement?"

Lenowitz kept at a deliberate pace. "She did make a rather concerted effort to conceal her departure, including canceling her booking on the *New Brunswick* only two days before, making business appointments she never had any intention of keeping for times after your launch, and even booking a flight back to Earth. And your early morning arrival at your ship was certainly meant to keep the subterfuge going."

Ed had to stand up. Sure, he expected this, but it was getting deeper than he thought. "It's not against the law or even that unusual to keep a lunar departure quiet."

Lenowitz remained seated, leaning on an arm to get more comfortable. "This was more than just keeping Ms. Westerhof's departure quiet. But you are right, it was not against the law. Yet I do have to question her motives behind these machinations, and why she canceled her seat aboard a doomed ship. That makes her my prime suspect. And since you helped to keep her departure 'quiet,' you could be construed as an accomplice."

"That sounds pretty thin to me."

Lenowitz shoved the tablet in a pocket and stood up. "For now, it's a line of questioning to follow." He turned to leave.

"But you haven't asked me anything."

Lenowitz stopped. "True." He turned back toward Ed. "Why did Ms. Westerhof want to keep her departure secret?"

Ed smiled and shook his head. "I'm afraid you'll have to ask her."

Lenowitz returned the smile. "That, I already knew."

"But captain."

"Yes?"

"If you don't like the answer she gives you, ask me again."

Lenowitz looked up at the domed, rose-tinted sky. "You know, It just may turn out to be a nice day after all."

Chapter 5

Whispers

Ed watched Capt. Lenowitz drive the electric cart over to his uncle's farmhouse where Faizah was staying, then he quickly dressed and headed for town. Ed had already decided that if Faizah didn't fill in Lenowitz on the threat she had received, he would tell the captain himself what little he knew. But Ed wanted to delay a second round with Lenowitz, and didn't want to risk the captain stopping by on his way back and being more blunt: "Here's what she said. Now tell me the truth."

So Ed decided to clear out for a while – because he didn't know the truth.

The investigator was nibbling away at the edges before, giving Ed a chance to spill something, but not pressing too hard, staying casual, friendly. Ed didn't have much to spill, but he worried that sharing what little he did know would reveal something much grander – something his uncle hoped would stay secret. It was clear the stakes were high. He just needed to know what the game was.

But if Ed was going to confront Faizah and his uncle about that, he was going to have to do it later when Lenowitz wasn't around.

Ed drove the commuter cart he had used the night before back to the mag-lev station, parking it so the bumper connected to the re-charger. He waved his electronic pass at the gate just as a northbound train pulled in. Only a few other passengers were on the platform, and in seconds, the automated train pulled out and entered the tube for Tiu City.

The tube kept the train in the dark less than a minute until it bored through a crater wall and shot out above the floor of Tiu Vallis.

Transparent panels gave passengers a vista of the broad, boulder-strewn floor created by the deposits of an ancient flood that spilled into the Chryse Planitia, the low-lying plain to the north. While the floor had a gentle slope, the rugged valley walls rose sharply to a height of two kilometers at this point, as high as five not too far up the valley to the south.

Tiu City is near the valley's mouth, taking advantage of the walls of another canyon branch to anchor the roof domes of the settlement. Calling it a city was a bit of a stretch. There were only about 18,000 residents of Mars, spread mostly between Tiu City and three nearby agricultural valleys. A fourth was being built. Several science outposts with permanent residences were spread out across Mars. Many people who had addresses in Tiu actually spent much of their time in space: at the Phobos shipping and maintenance docks, in mining operations in the Asteroid Belt, or as researchers and pilots. Of course, the numbers in the city swelled during the four-month tourist season.

The train slipped into the dome of Tiu City, and ran through the town on an elevated magnetic bed, dropping to wheels as it slowed to its first stop in a residential district.

The architecture of Tiu City has been called Martian Pueblo. It was inspired mostly by the American Southwest, though the international background of its residents brought in a Middle Eastern influence as well. The buildings were "printed" mostly of adobe materials, some covered in stucco, their reddish and sand coloring not too different from traditional earth tones. Corners were rounded, windows and doors set deep into the walls, and the flat roofs of multi-story buildings were stepped to give occupants open space for urban gardens. Mars didn't have any wood to spare for building material, so plastic and metal spans replaced the exposed timbers found in New Mexico. Architects took advantage of the lighter gravity to make extensive use of archways and supporting beams that seemed too frail to people who just arrive from Earth.

Ceramic tiles adorned many of the buildings, both residential and commercial. Designs ranged from abstract to pastoral Earth, depending on the personality of the people inside. Some occupants mounted only a few tiles on their outer walls as accents. On other buildings, the tiles created a mural that covered nearly the full breadth of the structure. Yet the tiles were unified in their vibrant colors that raged against the reddish sands of Mars and echoed against the planet's loneliness.

Tiu City is long and narrow, following the contours of the branch canyon. It broadens at the north end for the industrial district, the train's last stop in the city.

This train, however, was continuing on to nearby Chryse Marsport and, farther out, the much larger Pathfinder Spaceport. The former was the jump-off point for all other locations on Mars. The spaceport, just southwest of the historic Mars Pathfinder landing site and museum, was where the *Zach* was getting an overhaul. Ed thought about going out there, but he stepped off at the downtown stop instead.

Sagan Boulevard was nearly deserted, though shop keepers were busy in their storefronts switching over displays and stock to cater to the locals until the next Earth window. At a convenience store with a banner proclaiming "Open 24.6/7," the owner keyed in a command to change the sale item on the window poster from motion sickness patches to home repair kits.

Where there were two or three people together talking, the conversation seemed the same as Ed passed by.

"A bomb? Why would someone want to plant a bomb?"

"Maybe someone wants to frighten people off from coming to Mars."

"Maybe the pilot was sleeping with somebody's wife."

"For that you crack the guy's face plate and let vacuum suck the life out of him. You don't blow up his ship and take six other guys with him."

"I thought bombings only happened on Earth. That's one of the reasons I came out here, to get away from all that."

In front of Viking Electronics, the shopkeeper recognized Ed and gave him a quick, embarrassed wave. The shopkeeper's conversation with two women died down as Ed passed; a few whispers, more stares his way. He turned onto Burroughs Street, and the activity picked up. University of Arizona – Mars Campus was back in session, and students circulated in the art galleries, tech shops and sidewalk cafes. The lunch crowd was just starting to filter in. Ed stopped in at the Barsoom, a place usually too jammed during the Earth window, but it had a much more comfortable mix of artists, students and faculty the rest of the Martian year.

A half-wall enclosed the outside tables, but Ed stepped inside and went up to the bar to grab a menu. Before he could decide on lunch, however, the news on the screen stole his attention.

"Confirmation this morning that a bomb destroyed the *New Brunswick* has sent a chill through Tiu City and the rest of Mars, and has everyone asking who planted it and why?" said a female reporter in an urgent, dramatic tone. Ed didn't recognize her. Mars News Network only had four reporters for its on-air and 'net newscasts, but one had just landed a job on Earth, so this must be the new one.

"On Earth, Sen. Decker has called for hearings on the security of space travel. Investigators on the Moon have not identified any suspects, but clearly one of the people they want to talk to is not on the Moon but ironically here on Mars. She is Karen Faizah Westerhof, identified as a business consultant to 4th Orbit Enterprises. She was aboard the *Cydonia Zach* when its pilot made that dramatic rescue of the 40 survivors of the explosion halfway to Mars. Ironically, Westerhof canceled a reservation on the *New Brunswick* only two days before it left Luna."

"I wonder if she can say ironically a couple more times," Ed muttered.

"Investigators have not called her a suspect, but Capt. Lenowitz of the OSAR law enforcement division interviewed her this morning at 4th Orbit Farms. We talked to Capt. Lenowitz just a few minutes ago as he left."

Forget lunch, Ed thought, tossing the menu back on the bar. He started to walk out as Lenowitz offered his denials and no comments. But then he heard his name and stopped. "Capt. Lenowitz admitted he talked with the pilot earlier this morning, though it's not clear if he's suspected of any involvement in the bombing. But when we tried to talk to Mr. Ferald, there was no answer at his home except," the camera panned to Ed's front door and veranda, and a barking dog, "for this angry dog barring our way. Now for reaction at Pathfinder Spaceport ...."

"Way to go, Ariel," Ed chuckled. He left the bar and walked down Burroughs to Edgar's Rice for some take-out Chinese, then headed back to Sagan Boulevard and the offices of 4th Orbit.

For an operation that extended from Earth orbit to the moons of Jupiter, 4th Orbit offices were fairly modest. But a polished wood veneer door, made from trees harvested at the farm, set the building apart. The building held the offices for three divisions of 4-O: Agriculture, Transit, and Products. 4-O Products included the leather coats and art items sold in the stores on Sagan and Burroughs, and at the Mars Emporium on Luna.

The artists were primarily spouses, students, and space workers on down time. The building also held the office for the 4th Orbit Foundation, which sponsored art programs and underwrote the university's Artist in Residence program. The latest artist in residence had been on the *New Brunswick* and came through with a broken left arm.

Ed barely came through 4-O Transit's office door when the local manager accosted him. "Where the hell have you been? Don't you have your com on?"

"Nice to see you, too, Hafiz. Mind if I have my lunch here?"

Hafiz waved Ed to a conference table next to his desk. In his Earth-20s with thick black hair, Hafiz's face showed his Middle Eastern roots, but his family had been solid U.S. Midwest for a couple generations, settling in Michigan. In a couple of months, Ed and Hafiz would be arguing hockey. For now, there was clearly something else on Hafiz's mind.

He sat down across from Ed and didn't wait for him to open up his sweet-and-sour chicken. "That run you're making for Ceres in a couple of weeks? It just turned into a passenger run."

Ed dug out the fork and stirred the sauce into the rice. "OK, I can handle that. It means we have to add some crew, but what's the problem? We can.... Wait, you don't mean the passengers from the *New Brunswick*?"

"Some of them. Eighteen were scheduled to go on to Ceres. A few are too banged up to go now. Two of them are dead. The mining companies are looking for replacements for them, so I don't know the final passenger list yet."

"Don't you think things are kind of hot right now for me to be taking the survivors on their next trip? Didn't you see the news this morning? They think I'm a suspect. Do you want to give that idiot reporter a chance to say 'ironically' a few more times?"

"Why not?" said a voice behind them from the counter. "Irony is beginning to run rampant in this case."

Suddenly Ed wasn't hungry any more. "Capt. Lenowitz, what brings you here?" He didn't turn around, but instead glared at Hafiz. "Why didn't you tell me he came in?" Ed whispered.

Lenowitz took out his tablet and laid it on the counter. "Just a small detail that I have to take care of with Hafiz. But I couldn't help overhearing. You know, Hafiz, Ed may be right. I do not personally consider him a suspect, but appearances may suggest he was unwittingly involved. I can not charge him for being duped, but until we get to the bottom of this, it may not be a good time for him to leave the planet, particularly with the survivors."

"What am I supposed to do?" Hafiz said. "With the New B. gone, Trans-Orbit Express doesn't have any tugs left on Mars to take the run. Trans-Orbit called us since we were already heading for Ceres."

"It does not matter if the *Zach* makes the run," Lenowitz said. "It is the pilot I am concerned about."

"Wait a minute!" Ed stood up and leaned over the counter to glare at Lenowitz. "The *Zach* is my tug. If it launches, I'm at the controls."

Lenowitz kept his eyes steady on Ed, but after not quite five seconds, the captain shifted his gaze and leaned back. "There may be difficulties, but then again, maybe you can help me clear some of this up by then. Though I admit, after this morning, things seem to be getting murkier instead."

"Because of your conversation with Faizah?"

"Yes. It was short, but she told me about the death threat she received, a threat she omitted to reveal in her statement she sent from the *Zach*. Faizah said the omission was to give her company time to protect its sources on and around Earth. InterCorporate Resources backed her up in a statement she had ready for me this morning. It does explain her switching flights and her desire to hide her passage on your tug."

Ed was relieved Faizah gave him that much. "So why does that make it murkier?"

"Because I do not know if I believe her. Ms. Westerhof can not tell me who made the threat, or give me any satisfactory information on why anyone would want to threaten her. Nor can her company. She may be the intended victim, but she is still my chief suspect."

"She can't be both."

"No, in the end she must be one or the other," Lenowitz agreed. "The threat, this is the story she told you?"

"Yeah," Ed said, "though she didn't give me many details."

"There may not be many details to give. When did she tell you?"

"Back on the Moon, the morning of the launch. Marta back at Lunar 4-O can confirm that."

"So does your uncle. But I'll have someone on the Moon reinterview this Marta."

Hafiz, who had been nibbling on the sweet-and-sour chicken, put an extra fork down and came up to the counter with Ed. "So what did you want to see me about?" he asked the captain.

"I just need to resolve a minor discrepancy," Lenowitz said. "The manifest you gave me for the *Zach* before it landed does not match with the report from customs. One shipment is missing."

"What?" Hafiz took Lenowitz's tablet to take a closer look. "This is what Marta on the Moon sent me before the *Zach* left."

"How long before?" Ed asked.

"Why?"

Ed slid the tablet over to himself and checked the time stamp on the manifest. "Didn't she send you an update the morning we took off?" He flipped the tablet around so Lenowitz could see and pointed to a line. "The S-47 mining drill never showed up. Marta was pretty pissed about it the afternoon before. She ended up keeping the shipping deposit and selling the slot to someone else. It took two of us to load the replacement shipment into its spot in the cargo module, which is what we were doing at 4:45 in the morning."

Hafiz, back at his desk, looked up from his computer screen. "4:45? Why were you at the loading docks that early?"

"Never mind. Did you find the updated manifest?"

"Yeah, I missed it before." Hafiz tapped in Lenowitz's address and sent the file over. The investigator called it up on his tablet. To protect his lunch, Ed grabbed the sweet-and-sour chicken and took it up to the counter. "Why so concerned about my missing cargo?" Ed asked between bites.

"It may be just a curious coincidence." Lenowitz called up another page on his tablet and showed it to Ed. "But the S-47 was also on the manifest of the *New Brunswick*, its spot reserved in the luggage hold of the passenger module you brought back to Mars. Yet Customs reports the drill was not on board."

"Maybe it didn't show up for them either," Hafiz said while Ed studied the manifest.

"That is possible. But Customs said the hold was packed solid, mostly baggage. Even if it had arrived, there was no room for it. Another crate was also missing."

"So what? Baggage often takes up more room than planned," Ed said. "When that happens, cargo crates get shoved to wherever they can fit. Since the New B. carried a crew module this trip, no one would have been using the spare bunk in the tug. It could have fit there. And especially if it arrived late, that would have been the easiest place to put it."

"Now that is very curious," Lenowitz said. "Do you know how an S-47 drill is used?"

"To plant deep," Ed paused, realizing where the captain was heading, "explosives when mining asteroids."

"So even if it triggered an explosive sniffer alarm at the lunar docks," Lenowitz explained, "the workers would have assumed it was just remnants of chemical from past use."

"Explosives could have been hidden in the drill shell and pipe extensions," Ed said

"And with lunar security as lax as it is, it would have just slipped through," the captain finished for him.

Hafiz looked in shock. "So this was the bomb? And it almost ended up on our tug?"

"Who sent it?" Ed asked.

"A small mining company, but the company rep denies knowing anything about it. It appears someone faked the shipping order."

"What about the guy who made up the order?"

"They are checking on it now."

"But you're betting that person's ID was faked as well."

Lenowitz picked up his tablet. "My suspicion is growing. The shipment may have arrived late at the lunar loading dock by design to protect against discovery, but the bomber may never have intended to load it on the tug itself where it set off the fuel tanks with disastrous results. If it had exploded in the luggage hold instead, it is possible no one would have been killed."

"So what was the target?"

"I do not know. There was nothing in the luggage hold of high value."

"You said there was a second crate missing?" Hafiz said.

"I have someone checking on that."

"Could the bomb have been meant for the New B's pilot and crew?" Ed asked.

"Possibly," Lenowitz said. "The bomber may have delayed delivering the drill crate to the lunar docks until there was nowhere left to put it but on the tug itself. But if it was meant for the New B's crew, why reserve space on your tug as well? If the S-47 did hold the bomb, it appears the bomber was keeping his options open, waiting until the last possible moment to decide which tug to ship it on, the *New Brunswick* or the *Cydonia Zach*."

"But wouldn't that support the idea of Faizah being the target?" Ed said. "She's the only connection between the two ships."

"If we are to believe Ms. Westerhof was the target, the bomber was extremely sloppy," Lenowitz said. "She had canceled her reservation on the *New Brunswick* quite publicly, and even if she had been aboard, it is likely she would have survived, no matter where the bomb ended up."

"Two passengers did die," Ed protested.

"But 38 survived. The two passengers who died had tragic luck, but there was no way the bomber could have predicted which passengers if any of them would have been killed by the explosion. Yet you are right when you say Ms. Westerhof is the only connection between the two ships."

"Which goes back to making her a suspect," Ed admitted. "You sound like you're about ready to arrest her, captain."

"No, not yet," Lenowitz said. "She is a convenient suspect, but we have nothing to connect her directly to the bomb, nor any reason why she would plant it. But if you do pilot that trip to Ceres, don't plan on taking Ms. Westerhof with you."

CHAPTER 6
Contradictions

Lenowitz left 4th Orbit with at least one answer, but more questions. Hafiz's sweet-and-sour chicken – or was it Ed's? – also made him hungry for lunch. But Lt. David Carstol was waiting for Lenowitz on the street, and the young officer was always broke.

"That didn't take long," Carstol said, joining him as they headed for the OSAR city headquarters. "Did you find out much?"

"Yes, and no," Lenowitz answered. "I am confident I know how the bomb was brought aboard the *New Brunswick*, but no closer to who did it. Perhaps I am even farther away."

"Hey, if you know how the bomb was put on board, that puts us a step ahead of the FBI."

"Only for a short time," Lenowitz said, bemused at the lieutenant's eagerness.

"So was the bomb in the drill crate?"

"Yes, I am sure of that now. To be fair, even the FBI was looking at last minute shipments put on board the *New Brunswick*. But no one ever thought to compare the *New Brunswick*'s manifest with that of the *Zach*."

"Until yesterday."

"When I saw the S-47 had been booked on both ships, and showed up on neither – at least on the parts of the ship that reached Mars, it was a glaring anomaly. Ed tells me the drill never arrived for the *Zach*, and they put in another shipment in its place. We'll see if the *New Brunswick* steward is awake enough this afternoon to talk, but I think he will confirm that overflow baggage bumped the drill out of the hold and into the tug's cabin."

"Wait 'til you tell that to the FBI."

"I can wait," Lenowitz said, and added disdainfully, "and so can they for a change. The Americans are using the bombing as an excuse to throw their weight around again, not that they ever needed much of an excuse. The FBI keeps forgetting it is not an American Moon, but they usually leave Mars alone, except for an occasional corporate scandal."

"Yeah, but this case is too unusual, too spectacular for the Feds to resist – or for anybody to resist, for that matter," Carstol said. "Interpol, the FBI and OSAR began arguing over jurisdiction as soon as we heard about the bombing."

"I have to admit, it is hard for me to resist as well. I have been on the criminal investigations desk for not quite a Martian year, but there has never been anything like this. We had the criminal negligence cases, drug labs, thefts, and assorted other crimes you'd expect with 18,000 people living under a few domes on an otherwise deserted planet. But this is, in your word, the most spectacular crime out here since humans first arrived on Mars."

"It would be a great way for you to go out if you could solve this case before you take command of the *Ed White*."

"That is, thankfully, still a few months away."

"You used to be excited about having your own command."

"It is a great honor, but I have become – intrigued – by the challenges of criminal investigations. And the sabotage of the *New Brunswick* is the most challenging case of all."

"So do you really think Westerhof did it?"

"Patience, Lieutenant. Westerhof is my prime suspect only because I have no others at the moment."

"I don't know. The bombing still seems like the act of an extremist to me."

"You think it was someone from the assorted Earth First groups which claimed to be behind the bombing? The People's Republic of Earth, perhaps, or Greenspace, even a couple I never heard of before such as the Mother Earth Defense Alliance and Gaia's Children?" Lenowitz shook his head with an irritated impatience. "Ah, groups with passionate aims and tiresome names."

"Mars has its own fringe element," Carstol said, and pointed his thumb to the building they were passing. "You just have to look at the posters on the wall to find 'em."

"Wait, don't step too close."

"Terraform Mars now!" bellowed a poster glued to a store's side wall. The headline used to scream until Public Safety enforced the local sound ordinance. Approaching pedestrians set off its 15-second appeal to launch a global attack on the Martian environment.

"Why build a city under glass when we can rebuild a world under an open sky?" the poster went on, put up by the radical terraformers who had no patience to wait for generations to walk under an open Martian sky. "For the cost of a comet or two we can melt the ice caps, replenish the atmosphere and resurrect the oceans...."

Beneath the poster's headline, a holographic orbital view of Mars continuously shifted from a red planet to green to blue, then the cycle repeated.

"David, you've been on Mars long enough to know you should stay on the street side of the walk and not set these posters off."

"Better red and dead!" answered a second poster in opposition to the terraformers. "Can you really imagine a blue Mars, destroying its scientific insights on the origins of the Solar System...."

The second poster was put up by the Ten Percenters, who argued to preserve a pristine Mars and limit the human footprint on the planet to 10 percent. During busy days on Sagan Street, the two posters were locked in continual debate on Mars eco-future.

"Sorry," Carstol said. "I forgot about getting too close."

"It is all right. Maybe we needed to be reminded there are plenty of extremists in any orbit to consider as suspects. Nevertheless, Faizah Westerhof presents an interesting wrinkle to this case."

"As the target or the perpetrator?"

"I do not yet know. It is clear she did not tell me everything this morning, and what she hid of her past and her business on Mars is enough to make her a suspect. That her business was with Carl Chubeck, however, gives her claim of being threatened credibility."

"Do you think so? I thought everyone on Mars liked Chubeck."

"Apparently you have not been on Mars long enough after all if you think that. Chubeck is a hero to many on Mars, but he is also a fierce competitor. That Chubeck regularly goes up against Earth-based corporations means his enemies are few but powerful."

"But would those enemies be desperate enough to blow up a whole ship just to get Westerhof?" Carstol said as they reached the OSAR offices.

Lenowitz stopped outside the door. "Perhaps rich enough not to care who else they killed, simply to stop a new advisor that would give Chubeck some unique advantage that I do not yet understand. The problem is, those enemies are also smart enough not to put the bomb on the wrong ship."

CHAPTER 7
Trust

When Ed did turn on his com, he found the messages had piled up: a request from his uncle to come to dinner at the farm, 1800 hours, dress neatly (must mean guests); a notice for a memorial service for the *New Brunswick* victims scheduled for the next day; a voice message from Paul. Ed had heard from Paul a couple of times after the explosion when they were still en route to Mars, but this one was flagged urgent. He put on his earpiece and tapped the control to hear it.

"Ed, I hope you check your messages soon. The FBI seems to be asking an awful lot of questions about you the past few days, rather odd questions. They are suspicious of you, my friend. And I think their suspicions are being helped along by someone on The Moon. Be careful."

A bit late, Ed thought. There were also a couple of calls on the same subject from Jeff, a reporter Ed knew pretty well at Mars News. Jeff's editor was pressing for some type of comment from Ed, and if he didn't call back, the editor would hand it over to the new reporter, and she might end up back at his house that night. That wouldn't do, not with his uncle's dinner party going on.

So Ed called Jeff back and agreed to meet him outside the 4-O offices for a few minutes of no comment, though Ed was able to get in that Capt. Lenowitz did not consider him a suspect. He hoped the captain would back him up when Jeff made his follow-up call.

That evening, the sky above the dome had turned violet with strands of high, blue-white clouds when Ed walked over to his uncle's house, much grander than Ed's with three levels, balconies perched on stepped roofs, and tall arched windows on the first floor.

Voices and lights from the rear confirmed the dinner would be on the walled veranda out back. Faizah was on the southern side of the house, walking slowly along a meandering path through flowers of blue, gold and orange. She wore slim black pants and a shimmering blue shirt that flowed around her. Unlike the first time he saw Faizah on the Moon when she seemed to blend into the background, her look tonight demanded attention, as did the jasmine scent of her perfume as he approached. But Faizah didn't seem ready to accept attention, yet.

"Not all the guests have arrived, I take it," Ed said as he joined her.

Faizah looked up and smiled. "Perhaps we're still waiting for Capt. Lenowitz. At least I wouldn't be surprised if he showed up."

"Is he giving you a rough time?"

She shook her head. "No, he's been quite gentlemanly about it. But he has made it clear I am his chief suspect. Hell, I'm everybody's chief suspect." Faizah turned and took a couple of steps down the path. "Yours too, I imagine."

"I don't know enough to think you'd plant that bomb. Then again, I don't know why anyone would want to kill you either."

Her fingers strayed softly across the petals of a pink rose. "Maybe I wasn't supposed to be killed. Perhaps I was just supposed to take the fall." Anger slipped into her soft tones. "It's at least ruined my purpose here. I was supposed to spend the next 21 months advising Chubeck, working with your uncle and others to protect what you've done out here from some dangerously shortsighted people back on Earth, maybe even turn it to our advantage. I was supposed to be subtle, working with Earth contacts through back channels so our defense didn't seem like the shrill protests of special interests."

"So much for blending into the background." Ed tried to make it sound wry and light, but he really wasn't very good at wry.

"Now I don't know what I'm going to do for the next two years, provided I'm not in jail."

Three more guests, two men and a woman, arrived at the house and walked around to the back. Ed recognized the woman as CEO of the Phobos maintenance docks. One of the men held agricultural interests in the Serling Heights dome.

"What is happening tonight?" Ed asked Faizah. "Why are we here?"

"In light of all that's happened, Chubeck thought I should give a formal briefing to the friends and associates of 4th Orbit. I wouldn't be surprised if half of them walk out."

"Don't worry, no one walks out on my uncle's dinners. Should we join them?"

Faizah smiled gratefully, and took his arm as they walked around to the veranda.

Carl Chubeck's dinner parties were legendary affairs on Mars. Sometimes raucous cookouts, sometimes sumptuous feasts, this one looked to Ed to be quietly elegant. There were about 30 guests all told, representatives from the agriculture co-op, independent shippers, research scientists, the dean from UA-M, Martian manufacturers, and a ship builder from Ceres. Space operations entrenched in Earth corporations were noticeably absent, such as Astech and Interplanetary Drive Systems. Independent mining companies were represented, and there were a few people Ed didn't recognize, though he bet that, like the others, they were among the power brokers on Mars – what power there was that slipped out of Earth corporate control.

"What am I doing here?" he whispered to Faizah.

"Your uncle said he needed you in the know," she said.

"About time," Ed muttered. "I didn't realize it was going to put me in such high company. This looks like a gathering where everyone should be drinking wine or martinis, and all the men wearing ties."

"Do they even have ties on Mars?"

"Can't recall ever seeing one."

"We already know about the wines. How's the vodka and gin?"

"Pretty good, actually."

"Then why don't you have one now," Faizah said. "You look like you could use it. I know I could, but I'll have to save it for later. Excuse me, I have to talk to Carl before this starts."

Ed decided to take Faizah's advice and headed for the portable outside bar for a vodka martini. A balding man whose waistline suggested he took advantage of Mars' lighter gravity – to his disadvantage if he ever returned to Earth – stepped up after Ed and ordered a gin and tonic.

"I saw on the news that OSAR doesn't consider you a suspect after all," he said, and offered his hand "Arthur Strand, operations manager, Ares Manufacturing ."

"I was hoping that word would get out, though I don't know if the FBI and Interpol are convinced of my innocence. This whole thing made our arrival much more public than I think my uncle wanted."

"More public than any of us wanted," Strand said. "I was happy to see Chubeck had some of his men and dogs out to make sure reporters or anyone else didn't creep up to listen in."

"Dogs? I hadn't noticed that," Ed said. "The dogs are herders, not watch dogs, but I suppose they'll make enough noise if someone shows up. I didn't realize tonight was so critical or confidential."

With his drink hand, Strand motioned to the group. "When this many Martian independents show up, it has to be critical. And after that bombing, it better be confidential. Excuse me, won't you? Charlie, how was your trip to Olympus Mons?"

Charlie McKracken, the Ceres shipbuilder, was tall and thin, in his early 40s. Ed overheard him telling Strand about climbing the cliffs on the edge of Olympus Mons. For the most part, climbing the largest volcano in the Solar System would involve a very long walk up gentle slopes. But the escarpment that rings the volcano can range from two to six kilometers high, a challenge for climbers no matter how light the gravity.

McKracken was an adventurer, usually of a type that seems in a race to see what will happen first, death or bankruptcy. He had been lucky on both counts so far, though McKracken had his share of physical and financial close calls. His Ceres Shipbuilding yard built mostly robot explorers and a few manned tugs for the Belt, and provided steady maintenance on Ceres for both.

A few more guests congratulated Ed on his rescue efforts, assuring him they never believed he was involved in planting the bomb. He saw Faizah talking with two others in a corner beneath a small cherry tree that glowed softly in a lamp's yellow light. While Ed knew many of the names, or at least the faces, of those in attendance, Faizah was the only one there he felt comfortable talking to – except for his uncle. But neither one of them was having casual conversations that night. It was all business.

Ed was looking to plant himself against a wall when someone tapped him on the shoulder.

"Mr. McKracken," Ed said, surprised. He had met the man when they were both on Ceres years ago, Ed earning his pilot rating on mining tugs, McKracken just getting his ship building and maintenance yard going. But they had hardly talked since. "I overheard you telling Strand about climbing the cliffs of Olympus Mons. I'm not sure I'd want to try that."

"Make it Charlie, please," he said. Ed thought he seemed a little ill at ease. "I wouldn't have wanted to try what you had to do on your last trip. But I'm not looking to trade adventure tales. There's something else I need to ask you." McKracken guided him to a vacant spot along the wall. "When you were piloting the mining tugs, you had a friend with you, Paul I think it was. Didn't he go to work for Astech?"

"He still works for them. I'm surprised you still remember him."

"I keep coming across the name Paul Cherault on Astech orders from the Moon. Is that your friend?"

"Yeah, I had dinner with him when I was there. Why?"

"In any of your conversations with him, did he ever mention Astech moving into shipbuilding?"

"I know they're expanding their fleet, and are nosing around for pilots. IDS is building an interplanetary transport for Astech now in their L-1 shipyard. I saw it. But Paul never mentioned anything about Astech wanting to build the ships themselves. Are you afraid of competition if they're interested in getting into the business?"

"Actually, they are interested in getting into the business – my business."

"Astech wants to buy you out?"

"More like wanting a stake in Ceres Shipbuilding, but that's pretty preliminary. A company rep approached me since I've been on Mars. Look, don't spread it around. I don't know if it'll come to anything. The thing is, they seemed interested in a more extensive operation than the market will bear. I'm just not sure where they're coming from. But if they want to make the move, I'm not sure I can refuse."

"Why not?"

"For one thing, the offer they're talking about may be too good to turn down. More to the point, the pressure they can bring if I don't take the offer may be too much to stand. The whole thing makes me nervous. But if you pick up any hints on what Astech's up to, let me know, will you?"

"Sure. How long are you on Mars?"

"I'm going with you back to Ceres. I'm booked on the *Zach*."

"Then I'll see you at launch."

The call came for dinner, then, and the group sifted between the tables to find seats, about six per table.

Chubeck was at the head table, of course. He was a tall man, though he said he added an inch or two since he left Earth for Mars. He added more than that around his girth, but he was of solid build. The weight and the solidness both came from the farms he started and still worked. He was 62, but had an ample head of salt and pepper hair and a full beard. He wore a light brown shirt and a dark brown leather vest with a small 4-O logo branded over the left pocket. Chubeck was quick to laughter, as he showed frequently that night. But Ed knew he was also quick to anger.

Faizah sat next to him, and both of them held urgent conversations with the others at their table. She still looked nervous, but Ed thought her nerves eased whenever his uncle put a reassuring hand on her arm. At one point she seemed to lean into his shoulder. But Faizah quickly straightened when she saw Ed looking their way.

"Is it something more than business between them?" Ed thought. Uncle Carl never mentioned her before, and on their trip to Mars, Faizah always dodged the question of how long she knew his uncle. Yet Faizah said she'd never been to Mars before, and his uncle's trips to the Moon are pretty hectic, when he makes them. Besides, Ed figured she couldn't be much older than himself, and probably a whole lot younger than his uncle. He filed the thought away.

Ed was sitting at a table farther back, grateful to be away from the focal point of the evening. He found himself next to the dean of UA-M, Anne Gadient.

"Your uncle looks like some ancient land baron of the American southwest," she said. "Given the veranda, the adobe style house, even this canyon, you'd think you were in New Mexico if it wasn't for the gridwork of the dome above us."

"He fits that spirit," Ed said, putting his drink down. "He's a Martian pioneer who made good, and he seems to have brought most of the like-minded independents together tonight."

"Chubeck helped many of them get started," Gadient said, picking at her salad. "One thing I never found out, though, in the four – that is, two Martian years I've been here. Who helped Chubeck get his start?"

"It dilutes the legend if most people knew that. But he had connections with life science companies on Earth, and found favor with some major investors. Even I don't know all the details. He came to Mars on a research grant to improve hydroponics."

"I always heard his first project was in cattle."

Ed took a bite of tomato, then went on. "Raising cattle was always his intention. But that didn't have favor with the old Martian Development Initiative. Cattle took up too much land and energy, and a heavy meat diet wasn't as healthy as a vegetarian one. But my uncle knew that the asteroid miners, space jockeys and anyone else out here would kill for a steak. He figured if he could sell it to them at a price of something less than homicide, they'd call it a bargain. So his investors backed a side research project on the feasibility of raising cattle on Mars. It was supposed to be a small project."

"It wasn't, I take it."

"He didn't bring many calves with him, but he brought a lot of frozen sperm. The first thing he did was improve the efficiency of the hydroponics so they overproduced."

"And the excess provided feed for the cattle," Gadient finished for him.

"It still does. But my uncle also integrated his new cattle and dairy farm into the Martian ecology, things like manure for soil generation. Leather jackets became a big hit during the winter when the temperature drops beneath these domes. Even the methane his cows produce add to the greenhouse gases we're pumping into the natural atmosphere to warm the planet."

"The Mars-DI let him get away with it?"

"It didn't have much choice. He gave away some of the research at a cookout, and the demand for fresh meat and a varied diet became too strong to deny. Meat consumption per person on Mars is still far less than most developed countries on Earth, but it became vital to our society. Mars-DI was thinking subsistence, and my uncle was thinking quality of life. He sponsored and integrated many elements of a community economy. He expanded food production into poultry, pork and fish. He helped a sheep farmer get started, then began a small woolen mill. My uncle brought in variety wherever he could. Before, a permanent colony meant shelters waiting for the next crew rotation. My uncle really brought home the idea of people coming to Mars to live."

"That's why he can bring all these people together," Gadient said.

"That's why he sometimes butts heads with corporate companies out here, because he's created such a strong independent base."

"Really?" The dean looked genuinely puzzled. "I've talked to a number of corporate officers since I've been here. They speak very highly of Chubeck."

"They need him," Ed said. "He feeds their people; he helps them be content. My uncle excites people about living and working out here. In some ways, I think he excites corporations the same way. So they put up with him being a pain in the ass sometimes."

Gadient chuckled. "He's a dangerous friend for the Earth companies to have out here." But she quickly turned serious. "It's too bad everything Chubeck's done may not be enough."

"You mean the politics back on Earth, the funding cutbacks?"

"That's part of it, but popular support comes and goes," she said. "The real problem may be here. You can see it in our students."

That puzzled Ed. "I thought you had no shortage of kids wanting to come to school here."

"Earth kids, yes. And many of them want to stay out here for a time, a long time, even. It's the Martian kids, the ones that grew up here. Many of them leave for Earth before graduation, and most of the rest head for the home planet soon after."

"I stayed."

"You're the exception," Gadient said. "Our surveys show students who study to be pilots, naturally enough, stay out here. But the isolation is too much for most of the rest. The same is true on the other end of the age spectrum. No one retires here, and I mean no one."

"What? You're saying there are no old people on Mars?"

Gadient shook her head. "I don't mean that. But anyone older than 70 who's still on Mars stays because he or she is still working. Not always full time, yet still very active in a professional pursuit. But no one stays on Mars just to kick back and relax. Even long-timers usually stay for 20 or 30 Earth years, not a whole career. The average is much less. They mean to stay longer, according to the surveys. But every window for Earth, a major part of the Martian population turns over. The Mars colony has stopped growing."

"That's why the big passenger runs, the cheaper and slower ones, are still mostly full both ways."

"We have new people coming to Mars all the time, but just as many leaving, and recently more. The Earth to Mars runs aren't always full."

"Particularly over the last two windows?" Ed asked.

"It's been more pronounced, but the trend actually goes back much farther."

"Like about the time my parents decided to leave?" Ed suggested, with a touch of wistfulness.

"Your parents were probably like so many others," Gadient said. "They made their mark out here, and people like your uncle made it easier to stay out here. But Mars was still too alien. They had to go back."

Ed sipped at his gin, not taking much of it, but taking his time. "So how do we change that for the people on Mars now?"

"We end the isolation," she said. "We somehow make the trip from Mars to Earth quicker, and we expand the launch window."

"That takes physics."

"And that takes funding..." Gadient began. Ed joined her to finish the thought.

"... and that takes politics," they said in unison and laughed.

"Maybe that's why we're here," Gadient said, "to hear about the politics."

"We'll find out soon enough," Ed said.

They changed topics and went on to talk about the Wildcats' prospects in the coming college football season back on Earth. The caterers brought out the main dishes, an assortment to suit varied tastes, including vegetarian. But most seemed to choose the *Carbonnades a la flamande*, a Belgian stew made with beer, a specialty of the chef.

By the time dessert was served, the stars were out, noticeably dimmer on the south side where robot cleaners had yet to reach to clear off the panes from recent dust storms. Above and to the north, however, the stars sparkled through the grid, and Saturn rose spectacularly bright above the Eastern ridge line.

The wait staff cleared plates and served second cups of coffee for those who developed a tolerance for the local variety. As the catering staff packed up and disappeared, a couple of 4th Orbit staffers placed an electronic paper report in front of each guest. Ed noticed Roger at the gate nodding to Chubeck. Ariel, who was with Roger, noticed Ed and wanted to join him. Her barks drew some laughter as Roger dragged her off. She was a working dog, but tonight's duties clearly struck her as strange.

Chubeck stood up, and the guests, engaging in some soft chatter after the meal, quieted down. Ed knew his uncle wasn't going to ease into the topic, and from the look on all their faces, they knew the same thing.

"We have two issues to deal with tonight," Chubeck began. "The second is why I've asked you to attend. But to open our minds for the second, we must deal with the first.

"We were all shocked by the bombing of the *New Brunswick*, and I was happy to see on the news this evening that my nephew, Ed Ferald," Chubeck pointed to Ed, "is no longer considered a suspect by the local OSAR investigator. I don't think Capt. Lenowitz ever seriously considered Ed as such, so after a short time of doubt some of you may have had today, we can go back to honoring Ed for being the hero he is." The group applauded and Ed acknowledged them with an embarrassed half wave.

"I'm afraid we have no such reassuring statement from investigators concerning our special guest, Faizah Westerhof. Circumstances have made her a suspect in their minds. But if we are to find her information credible, and judge her counsel wisely, we have to clear that suspicion from our own minds at least."

There was a murmuring from the group, not a particularly encouraging one.

"The circumstances that have placed her in this precarious legal position came about because of a threat to her life. The threat warned her not to come to Mars. Inter-Corporate Resources, the company that employs her, received the threat through its operations in Seattle and forwarded the information on to Faizah, who by that time was already on the Moon. She took precautions, including canceling her reservation on the *New Brunswick*. By my direction, she worked with the 4th Orbit staff to secretly take passage on the *Cydonia Zach*. They took extra measures to ensure the safety of the *Zach* and of Faizah, including establishing a public schedule that had her seemingly remaining on the Moon for another two weeks before returning to Earth.

"We did not warn the *New Brunswick* crew. That was my decision." Chubeck let that sink in on the group for a few seconds, then continued. "The threat was directed against Faizah, not the ship. Once it was clear she was no longer going on that ship, I assumed the *New Brunswick* was safe. It may have been a mistake in judgment that doomed the crew and two passengers of that ship, and if so, the mistake was solely mine, and I deeply, deeply regret it. But there is no evidence that Faizah was involved in the planting of the bomb, and there isn't even a hint of a suggestion of a motive for her to do so. The actions she took on the Moon were for her safety and to allow her to talk with us tonight, and work with us for at least the next year to circumvent an even larger threat from Earth that looms over our way of life. She has the solid backing of Inter-Corporate Resources, and I trust her without reservation. You know me, so you know my trust doesn't come easily. All of us need to listen."

Without reservation? Ed didn't think his uncle ever trusted anyone without reservation, and by the look on their faces, many in the group weren't willing to share his uncle's trust. But they all stayed to listen, and that was all his uncle asked.

CHAPTER 8
Moratorium

She-Who-Is-Victorious never felt so much on the edge of defeat. Her reputation on Earth had been solid. Faizah didn't just uncover business trends. She found out what was happening in back rooms, board rooms and bedrooms, what government was about to fall and who it would fall upon – and who would profit. She would pour over accounting data, slip into parties and break into networks to find out what a client needed to know. And she had a grasp of how societies reacted, how a seemingly little thing would drive a populace crazy, and how a disaster would unite a citizenry and make them strong. She knew who to talk to. She knew when to listen.

But Faizah never felt directly responsible for the deaths of seven people before. She knew lives often depended on the information and advice she gave, and there was no way to predict or often discern ripple effects of her work. But the *New Brunswick* crew shouldn't have died. Carl couldn't take that responsibility away from her.

He asked this group to listen to her. She knew she better have something to say. Faizah touched a control in her hand, and a photo appeared on each of the electronic sheets placed before the guests.

"U.S. Senator Franklin Decker by all accounts is a loose cannon. He is generally considered a liberal, and often branded a radical. He knows how to create a simple message that resonates with the public. He is running for president in the U.S. election set for the next Earth year. Pollsters are finding he is making some surprising gains, but they don't expect him to be a major factor. They are wrong."

Faizah switched the display on the sheets. "Many people don't know him yet, but his ideas have found surprising support across a broad

range of demographics. The talking points he's raised about space operations are what concerns all of us here, of course. If he's successful
in cutting back half the funding and subsidies he argues against, and
he might, even if not elected, the cutbacks will be felt from Earth to
Saturn. It is what Decker will do in two months, however, that will
make him unstoppable."

"Wait a minute," spoke up Strand. "You know what he's going to
do in two months?"

Faizah smiled a little and shrugged. "That's our job."

The displays switched again. "The senator will announce his plans
for a total moratorium on space exploration, military development,
science and technology advances of all kinds that are not directly re-
lated to health and the social condition of Earth. For 10 years, Decker
proposes the U.S., and because of its lead, the world, should put all its
resources into fixing Earth."

"That's crazy," someone said. "It wouldn't work."

"Most likely. But it will get him elected."

"Even if it did," said the university dean, "America doesn't have the
power it once had."

"What power it does have, it holds onto dearly, and its cultural
influence is widespread. More importantly, there is a growing belief
among the American public and the populace of the rest of Earth
that space is for the elite, a place for science that most people don't
understand, a corporate boondoggle, and an exotic playground for
the rich. He proposes to cut off all support for Mars and beyond,
even bring us all back to Earth if need be. Decker would maintain
only minimal support for the Moon, and to return to space only
when the critical problems of the world are resolved or at least the
planet is on the road to recovery. The Americans among you know
the turmoil Congress will be in when it attempts to deal with this
moratorium. Its members will be torn between connecting themselves with a popular idea and protecting special interests. Some
corporations will position themselves well in the political battle.
Others will go bankrupt."

"But no one's going to protect our interest," Strand said. "No one
will look out for Mars."

"Precisely." Faizah saw that maybe they believed her after all. At
least they were listening. "At best, independents will be squeezed out

of space in a supposed effort to consolidate operations. At worst, by the end of Decker's first term, Tiu City will be a ghost town."

Faizah's presentation went on for 30 minutes, interrupted frequently by questions. She knew Decker's 10-year moratorium was an elegant plan that, if done effectively, could in fact go a long way toward improving life on Earth. But it wouldn't go as planned. Everyone in the group knew it, but as Faizah talked, she saw the realization come to their faces on how disastrous even half measures, especially half measures, would be for Mars and the independents. In space, corporations would carve out new niches, the use of robots would expand again, and the number of people living in space would drop – drastically. The permanence that people like those in front of her were trying to establish beyond Earth orbit would drift away.

"You're just guessing," said the CEO of the Phobos docks. "How can you be so certain Decker will find support? People love space."

"People love movies about space," Faizah answered. "Always have, even before men reached orbit. But not the reality of it. InterCorporate interviewed, polled, sifted the moratorium through focus groups and listened in on whispers in government hallways. We scoured news stories and digested statistics. What we found was that most people weren't just disinterested in space and science, they wanted to be rid of them. Sure, there is a percentage that is very supportive of what we do here, and still come out here to work and live, but not enough. The bottom line: the majority of people will believe in Decker's plan because they want to believe in it. The people of Earth are exhausted from constantly evolving technology that's bewildering at best, and at its worst further separates the privileged from the majority of poor souls just trying to get by. They want a break from progress."

"But once they have that break," Gadient asked, "will they resume progress again after 10 years? Will they return to Mars, or will our society find itself on a plateau and believe that's good enough?"

"I don't know," Faizah said, "and I wonder if all of you realize how frightening an admission that is. We've asked – desperately, we've asked. Yet in all my time studying trends and discovering schemes, in the history of my company and all its years of uncovering plots and shaping opinions, we've never come up with a more unanswerable question. The last time people turned their back on progress, it lasted for centuries. If it wasn't for Europe's Dark Ages, we might have reached the stars by now."

Faizah saw they understood. If not the complexity of the politics, they realized the uncertainty of their future.

McKracken broke the silence. "So how do we stop Decker?"

Faizah turned to Chubeck, who had said nothing since his introduction. He stood up to answer the question.

"We don't. In fact, we endorse him."

The group erupted in denials and disbelief. Chubeck held up his hands to quiet them, but it took a while until the last of the anger and questions about his sanity died down.

"Understand the details. Decker doesn't want us off Mars. He just doesn't want to pay for us to be here. He doesn't want to pay for the tremendous subsidies that corporations – Earth-based corporations – say are needed to continue to do business in space. We need to show that the assumptions, profit and loss statements, costs overruns on which the subsidies and inflated contracts are based, are a lie. We can use Decker's candidacy to show that."

As he talked, Chubeck stepped around the table and approached a table of miners and shippers. "Independent miners have accused Astech for a long time of cooking its books and getting an unfair pricing advantage from the U.S. Am I right?" Half the table nodded. "Interplanetary Drive Systems has a monopoly on fusion reactor drives enforced and funded by the U.S. and China. You can only lease the drive, and they keep the number of drives small so they can keep the charges high." The other half nodded. "Euro's space plane is heavily subsidized, yet ticket prices are outrageous. The number of new people coming into space to explore and work has dropped to a trickle compared to what it should be because of cost. And protectionism – supposedly to save jobs, but the only ones they save are in the board room – prevent the resources of space that would truly show its value – energy and metals – from reaching Earth in abundance."

Now in the middle of the full group, he turned slowly, making eye contacts down the line as would a lawyer giving a summation to a jury. "Operations around the Moon, Mars, the Belt and Jupiter already provide enough food, raw materials, energy, and products for us to survive on our own. We would already have a viable economy if it wasn't for this gaping hole of manipulated costs that keeps us from expanding the way we should, and saps national budgets on Earth. I don't know if Decker is a madman or a visionary, but we can use him to plug that hole. From what we know of his plan, it calls for a major cutback in space and eliminates subsidies. The plan assumes most of us will have to be brought back to Earth, which would be incredibly expensive and delay plans to reinvest in Earth.

"Let's offer an alternative. We stay out here. Earth corporations can continue in space without subsidies, or the government buys out their space-borne assets – at discount – and transfers them to us. It would still cost far less than bringing us all back to Earth."

"Wait a minute, Carl," McKracken said. "Do you think IDS will just pack up and de-orbit? All they have to do is jack up the prices on the drive leases."

"Not if Decker breaks their monopoly on fusion drives."

"Will he commit to that?"

Faizah took the answer, feeling a touch triumphant as she gave it. "He already has."

It seemed to Ed an amen was called for, but the shouted questions and sudden side discussions would have drowned it out. He leaned over to Gadient. "I don't really know if my uncle is a madman or a visionary."

Gadient grinned. "I wouldn't want to poll this group on that question right now," she said. "Vision or delusion, though, his view is addictive."

She touched the report sheet in front of her to show another page. "I read ahead. Mars operations are also heavily subsidized, but from what I'm seeing so far in this report, most of the money never reaches the planet. It pays off mostly indirect costs that InterCorporate claims never should have been charged to Mars in the first place. This is only a summary, but if it holds up in the details, this information alone would be enough to get Decker elected."

"Would it be reason enough for murder?"

"With the money this report talks about, certainly. But even if Ms. Westerhof had been on the *New Brunswick*, it wouldn't have stopped this report."

"But even if my uncle gets the independents out here to go along, doesn't that make Mars even more isolated?

"Certainly it does politically," Gadient said. "Economically, it may attract more entrepreneurial pioneers. But I don't see how that attracts enough money to solve your physics problem. That piece of the puzzle is still missing."

The noise level rose as people started splitting off in threes and fours trying to make sense of the evening. Faizah and Chubeck were working different tables, clarifying the report or explaining their plan to co-opt Decker. Ed got up to leave. The report had an overprint that said it should be left behind, so he left the sheet on the table. He caught his uncle's eye and gave him a quick wave. Chubeck gave him a nod back, which Ed took to mean his uncle would talk to him more about this later.

Ed ducked out a side gate and walked across the road toward his home, glad to be away from the crowd.

"Leaving the party so early?" came a voice from Ed's patio.

Ed peered into the shadows and saw Lenowitz, petting Ariel's head in his lap. "I was telling somebody back there that these dogs are herders, not watch dogs."

"Not so. This dog has kept watch on me for much of the evening. She just apparently saw no reason not to be friendly about it."

Ed couldn't help but laugh. "What are you doing here, captain?"

"A public safety officer saw all these rather important people boarding the train, and overhead someone mention a meeting with Chubeck. He thought I might be interested. I was."

"But what are you doing on my porch?"

"Ah, that. The caterers were packing up, and the chef saw me in the commuter cart. We are friends. I eat at his restaurant all the time, except during the tourist window. So he gave me some leftover Belgian stew, and your veranda seemed a much more pleasant place at which to eat it. It is over this stew that this wonderful dog and I became friends."

"You know, that goes great with beer. Do you want one?"

"I already have one," Lenowitz said, lifting a bottle.

"Wait a minute, did you get that from my refrigerator?"

"The door was unlocked. Besides, I needed to go in anyway to find a spoon for the stew, and the dog needed water."

"Her name is Ariel."

"Nice to meet you Ariel," Lenowitz said, bowing his head closer to the dog. Ariel licked his nose.

"No accounting for taste, I guess," Ed said, going inside to get a beer for himself. "You're sure you don't need a second one?" he called out.

"This is my second."

Ed came back out and pulled up another chair.

"It sure is a nice night," Lenowitz said. "There's no rain coming, is there?"

"Maybe in the morning again. My uncle asked for it to be dry until 4 a.m."

"He expects to go that late?"

"It just might."

They both sipped their beer. Ariel laid down between to them.

"You know what your uncle should do?"

"What?"

"He should have the village put up a row, a few rows, of holographic panels across the dome, east to west, and program it to show a moon going across the night sky. A real moon, like Earth has, not the piddlin' rocks we have up here."

"You sure that's just your second beer?" Another moment of silence. A few more sips of beer. "Did you go over there to listen in?"

Lenowitz shook his head. "That would have been too embarrassing if I was caught, and too embarrassing for your uncle if I wasn't. I thought I'd just ask you instead."

"You expect me to tell you what went on over there?"

"At least tell me one thing. Did what you hear convince you that Ms. Westerhof was the target of the bomb?"

"No."

Lenowitz leaned forward as if to get up.

"Then maybe I best go over there and arrest her."

Ed put his arm out to stop him. "After two beers? Why don't you wait until tomorrow? She isn't going anywhere."

"Good point."

Several guests were leaving, and the conversations from across the way grew quieter. They could hear the burbling of the irrigation stream.

"Besides, what I did hear convinces me even more she didn't do it."

"But as we said earlier, she is either the suspect or the target."

"No, we said she couldn't be both. But what if she's neither?"

"But she herself said she was threatened."

Ed shook his head and leaned forward, putting it together in his mind. "That's just it. She wasn't threatened to be killed. She was warned not to be on the *New Brunswick*."

"You are suggesting there was another target and someone was protecting her?"

"I've been thinking about it, and it makes more sense. The bomb would have been a pretty sloppy and probably ineffective way to kill her. You said so yourself. And you haven't found the slightest hint of a motive for her to be the bomber, have you?"

"No. And to be honest, not much evidence. But if not her, who was the intended target?"

"Or what. The bomb was moved at the last minute from the luggage hold to the tug. The bomber couldn't have known that. And you said it was larger than it had to be to ignite the fuel. But if it was meant for the luggage hold, the size was right to destroy anything in there."

"But there was not much in there," Lenowitz said. "I inspected all the luggage and packages that were in the hold. There was nothing worth destroying."

Ed leaned back and put his feet up on an empty chair. "Maybe it will come to us in the morning."

Lenowitz finished his beer. "You know, the FBI still thinks you did it for the glory. They were angry with me for admitting to a reporter that I did not consider you a suspect."

"To hell with the FBI," Ed said, lifting his beer in a toast.

"Here, here." Lenowitz answered. After another sip of beer, he reached down and petted Ariel. "So what was going on at your uncle's place tonight?"

"The First Martian Continental Congress, I think."

That puzzled Lenowitz for a few seconds until he remembered his history. "You mean that American 'Give me liberty or no taxation with representation thing?'"

"Yeah, that's it."

Saturn was high above, and clearing the eastern ridge was its larger rival, Jupiter.

"Did they sign anything?"

"Nope."

Lenowitz leaned back and sighed. "Then I will not worry about it tonight."

"You want another beer?"

"Sure."

CHAPTER 9

Fire & Dust

The monastery of St. Joseph of Cupertino is the last hope for all spacefarers. When miners go bust, when pilots lose their nerve, when researchers lose their grants and stretch projects too far until they're stranded on Ganymede, they find their way here. The monastery offers them a haven while they earn a stake and recover their confidence for a fresh start, or scrape together enough to return to Earth.

Anyone seeking the monastery on Mars or its mission on Ceres has free passage from anywhere off Earth. Tug operators bill the monastery, but make no attempt to collect. They may need passage to the monastery themselves someday. Besides, St. Joseph's collects a highly skilled if down-on-their-luck workforce in many disciplines and trades, and hire them out with major discounts. Though it's never quite certain what skills are available at any one time, St. Joseph's often has a specialist on hand who is rarely needed, but is irreplaceable when that skill is called for.

The Martian monastery's broad reach takes in desperate people from many different pursuits. Some have turned from navigating in the belt to tending a shop on Sagan Street. Others found employment in Tiu City's industrial district. All of them needed time to find their direction, and often their soul.

The monastery buildings echoed the same desert style as the rest of Tiu City. Its perimeter wall incorporated the rim of a small crater left after the land was domed. The chapel was set in the center, its steeple resembling a crater's ragged center peak, but loftier so it could be seen beyond the crater walls. Workshops and dorms extended on either side along the crater's diameter. From outside, what was left of the crater's natural walls formed only a slight rise surrounding the monastery, with the main entrance to the grounds opposite the chapel front door. A walkway descended onto the crater floor, where the open land was filled with gardens and meandering paths.

"Ed! Ed, over here."

Ed was walking up the steps to the chapel's front door when he heard the voice behind him. He turned to see the steward from the *New Brunswick* rushing up to join him.

"Jessica. How are you? You're looking great. Did the doctors give you a clean bill of health?"

"Yeah, I'm fine," she said, touching his arm lightly as she reached him. "A lot better than George, anyway."

"Will he be here?"

"A couple of nurses already brought him in, but they're taking him right back to the hospital after the service. Listen, Ed, is it all right if I sit with you?"

"Well, yeah. Sure."

"It's just that I'm supposed to read a message from the sister of one of the dead passengers, and I'm a little nervous. I don't now, it just seems ...."

"It's all right. No problem."

"Thanks."

Ed surprised himself that he noticed her sandy-colored hair was freshly trimmed above her shoulders and styled. Even during the catastrophe on board, Ed thought she was pretty, but with the dirt and bruises gone, no one could have any doubt. Jessica's blue eyes pierced the gloom of the chapel as they entered, showing an overwhelming sadness now, but he remembered an unexpected determination in them as she dealt with the injured.

The chapel was a dome, its arc extending to the floor. Where churches on Earth have skies and clouds painted on their ceilings, St. Joseph's surrounded its congregation in stars set against a violet blue background above, fading to a rose hue along the sides. Four stained-glass windows, set on the compass points, arched across the dome from the floor until they meet in a circle at its apex.

St. Joseph's was chartered by the Franciscans, and was named after a Franciscan priest of the 17th century who, among other religious ecstasies, was said to periodically float in midair. That's why he eventually became the patron saint of astronauts. A depiction of a rather stiff looking Joseph floating above a group of amazed friars in a church, based on a 1682 woodcut, was set in ceramic tiles near the entrance. The mission store sold a similar sculpted relief, but the background was the blackness of space. His silvery halo struck some as a depiction of a space suit's helmet.

While many who visit the monastery doubt the story of Joseph, Fr. John, the first priest to study for the priesthood entirely on Mars and be ordained on the planet, points out that everyone on Mars has spent at least a few days floating between orbits. He insists Joseph of Cupertino was just ahead of his time. No one chooses to argue.

It's officially a Catholic monastery, but in practice much of its activities were nondenominational and even secular. Yet it held true to its mission of offering hope and new direction to the people who find their way to the monastery. As its popularity grew, it became a center for the celebration of life amid the stark realities of space, and a gathering place for honoring the dead.

A crowd of 1,000 filled St. Joseph's chapel for the memorial service for the seven who died in the *New Brunswick* explosion. Ed saw some of the passengers from the New B. greeting Faizah. She wanted to skip the service, thinking there was still too much suspicion on her. But it looked like the passengers were pleased to see her and gave Faizah their support.

Ed and Jessica joined Hafiz near the center of the circular rows. Faizah took a seat with Chubeck a few rows behind them. Lenowitz showed up late and stayed in the back. A solid contingent of pilots attended, along with the mayor of Tiu City, Pathfinder Spaceport officials, and friends of the crew. Ed didn't think anyone on Mars knew the dead passengers, the one who died immediately and the one that succumbed to injuries three days away from Mars.

Ed knew most of the crew by sight, but only had social contact with the pilot, John Gaitlin, an Australian who had been running the space lanes for six years. It was hardly a friendship, though the two often met for racquetball between runs, and beer after the matches. Organizers of the service asked him to speak for Gaitlin. Ed reluctantly agreed. People expected him to say something as the rescuer of Gaitlin's passengers, and when the time came, Ed kept it short with some platitudes about the dead pilot and crew, and the "dangers we all willingly face to expand humanity's horizons." The mourners seemed to like it.

Minglong Chi, who ran the mission's Ceres shop on reactors and power plants, had sent a video eulogy on Gaitlin, played after Ed finished speaking. Minglong had his certification in fusion drives when he went into space, but he became a master only after a reactor accident left him two withered legs. The mission gave him a second chance when the transport companies wouldn't touch him, and Ceres allowed him to use his legs in the asteroid's microgravity.

Many pilots when they docked at Ceres sought him out to maintain their drives or hear his philosophy. Gaitlin in particular spent hours with Minglong during stopovers at the asteroid, and the monk described how their talks grew into a strong friendship.

"I actually knew two victims of this tragedy," Minglong said. "John I knew for years, and treasure the times we spent together talking philosophy on a barren rock. But over the past year I've also come to know Tim Averink, a passenger who died on the *New Brunswick*. In his discourse with me over the InterPlanet, Tim seemed to comprehend innately a passage from St. Joseph that John grasped only after hours of conversation: 'The will is what man has as his unique possession.' That is especially true out here, where we must fight against the influences and forces that would bend or break that will. These men left their lives with their will intact."

After others spoke on the remaining crew members, Jessica read a message from the sister of Fran Oster, the passenger Faizah and Jessica couldn't keep alive. Fran had been a geologist, a grad student on an internship scheduled to split her time between Mars and the Belt. She was on her first trip into space. Jessica was in tears when she returned to her seat. Ed put his arm around her.

The pilot was surprised when he saw Kurt Weller walk to the front. Weller was a physicist who saw his theories spiral in at a Jupiter research station. He had a return ticket to Earth but knew he'd never get back into space if he used it. He hitched a ride to Mars instead, donated the ticket to St. Joseph's for anyone else there to use, and took whatever job the monastery could find for him. Weller often ended up in the fields beneath the agridomes, and learned things about the universe that his studies had never touched upon. Eventually he took over a vineyard and became a self-taught vintner, struggling to come up with passable wines. But he had high hopes for the coming harvest. Weller learned much about time in the orbits of Jupiter, but he never fully experienced time until he spent it among the vines of Mars.

Weller took a moment at the lectern. There was not just sorrow in his eyes, but a barely controlled anger.

"Minglong spoke briefly of Tim Averink," Weller began, "and he was right when he said Tim left this life with his will intact. He would not bend his will for anyone. Tim was a colleague of mine, not in growing grapes, but in plasma physics. Yet where I reached a dead end at Jupiter, his research took some interesting side trips back on Earth. He even started his own company, Polaris Enterprises, really not much more than him and two research assistants. Tim told me he was taking a new look at fusion drives and plasma efficiencies of helium-3. It wasn't just a matter of professional advancement. He was impatient – over the time it took to get to Mars and Jupiter, the narrow windows, the slowness of humanity's expansion into the Solar System. From what he sent me over the last few months from Earth's Moon, Tim believed he had a breakthrough that would change everything. Maybe that belief was too dangerous to survive."

Weller paused, but not for tears. If he was a stronger man, his grip might have ripped the top off the lectern. "Tim's dreams were grand, his murder that much more tragic because of them. I don't know if anyone can pick up the threads of his dreams now sailing somewhere beyond the belt. Tim's legacy is incomplete, and, I'm terribly afraid, lost to us."

Ed still had his arm around Jessica, but he hardly noticed her. He could barely keep his seat as Fr. John rose to close the service.

"We travel beyond Earth on Moon dust, and build our homes from the sands of Mars. We are born of the stars."

The mourners responded in muted unison, "And to the stars we will return." A prayer. A mantra. An oath.

After the service, as the crowd gathered outside, Jessica excused herself to help two med techs get George into a commuter cart to take him back to the hospital. Several of the *New Brunswick* passengers stopped Ed to thank him again for bringing them to safety. Ed was gracious, but broke away from them when he spotted Faizah standing with his uncle and walked towards her. Chubeck was in urgent conversation with a mining official and didn't notice when Faizah left his side to meet Ed halfway.

The pilot put a sympathetic hand on her shoulder, bent his head low and spoke in a soft, comforting tone. "So what do you or InterCorporate know about Polaris Enterprises?"

Faizah gave him a mock grateful look and spoke just as softly. "Give me 'til this afternoon. I'll know more then."

The two casually walked toward a garden path to keep out of earshot. Ed kept his sympathetic demeanor for anyone watching. "That frantic call we got from Polaris and Averink's death couldn't be coincidence."

"Not if you believe Weller. Do you think anyone picked up on that?" Faizah asked.

"Lenowitz, probably. At least enough to pique his interest. And perhaps one other."

"Who?"

"If Averink's death isn't coincidence, whoever is behind the bombing couldn't have depended on the explosion killing him. Somebody would have had to be on board to do it."

"The killer would have been putting himself in for a wild ride."

"Perhaps it was more wild than he expected."

"Why?"

"Lenowitz thinks the bomb was just supposed to blow up the luggage, not the whole damn tug."

"Does Lenowitz know about Polaris' call to save their shipment?" Faizah asked.

Ed shook his head. "I don't think so. The call was on a commercial channel and most likely sent on a directed signal. It probably never reached Mars, and I never recorded it. I never mentioned it to Lenowitz because, frankly, I forgot about it until now."

"Don't mention it the next time you see him, either," Faizah said.

"Aren't we on the same side? Don't we want to see this solved?"

"Lenowitz thinks I did it, and the FBI on Earth thinks you did it. I wouldn't call that the same side. And with everything else that's going on, I'd like to get ahead of the curve on this for a change. Don't worry, if we find evidence, we'll share it with Lenowitz. Are you going to talk to Weller?"

"After I hear from you on what you find out. While you're at it, send a secure message to Marta. See if she can find out what Polaris was shipping."

The crowd had thinned when the two of them returned to the front of the chapel. Faizah rejoined Chubeck, and Ed found Jessica talking with Hafiz and Lenowitz

"Ah, there you are," Hafiz said brightly. "Jessica here said she needed to escape some of this gloom, and I told her I know just the place."

"The Wahoo," Ed said resignedly, still suffering a bit of a hangover from the night before.

Jessica looked doubtful. "The Wahoo?"

"It's a bar not too far from here," Hafiz said. "A lot of pilots and crew frequent the place. You'll love it. Captain, will you join us?" Lenowitz put up his hand to wave off the invitation. "I had enough drinking with this pilot to last a while, thank you. Ed, a moment, please."

The two walked a few steps away to talk in private. "Jessica tells me she did not get to know this Averink well on the trip. But you know Weller, correct?"

"I've been trying to sell his wine on the Moon, and we talk sometimes about his vineyards. I didn't know he was friends with Averink."

"You have not talked to him since you came back?"

"No."

Lenowitz folded his arms and looked out over the gardens, struggling to gather threads of thought together.

"It is interesting that Weller was the only one angry enough this morning to call it what it is, murder. Everyone else seemed to dance around the term, even now too shocked to accept it."

"Was there an autopsy done on Averink?"

"On all four bodies recovered. The examiner conducted them on Sundim, soon after you landed. The conclusions were all the same: died as a result of the explosion. In Averink's case, it appears he was thrown against a bulkhead and broke his neck. Whether we can determine now if it was the explosion or someone else who threw him against that bulkhead, I do not know."

"Have you talked to Weller?"

"No, he left too quickly. I will catch up with him. Of course, there are seven legacies left unfinished. Who knows what grand plans any of them had?"

CHAPTER 10

Wahoo!

The Wahoo! sits in the heart of Tiu City's industrial district and a block from the last passenger stop on the mag-lev line heading north. Soon after they pumped air into the dome, space crews and construction gangs homesteaded the site for a bar, much like neighborhood kids taking over a vacant lot and piecing together crates and plywood for a clubhouse.

It started with a cylindrical construction pod contractors used when they were putting up the dome and reshaping the land. The pod was marked as surplus, but instead of taking it outside for disposal or storage, the workers dragged it over to the lot for their tavern, and cut off the roof and part of the wall so they could use the second deck as a balcony. It was supposed to be replaced someday with a real building, but instead they just added on to it. A couple of adobe walls butted up against the pod, and a new opening was cut out for an entrance to what could loosely be called the interior. A roof over the adobe walls came gradually, its support struts scavenged from a cargo module that took too hard a landing on Mars. The place looked like a bunch of jigsaw pieces jammed together, all from different puzzles.

Pilots who had been at the memorial were starting to fill up the place. A band of part-time musicians with a multi-cultural mix of instruments were playing a Martian version of the blues for the wake. Hafiz found three stools at the bar near the back and waved Ed and Jessica over. The bartender, a husky woman with a jovial face came over to wipe the bar top as they sat down.

"Ed, the first one's on me," she said. "What'll you have?"

"Bloody Mary, but light on the vodka," Ed answered.

"Since when?"

"Since I had too many beers last night, er, this morning."

"Suit yourself. How about you two?"

"Mariner's Ale," Hafiz said. Jessica stuck with the ale as well.

"You're right, Hafiz," Jessica said as the bartender poured their drinks. "This place is certainly, um, eclectic."

Hafiz and Ed laughed. "That's a kind word for it," Hafiz said. "See the back wall. That's what's left of *Asteroid Annie*. She was a mining tug that got too close to its work. They brought her back to Phobos in chunks for repairs, but she was a lost cause. So somebody slapped a heat shield and parachutes on it and dumped her down on Mars. Some pilots scavenged it for this place. The restrooms and part of the galley came from Annie, too. That's her name plate up there over the bar."

"This bar top," Ed interjected, "is standing on pipes and struts from the long-hauler *Rings of Fire*."

A couple of pilots nearby who started the wake early heard Ed, took their glasses and rose rather unsteadily to their feet.

"The *Rings of Fire*," the two toasted, not quite in unison, but loudly.

The rest of the bar heard them and rose to complete the toast, as did Hafiz and Ed, catching Jessica by surprise. The band halted in mid-chorus.

"The *Rings of Fire*," the crowd called out, raising their glasses. A moment's silence, then glasses banged down on tables and the bar top. The music resumed and conversations began again.

"What was ...?" began Jessica

"Don't ask," Ed said.

Hafiz picked up the descriptions again, sliding his hand across the space in front of Jessica. "For the bar top, they pounded out the skin of the British probe Beagle VII."

"No toast for the Beagle?" Jessica asked.

"Robot," Ed explained.

"Ah, of course."

"Did you notice the ceiling fans," Hafiz asked her.

"Yeah, solar panels, aren't they?"

"From the ore processor *Tianyi*."

"The tables were made from the remains of the passenger liner the *Mars Express*," Ed said. "The floor is from the decks of the first Belt rescue vehicle, *Tom Corbett*. The tiles behind the bar there come from the old NASA space shuttle *Columbia*. I don't know how they got here. All along these walls hang the flotsam of dozens of ships – and memories of the souls they carried beyond Earth."

The portion of the crowd near Ed grew quieter as the pilot ticked off the names of the legendary wrecks. When he finished, the bartender took a glass and pounded it on the bar top, quieting the rest of the crowd.

"Ladies and gentlemen, to the *New Brunswick*."

This time the crowd rose more solemnly to answer the toast.

"The *New Brunswick*."

The silence was a couple of seconds longer this time, and conversations a bit more subdued as they resumed.

"I admit, when I first came in, I was thinking more junkyard than bar," Jessica said. "But the spacers have really put their soul into this place."

"We've also put a lot of partying into this place," Ed said, sipping at his drink. "The junkyard look is seasoned by abuse from space crews, port workers, science station researchers, and oddly enough the staff of the Mars Development Council's planning and design office."

"You're kidding."

"They come here to escape the building codes and design regs the council tries to enforce on the rest of Mars."

"So why is this place called the Wahoo!?"

Hafiz took the question. "It's named after a crater northeast of here."

"There's a crater named Wahoo? What, did some astronaut stumble across a crater and name it the first thing that came to his mind?"

"Not quite. It's named after a town in Nebraska," Ed said

"Which, I suspect," added Hafiz, "was named by a pioneer who stumbled across the place while looking for somewhere to live, and named it the first...."

"I get it," Jessica said. "But why name it after a town in Nebraska?"

"I don't know that story," Ed said. "A number of craters have Earth city names, and someone couldn't resist Wahoo."

"Well I don't know about the craters, but I like the bar," Jessica said. "It reminds me of some places I've been to in north Chicago."

"Is that where you're from?" Ed asked.

"I went to school there, and still had an apartment on the northside until I took the job with Trans Orbit."

"Chicago, huh?" Hafiz piped in. "So, do you believe those Cubs?"

Jessica reached for her beer. "I don't want to talk about it."

The two men laughed and reached for their own drinks.

"Is Trans Orbit picking up your pay until it has a flight for you again?" Hafiz asked.

"That's something else I don't want to talk about."

"Why, what happened?"

Jessica took another swallow of beer then set the glass down. "Trans Orbit looks like it's going under. They have insurance, but they tell me there's no interplanetary tug for sale on Mars or Phobos to replace the *New Brunswick*. The company was already in debt, and without the anticipated income from the Ceres run and others the New B. was supposed to make the next couple... that is, this year, Trans Orbit will have to default. I got a layoff notice late yesterday."

"That's pretty cruel," Ed said. "They just released you from the hospital."

"George was still in his hospital bed when he received his notice." Jessica took another swallow. "At least he'll be on worker's comp and medical until he recovers. T.O. gave me two-weeks severance and a note to wish me luck. The company said it would do its best to help me find another job, but most of the insurance money is being spent in finishing the run of its remaining tug and closing the company down."

Hafiz leaned back and gave Ed a questioning look. Ed realized immediately what he was asking and tried to subtly shake his head so Jessica wouldn't notice but still wave Hafiz off, but Hafiz just mouthed, "Why not?"

Jessica noticed Ed's look. "What?" she asked.

Something nagged at Ed that this wasn't a good idea. Yet, he gave in. "Are you willing to go right back into space?"

Jessica shrugged her shoulders. "On our approach to Mars, I thought about staying on the ground for a while. But suddenly facing no paychecks, I have this urge to get back to doing what I know. I was on Earth-Moon runs for about two years before taking the job with Trans Orbit. I wanted to be out here, and I don't want to end up at St. Joe's. Why, do you have something?"

"As a matter of fact, we might," Ed said. "I'm taking the *Zach* to Ceres in a couple of weeks, and Hafiz tells me it's turned into a passenger run. About 20 passengers, many from the New B. I haven't put together a crew yet, but I know I'll need a steward. Would you be interested?"

"Would I! I heard some of the *New Brunswick* passengers say they caught a new flight, but I didn't hear with what ship. I don't know what I'll do the rest of the Martian year, but this is a start."

"It may be more than a start," Hafiz said. "If you're right about Trans Orbit going under, we may be picking up more passenger runs and other shipments."

That caught Ed even more off guard. "I thought our schedule for both 4-O tugs was pretty much maxed out"

"It is," Hafiz said. "But if this proves to be an opportunity to expand our market share, I think I know a used tug that will be up for sale shortly."

"You're starting to sound like a vulture," Jessica said.

"Hey, there's another Trans Orbit pilot and crew out there that still need to eat, and people and cargo that still need to get between the Belt and Mars. If 4-O can pick up the pieces and keep everything going, so much the better for all of us." Hafiz drained his beer and stood up. "I have to get back and send a message to Marta. Maybe we can come up with a proposal for your uncle to buy that tug, if not tomorrow, at least by Thursdim."

Hafiz left quickly, leaving Jessica and Ed staring at their drinks and facing a sudden lull in their conversation. Ed tried desperately to think of something interesting to say, and was grateful when Jessica broke the silence first, hesitantly.

"Am I the only steward you're hiring, or will you be adding someone else?"

"Frankly, Hafiz and I haven't had a chance to talk about a crew yet. He just sprang the Ceres run on me yesterday. But if we hold the passenger list to 20, I think one steward would do it."

"Wow, that would make me chief steward, even if it is just a staff of me. I've never been that before. But I suppose if the passenger list goes higher, you'll hire someone with more experience to be chief."

"I'm not sure what we'd do, but don't sell yourself short. You did pretty well out there with your chief out of commission and the ship a wreck. You kept your passengers from panicking and helped them survive."

Jessica shook her head. "I couldn't have done it if Faizah hadn't come up to help after you docked." She placed her hand softly on his arm. "None of us on board might be alive if it wasn't for you."

It was Ed's turn for denial. "I only did what any pilot would have done. That's why we make these flights in pairs."

"Aw shucks, ma'm, 'twern't nuthin," Jessica said, mockingly. Smiling broadly, she leaned into Ed and slipped her arm around his. "C'mon, I never had a guy ride to my rescue before, so don't spoil it. Besides, I met a lot of space pilots. I'm glad it was you who came to my rescue and not any of them."

The softness of her shoulder and the slight scent of raspberry from her hair were pushing thoughts of murder plots and conspiracies out of his mind.

"Ed?"

His prelaunch workload seemed to drop in priority, and he wasn't even too concerned about the voice behind him.

"Ed?"

The voice was firmer, and Ed began to wonder if it was for him. A tap on his shoulder brought him out of it. Ed reluctantly swung around on his barstool to find a tall woman standing next to him with an athletic build – very athletic – wearing tight, black pants, and a low-cut red tank top.

"Laura!" Ed said in surprise, and looked up. Laura had short-cropped blond hair, and a silver chain around her neck holding a polished stone that Ed knew came from the Belt. She spoke in a cockney accent.

"I'm sorry to barge in, love, but I couldn't help but overhear you're looking for a crew to make a run to Ceres. I imagine you need a co-pilot. I'm available if you're interested."

"Um, yeah... I mean, we haven't put a call out for crew yet, and I don't know if Hafiz has anyone in mind, but sure, we can put your name down."

Laura sat down on the stool next to his. Jessica on the other side of Ed undid her arm. "I take it this is a passenger run?"

"Yeah, a small module, about 20 passengers. Jessica Cantrell here will be the steward."

Laura looked over Ed's shoulder at Jessica. "You were on the *New Brunswick*, weren't you?"

Jessica leaned back to make eye contact. "Yes."

"Very well done, girl. From what I heard, not many stewards I know would have held up as strongly as you did."

Jessica gave a wan thank-you smile and returned to her beer. Laura turned her attention back to Ed. "You'll be needing one or two system engineers. I believe Manny can free up his schedule if you wish to hire him as well. And he can also double in the third shift pilot seat."

"Did he get his second class license?"

"Just. He'd be eager to earn some flying points, even if it's only to sit on the night shift and make sure nothing goes wrong."

Ed frowned at the remark. "After my last trip, I don't take that for granted anymore, which is why I'd love to have Manny as system engineer. With any luck, we can work in some maneuvering time for him at the controls."

Finally, Laura showed a smile, a soft smile in contrast to her hard-edged demeanor. "That would be terrif. Manny would love that. He's been itching to have some real time."

"Send a contract application off to Hafiz this afternoon and tell him you talked to me. I'll let him know you're on my short list. We'll get back to you in a day or two."

"Brilliant. Thank you very much." Laura stood up and nodded to Jessica. "Jessica, very nice to meet you." She turned smoothly to leave, her heels clicking on the floor tiles, drawing stares as she passed.

"Ed?" Soft, but insistent. "Ed!"

"What? Oh, I'm sorry." Ed quickly shifted his attention back to Jessica. He noticed her eyes didn't have that hero-worship look anymore.

"Putting together a crew seems to be pretty easy for you," she said.

"It was just luck running into Laura. She's really very good in the pilot's seat."

"I'm sure she's very good wherever she chooses to be."

Warning lights were blazing in Ed's head, and he shifted into a mid-course correction. "Actually, she and Manny make a wonderful team. He's a crack engineer. He can fix anything."

"So who is Manny?"

"He's her husband. And if we do hire them, and I think we will, one warning: Don't flirt with Manny."

"What?"

"Even if it's just joking around, don't do it. They're madly in love with each other, and plan to get their own tug someday and ply the Belt. That's why he's studying for a pilot's license. But she tends to get jealous, and you don't want to get on her bad side that way."

"I don't think I want to get on her bad side in any way." Jessica was giving Ed a more bemused look.

"Once you get to know Laura, she's fine. And we'll get to know them both on this trip."

Jessica didn't say anything for a moment, but then decided to take the opening. "I'd like to get to know you better while we're still on Mars. Are you doing anything the rest of the day? Maybe you can show me some of Tiu City."

Relieved, Ed declined gently. "I'm afraid I have to take care of some things this afternoon, finalize the crew with Hafiz, other launch preparations. But if you're free tonight, how about dinner?"

"I'd like that."

∞∞∞∞∞∞∞∞

Ed didn't take long at the 4th Orbit offices, and was soon back in Viking Glen, heading directly for his uncle's place. He found Faizah in a second floor spare bedroom she turned into her office. An arch window looked over a small apple orchard, with pastures beyond. Faizah motioned for him to close the door.

"I take it you turned up something." Ed pulled up an imitation wood chair next to her work table.

"Mostly that it's a good thing you didn't take Polaris up on its offer to rescue their shipment," Faizah said, handing Ed an e-paper readout of the company's credit report. "They couldn't have bought you a cup of coffee."

"Hey, a cup of real coffee is pretty expensive on Mars."

"Maybe that's what they were shipping. There's no indication they were successful at developing anything else."

"Are you saying Polaris is a dead end?"

"I'm not sure yet, but it doesn't add up. Averink was working on fusion plasma propulsion, as Weller said, trying to improve efficiencies. I actually looked into his project when I was on the Moon. He moved

his lab to the Moon about two years ago so he could have a ready sup-
ply of Helium-3."

"That's still pretty expensive on Luna, even if it is laying around in
the moon dust," Ed said.

Faizah touched a button on the screen, and the display in Ed's hand
changed. "He had money when he came to Luna. That's how he got
the lab in the first place. He just ran through his funds pretty quickly."

Ed studied the names of Polaris' investors. "They put in pretty good
money, but I don't recognize any of these investment companies."

"You wouldn't. The money's been laundered."

"Averink was using dirty money?"

"Well, that's usually why money gets laundered, but that may not
be the case this time." Faizah walked over and pointed to three companies she highlighted in the readout. "These firms specialize in investing
funds for clients who don't want publicity. But they're often legitimate
transactions."

"Excuse me for being dumb about this, but if it isn't mob money or
something like that, why launder the investment?"

"Economic repercussions if the investments became known. Political
ramifications. Stock prices. Competitive advantage. Somebody wanting to stick it to a rival. Who knows?"

"So why did Averink's money run out?"

Faizah reached and touched another button. "This report's been
circulating for a few months now. It's supposed to be confidential, but
Averink has apparently been a topic of discussion in his field for some
time, and someone leaked it on the 'net. I don't understand half of it,
but the summary is pretty clear. Averink's claims for improved efficiencies for plasma thrusts were unsubstantiated, his theories faulty, and
his research questionable and possibly fraudulent."

"Who did the report?"

"It was part of an audit for the investors. They put a lien on his lab
equipment, his records, and a working model of a plasma engine component he was developing."

"If it didn't work, why did they want it?"

"I think they wanted to get something for their money, do their
own tests. But Averink must have already had the prototype loaded
on the *New Brunswick*, along with all his records. Marta tells me the
lab is bare."

"Why was he coming to Mars, then, just to run away?"

Faizah shook her head as she touched a key again and blanked the sheet in Ed's hand. "He was actually traveling on to Ceres, but why, I don't know. I'm trying to track down Averink's two research assistants. It must have been one of them that radioed us, but they left the Moon soon after the explosion, and no one knows where on Earth they are. I asked InterCorporate to track them down."

"Does this add up to Averink being a target?"

"Not in my mind, it doesn't," Faizah said. "It's still a damned striking coincidence, but even if the investors were hopping mad that Averink was running off with the model and his notes, they wouldn't have used a bomb when a court injunction would do. There are a few more things from Earth I'm waiting on, just to be sure. You weren't going to talk to Weller tonight, yet, were you?"

Ed hesitated. "Actually, I have plans tonight, for dinner."

Faizah raised an eyebrow. "With Jessica?"

Ed nodded his head and gave an embarrassed smile. "Well, yeah. Hafiz and I hired her today as steward for the Ceres run. After Hafiz left, Jessica and I just kept talking, and I ended up asking her out."

"I'm sure it was all your idea."

"Well, yeah – kinda."

"Ed, she was trying to make connections with you before we reached Mars, though I think it was mostly about getting another job. She talked about needing to get to Ceres and asking if you'd be taking the flight. I didn't know at the time. But I heard her talking with some of the other passengers today before the service about what ship they were taking. After they told her it was the *Zach*, she ends up seated between you and Hafiz."

"Jessica said she didn't know I was making the run."

"Really? Did she just bat her eyes and talk woefully about being out of a job?"

"Sorta."

"And you fell for it?"

"It's not like it was a hard fall. She could have just come up to me and said, 'I need a job,' and I probably would have hired her. She didn't have to put on an act."

"Which makes me wonder why she did. Maybe 'probably' wasn't good enough odds for her. It doesn't matter. She's probably a good hire.

But if she bats her eyes at you again tonight, you might want to find out what she really wants."

"Maybe she just wants dinner with a charming space pilot."

"Wait 'til she gets to know you. After spending a month in a space tug with you, believe me, you're not that charming."

As Ed walked back to his house, he tried to sort everything out. He was willing to pass off Jessica's actions, though they nagged at him. As for Weller's accusations and Faizah's findings, she was right, they didn't add up. He could put that off for a while tonight, but not entirely. Ed wasn't sure why he didn't tell Faizah that he and Jessica were having dinner at Weller's restaurant.

CHAPTER 11

Vines and Webs

Ed still brooded over his suspicion and fears that evening on the commuter trip back to town Tuesdim evening, but those thoughts dissipated when he spotted Jessica waiting for him on the downtown platform. She was wearing a floral print dress of red and green against a white background, and a long sleeve white jacket.

"New?" he asked as she stepped up.

Jessica smiled broadly. "I saw this on Sagan Street and had to buy it. After all that's happened, I needed something bright. I just hope it's warm enough for your Martian nights."

"It should be, for a few more weeks at least. When winter comes on, though, and the sun stays lower on the horizon, we don't collect as much solar warmth beneath the domes. We don't let it get Chicago-in-January cold, but it's definitely cooler."

"Nice jacket you're wearing," she said, fingering the thin suede sport coat.

"Part of my commission. But c'mon, we have to hurry to catch the next southbound." He took her hand and led her to the steps for the cross-under to the southbound platform.

"We're not eating downtown?"

"I made a reservation at a restaurant in Serling Heights – The Rose Lake Vineyard."

"I could have just met you there."

"I had to come into Tiu City anyway to make the connection."

The two reached the southbound platform just as their train pulled into the station.

"Rose Lake," Jessica said as they sat down, "isn't that the winery Kurt Weller owns?"

Ed was hoping she didn't know that. "Yeah. They serve great seafood. The fish are raised in Serling Heights. And the Rose Lake Chardonay is not bad."

Jessica gave Ed a quizzical, not quite suspicious look. "And it gives you a chance to talk to Weller?"

Ed sat back in his seat, loosening the hold on her hand. "The guy who took the reservation said Weller would be there tonight," he said, torn between needing to know more about the plot and wanting to simply enjoy the evening with her. "I don't know if I'll get a chance to talk to him, but I need to try. I'm caught up in the middle of all this, Jessica, and no one understands yet why the bombing took place."

Ed expected Jessica to be disappointed to have the past horror invade their evening, but she gave his hand a squeeze and held on. "I was the one who found Averink, and couldn't do anything but watch when Fran died. It was luck I was strapped in, or I could have died, too – and others. I want to find out why as much as you do."

Ed didn't want to fill her in on the details he knew with other commuters around, so the conversation turned light again as the train cruised through the city and slipped into the tube on the Martian surface. It was a five-minute ride and a sharp rise to Serling Heights.

"You know, I can't believe I'm on Mars," Jessica said. "It's going to take me forever to adjust."

"You'll be surprised how quickly you get used to this place," Ed answered.

"I don't know about that. I'm having a hard time remembering it's a sol and not a day on Mars, and the sols of the week are Mondim, Tuesdim and so on. Why do Martians do that?"

"A lot of people here still call it a day, but naming them Wednesdim and alike was necessary"

"Just to be different from Earth?"

"Our days are different from Earth. Because the Martian days are longer, the days of the week never stay matched up. Today's Tuesdim, but I think it's Saturday on Earth. The different names keeps things straight when communicating off planet."

"But you don't say 'tosol' or 'todim'?"

"That would be too Martian."

Jessica chuckled, then looked out the window. "Are those lights where we're heading?" she asked, nodding to a glow in the distance.

"No, that's a new agridome. No name for it yet. Serling is just around the bend." As the mag-lev rounded a curve, they entered a canyon with a buttressed steel barrier that stretched between the canyon walls. Serling Height's dome rose above the barrier.

The train slowed as it bored through the barrier and eased to a stop in a small village. Gold tinted street lamps gave the village a quaint look despite the glass and metal dome rising above it. A number of people walked the street, couples mostly, waiting for the next train back, or a restaurant table to become free. There were only a few shops on the street, including a fish market closed for the night. But three restaurants were doing a steady business.

Jack's Fish Shack was boisterous that evening, with loud music and aromas of fried fish and steamed crab wafting onto the street. Fake wood piers and ramshackle siding gave it a rustic look, but unlike the Wahoo!, it was by design, not neglect. Even though it was a weeknight, it was packed.

Martian Rivers was quieter, a family restaurant with an earlier crowd that was just beginning to thin. Three children ran ahead of their parents and nearly straight into Ed and Jessica.

"Slow down," their mother called out. "Watch where you're going."

"I'm sorry," their father said, but Ed just waved him off with a chuckle.

"No problem, really," Ed said.

"Aren't they a little young to make the trip here from Earth?" Jessica said quietly to Ed as they walked on.

"Most likely they were born on Mars," Ed said. "They're part of our first generation of native Martians. We've had births on Mars before, but it's only been in recent years that parents of new born are becoming permanent, or at least long-term residents."

Rose Lake Winery was at the end of the street, on a hill overlooking the lake and vineyard. Rose Lake is the largest body of water on Mars, and takes its name from the color of its surface during the day as it reflects the Martian sky. Seeing it now at dusk, the lake was a ribbon of violet and red set among the lush green vineyards. Its surface rippled from a breeze directed down the canyon, a breeze that carried with it the sweet smell of ripening grapes. Small sailboats were moored below the restaurant and along the far shore.

Jessica leaned against a walkway rail to get a better view of the boats. "I heard they had sailboats here. Where do they get the wind?"

"The dome's circulation system provides a prevailing breeze along the valley. It's enough to fill a sail."

"Can we rent one sometime?"

Ed was skeptical. "I've never sailed in my life."

Jessica was undeterred. "No problem. I learned to sail on Lake Michigan. You can be my crew."

"Aye, aye, captain." Ed gave Jessica a mock salute. The two laughed as they walked up to the restaurant.

Rose Lake Winery presented a French Mediterranean look rather than the common Martian Pueblo. The outer walls were painted white, with metal grillwork over the second story windows. The interior exuded a simple elegance: rustic black metal chairs and tables with flowered cushions and white tablecloths, lit by candlelight. The music was soft, French. The menu held a mix of cuisine, and the smell of garlic, rosemary and other herbs mingled with candle scents of lemon and vanilla.

The maitre'd seated them at a table by a window overlooking the lake. Ed asked to see Weller if he was available. The maitre'd sniffed a noncommittal "I'll see what I can do." Ed didn't mind. He was beginning to hope Weller would not make an appearance. Why spoil an evening that was turning out perfect?

Ed and Jessica talked easily and laughed frequently, sampling each other's plates and their lives. They talked of growing up, he on a Martian farm, she in Milwaukee. They compared college classes in north Chicago with those in Jupiter's orbit, and shared memories of family and friends. Halfway through dinner Jessica removed her jacket, revealing spaghetti straps and a low cut u-shaped neckline.

"I can see, now, why you asked if the dress would be warm enough for Martian nights."

"Do you think I'll get cold?"

"I doubt it. In fact, it seems to me the evening is warming up."

"That's what I thought," she said, putting a hand on his.

Ed responded by gently intertwining his fingers with hers. Thoughts of the explosion and murders were as far away as the point in space where the tragedy occurred, as if the 37 million kilometers made a difference.

 oooooooooo

Only a few diners were left by the time Ed paid the bill. They were talking of a final after-dinner drink in the bar when a hand dropped a bottle and three aperitif glasses on their table.

"I heard you wanted to see me," Weller said. He uncorked the bottle and poured a rich, translucent port into each glass. He pulled up a chair and sat down opposite Ed, with Jessica to his left.

What a time for reality to return, Ed thought. "Hi, Kurt. Glad you stopped by."

"I didn't want to disturb a romantic evening too early, but I did want you to try this port. We actually were able to age this in small barrels cut from your uncle's estate. There isn't much in this batch, but I should have enough ready for export in the next window." He handed the filled glasses to Ed and Jessica. "But then, you didn't wish to talk about pitching my wine on Earth's Moon, did you?"

"No. I wish that's all it was. It's about your eulogy of Averink this morning."

"I thought we all touched the mourners with what we had to say," Weller said, his tone carrying an edge of mockery. "You were quite elegant in your kind words of the crew. And, Jessica, isn't it?" he nodded toward her. "That letter you read was very moving. Murder is such a sad business." Weller raised his glass in a toast. "To the victims of the *New Brunswick*. May they float free in peace." A prayer. A taunt.

A silence as they sipped their drinks. Ed was surprised to find the port quite excellent, surprised that a part of his senses even noticed. He put that thought down with the glass. "They were all victims of murder, Kurt, but you suggested Averink was the true target."

Weller sat back and draped his right arm over the back of his chair. "True? There's some debate as to how true Averink was. But I made no suggestion. He was the target."

"I saw the audit report on his research," Ed said. "His fusion drive component didn't work. He wasted money. His backers suspected him of fraud. They didn't need to kill him. They just had to write him off as a tax break."

Weller jerked across the table to stare intensely into Ed's eyes, a flash of anger reflected in the candlelight on his face. "You can't write Tim off that easily. Did you read anything more of that report than the summary? It was just a bunch of lies. They cut his funding to stop him. They discredited him to stop him. And when they saw that didn't do it either, they killed him, and destroyed his work. They apparently didn't care if six others had to die as well."

"Who are 'they,' and why was Averink's work such a threat?"

Weller's face stayed where it was, grim, almost demonic in his candle-lit anger, the flame's flicker disguising the barely perceptible shake in his head. Then he relaxed, leaned back, and took another sip of port before answering.

"I don't know who they are, not really. Tim didn't even know. When he received his funding for his lunar lab, he thought it was old money from Seattle, the latest round of spoiled offspring who finally decided to do something with all the credit their grandparents and great grandparents earned or pirated for them. But somebody in that group became afraid when they realized they couldn't control what Tim was creating."

"And what was that? The fusion drive is going about as fast as we can push it now. If Averink could squeeze a bit more efficiency out of, it could make him rich, but it wouldn't have shaken the Solar System."

"Try increasing the thrust from your constant drive by a factor of 10."

Now Ed's face was motionless in surprise. Jessica was puzzled by his expression. "Why, what does that mean?"

Ed still stared back at Weller, trying to read how much was true. "It means we get to Mars in as little as two week's time instead of four," Ed said.

Weller shifted his attention to Jessica. "More importantly, the window expands. With a thrust of .1g, the opportunity for business increases, the demand for travel. It could have been boon time for us on Mars. That's what Tim set out to create. The Earth corporations were afraid they weren't going to control it, or even get their hands on it. So they tried to keep a lid on it."

Jessica was incredulous. "Whoever they are will kill for moving a decimal point in the thrust equation one space to the left?"

Weller shook his head and took another sip. "No, not for one. But 12 months ago, Tim discovered he could move it two."

Ed barely gulped his mouthful of port in time. "One-g constant thrust?"

"What does that mean?" Jessica asked.

Weller kept his attention on her. "It means Earth to Mars in four days. Jupiter in less than two weeks. Launch windows? Wide open. We could go anywhere in the solar system, any time. At point-one-g, there was great money to be made and lost, but Interplanetary Drive Systems and their cohorts could have made sure they had their cut. It would have been a struggle, but they could have kept things under control. It may have been worth a lawsuit or two, but not murder. But open up the Solar System to travel at a full g, and the situation explodes. IDS could never maintain a monopoly under the demand, and Tim never wanted to give them the rights."

"IDS wasn't behind the funding of Averink's lunar lab?" Ed asked.

"Not directly, not from what I learned. But Tim was afraid IDS had an in with one of the backers. IDS, though, wasn't the only one at risk. Think about it. Earth Firsters would suddenly see their cause melt away as people clambered to get off Earth. The Belt could become a new gold rush. And look outside," pointing to the serene, darkened vineyard and reflected lights on the lake. "We've created a mini paradise on Mars, but the emphasis is on mini. We have about 18,000 people on this planet. Move that over by a decimal point, or two, all in a rush. Everything we know out here would be out of control. Ask your uncle what he thinks of that...."

"People still have to get off Earth," Jessica said, "and that's still pretty expensive."

"It's expensive because not enough people want to get off Earth. Rich tourists aren't enough to do it, and they can be overcharged. But create the demand and someone will find a way to get them off planet. If not the U.S., then Japan, or Europe, China even. But that will throw Earth politicians in a tizzy as they try to keep up. No one would be prepared for it if Tim sprang this on us. It would be chaos."

This was all a bit much for both Ed and Jessica to take in, even as Ed tried to fit what he was hearing into what he already knew. But it was Jessica who asked the obvious question.

"If you saw all this, why didn't you warn him?"

Weller broke eye contact and shifted his gaze toward the window. "I didn't see it in time. Tim's enthusiasm was infectious. He wasn't thinking of repercussions. I saw it all poetically as freeing us from Earth's bounds. It wasn't until after the explosion and I heard Tim was dead that I began to think it through, to put all the pieces together that he wrote me about the past year he was on the Moon. He went there just before last year's window, two Earth years ago," he added for Jessica's benefit. "I almost went with you, Ed, to see him. Maybe I should have. I would have known more of what he was trying to do, and maybe see the risks more clearly. I wish I could have warned him to take it slow, but it wasn't his way."

Jessica reflectively put a hand on his shoulder. Weller smiled at that, and went on. "I shouldn't even be telling you all this. Someone tried to warn me off today."

"You were threatened?" Ed asked. "At the service?"

"Not at the service. I stopped off downtown for a few hours. When I got back to the station, somebody slipped a note into my pocket. It was a rush hour crowd, so I didn't see who it was. The note just said, 'Stay quiet, or there will be trouble.'"

"Not much of a note."

"Not much of a threat. Stay quiet from whom? Should I just not talk in public, or shouldn't I even talk to you? And what trouble? Is this a death threat, or is this somebody not liking what I said this morning and wanting to punch me in the nose? Do I even know enough to worry someone? What I told you, without proof, just turns into legend."

"You don't know how Tim's fusion component works?"

"No. At least I don't think I do. Tim sent me bits and pieces of what he was working on, trying out parts of theory on me, but there was never enough to see clearly what he was doing. It was analogous to a supercharger on an old car engine, but I don't really know what he was trying to do with the plasma. Tim was going to show me how it works when he reached Mars."

"Why was he going on to Ceres?"

"To study under the master," Weller said with a half laugh. "He was going to work with Minglong at the mission. They had communicated, and Tim thought Minglong could help him bring it off. Tim believed the mission would also give him legal and political cover, sanctuary."

There was only a thin layer of port left in Ed's glass as he swirled it around slowly. He wanted to be mesmerized by it, but instead lifted his gaze to Weller's eyes. "Do you know for certain that Tim's fusion drive did work?"

Weller's return gaze was steady. "I didn't know until they killed him for it. Why else would they do it?"

ooooooooo

The air had chilled by the time Ed and Jessica left the restaurant. Jessica's light jacket turned out not to be warm enough, and Ed draped his sport coat over her shoulders. But he was too distracted to be gallant about it.

"How do you know he was the one they wanted to kill? Because it worked. How do you know it worked? Because they killed him for it!" Ed looked for something to throw into the lake in frustration, but just pounded the handrail hard with his fist. The thump echoed across the lake, but did nothing to ease his frustration.

Jessica pulled the sport coat closer around her. "Didn't you learn a lot more from Weller tonight?"

"Sure we learned more, but I don't know if it gets us any closer to who did the bombing. In fact, the list of suspects just grew. IDS, Earth Firsters, the Martian Development Council. Hell, even my uncle." Ed stopped.

"Your uncle?"

For a second, Ed wondered if his uncle would see this sudden advance as a threat to his own plans, then dismissed the thought with a wave of his left hand. "It doesn't matter. Everything about Averink hangs on supposition, and even if true, there really isn't anything to go on as to who killed him."

"Then let's leave it for tonight." Jessica slipped her arm into his. "It's been a beautiful evening. I had a wonderful time. But it's getting cold out here, and maybe we should move on."

Ed felt his frustration slip away. He allowed himself to hear the soft sounds that had taken over the night. The music on the street had ended, and there was only the muffled clink of plates being stacked inside the restaurant, the lap of water on the shore, the raspy footfalls of a late night jogger in the sand passing below them.

"All right, forget the intrigue. We can talk about it in the morning."

She looked up at him slyly. "We will?"

Ed stifled a half-embarrassed smile. Then he wasn't embarrassed at all. He brushed her cheek with his left hand, then bent his head down.

There is something special about a first kiss – a charge of excitement, a knot of doubt, resolved in a moment when the lips touch. Not that they touch for only a moment.

They held each other for a few moments longer, then with his arm around her shoulder, they began to walk to the commuter station. Ed drew her in a little closer as she started to shiver from the cold. The cold nagged at him. The heat was escaping too fast from the dome for this time of year, he thought. The system never allows that before the harvest.

Jessica stopped and looked up into the glow of a street lamp. "Is that snow?"

Flakes drifted gently down from condensation on the dome, their sparkle reflecting the lamp's golden hue. It wasn't that unusual, but Ed knew it shouldn't be happening now.

"Something's wrong."

Even as they stood there, the snowfall was getting heavier. "Village public safety is just down the street. Let's go there." They hurried down the block, but only reached halfway when a loud, explosive thump sounded before them and echoed across the valley. The gentle breeze swiftly changed in a wave that swept up the valley and turned into a torrent against their backs. Within a second, the whoops of ear-splitting sirens wailed through the agridome.

"Breach!" Ed yelled. "Get inside, quick."

The wind began tearing off the faux wood siding of Jack's Fish Shack, hurtling it down the street. Dust and leaves pelted people as they struggled to get indoors. Ed and Jessica ran the few yards to Public Safety, but their momentum assisted by the wind pushed them past. Ed took hold of Jessica and pulled her back to the door. They entered a confusion of running bodies, shouted orders and blaring alarms.

"Open up the shelters and get people on the street into them," the desk sergeant yelled. "Somebody find out where the breach is."

Other civilians joined Ed and Jessica in the lobby. An officer started nudging them toward a doorway to the station shelter. "Down the stairs, down the stairs. This will be over shortly, but it's better to be safe." The tension in his voice belied his assurances.

"Shouldn't the robot sealers have taken care of this by now?" Jessica asked.

"The hole must be too big, and I don't think it's in the dome. The wind would be going up, and this is all horizontal."

"Sergeant, Maclaren just called in," called an officer, a worried kid really, seated at the communication gear. Ed stepped aside to listen. "The hole's in the south barrier, all right. That temporary cargo airlock for the construction depot blew out, frame and all."

"Jesus, no wonder the robots aren't handling it. We need to get a crew out there to plug that hole, but in suits! Sure as hell someone's going to get sucked outside. Who's suit certified in here?"

Three of the officers, including the one nervously guiding people into the shelter, raised their hands.

"That's a start. Get suits on and get to the breach, see if you can at least slow it down. Tom, call the construction crew at the new dome. They may have the best chance of sealing it. It's their damned airlock anyway."

Ed turned and bucked the now steady stream of people heading for the stairs.

"Ed, where are you going?" Jessica called out.

"To see if I can help. I can wear a ground suit."

"Ed!" But the crush of the crowd pushed Jessica along and down the stairs, and Ed struggled to reach the sergeant's desk.

"There's no answer at the construction site's emergency number," he heard an officer, Tom, tell the sergeant as he got nearer.

"We've got the super's number somewhere. Find it!" The sergeant turned to Ed. "What do you want?"

"Sergeant, I'm suit certified, and experienced."

"Ground?" the sergeant asked.

"Space, but I have years in vacuum."

"That'll do. Suits are in back. Find one that fits."

Ed followed the other three officers as the sergeant's attention turned back to the construction crew.

"Sarge, I reached the construction supervisor, but he doesn't sound too coherent. I think he's at the Wahoo."

"Give me that," the sergeant said, angrily grabbing the phone. "Listen, your temp airlock just blew a hole out the Serling Heights wall. Get your … What!? You're useless. Put the bartender on. Now!… Joe, we've got a breach at the Serling Heights wall. Sober him up and have him send his crew out here…. What do you mean half his crew is there!? Sober them all up. No, wait, use his com and try to reach the other half at the worksite. With any luck…."

That was all Ed heard in the noise as he continued on and reached a cluttered locker room with 10 white vacuum ground suits hanging along one wall. The suits had fluorescent orange stripes on the legs and arms, and numerals on the chest and shoulders. He took No. 6.

The officer from the stairs was climbing into No. 4, the obvious nerves from before creeping into fear. "I don't know what we're supposed to do. How are we going to seal the breach?"

Ed just grinned at him. "We'll figure that out when we get there. Get your helmet on and let's go."

A woman, already suited with No. 3, her helmet in hand, tapped Four on the shoulder. "Bill, grab a suit, large, for Maclaren. Six, grab one, too, for his partner. Dump 'em in the laundry cart and we'll take that with us."

Ed dumped the dirty towels out of the cart, and he and Four – Bill – dropped the suits in. They barely had time to check their radios and the charge on their backpacks when all four headed out. They left by a back door and stepped into a maelstrom of debris, snow from above, and blinding mist from the lake.

"Everybody, don't run," Three called out. "With this wind, you'll tumble. Just walk quickly and stay calm. We'll do this by the book."

"I didn't know they had a book for a breach this big," from an unknown voice.

"Then we'll write it, one page at a time. Got it?"

"Roger."

"Three," Ed called on the suit-to-suit. "How fast is the pressure dropping?"

"The name's Lynn. Is that you, Six? The air in the dome and the reserve should hold out for a couple of hours. But the temperature is taking a nosedive. The heat exchangers went out about an hour before the breach, don't know why. But we won't get any heat in here until dawn, and the new air we're pumping in is Mars cold."

"My name's Ed. Did one cause the other?"

"That's for somebody else to figure out."

They made their way down a side street, using it as a wind break. No. 7 took a tumble, but was unhurt. Ed and Bill were pulled along by the laundry cart, but somehow managed to keep it under control. The wall was not too far from the village center, and in 20 minutes they reached the area. They found Maclaren in a small building, a storage yard office holding up well against the wind. The warehouse next to it was ripping apart.

"Over here, Lynn," Maclaren called as they entered. "You can see the hole from the window."

They could barely see the hole from all the debris funneling through it. It was roughly square. The door had been big enough for two cargo transports side by side, but the frame around it was gone as well. The crush of air through the breach was deafening.

"The hole's too big for any of the debris to clog it up," Maclaren yelled.

"If that warehouse goes, that might do it," Lynn said, her visor raised so they could hear each other.

"It won't hold the air up much, and not for long."

"But maybe long enough to pile up dirt against it and make a patch," Ed called out. "Is there a bulldozer around here?"

"Yeah, I know where there's one," from Maclaren. "On the other side of that wall."

"Can we get to it?"

"There's a personnel airlock to the right of the breach that may be intact. But even if you reach it, you'll never be able to drive it through that hole."

"How far is the dome's landing port? We could drive it to the airlock there."

"Not quite a klick away, half a klick maybe back toward the rail line. The cargo airlock there will take it. But that's still a long haul outside at night. Can you drive a bulldozer?"

"No, I just came up with the idea. I was hoping someone else knew how to drive."

"I know how to drive a bulldozer," Bill said. "I mean, if no one else does."

Lynn looked around the group. "I don't see anyone else volunteering." Her gaze stopped on Ed.

"I'll go with him," Ed said. "We'll keep each other out of trouble."

With visors closed, and a line tied around them and secured to the yard office, Ed and Bill made their way to the wall, bracing themselves hard against the wind. They walked, stumbled and finally crawled their way to the wall, then edged along it until they reached the personnel airlock door.

"The pressure's too low inside," Ed said. "Not a good sign, but we'll give it a try." He cycled the airlock. The pressure in the lock raised, but it didn't hold. "I've got some pressure in there, but it's going to take both of us to open the hatch."

Despite being within meters of the breach, the pressure along the wall was still standard as the dome's air jammed up to escape through the hole. Bill grabbed the hatch with Ed, and they strained against the lower air pressure inside the lock. Finally they opened it enough for the air to equalize. But the hatch swung to the left toward the breach. The wind caught the hatch, flinging it open and slamming the two of them against the wall. Ed checked his suit indicators, and they still read green. Bill was on his knees, but gave a thumbs up. They crawled into the airlock, but closing the hatch after them was even more of a struggle. When they finally shut the hatch, it locked securely. Air was screaming out of the lock from a leak near the outer door, caused, Ed was certain, when the cargo airlock blew. He cycled the air, and the scream dropped to a whistle, to a whisper, to nothing.

Ed hadn't been on the unprotected Martian surface for a couple of years. The times he had stepped outside, he was always struck by the serenity of the virgin planet. He never saw it like this, with an eruption of debris and vapor vomiting onto the canyon floor and blotting out the night sky. The thin atmosphere softened the sound from the breach, but not enough.

"The bulldozer's over there," Bill said, pointing to a machine on the other side of the breach.

"Where did you learn to drive a bulldozer?" Ed asked. The two had switched their suit radios to a clear channel to avoid the confusion of orders coming from inside.

"My parents are in construction. They were on the crew that built Serling Heights. During school breaks, I picked up jobs with a later project, and in my senior year, they let me drive a dozer, a little."

That couldn't have been more than a year ago, Ed thought. The pair used parked construction equipment as protection from the flying debris as they made their way to the 'dozer. By the time they reached the machine, they were out of the worst of it. They quickly climbed into the enclosed cabin and sealed the hatch. The front bench seated two. Bill didn't wait for the air pressure to rise as he flipped on the controls and checked the vehicle's charge.

"We're all set," Bill said, and with a whine, the dozer took off. The look of fear had left Bill as he fell into a comfortable routine, adjusting the power and guiding the dozer as it bounded across the surface toward the lights of the Serling Heights landing port. The fear that fled Bill's face, however, found haven on Ed's as the dozer went airborne over a rise.

"Are dozers supposed to fly?" Ed said, hanging on tight as the machine came back down.

"This one does tonight," Bill answered.

Port staff were waiting for the two of them as they drove up and guided them immediately to the cargo lock. Within a minute, they were through and back into the maelstrom.

As they approached the breach, a firefighter wearing his standard gear but not a ground suit, waved them to hold position. Two fire trucks had moved into place on either side of the breach, and cables extended from winches on the trucks to the battered warehouse. Figures darted from the warehouse, leaving welding equipment and prying machines behind. The winches tightened and the wall of the warehouse groaned against its foundation. The near side broke free and flapped crazily in the wind, then the far side. The wind caught the siding as if it were scrap paper and flung it against the breach. The force of air sucked through some of the warehouse wall supports and siding. But the beams were wider than the hole, and a barricade against the storm began.

The firefighter ahead of them waved a go ahead. Bill lowered the blade and punched the dozer into gear, scraping a mound of soil against the beams and scraps of siding. Clouds of dirt flew over its crest, but much of the mound held. Bill see-sawed the dozer against the breach, heaping more dirt on the mound. Ed kept lookout for the figures darting before the dozer, fighting the hurricane force wind as they lodged more supports into the hole to catch the dirt and flying debris.

The sign from Jack's Fish Shack flew past the dozer and smacked flat against a break on the left side. Bill gunned the dozer and shoved a heap of dirt against the sign. Two firefighters who approached the mound from the side with a hose sprayed the dirt, wetting it down and freezing it into place.

Pieces of debris kept clanging against the dozer cabin, but it held. Not everyone on the ground was so lucky. The suited figures were better protected, but Ed saw several in regular gear go down, one just ahead of the dozer as Bill was shifting forward.

"Stop!" Ed yelled. He flipped down his visor, and jumped out of the cabin. The wind pushed him forward and he hit the ground rolling, struggling to stop. He didn't try to stand, but instead crawled into the force of the wind. The injured man, his head bleeding profusely, lay 10 meters ahead of him. Ed kept a low profile as he reached and dragged him away from the wall.

"You're clear, Bill," Ed yelled into his suit mike. The dozer gunned past him and slammed again into the mound. A helmeted firefighter on a safety line inched toward Ed from the yard office. Together they pulled the injured man to safety and carried him inside.

Two med techs had turned the one room office into an aid station for the men and women throwing themselves against the breach. The injured man Ed helped was the fifth in there. Ed started to head back out.

"Six, wait."

Ed turned to the med tech who called him.

"We've got enough people out there. With your suit, you're better off rescuing some of them who go down. Attach him to a line." The med tech wasn't making a request. Ed didn't object.

Three times he went out to bring an injured volunteer back. The last time, the wind had noticeably dropped. Regular construction crews reached the breach, bringing a front end loader to fill in the top of the mound. Firefighters began spraying a fast drying patching foam against the dirt and beam barricade, working it higher in layers. The sound had cut from a deafening roar, the pitch rising as the breach narrowed, then fell silent as it was finally sealed.

Ed walked outside, taking off his helmet, the steam from his breath rising in the frigid air, swirling and flowing back up valley as new air currents equalized pressure in the dome. The volunteers around the mound stepped back.

It was Bill, climbing out of the dozer cockpit, who gave the first joyous shout. In seconds, it was a chorus.

The construction crew moved in closer, checking the seals and taking over the job of making the patch permanent. The others, exhausted, frozen, fell back. An ambulance pulled up to the yard office and more med techs jumped out to help.

The other four suited public safety officers reached the dozer and were slapping Bill on the back, and soon others were too. A construction crew foreman offered Bill a job on the spot, at double his pay.

"Six," Lynn called out as Ed reached the group. "Nice job in getting our boy out there."

"Ed. And he did all the work."

With her helmet off, Ed could see her long red hair tied back, and a pretty face with brown eyes drawn and haggard from the night's work. "Not all of it. He was a scared kid when he went out. I don't think he would have made it to the wall without you. Now look at him. He's a damn hero. And I saw you pulling people back when they got hit, some of them my people. It felt good to have you covering our backs. What were you doing out here, anyway?"

"I was on a date."

"Just my luck. A hero comes out of nowhere to ride to the rescue, and it turns out he's on a date."

"I get that a lot, lately."

Lynn gave him a jaundiced, bloodshot eye for the remark. "Ah, what the hell," she said, grabbed the back of his head with her right hand and planted a deep, passionate kiss on him as Bill and the other four officers howled. Lynn then looked deep into Ed's eyes. "She better be a great date."

Ed could only take a deep breath.

Celebrating their success, relieved they came out of it alive, and promising to buy each other beers when things calmed down, the seven of them walked back to the village center. But as they entered the main street, they stopped. The village had taken the brunt of the hurricane winds, and before them was a mad scene of raked store-fronts, broken glass, a jam of emergency vehicles – one on its side, its lights still flashing – and scores of med techs, safety officers and volunteers helping dazed and injured people in the bitter cold.

Ed looked for Jessica, but missed her at first among those helping load injured onto what ambulances were left and a train to take some of the victims to the Tiu City hospital. Someone had given Jessica a set of public safety blue coveralls to pull over her dress, the blues stained by blood from the injured she was aiding. But as two med techs carried off the woman she was tending, Jessica turned and saw Ed instantly.

She ran, forgetting Martian gravity as she launched herself into his arms, but overshot. Ed took a step back and pulled her down in an embrace while turning to brake the momentum, like a downfield receiver hauling in an end zone pass back on Earth. It could have been a clumsy moment, but she was too glad to see him safe, and he was just too glad to see her.

"Hey Six," Lynn called over her shoulder as she headed for the locker room. "You're right about your date."

Emergency efforts had turned more orderly by the time Ed had shed his suit and rejoined Jessica. She was wearing his sport coat over the coveralls. Seven lent Ed a jacket to wear. Officers were directing people to the trains, but Ed saw Weller outside his restaurant. He took Jessica's hand and they went up the slick walkway to get to him.

Weller was hanging onto the rail, looking over the lake as it rapidly took on a sheet of ice. On the shore, his vineyards had turned into a crystalline web. "You know," he said as they reached him, "Mars is cold as hell, and the one thing growers on this planet don't worry about is frost. Go figure."

"Is your crop ruined?" Jessica asked.

"Don't know. Good chance it is. We may save some of it. I always wanted to try making an ice wine."

"Sam," Ed said, "did all this happen because of that warning you got?"

"It seems like overkill, doesn't it? But it was no accident. Two events. A cop tells me the heat exchangers went down an hour before the wall blows. There's no way one caused the other. If it was just a blow out, we'd have plenty of wind damage in here, but we'd recover. If it was just the heat exchangers, we might have had a light frost by morning, but the dome's insulated enough to hold enough heat in for one night. Combined, it's devastating. The breach sucked much of the heat right out, and we're pumping unheated air back in. It's -20 Celsius right now and dropping. It's 60 below outside, and we may get pretty damned close to that in here before the dawn. I don't know if anybody's crops can stand that."

Weller shoved his hands in his pockets and turned toward them. "You'd better get on the train and get out of here. But one thing. If this is because I spouted off, I get it. I'm not taking any chances, not with everyone's life in here. And I suggest both of you do the same."

CHAPTER 12

Bagels and Warrants

Ed was up, or at least on his bare feet, by 0930. He was exhausted, but his mind wouldn't let him sleep. He flipped on the wall screen to see if the news had anything more on last night, but cringed when he saw the rookie reporter from Mars News giving a live update.

"...when public safety officers and volunteers from off the street rushed to repair the breach. Ironically, one of the volunteers was the pilot from ...." Ed flipped it off.

He went into the kitchen to pour himself a glass of orange juice when a pounding on his front door jarred him, throwing off his aim. He reached for a towel to mop up the spill when the pounding started again, joined by Ariel's barking.

"All right, all right!" He forgot the towel and stumbled toward the door. Ariel's bark didn't have an angry sound, so Ed figured it was safe and opened it. He immediately had second thoughts when he saw Faizah.

"You idiot! You went to see Weller after all when you told me you'd wait. You didn't trust me, did you?" She stormed in, and Ed gave Ariel an accusing look. The dog just sat down and wagged her tail, waiting expectantly for a treat. Ed reached for a biscuit and gave it to her, but Ariel decided it was safer to eat it outside. As he closed the door, Faizah wheeled around and laid into him again.

"What were you thinking, seeing him before we knew enough? You're lucky you didn't get yourself and Jessica killed."

Just as Faizah finished, Jessica stepped out of the bathroom, wearing Ed's Maple Leaf jersey that nearly reached to her bare knees. "Oh, Faizah. Hi?"

Jessica's appearance surprised Faizah.... No it didn't. "Jessica, I didn't know you were a hockey fan."

"This? No, the jersey belongs to Ed."

"Maybe someday he can afford the rest of the uniform." Faizah turned back to Ed. "At least you had the good sense not to leave her alone last night, though I don't know if bringing her here was the safest idea. Did Weller tell you anything?"

"Yeah, he told us something."

Faizah cringed at the word "us." "Was it enough to nearly destroy all of Serling Heights over it?"

"I don't know. Somebody may have thought so." Ed walked back to the kitchen to get the remains of his OJ. Jessica already had the towel and was cleaning up his mess, at least the one on the counter.

"Did you tell Lenowitz what Weller told you?"

"Lenowitz wasn't there."

"What? That annoying little bergie has been everywhere. How could he not show up when someone tries to destroy a whole village on his own planet?"

"What's a bergie?" Jessica asked, then wished she hadn't when Faizah glowered at her.

"Ag, it's a Capetown thing."

"Maybe he was there and I didn't see him," Ed said. "I saw other members of the OSAR crime staff, but it looked like somebody else was directing them."

"Taking the night off, I guess. If only you had."

"Wait a minute, Faizah, this couldn't have happened because we talked to Kurt. This was too complex to pull it off right after we saw him."

"No, but it may have happened to try to stop him from talking. And if whoever did this saw you there – and everyone who's watched Mars News Network has seen you there – and realized you talked to Sam, what do you think they'll do to you? Or Jessica? She was on the news, too. It doesn't take much to surmise she was with you."

"I was on the news?" Jessica said.

"Yes, and now both of you are in danger. And how many others? These people don't seem to bother with a stiletto when a sledgehammer will do."

"What difference would it have made if I had waited, besides having Weller clam up because someone showed they could blow up his sky and freeze him out?"

"We might not have needed to talk to him at all. But you didn't trust me enough to wait."

Faizah stood there, glaring at Ed. She was about to say something more when a knock on the door saved him. There was no barking this time. Faizah was nearest, so she looked out a window then swung open the door angrily.

"Where the hell were you last night?"

"I was expected?" Lenowitz asked. Ariel was sniffing at a bag in his hand.

"When someone tries to blow up an agridome on Mars, yes, I expect you to show up."

"I am here now," the inspector said innocently.

"You're just in time. I think I'm ready to do great bodily harm to our pilot here in case the real murderers don't get around to it first."

Lenowitz glanced at Jessica coming out of the kitchen, then leaned closer to Faizah and lowered his voice. "You know, crimes of passion are usually handled at the village level."

Faizah lowered her own voice, ominously. "Be careful, my captain. If I get started on a crime of passion, I might turn it into a spree."

"That would be a pity. Perhaps we should calm down and have breakfast instead. Luckily I brought enough bagels from the village for everyone." He stepped into the living room, and Ariel followed him in.

"Good. Over breakfast Ed can tell you everything Weller told him last night. And Ed, I do mean everything. Since everyone knows you were there last night, the safest thing for you and Jessica is to get it all out in the open quickly." Faizah turned to walk out the door.

"You're leaving?" Lenowitz asked.

"I don't think I should stay. It seems Ed doesn't trust me any more, if he ever did."

Lenowitz shrugged his shoulders. "I do not trust you, and I want you to stay."

She stopped and eyed him down. "Do you have onion bagels in that bag?"

"Of course, and three kinds of cream cheese."

Faizah closed the door, grabbed the bag brusquely out of his hand and headed for the kitchen. "I'll see if I can find a toaster." She stopped next to Jessica, giving her a quick sideways look. "Get some pants on, girl!"

ooooooooo

There wasn't enough room for all of them around the table, so Ed sat on a stool at the counter. Jessica, with a pair of Ed's gym pants cinched up tight beneath the jersey, stood next to him. Faizah smoldered across the table from Lenowitz while Ed went over Weller's story. The captain listened impassively. Faizah seemed puzzled that Weller didn't know more of how Averink's fusion drive component worked. Ed skipped over the action at the breach, but picked up with Weller's decision to take the warning seriously and not say anything more.

"So tell us, captain," Faizah quickly cut in when Ed finished, "why weren't you there last night? You don't honestly think the blow out didn't have a connection with Weller?"

Lenowitz tore off a small piece of bagel and offered it to Ariel sitting next to him. "No, I do not believe Weller's statements and the Serling Heights explosion were mere happenstance. But it does not matter what I think anymore. I am off the case."

"What!?" That from all three of them. Ariel barked.

"Under the circumstances, everyone is on the Serling Heights case today. But I am reassigned. I was supposed to take command of the White when it returned to Mars in Januride. Instead, they gave me the Grissom, effective immediately. That's why I was not in Serling Heights last night. I was in orbit until a couple of hours ago. The good news, Ed, is that I will be following you to Ceres in two weeks."

"I hope that's good news," Ed said.

"Januride, that's...?" Jessica started to ask.

"Six months from now," Faizah told her.

"The former captain of the Grissom will head the law enforcement division for those Six months before handing it over to the captain of the White. Captain Keritan of the Grissom is not happy with the temporary assignment, either, even more unhappy with it today than yesterday. He expected to be back in space in two weeks.

I believe he hates Mars, something to do with an ex-love that is still here. Please, Ed, do not pass this on to your reporter friend, Jeff, but I do not believe Keritan has the right temperament to put into this investigation."

"So why did they push you back into space early?" Ed asked.

"The FBI and Interpol, particularly the FBI, were not happy with my efforts, even before you landed. No one told me this is why, of course, but this is true. My efforts did not fit their theories of the crime for the *New Brunswick*."

"And those theories include me?"

"No, not anymore. As I told you the day after you landed, your time is too easily accounted for. It was too complex to include you. The FBI had a simpler solution yesterday. They did not make it public, but they did inform OSAR of it, just before I was reassigned. It appears Tim Averink's research drove him over the edge. He was a failure and couldn't deal with it. The FBI concluded Tim Averink planted the bomb himself, and expected to die in the blast."

"That can't be," Jessica said, surprising Ed and Faizah. "I mean, look what Weller said. He believed in him."

Lenowitz was unmoved. "Averink was very expert at convincing people of the value of his ideas. He was not so expert at turning those ideas into something tangible. If his backers had dug deeper, they would have found a string of failures dating back to his graduate days in Madison. It is amazing the University of Wisconsin ever gave him his degree."

"No, that's not true!" Jessica protested. "He graduated with ... he said he graduated with honors."

"So, you were able to get to know him after all?"

"No. ... Some. I ask every passenger a little about themselves. He wasn't a failure."

"I see. Faizah, I'm sure you researched Mr. Averink since Mr. Weller's statements yesterday at the memorial. Did you turn up anything?"

"Nothing convincing."

Jessica turned to walk into the kitchen. Ed could see her tense up with anger during her exchange with Lenowitz, and with her back turned, he gave the captain a questioning look.

Lenowitz ignored it. "Of course, all of that was yesterday's theory," the captain said.

"I thought so," said Faizah. "Averink doesn't make sense as a suicide bomber after last night. The FBI can't believe the *New Brunswick* and Serling Heights were not connected."

"No, even the FBI could not ignore that, though it is keeping Averink as a suspect in reserve. I think he is simply inconsequential. But luckily for the bureau, it had a second theory, one which it raised to the top spot this morning and did make public: Terrorists from the Earth First movement carried out these acts. A fringe group has even claimed credit for it, the Mother Earth Defense Alliance."

"MEDA!?" Faizah said. "They couldn't carry out a transfer on the London tube."

"You know of them?"

"InterCorporate keeps track of all known anti-space groups for our off-Earth clients. Some are quite capable politically, and some groups stage protests that threaten operations. But MEDA? They're big talk, with no cash and no smarts."

"They have advocated violence in the past."

"But outside of macing a few guards at space ports and spray painting a booster in storage, they haven't succeeded in executing any violence. Anyone who would have reached Mars to pull off last night's attack would have been too technically knowledgeable or too rich to buy into MEDA's message."

"Everyone believed as you did." A beep in his pocket interrupted Lenowitz. He casually read the message on his com unit, looked puzzled for a second, then continued. "There were many claims for the *New Brunswick* explosion, and MEDA's was placed way down on the list. But they were the first to make a claim last night. And they gave details on Earth before we knew all those details here on Mars."

Faizah shook her head. "It still doesn't make sense. They can make all the claims they want on Earth. It was still somebody on Mars who did it."

"And it will not make sense until we catch whoever did it. Cases like this don't depend on motive. We need to narrow down who had the opportunity and the capability to execute the crime." Lenowitz focused solely on Faizah. "We're looking for two areas of expertise. One, demolition. It took an expert to blow out that cargo airlock, knocking out just the right supports and letting air pressure blow the rest of it away.

"Knocking out the heat exchangers required something more subtle. We didn't find it in the program until after dawn. Our programmers kept rebooting and replacing the program and it still wouldn't work. It was maddening, for the temperature parameters were correct. Someone finally realized the system was pulling definitions from outside the program, and the definition of the temperature scale was changed, from Celsius to Kelvin. The sensors were reading temperatures in the dome well above zero – well above absolute zero, or 273 degrees higher than it really was. Climate control was actually trying to cool things down further. It took a very skilled programmer with a very soft touch to work that change into the climate system and have it go unnoticed for so long."

Faizah seemed resigned to what was coming. "You think I have that soft a touch. I'm flattered."

"I know you have the touch," Lenowitz said. "And you had the opportunity."

"Wait a minute," objected Jessica. "Are you arresting her?"

"No, we have no evidence for an arrest."

"But you do have a search warrant," Faizah said. "Was that the message you got?"

"Yes, and that my computer techs arrived. We'll be going through every computer you may have had access to at Chubeck's."

"I thought you were off this case," Jessica said.

Lenowitz softened and shrugged his shoulders. "As I said, everyone is back on the case this morning. This is the assignment I drew. This may be my last assignment on the case."

Faizah stood up. "Let's go then. I'm sure Chubeck will have called a lawyer by the time we get over there."

Ed and Jessica were quiet until Faizah and Lenowitz left. But as they closed the door, Jessica turned to Ed. "Why didn't you say anything? I don't know much about her, but after spending nearly two weeks with her in a battered spaceship taking care of my passengers, I find it hard to think she'd have anything to do with last night. How could you just let him do that?"

"What could I do? I'm no lawyer. I couldn't stop them from executing a search warrant. I'm not sure I'd want to."

"You don't trust her?"

"No," Ed admitted. "I like her. I felt confident having her in the *Zach* as we tried to dock with your module, and I know she was invaluable helping you. I want her on my side, but I don't know what side she's on or what game she's playing. I don't know what game anyone's playing in this. I just know the stakes are too high."

"Do you trust me?"

"I think so, but it seems like you know more than you're telling."

"Don't we all?"

CHAPTER 13
Hip Chips

Faizah leaned against her office doorway, a look of bemusement and quiet disdain on her face as she watched the tech struggle through her computer files. "You don't really expect to find anything, do you, captain?"

"You believe this is all for show?" The sour taste from his stomach that Lenowitz had since yesterday churned up again, and it wasn't the onion bagel. He waved another tech into the office. "Download her watch, too."

Faizah deliberately undid her watch/com and dangled it in front of the second tech. "No. I believe all of this is you dutifully following orders from the head of investigations."

"Were I still in charge, I would issue the same orders. If you were involved with last night, we may not find what the Americans call the 'smoking gun,' but there would be traces of powder burns in your files. And even if you are not responsible for last night, you are involved."

"So you're just going to sift around my confidential business files to see what turns up? I think the Americans call that a 'fishing expedition.'"

"Frankly, I rather enjoy fishing, even if I do not have much success on Martian streams."

"Maybe you should try ice fishing today. You might have more luck."

"I do not believe the lake ice will hold for very much longer."

"Damn, you're too quick for me."

The lieutenant downloading the com's memory couldn't stifle a snicker in time. Lenowitz wanted to smack him in the head, but instead picked up the scanner, a small black tube with a digital readout. "You have scanned everything in the room?" he asked the officer, Lt. Carstol.

"Everything except her," Carstol said.

Lenowitz handed the scanner to a tech, a junior grade officer. "Scan her for any other electronic devices."

"You want me to scan her body?"

Faizah straightened up and took a step into the room. "I think he already has."

"I do not trust his eyes," Lenowitz said.

"I don't trust his hands."

"Don't worry, ma'am," the tech said nervously, "I don't have to touch you with the wand."

"You'd better not," Faizah said, "or you're the one who will have something to worry about."

The tech gingerly waved the wand around Faizah, the scanner beeping when it turned up a digital pen/recorder in a shirt pocket, a foldable notebook in a hip pocket, a button mike attached to her collar, a tiny earpiece attached to an earring, and a couple of small discs in a front pocket. Even with all that laid out on her work table, the scanner still beeped when waved around her left hip. The tech looked at Lenowitz, unsure of what to do next.

Lenowitz grimaced. "Please do not tell me you are hard wired."

"I'm afraid so, captain," Faizah answered. "A transceiver and memory chips embedded in my hip."

Lenowitz took the scanner from the tech and slowly moved it toward Faizah's eyes. The scanner beeped again.

"Visual as well as auditory input?"

"Of course, and heads up displays through my contacts."

"How do we download all of that?" Carstol asked.

Faizah stared down the young lieutenant. "You don't."

"She is right, lieutenant," Lenowitz said, handing the scanner back to the tech. "By international treaty, downloading data from chips embedded in the body capable of inputs such as these is considered a form of self-incrimination. Without a grand jury and a grant of immunity, we cannot touch it."

"And it's too early to be handing out grants of immunity, isn't it?" Faizah said.

Lenowitz shrugged his shoulders. "It will not be my concern. My job is only to execute the search warrant. Any secrets you have will stay in your hip – for now. Of course, you understand ...."

"Erasing anything now could suggest I'm destroying evidence," Faizah said. "Yes, captain, I understand, perfectly."

It took a couple of hours for the tech crew to search through the rest of the computers in Chubeck's house and download all their files, but Lenowitz was certain they would find nothing incriminating. If Faizah was good enough to hack in and sabotage the climate control system, she was good enough to hide her tracks.

Except he wasn't supposed to be the one reviewing what the techs found. That was Keritan's job, if he didn't just forward the files to the FBI. Lenowitz wasn't sure what would be worse: Keritan bungling the investigation while he marked time to go back into space, or acquiescing to the FBI and handing it all over to them to screw up. Lenowitz's only hope of getting back into this case was if the trail led to Ceres – where, after all, Averink had been heading. So was the *Cydonia Zach* and nearly half the passengers of the *New Brunswick*. And as the captain of the Grissom, Lenowitz would be the law when he reached Ceres. Too bad Faizah was staying on Mars.

Lenowitz stopped the lieutenant as he was loading his equipment into a van. "David, you normally just make one backup of these files before making your report and sending them on to the lead investigator, correct?"

"Yeah, that's right."

"Considering the sensitivity of this case, and this suspect, would it not be wise to make two backups?"

The tech was confused for a second, until he caught Lenowitz's drift. "Yeah, that probably would be a good idea, and another backup of my report, too. But it wouldn't be secure to keep them in the same place," he said deliberately. "Unless you would like to take charge of them. I'd feel better about it that way. And since you used to head up investigations, that would be logical."

"Quite logical."

Carstol went back to loading his equipment. "Man, I didn't believe all the e-gear that Westerhof woman wore and had inside her. She should carry a sign warning anyone with electric heart pumps to stay away, or risk having their hearts zapped into an overload."

"I'm sure she has that effect on natural hearts, too, David, without electronic assistance."

ooooooooo

Faizah stood by the window in Chubeck's living room and watched the OSAR crew pack up. Chubeck stepped up behind her, and placed his hand gently on her shoulder.

"They didn't find anything?" he asked.

"No – no information, anyway. They did find my embedded chips, which surprised me. Those are the latest chips. When I left, they were just testing the upgraded scanner that could detect them. I didn't think OSAR's scanner upgrade would be ready in time to ship during the window."

"Will Keritan seek a grand jury to look at those chips?"

"Maybe, if the FBI insists on it. I don't think Lenowitz would bother."

"How bad would it be if they did grant you immunity and ordered the download?"

"Embarrassing, but not disastrous. The trend reports and the Decker files are there, some of the info on Averink, though I left the audit report on the computer out here where they could find it."

"And our plan for Decker's moratorium?"

"I erased and scrubbed all those files earlier, after running a print out. I stuck that underneath a mattress. As I figured, they just used their scanner for the search."

"I don't know how much longer that will stay secret anyway, if it's secret now."

"Should we try to get Decker to move up his timetable?"

Chubeck shook his head as he walked over to his liquor cabinet. "No. After last night, I'm not sure our plan is viable any more. You look like you could use a drink. I know I could."

"A short one. Was the damage that bad in Serling Heights?"

"Yeah, it was that bad. Crops are a near total loss. The water system's a mess. We may need emergency food shipments from Earth, and that pretty much undercuts my argument we can stand on our own. There's no estimate on the financial loss, yet, but 4th Orbit was heavily invested in Serling Heights. We'll take a big hit."

"I hate to bring this up, but ...."

"Astech again?" Faizah saw the anger build up in Chubeck so quick-ly she thought he was going to hurl his glass against the wall. But he stopped, relaxed the grip on his glass, and slowly took a sip. "Damn, I don't want to bring them in."

"But they have the resources. They have the finances. They may be Earth based, but they're committed to the Belt."

"They're committed to driving independents out of the Belt."

"They may have a broader vision than you think."

"I don't trust them."

"I can talk to them."

"On Ceres?"

"Yes."

Chubeck raised his glass again and took a deeper drink. "Lenowitz would never let you go."

"I think he would." Faizah walked to the small side table where Chubeck had poured her drink, a bourbon, distilled on Mars but as close to Kentucky as you could get without branch water. She swirled the am-ber liquid slowly around the ice. "He's lost control here, but Lenowitz still wants to solve these bombings. He believes all the trails lead to Ceres."

"Is he right?"

"Probably, and my going to Ceres will just seal the deal in his mind. He'll want to keep his chief suspect close, and on Ceres, he'll be in charge again. Hell, he's probably trying to figure out a way to convince me to go to Ceres."

"You'll be taking a risk."

Faizah turned and walked back to the window, still swirling the bourbon slowly around the melting ice. "That started when I met you."

ooooooooooo

It wasn't long after Lenowitz left to begin his search that Ed sud-denly found himself alone. It wasn't that he minded being alone. He enjoyed it, most times. But it was like the whirlwind of people that surrounded him the past few days, engulfed him last night, and swept through his living room that morning had unexpectedly blown itself out. The last wisp left when Jessica breezed out the front door to grab the commuter cart back to the station.

"Why did they call you?" he said as she was leaving.

Jessica, wearing the coveralls from the night before, turned around to answer, still walking backward towards the road. "They need help with the volunteer recovery crews, and someone from public safety remembered my name from last night. I told them if they could find me some fresh coveralls, I'd be right there."

"Doing what?"

"I'll find out when I get there," she said as she climbed into the cart. With a quick u-turn, she drove off.

"No one called me," Ed muttered to himself, then looked down at Ariel. "At least you're" – But a sharp whistle from across the road perked up Ariel's ears. In a dash she was over the wall and bounding toward the pastures – "still here."

The idea of having the house suddenly to himself seemed very un-appealing to Ed, particularly with his mind still racing on possible plots and perceived threats. He needed some air, some high air.

Most Martians maintained a strict regimen of exercise; it was near-ly a religion. Ed's uncle was an agnostic on the subject, but most of the rest strove to keep their bodies in shape for the day they may re-turn to Earth. Immigrants to Mars rationalized their commitment to the planet, but emotionally kept their ties to the home world, never wanting to cut themselves off from the option of going back. If they let their bodies atrophy under Mars light gravity, they could become prisoners there instead of willing pioneers.

Ed barely remembered Earth, but he saw the blue planet often enough, if only from Lunar orbit, to have a desire to go back. The only started growing in him about four years before. He knew he wouldn't stay, but the appeal of an open sky was strong, even if it was an Earth sky. Part of him also hoped that what Weller told him last night was true, that there was a way to push the fusion drive's constant thrust to one-g. Pilots would have to be in shape to fly that.

Ed's flying today would be different. True flying. No buttons, no computers, no engine. Just him strapped to a wing, soaring high above Viking Glen. But he had to climb the canyon cliffs first.

The path up the cliff wasn't too rugged, even with the collapsible wing slug across his back. It certainly was nothing like Charlie McKracken had to go through climbing up the escarpment of Olympus Mons in a pressurized ground suit. But it was still a long climb, and by the time he reached the top, Ed couldn't wait for the valley's cool air to rush across his body as he gently spiraled his way down. But he stopped first to gaze out the dome's clear hexagon panels onto the native Martian surface. The arch of the panels were anchored into the top of the cliffs a short distance from the edge. The sun was high, and the view outside was harsh, the shadows short but sharp.

His shoes crunched on the native pebbles and sand that still capped the cliff tops, unlike the regenerated soil that filled the farmland below. The air up here had that tang of iron and rust, the scent of Mars that normally only outside crews could smell, and then only after they came back in and began to shed their ground suits, dusting off the sand that had collected on their boots and legs.

"We're not leaving," Ed said under his breath. "Whatever the politics on Earth or the plots hatched on the Moon, they're not going to chase us off Mars."

There were three other fliers unfolding and rigging their gear near the cliff edge. Ed saw several more in the air above the valley, tracing lazy circles with their brightly colored delta-shaped wings.

"Hey Ed, you want to see which of us can stretch our flight the longest?" said one of the fliers, a member of Astech's staff on Mars.

"Not today," Ed said. "I just want to fly solo."

"Suit yourself," said the younger man, completing the connections to his wing, decorated with a brilliant red design of Ehacatl, the ancient Aztec symbol for wind. With a short hop, the Astech staffer jumped off the edge of the cliff and began his slow glide to the canyon floor.

"Do I really want to fly solo, or am I just being paranoid about flying with someone from Astech?" Ed thought. He shrugged it off, but made a mental note to get in touch with Paul later. He unfolded his own wing, etched with an image portraying white clouds above a Martian lake along a red shore – as it might have been or could be again.

He finished making the connections, strapped himself in and hopped without hesitation off the cliff and began his own flight across the canyon. He drifted away from the houses of Viking Glen, soaring over crests of hills and diving low to skim over the trails that twisted among the pastures. Air circulation always kept the smells of cattle away from the village, but not here. But that, too, was part of Ed's growing up on a Martian farm.

With the velocity gained from his dive, Ed gained altitude again, slipping from updraft to updraft before feeling the rush of air as he dove again.

He flew like that for quite a while, far longer than the flier from Astech, he noted with satisfaction when Ed spotted the company man on the ground packing up his wing. Ed was sailing over his uncle's pastures when he heard Ariel's bark. He maneuvered above Ariel and Robin as the two dogs worked a small herd, cajoling them back toward the barns. Ed circled to watch the two dogs work on opposite ends of the herd, then spotted his uncle under a small grove of trees. He had yet to have a talk with his uncle alone since he came back to Mars. This was the time.

The grove was about three kilometers from his house. It seemed to be Uncle Carl's favorite place to escape. As he was growing up, Ed loved the times he could join him as together they watched the agility of the dogs matched against the sturdiness of the cows. It had been a long time since they sat together beneath these trees. His uncle was leaning against one of them as Ed touched down nearby.

"You know, Ed, cows must be the only animals we've brought here that don't take advantage of Martian gravity," Chubeck said as Ed unstrapped his wings. "They plod along just as if they were on Earth, and if something does startle them so they kick extra hard and send themselves flying, they just get this confused look about them and tumble."

"Unlike pigs," Ed said, "who seem determined to prove us wrong about their flying ability."

Chubeck chuckled and folded his arms. "So what trouble were you trying to escape today?"

"Me? You're the one who had cops in your house this morning crawling through your computers."

"They went through the 4-O office computers, too. Didn't find anything, that I know of."

"Was there anything to find?"

"Not about last night. Faizah made sure about the rest."

Ed grimaced at that as he joined his uncle under the tree and sat on the ground. "That's what worries me. How do you know she had nothing to do with last night?"

"Faizah said you didn't trust her."

"Do you?"

Chubeck didn't answer right away. He watched as Ariel jumped on a recalcitrant cow's back to harangue her, then launched her self off before the cow could buck her off. Robin just trotted out of the way as the cow did buck, sending herself into a clumsy somersault, landing on its back in a slow motion bounce. The cow stumbled to its feet, dazed and obedient as Ariel urged her back with the herd heading for the pens.

"Do you notice how Ariel tends to bully the cattle, while Robin seems to negotiate with them?" Chubeck asked.

"It's what makes them a good team," Ed said. "Good dog, bad dog."

"Different approaches, but they work. Yes, I do trust Faizah. I met with her three windows ago, when I went with you to Luna. I've worked with her ever since. I've worked with InterCorporate longer than that, but not as closely as when Faizah became my agent. She's more subtle than I am, but we make a good team."

"I've never heard you talk about InterCorporate or Faizah."

"There's been a lot I haven't shared with you."

"Isn't it time?"

For the first time, his uncle looked Ed in the eye. "You don't trust me, either?"

Ed's own stare didn't flinch. "Trust you do to do what?"

"To do what's best for Mars and everything we've built out here."

"Whatever it takes?"

"I've been doing that for years."

"And has everything you've done finally caught up with you?"

Chubeck's voice rose, bordering on the anger he rarely but effectively used on Ed when he was growing up. "You think everything that's happened is my fault?"

Ed's gaze finally shifted. "I ... I don't know. But I saw a tug blow up in front of me from a bomb that could have just as easily been on my tug. I felt the force of air being sucked out of a dome and the numbness of Mars cold rushing in. People have died, and we came close to having many more die last night, and still nobody knows why. I think it's time you tell me what you do know."

"You think you have a right to ask, to demand that?"

In earlier years, such a question would have made Ed back down. Not this time.

"I'm piloting a flight to Ceres for 4-O. About half my passengers and one of my crew were on the New B., and there's a good chance somebody among them was involved in the bombings. There's also a good chance, and there's nothing I know so far to disprove it, that the *Zach* could be the next target. Yeah, I think I have the right."

"Marta said you pulled the same thing on Luna."

"She said then you'd back me up."

"You don't think Faizah had something to do with the *New Brunswick* and last night?"

"I don't know."

"You don't think I had anything to do with it?"

Quietly, Ed answered. "That's just it, I don't know."

That seemed to shock Chubeck, but he didn't respond with anger as he looked away. "Now that's a problem. Sad thing is, I don't know either. I can tell you I had no intent in those crimes, and I hope you believe that because of family and the years I helped raise you. But I don't know how much I started, and how much are from events already set in motion."

"It seems like nearly everything in motion on Mars comes at least in part from something you started. And now you're trying to see if your reach can go as far as Earth. Is it any surprise that your enemies might fight back?"

"So you think I'm the target of all this?"

"Do you?"

"It's possible, but I didn't expect this violence. Backroom deals and smear campaigns, yes, but not bombings."

Chubeck took a step toward the pasture, his arms folded across his chest. "So go ahead, what do you want to know?"

Ed started with a question he always wanted to ask. "Who gave you the money to get started on Mars?"

Chubeck turned back toward his nephew. "You want to go back that far?"

"Faizah said she recognized some of the firms that fronted for the investors backing Averink. Maybe because they backed you when you were getting started?"

"They were the same firms, but that's not why she knew them."

"She knew them because now you're one of the investor's they're fronting for, right? You were using the same firms to funnel funds to Averink."

"His and other projects."

"Did you know him?"

"We never had direct communication. Faizah wanted me to keep my distance. I thought his work had promise, but her information said his chances for success were slim. I wanted to meet with him when he reached Mars. But I think he saw 4th Orbit as not much better than Interplanetary Drive Systems."

"So who backed Averink now who backed you then?"

"Seattle and California money, mostly. I could give you a list, but you could guess. IDS for another."

"You were in bed with IDS?"

"Hell, yes. They had the fusion drive that made Mars colonization possible. It took longer than now, but the trip didn't take the nine months or more that it did in the old days. But IDS needed people like me, too, to help feed the ship builders in orbit and those on the Moon who were mining helium-3 to fuel their drives."

"Weller said Averink didn't know but suspected IDS was helping fund him."

"They tried to hide their involvement, as did Astech."

"Astech? Did they give funds to you, too?"

"Sure. Their prospectors in the Belt need to eat."

"If you knew who backed your project, how come Averink didn't know who backed his?"

"Probably because of me." Chubeck absently tore off a tree leaf and rolled it between his fingers. "I didn't do things the way many people planned. The IDS subsidiary, Solar System Shipping, was supposed to have a monopoly on high-speed runs because of their exclusive rights to use the fusion drive. I raised a stink among independents – shippers and producers alike – to break their monopoly. That's when I first became involved with InterCorporate. They helped me find support on Earth and get the Treaty regulations changed, forcing IDS to lease its fusion drive to anyone and not just Triple-S."

"I don't get it. That's why IDS doesn't trust you any more – that and you started your own shipping company to compete with Triple-S. But what does that have to do with Averink?"

"The company wanted to keep its eye on Tim without him knowing it, or anyone else. This is all from what Faizah was able to piece together on Earth and Luna."

"Yet Faizah seemed pretty surprised at the memorial when Weller suggested Averink was the target."

"She considered him a minor issue, and neither of us thought his project had anything to do with the explosion until Weller brought it up yesterday. We're still not sure it does. IDS was afraid of Tim, apparently because they thought he was on to something. I don't know if he could have reached the 1-g constant thrust Weller told you about last night. This is the first I've heard of it."

Ed interrupted his uncle. "But what if Averink could get to 1-g thrust? Wouldn't that blow a hole in your plans to support Decker and cut off all subsidies beyond Earth?"

"Are we going back to believing I had something to do with Averink's death?" There was exasperation again in Chubeck's voice, but not as much anger.

"I'm just trying to figure out the angles, see who wins or loses in all this," Ed said.

"That's not easy to do, Ed. It's all a matter of timing. You're right. If Averink's drive became known too early, and he could prove his claim of 1-g constant thrust, or at least seem credible, there would be a burst of interest from the public. The time it takes to get out here is what's stalling our development."

"But that burst of interest would stall Decker's campaign, right?" Ed said. "And if Decker loses, the big corporations keep their subsidies, and their control out here."

"It doesn't even have to be before the election," Chubeck said. "It'll take time to cut those subsidies, and to get the rest of the world to follow suit. And if you're about to say that's enough of a motive for me to want to keep Averink's drive buried, don't bother. If Averink's drive became known too early, it would be a legal and political free-for-all. I don't know who would have come out on top. But remember, I didn't know if he could even reach the point 1-g thrust he did claim to the investors. Still don't. That audit report was pretty damning."

"Weller thought someone fabricated that report."

"That's possible, though InterCorporate didn't think so. If it was falsified, I'm sure IDS was behind it. The company became involved to keep an eye on Averink's research, to defend its own patents and wrap up any new ones. Company officials may have got wind that Averink was working on a one-g thrust drive and were afraid he would come up with a new design and not just a modification of the existing patents."

"Would they blow up the *New Brunswick* to protect its monopoly on building fusion drives?"

"Maybe they would, or at least some rogue in that company would, particularly if they believed Averink's drive could go as fast as Weller said and they couldn't get legal control of it."

"But as investors, wouldn't they have legal control?"

"Only a minority interest. For a physicist, Averink was more shrewd on business matters than I thought he could be."

"He outsmarted IDS?"

"Only when they weren't looking, when they thought he was a young researcher with some mildly interesting ideas. I think when someone in the company realized it was more than that and IDS didn't hold the strings, the actions became more drastic. I'm afraid I may have pushed them over the edge."

"How?"

"I had hoped Tim could break the IDS hold on fusion drives, and his original work showed promise. When the results seemed to turn and it looked like his project was reaching a dead end, it still burned me that IDS, or someone acting for IDS, was doing everything possible to make sure he'd reach that dead end quickly."

"Why would they bother if the project already seemed doomed?"

"That's what nagged at me. Maybe Averink was on to something after all, and IDS was just throwing up roadblocks. So, over Faizah's objections, I had her book a flight for Averink to get him off the Moon, giving him passage to Ceres to work with Minglong."

That sent a chill through Ed. "Faizah booked his passage? Does Lenowitz know that?"

"No, I'm sure he doesn't."

"You're probably right. He would have come this morning with an arrest warrant if he had known."

"She had nothing to do with Averink's death. There's no evidence that she had."

"No evidence? I'll admit it's all circumstantial, Uncle Carl, but the evidence is piling up. She has the hacking skills to fake the shipping order that put the bomb on board the New B., and she probably had the skill to pull off last night's freeze-out. My guess is she didn't get that warning to stay off the *New Brunswick* until after she booked Averink's passage on it – or created the warning herself. From what you just told me, she's been trying for a long time to convince you that Averink's drive component didn't work. And come to think of it, Faizah was the one who took the call from Averink's company, Polaris, when his research assistants tried to bluff me into saving the prototype in the New B. cargo module. She told them in no uncertain terms to put that module someplace where the sun don't shine, and that's just where it ended up, on its way to the Oort Cloud."

"That's absurd. You've been watching too many of your old vids on your trips. She has no motive. She's loyal to me."

"Damn it, Uncle Carl, she's loyal to you because you pay her. Do you think your charm has such a hold on her that she wouldn't switch clients if someone paid her more?"

"She may switch clients, but she wouldn't work against me."

"Even if she was paid a lot more?"

"She wouldn't betray me like that."

"What planet are you on? Or more to the point, remember what planet she's from."

"Is there anyone you trust?"

"The list keeps getting shorter."

CHAPTER 14

Theories and Doubt

"Did you hear? They know who did it."

Ed had barely walked through 4th Orbit's door Fridim morning when Hafiz blurted out the news. "The Serling Heights blowout? There was nothing on the morning rundown." Ed said, putting his take-out "coffee" on the counter. "Who was it?"

"It just came through. Some guy on a fake passport and Mars tourist visa. They think he's back on Earth now."

"Wait a minute. Some guy on a fake passport who they think is on Earth hardly qualifies as knowing who did it. Who's they, anyway?"

"The FBI. Did you happen to buy any donuts with that coffee?"

Ed tossed a bag on the counter. "Save me the cinnamon. How long ago is the FBI saying this mystery tourist planted the bomb?"

"Actually, it was four charges that blew out that airlock. They say the charges may have been planted almost two months ago."

"What's OSAR saying about this?"

"Mmm-nnn" was all Hafiz could get out after biting down on a powdered sugar donut. He shrugged his shoulders.

"Never mind." Ed pulled out his personal com and switched to news, scanning quickly.

"Here it is. 'Capt. Keritan said the evidence at the site is consistent with the FBI theory on the case.' Hell, that just means they haven't found enough to prove or disprove anything. It's only been a day. What about the freeze out?"

Hafiz swallowed a swig of his own coffee from the office pot before answering. "They think the temperature drop triggered the explosion. They found a control device that was monitoring the dome's environmental sensors. When the temperature dropped, boom."

"So what triggered the temperature drop?"

"The FBI suspects a signal was sent over the InterPlanet, probably from Earth."

"C'mon. I've never heard of a hacker on the Earth Internet getting far on the InterPlanet, particularly on sites beyond the Moon. Security is too good, and the time delays in cache transfers too frustrating. Someone just can't sneak in from Earth."

"The theory goes the tourist hacked in while on Mars, and either set a timer in the program or sent a signal from Earth that set off a bug."

"But who is it?" Ed got out between bites of his cinnamon donut.

Hafiz tossed Ed a napkin. "So far no one seems to know him. Interpol discovered him while double checking the passenger lists for this past window. I forget what name he used."

Ed checked his com again. "It says here, John Harrington. A couple of people barely remember him. Black and gray hair, mostly gray beard, heavy set. He stayed at the Far Horizons. That's where Jessica's staying."

"Not anymore," Hafiz said.

"What do you mean?"

"She's moving in with somebody at the college who needed a roommate. She stopped here this morning before heading out to Serling Heights. She had me lock up a small duffel for her in the safe, and she left a note for you." Hafiz walked over to the office safe and pulled a plastic note off the duffel. "Jessica didn't want the note in public view, but she didn't seem to mind me seeing it." He handed the note over.

"Ed, can you take this bag home with you? Taking rest of gear to new place. Will explain. Lunch, Fish Shack, 1130? – J"

"It's only 9 now," Ed said. "When was she here?"

"Jessica had me meet her here at 0730."

"She called you?"

"I called her, yesterday. I didn't know she was on the emergency crews at Serling. She asked when you were going to be here again, and when I told her, she wanted to meet me here early. She didn't tell me why at the time, but when she got here she said she was worried about her duffel and wanted it kept safe until you could pick it up. Her passport and other valuables must be in it. You didn't know she was moving?"

"It's news to me. I hope her new place is secure. With everything going on, I didn't think it was too safe for her to go back to Serling Heights. But she didn't think my pueblo would be that much safer."

"She's got a point. You rarely lock your doors when you're on Mars."

"I do, now. I dialed up the security settings to keep out mystery tourists from planting bombs, or Capt. Lenowitz from stealing my beer."

"I'm not sure that will stop either one."

"Why did you call her?"

"I need you two to do the walk through of the passenger and crew modules we're leasing. Jessica said she could do it at 0800 tomorrow. Can you make it that early?"

"You know, we have an extra 40 minutes in the Martian day. Why do we have to be in such a damn rush to get it started?"

"It sounds like they need more than 40 minutes per day to get things cleaned up in Serling Heights. Jessica said that was the only time she could make it."

"OK, I'll be there. Hey, is that message you sent last night right. Our buyout of Trans-Orbit already went through?"

"Yeah. It turns out Trans-Orbit approached your uncle soon after the *New Brunswick* was destroyed, and he and Marta were working on it days before you landed. While I was rushing off to give him a proposal, he was way ahead of me and signing the deal. So you and I have a lot of work to do."

Ed and Hafiz went to work on their morning's task, juggling shipping schedules. Marta sent her priorities over on which of the contracts from newly acquired Trans-Orbit she wanted to fill, and which she wanted to peddle off to other shippers. Trans-Orbit's remaining tug, the *Halifax*, had arrived at the Moon after the *Zach* and *New Brunswick* launched, and laid over for two weeks before heading for the Belt.

Ed's eyes began to blur as they devised the schedule out to 12 months for the *Zach*, *Halifax*, and *Zach*'s sister tug, Wayfarer. "Wait a minute, back up," he said. "The Halifax is going to arrive at Ceres two days after I do ...."

"No, two days before," Hafiz said.

"Yeah, I mean before. The Wayfarer is two days after. We come back to Mars together. Then *Halifax* and *Wayfarer* sit for weeks while you send me back out again. When the hell do I get a break?"

Hafiz shrugged his shoulders. "I'm sorry. The other two tugs are due for overhauls, and Marta doesn't want to delay that, particularly after just buying the Halifax, and the Wayfarer just getting back from the Belt."

"But there's no let up, even later. With us taking on Trans-Orbit's schedule, we need a fourth tug."

Hafiz stood up to get another cup of coffee. "Need a refill?"

"Nah, I've had enough."

"Buying another tug was in the works. Phobos could have had one built for us in six months. But your uncle nixed the idea yesterday."

"Why?"

"The Serling Heights blow-out."

"Uncle Carl did tell me 4th Orbit was heavily invested in Serling Heights. We took a big hit there."

"Right. Marta thinks Chubeck wouldn't have gone through with the purchase of Trans-Orbit if the blowout happened before the sale. But they closed the deal a few hours after the wake."

"And a few hours after he signs the purchase, the blowout happens."

"Yeah," Hafiz said, "and the buyout is no longer such a great deal."

Ed and Hafiz finished by 1100. Ed sent a message to Jessica confirming lunch, and then caught the commuter mag-lev for Serling Heights.

Ed stepped out of the commuter into a hectic, dizzying scene of activity as workers and recovery crews labored to restore the village. The staccato and whining sounds of construction replaced the street music of two nights earlier. But as he walked down the street, he noticed the mood seemed upbeat. Serling Heights took a horrible hit and survived.

"Six!" Ed turned quickly to his left to face the call.

"Lynn, haven't you got this place in order yet?"

The public safety officer grinned as she walked up and shook his hand. "If they gave us real guns, maybe we'd make more progress. But despite the confusion, everybody's been great. What are you doing here?"

"I'm supposed to meet a friend for lunch at the Shack – the woman I was with the other night."

"You mean Jessica?"

"You met her?"

"This morning. She's organizing the college kids trying to rescue what they can of the crops, though most of the harvest is a total loss. She's doing a great job. I was just breaking for lunch. Sit with me until she arrives?"

"Sure."

Jack's Fish Shack had set up long tables in front of the restaurant, extending well beyond the sidewalk and into the street. Workers with recovery staff badges ate for free, and almost everyone there was wearing a badge. The restaurant replaced menus with a cafeteria line.

"Why don't you grab lunch for you and Jessica now?" Lynn said. "The line's going to get pretty long in a few minutes." She took a sandwich for herself, and told the staff Ed was with her. The cashier waved him through.

"I could have paid for my own lunch."

"After what you did the other night, the village can buy you a damned sandwich."

They took seats at the end of a table in the street, in easy view for anyone walking up.

Ed put his sandwiches aside to wait for Jessica, and opened his ginger ale. "So how bad is it, here? It seems amazingly lucky that no one died."

"Quite a few people were hurt, some pretty badly. The air pressure isn't as bad as yesterday, but it's still pretty low."

"Yeah, I noticed my ears popped when I stepped off the train."

"We're back to the equivalent of Denver, I'm told. As for damage, in town, it's mostly just a mess. It won't take long to put it back in shape. Can't tell yet how hard a hit the growers and producers took. It's not just the harvest, but the irrigation system and fish hatcheries. It's going to take a while to get all that back in order. And who knows how much it's going to cost? Only one case of looting, so far."

"Where?"

"Rose Lake Winery. Someone ransacked the downstairs office during the blowout. The staff reported it. But I went there after daybreak, and Weller, the owner, didn't want to pursue it. He claimed it was wind damage."

"You don't think so?"

"No. Windows in the office open onto the beach, and the wind blew them out. But from what I saw, the wind damage inside was superficial. Yet files had been taken out, drawers opened and contents dumped on the floor. A waiter said the office computer was missing. But if the owner doesn't want us to investigate, what can we do? I'm beginning to think somebody doesn't want us to solve anything about the blowout anyway."

"What do you mean?"

Lynn took a swallow of her soda, and seemed to be trying to decide if she should say anything. Finally she leaned forward and lowered her voice. "You heard the news this morning, claiming the explosives could have been laid two months prior, and placing the suspicion on a tourist with false I.D.?"

"Yeah. It seemed a bit far-fetched to me."

"It seems impossible. I talked to Bill this morning, your partner in the bulldozer. He took the job with the construction crew. He seems happier. But he tells me this morning after the news broke that another worker had done some maintenance on the cargo airlock last week, and even inspected the supports where the charges were planted. Nothing was there. I went and talked to this guy, took a statement and filed a report. But when I contacted OSAR investigators, they told me to forget about it. The worker must have been wrong because it didn't fit the evidence they already had."

"Did they actually find any evidence?"

"No, at least not that the charges had been there ahead of time. I talked to an OSAR investigator yesterday, a friend of mine. He told me about finding a controller, an unassigned personal com unit that was still intact. That's how they found out about the link to the temperature readings. Even yesterday, he didn't think it had been there long. The com unit was still strapped to a brace that would have been in plain view from the outside where the worker had done the maintenance."

"Who gets to see your report?"

"Nobody. It's been erased. And that's not supposed to happen. Its priority can be downgraded. The chief can even stamp a note to it denying its credibility. That happens to witness reports all the time. But the computer record is supposed to be complete. If you dig down deep enough, any report is supposed to be there. But my report was deleted an hour after I filed it. And the chief told me OSAR called him and chewed his ass out, telling him to just leave the investigation to OSAR and the FBI."

"Who from OSAR called your chief?"

"Their head of investigations, the new one. Lenowitz was never like that."

"No," Ed agreed. "That's probably why he's no longer head of investigations. Who was the investigator you talked to yesterday?"

"I don't want to get him into trouble."

"Lenowitz and I are drinking buddies. I can slip a word to him. Maybe he can find out something unofficially."

"OK, but he better be careful for his own sake. Stan Olas is the guy's name. I haven't seen him around today."

As the two talked intently, neither noticed Jessica walking up behind Ed.

"Here I am , just a few minutes late for lunch, and I find you two huddling together." Ed cringed involuntarily, but Lynn was smooth in her response.

"It's no big deal. Six and I were just making plans to meet at my apartment while you're still in the fields."

Jessica looked bemused as she put a hand on Ed's shoulder. "Six?"

"It's easier to keep 'em straight if I just give them numbers."

"Well, as long as it's while I'm at work."

"See, I told you there'd be no problem." Both women laughed at Ed's expense as Jessica sat down next to him. He handed Jessica a chicken sandwich.

"I have to go back on duty," Lynn said, standing up and picking up her sandwich wrapper. "Besides, the place is starting to get crowded. They need the seats. Jessica, I hope the college kids aren't giving you too much trouble."

"They're doing fine. Thanks for your help this morning."

"Sure thing. And Ed," placing emphasis on the name, "be careful."

"I didn't mean to crimp your style," Jessica said as Lynn left, "or hers."

"I don't think anything crimps her style. So Hafiz tells me you're moving."

"The hotel was just too expensive. Do you remember Amy Chen on the *New Brunswick*, the one coming to Mars to be the artist in residence at the university?"

"Yeah. She broke her leg in the explosion, didn't she?"

"Her arm. Luckily it was her left arm and she's right handed. We talked on the trip about finding a place together. She was here yesterday, making some sketches, when I ran into her. She told me she found an apartment near campus, but she still needed a roommate. I went to see the place last night and I loved it. Some of the guys are helping me tonight to move my stuff there from the hotel after we're done."

"I could have helped."

"We'll be done late, and the guys live in that area anyway. But I will see you bright and early tomorrow."

"Yeah, Hafiz told me about that, too."

"Sorry. I couldn't make it any later and still get here at a reasonable time."

"How long will you be working here?"

Jessica leaned back and spread her hands to take in the sweep of the surrounding scene. "It could take months to put all this together. My job is helping organize volunteers. I told them my last day is Wednesday so I can get ready for the launch, but the development council staff already told me they could use me again when we returned."

"So could 4-O. We have another run right after we get back, and a third run down the road."

"Are you guys going to put me on a long-term retainer?"

"That's up to Marta back on the Moon. Hafiz and I put in that recommendation. Same for Laura and Manny. You don't have to take the retainer if you'd rather work on the ground."

"It's nice to have choices, but your pay is better. We can talk about that when Marta makes her decision. Is it all right for you to take my duffel back home with you?"

"Sure. What's in it?"

"My passport and some other stuff that's important to me. The apartment I'm moving to seems pretty secure, but it's a student area, so who knows. I'd feel better if you took it back home with you."

"It's probably safer where it is in the 4-O safe."

"Not if OSAR decides to search that office, again. Hafiz told me they searched it yesterday. I don't want them going through my stuff."

"I doubt they'll search 4-O again. With the new head of investigations more willing to do the FBI's bidding, they're more likely to search my place."

"I thought you were cleared."

"They moved me down the list, but the FBI still has their eye on me."

"OK, then, keep it in the 4-O safe, at least for now."

Ed wanted to ask more, but stopped when a man pulled out the chair opposite them. "Ed, Jessica, I haven't talked to you since we landed."

"Juarez," Ed said, noticing the volunteer badge he was wearing. "I saw you at the service, Wednesdim. I'm sorry I didn't get a chance to talk. You know, the way you helped clear the *New Brunswick* wreckage so I could dock out there, I'd give you a recommendation anytime you want. What do they have you doing, here?"

"Outside work," Juarez said as he sat down. "I was helping clear debris and prep material outside for the permanent wall repair."

"So that was you I saw yesterday," Jessica said. "You had your helmet off and were with a group of other workers who had just come through the airlock."

"Yeah, probably was. It seems most of the outside construction workers on Mars are working on a new science station on the other side of the planet. A call went out for suit workers, and I caught the first train here. I see you have a badge, Jessica, but Ed, you don't. You're not working here?"

"No, I just met Jessica for lunch."

Juarez smiled and leaned slightly forward. "So you two were together the night of the blowout. I saw each of you on the news, and I wondered. Let me guess, you had dinner at Rose Lake."

Jessica started to answer, but Ed was quicker.

"No, we came to the Shack for the music."

"You didn't happen to see where Jack's sign went, did you? He paid good money for that sign and was hoping to get it back. He asked us to look for it, but we couldn't find it outside."

"It's buried beneath a couple of tons of dirt, foam and debris. It hung up in the breach and we used it to help hold the patch."

Juarez laughed. "I'll let you tell him that if you want. But it may be better off to let him keep wondering."

"I have to get back to work," Jessica said. "Juarez, be careful outside."

"Yeah, I should get going, too," Ed said. "Maybe next time I see you, I can buy you a beer."

"If you have time, leave me a message at the Far Horizons. I'm staying there until I launch with you."

"You're taking the *Zach* to Ceres?"

"Yeah, I'm meeting a mining ship there."

"Well then, see you at launch."

Ed and Jessica didn't say anything as they left until they rounded a corner and were well out of sight of Juarez.

"Why did you tell him we had dinner at the Shack?" Jessica asked. "Do you suspect him?"

"I'm suspicious of everybody, but if you knew a bomb would go off in your ship, wouldn't you want to have a spacesuit handy?"

"He wasn't the only one on board with a spacesuit. Three or four others had them on, too."

"But he had his suit on pretty quick, and he's the only one to run into us here, and the only one to ask us if we had dinner at the winery. He may have been trying to find out if we talked to Weller."

"If that's so, at least you were quick enough to tell him we went to the Shack instead."

"That might not have been so smart. The whole idea of talking with Lenowitz yesterday was to get everything out in the open. If Juarez is involved and thinks I lied to him, he'll wonder what else we have to hide, what information we haven't shared. Damn, that was dumb."

"He may not be involved. There were a lot of us on the *New Brunswick*."

"And a lot of them will be on the *Zach*. With the FBI chasing ghost conspirators on Earth, we're on our own if we want to stop someone from doing to the *Zach* what was done to the New B. – or Serling Heights."

"Or just to us?"

"Anything's possible. Stay in a crowd. I hope there are a lot of students helping you move tonight."

"Not a lot. But they look pretty strong." She kissed him, then went off toward the vineyards.

Before heading for the station, Ed looked around for a public safety officer. When he found one, he asked the officer where Lynn was stationed. It turned out she was only a block away, arbitrating a street dispute between a trash hauler and a contractor trying to use the same vacant lot. It looked like the trash hauler had been there first, but it didn't look like he was going to stay there long.

"Tell that to the bureaucrat who's supposed to be running this show," protested an angry and grizzled man covered in dust and grime. "She told me to dump it here, so I did."

"Actually, she told you to dump it two blocks away," Lynn answered. "You didn't check your map."

"So I'm just supposed to pick all this up again and move it?"

"Exactly," gloated the contractor, thin, with surprisingly clean bright blue coveralls.

Lynn turned to him angrily. "You, just go to lunch. Don't make more trouble." She turned back to the trash hauler. "While he's at lunch, you have an hour to get your robo-haulers over here and cart this stuff away, or I'll haul you away."

The trash hauler grumbled under his breath but made a call for the robo-haulers return. The contractor went off in a huff toward the lunch line as Ed walked up.

"Lynn, how late are you on duty today?"

Lynn gave him a sly smile. "We're all putting in long hours, but when would you want me off ... wait a minute, what's wrong?"

"Maybe nothing, but try to keep an eye on Jessica. Maybe you can tip off some other officers, too."

"Sure. Scared of something?"

"Someone. See the guy in the olive green shirt just leaving the Shack?"

She casually looked over her shoulder. Shrubs partially hid them from view, so she could look down the block without being easily seen from that direction.

"His name's Juarez. He's working with the outside crew."

"Yeah, I recognize him. I saw him yesterday morning at the wall."

"In the morning? He got here quick."

"Who is he?"

"He was a passenger on the *New Brunswick*."

Lynn turned to Ed with a demeanor that was all cop. "What's this about?"

"It may just be me being paranoid. He sat down with us after you left. Friendly talk, but he got around to asking where Jessica and I had dinner the night of the blow out. I told him the Shack."

"Why is that a problem?"

"It's only a problem if the wrong person finds out we had dinner instead at Rose Lake and talked with Weller that evening."

"I heard what Weller said at the memorial. You're in this deep, aren't you?"

"For several reasons, not the least of which is that many of the passengers I'm taking to Ceres were aboard the *New Brunswick*. One of them may be a killer."

"You think someone bombed a ship he was aboard? Pretty chancy."

"Maybe not so much if you had your own spacesuit with you. There were 40 passengers on board. Two died. Weller thinks somebody on board made sure about one of them."

"And you think Juarez may be that somebody?"

"I'm saying it's possible. That doesn't mean he planted the charges here, but he showed up pretty quickly. Admittedly a lot of people did. Juarez told me he caught the first train in when he heard the news."

"Did he say he caught a train?"

"Yeah, why?"

Lynn shifted her gaze to where Juarez was just rounding a corner and walking out of sight. "When I saw him, it was about dawn, heading for the wall with his suit on but helmet off." She turned back to Ed. "At the time, they were only letting medical staff come in by train. Construction crews were flying in from their building site, but those were only contract workers. The only volunteers who went outside were the ones already living here."

"Maybe I'm not being paranoid. Are you sure it was him?"

"Yeah, but I'll head down to the wall and double check the suit he's wearing. It was a space work suit, not a groundsuit, right?"

"Yeah."

"We had more of a mix of suits later, but at that point most were wearing groundsuits from just a couple of construction companies. I was trying to keep some track of who we had at the wall. The other spacesuits I saw were from the spacers I know who live in the village. Are you sure he's not staying here?"

"He said he was staying at the Far Horizons in Tiu City."

"So the question is, did he come here to help that early, or was he just trying to blend into the crowd to escape?"

"And come back?"

"Could be. In case somebody like me saw him here, he establishes himself as a volunteer. Hell, I've got enough to pull him in for questioning right now."

"But you're not going to, right?"

"Not after the call my chief got this morning. But you're still going to get a hold of Lenowitz?"

"You bet."

"Do it soon."

CHAPTER 15

The More You Know

"You call these security measures stringent?" Ed gripped the edge of the counter and glared at the junior officer. "I call them a joke, lieutenant. A cursory review of paperwork? A meandering inspection of cargo? You might as well put cots at checkpoints so your guards can be comfortable. They couldn't keep a 12-year-old out of the loading dock."

The beleaguered lieutenant at OSAR's spaceport headquarters took a step back from the counter. "W-we're doing everything we can, sir. But the FBI is certain the saboteur is back on Earth."

Ed leaned over the counter even further. "Lieutenant, I've seen a ship blow up in front of my eyes. I've had half of Serling Heights' air and most of its cheap siding sucked out around me. When I'm somewhere in the Belt, wondering if one of my passengers is a murderer, and if a bomb is stashed in my cargo hold, the FBI will be safe on Earth chasing phantom terrorists, and you'll be in some Tiu City bar trying to keep down one too many Martian beers."

"But sir, the Grissom will be trailing you on your trip."

"Will you be on it?"

"Well, no."

"Will your boss be on it?"

"My watch commander won't have space duty for a few more months."

"Will anyone from the security detail be on the Grissom?"

"No."

"So no one responsible for security will have to risk his life to save us if that security breaks down."

"Perhaps I can have the captain of the Grissom talk to you. He reviews security measures."

"You do that, lieutenant. I'll be on the *Cydonia Zach* the rest of the afternoon."

Ed turned quickly, smiling as he left before the lieutenant regained his wits to see if Lenowitz was available now. Ed didn't want to talk to captain at OSAR headquarters, nor did he want to call Lenowitz directly asking to meet him. He didn't want to risk having Lenowitz's superiors ask the captain the reason for the meeting. This way, Lenowitz was doing them a favor bailing out the security detail from having to deal with an irrational pilot.

Headquarters staff sees us commercial pilots as a nuisance, anyway, Ed thought.

The enclosed walkway out of OSAR headquarters connected it to the loading docks and maintenance hangars, and looked out over the open air landing field, a broad expanse of concrete laid atop the Martian plain. An orbital tug with a cargo module sat on pad 7, with only the pad's painted markings, inset lights, and a burst pattern of rocket exhaust soot setting it off from the rest of the concrete. A light wind blew a haze of dust across the field, blurring the distant hills and diffusing the shadows thrown by the harsh sunlight.

Ed turned a corner, cleared security, and took the stairs down to the commercial hangar. The *Zach* waited in Bay 15, minus one of its docking clamps damaged in the flight. Access doors hung open revealing gaping slots in the tug where the maintenance crew had pulled the long-range radar components, a couple of pumps, and the waste water treatment system. The missing equipment was at the shop for inspection and repair. No one was working on the *Zach* that afternoon.

Ed climbed into the tug and pulled out a tablet from his personal gear. He stepped into the cockpit and slipped into the pilot's seat. Might as well get comfortable while I'm waiting, Ed thought. He blacked out the cockpit windows, then started scanning through news reports on the tablet.

He soon dozed off, and didn't hear Lenowitz's soft footsteps on the ladder. Ed jumped, however, when Lenowitz clanged the outside hatch shut.

"Damn, you could have given me some warning, captain."

"Perhaps you should not be so quick to criticize OSAR security when you so obviously neglect your own."

"I'm sorry about giving that lieutenant such a hard time, but I needed to see you and I wanted to give you some cover. Sit in the co-pilot's seat." Ed switched on his communication gear again to be certain no signals from hidden microphones were going out. His instruments showed clear.

"I appreciated the hyperbole you employed," Lenowitz said as he sat down, "though I must inform you that no security detail in the solar system can keep out a determined 12-year-old."

"It's a good thing we're not looking for a 12-year-old bomber."

"Personally, I am not ruling anyone out, though I remind you, I am officially off the case."

"Which means nothing we talk about here will end up in an official file, right?"

"Correct. Why do you wish to see me?"

"I may have a suspect."

"Ed, we have no shortage of suspects. The FBI just added about half of Earth's population."

"Let's say I have some information that makes somebody more suspicious than the rest."

"Who?"

"Juarez, the guy who put the suit on out there and helped me clear away wreckage so I could dock with the New B., or what was left of it. I forget his last name."

"Santiano. I was taking a second look at him after Weller's statements at the service. If there was a killer aboard the *New Brunswick*, it seems likely he'd have a spacesuit ready when the bomb exploded. Four of the passengers did. But I didn't get very far before I was reassigned."

"He was at Serling Heights yesterday, and he still had his suit handy."

"Yes, we know that. We, that is the investigative staff, checked on the whereabouts of everyone who had been on the *New Brunswick*, and I read the reports. Juarez had dinner in Tiu City the afternoon before the explosion, and the following morning he answered a call for more outside workers to the disaster site. He signed up in Tiu City and boarded the train with the first group, around 1030."

"A public safety officer saw him in Serling Heights, at the wall with his suit on, around dawn."

Lenowitz pulled out his notebook and set it to record. "Don't worry. I won't transcribe this until I'm back on the Grissom. This officer can make a positive ID?"

"Juarez had his helmet off at the time. The officer, her name's Lynn, was trying to keep track of who was going outside, and noticed him because most of the outside workers had groundsuits and he had a spacesuit. She figured it was someone who just moved to the village, because she recognized the other spacers who came to the wall. And only med staff were coming in by train at that time."

"So how did she later identify this man as Juarez?"

"Because of me." Ed went on to explain the details of his conversations with Lynn, Jessica and Juarez. He included the evidence of Weller's ransacked office, the vintner's refusal to file a complaint, and the erased witness report that contradicted the FBI's claim someone planted the explosives on the cargo airlock ahead of time.

"Your friend Lynn is right, this should have been enough to bring Juarez in for questioning, but not enough to arrest him."

"Can you convince Keritan to bring Juarez in?"

"Not a chance." Lenowitz switched off his notebook. "Keritan would point out that we already know Juarez was having dinner in the city, so he couldn't have been planting bombs outside Serling Heights. And if the charges really were planted months in advance as the FBI claims, his presence is irrelevant."

"You're not buying that."

"No. We only know his account was credited for dinner. That is too easy for someone else to accomplish to establish an alibi. As for the bomb placed there weeks ahead of time, the FBI states it with conviction because it fits their theory of the crime. But there is no hard evidence of that, and Lynn's erased report would have contradicted it. Yet no one will look into this deeper. This case is too political, and too many strings are being pulled from Earth. The *New Brunswick* explosion drew high interest from home, but not this much. The ship explosion could have been the work of one person, for any one of many possible motives. Serling Heights, on the other hand, needed a conspiracy, and it was an act of terror."

"But isn't that even more of a reason for OSAR to bring in Juarez? Don't you have to pursue any leads you turn up?"

Lenowitz leaned forward in his seat, slowly tapping the notebook against his left hand. "The Americans do not want OSAR to solve this, and they do not want anyone to solve this quickly."

"Why?"

"Understand Ed, we are not talking about one conspiracy here, but several. Uncovering one can reveal the rest."

The way Lenowitz said it made Ed think he wasn't as clever as he first thought in meeting the captain on the *Zach*. They needed a more secret place to meet, but where would they find that on Mars? "What conspiracies are we talking about?"

"First, we can start with your uncle and Faizah. The plot they hatched to support Sen. Decker's moratorium as a scheme to break free from the control of Earth corporations – it probably set everything in motion."

"I didn't know they told you the details."

"They did not. That night on your patio, I could see who attended Chubeck's dinner, and from what little he and Faizah did tell me – and you – I knew who to go to for prying out the rest."

"And here I thought you just wanted free beer. Why did my uncle's plan set everything in motion?"

"It made everything critical, including Averink's success or failure. American politics, corporate subsidies, your uncle's vision of an economic independence for Mars, they all reached a nexus. The *New Brunswick*'s destruction may have occurred to preserve profits for the current builders of fusion drives. The Serling Heights blowout-freezout certainly was an attempt to keep Mars dependent on Earth."

"Couldn't it backfire and allow Decker to pull us back from Mars?"

"I am not sure if anyone understands American politics, but usually when faced with extremes, Americans do nothing, and the rest of the world makes a lot of noise. And Americans have never wanted to pull back from anything in response to a threat. I suspect there could have been many powerful people afraid that Chubeck was offering a compromise, to make it easier to cut off funds from Earth without abandoning Mars. The American public would have grasped that, and the corporations may not have been able to buy the voters off this time. The rest of the world would have gone along. Averink was offering a means to make the compromise work, if his research panned out."

"You don't believe it did?"

"The evidence I have seen suggests otherwise. Averink's death and the loss of his drive prototype may yet be just happenstance, or someone not taking any chances."

"But if Averink's research did work and it became known too early, that could have undercut Decker's moratorium."

"As well as your uncle's plans. The means to travel to Mars and the Asteroid Belt in days instead of weeks, at nearly anytime instead of a narrow window, would have strengthened the perceived value in space travel. Chubeck may have feared the timing before the election would have strengthened the argument for continued financial ties and siphoned profits to Earth."

"I can't believe my uncle's behind all this. He backed Averink, and the Serling Heights blowout hit 4th Orbit pretty badly."

"You do not want to believe your uncle is behind the bombings. I sincerely hope you're right. But he has put Faizah into a position to be very involved."

"My uncle doesn't want to believe that." Ed hesitated. "But I think she could have been bought off."

"Do not discount loyalty. Your uncle commands it, and Faizah respects it. She is high on my suspect list, too, but it does not sit right in my mind. There is a missing piece in her puzzle. Did you know she was hard wired?"

"Faizah? You're kidding."

"We detected the chips during the search. Of course we couldn't access them."

"Actually, it makes sense now that I think about it. I thought she was a quick study on the *Zach*, handling the comm gear like a pro. She must have been reading the info on her contacts."

"It makes her even more capable of doing many things," Lenowitz said.

"It still could have been the First Earthers behind the bombings."

"I admit, their motive is straight forward. But the Mother Earth Defense Alliance? No. Yet they are convenient, and they volunteered to be guilty after the *New Brunswick* bombing. A number of fringe groups volunteered. Whoever was behind the Serling Heights blowout only had to pick one of them and give it a script – a willing frame-up."

"But why is the FBI so willing to buy it?"

"Maybe because the price of finding someone else guilty is too high. The U.S. administration may not be willing to endure the scandal if Interplanetary Drive Systems or some other corporation was discovered to be behind all this, acting to protect its current monopoly on fusion drives."

"But the administration would have much to gain if the FBI solves the case with someone convenient, is that it Captain? It reinforces their claim they need to protect American interests on Mars."

"A collision of conspiracies, an intersection of motives. Take your pick."

"At least I dropped down on their suspect list."

"Well, I'm afraid ...."

"Wait a minute. I thought the FBI lost interest in me."

"I said they dropped you down on their priority list. But since you once again were on the scene of a disaster and came to the rescue, the FBI has again taken notice. In fact, yesterday morning I was waiting for a search warrant for your house as well. For some reason, Keritan decided against it."

"He lets the FBI push him around on everything else, but he bucks them on searching my house?"

Lenowitz shrugged his shoulders. "Perhaps even he saw it was a waste of time, or maybe the FBI didn't want to tip you off that they were still interested in you."

"I think you just did."

Lenowitz sighed. "Yes, but this is an unofficial conversation, correct?"

"Oh, yeah. I forgot."

"There is, however, one possible conspirator we haven't talked about."

"Jessica?"

"She almost certainly lied to me outside the church about knowing Averink, and I do not mean just getting to know him as one of her passengers. But I still do not know why she lied to me. Do you know?"

"No. She lied to me about not knowing I was taking the *Zach* to Ceres until I hired her as steward. She made me think the hiring was my idea."

"Most interesting. But do not be too glum, my friend. The advantage you have with Jessica is she is a bad liar. She could not hide knowing Averink, or supporting him. She would not have conspired to kill him."

"But you think she conspired to do something?"

"Perhaps." Lenowitz stood and made his way to the hatch.

"Wait a minute," Ed said, hurriedly following him into the center cabin. "All of this still doesn't explain why OSAR is going along with the Americans in the investigation."

Lenowitz let his hand rest on the hatch. "No, it does not." He turned to Ed. "Part of it is the Americans, through back channels, let OSAR command know if we see things their way, we will get those two other ships for which we have been waiting for years. If we do not, well, we are U.N. chartered, but most of our funding comes from the U.S."

"You said that's part of it?"

"Yes, I did," Lenowitz said as he turned back to the hatch and left.

CHAPTER 16
Sidestreets and Shadows

The sun was setting over the Martian plain by the time Ed was back on the mag-lev from the spaceport for Tiu City. After Lenowitz left, Ed spent the afternoon checking on the shop work and reviewing navigation, the normal routine for a week prior to launch. But tending to routine seemed odd this time.

He called Jessica from the train, but she said she wouldn't reach downtown until 2030. She again told him not to wait, that she had plenty of help to move her stuff.

"Have you seen Juarez again?" he asked.

"No, but I think you've got me spooked," Jessica answered.

"Why?"

"Ever since I left you after lunch, I'd swear there were cops shadowing me. I mean, they're all around anyway, but this is different."

Ed frowned, and tried not to let on. "It's probably nothing. You're likely just reacting to the suspicion I planted in your mind. Still, be careful."

"I will," Jessica promised. "Now remember, don't wait for me downtown tonight. I'll see you tomorrow."

But Ed did wait. After getting off the mag-lev, he walked down Sagan Street in what he hoped looked like a casual manner while still trying to note the passers-by. There were quite a few, mostly from the cadre of Mars-bound office workers and bureaucrats dawdling downtown on a Fridim night. Ed was looking for anything unusual, but what was unusual on Mars? Still, he looked, stopping in a few stores, taking his time.

Ed ended up at Uncle Martin's Diner halfway between the station and Far Horizons. He took a window seat and tried to scan the menu on the tabletop screen.

"Here, hon, let me wipe those smudges off the screen for you," said a middle-aged waitress wearing a tan dress and a stained white apron.

She had worked at the diner as long as Ed could remember. "Coffee?" she asked as she took out a cloth to wipe the screen.

"Sure."

"The special tonight is tofu stroganoff – beef is extra. It was supposed to be a seafood platter, but the prices went way up. That Serling Heights thing, you know."

"Yeah, I know."

"Just tap out what you want, and I'll be right back with your coffee."

"Hey Frances!" a diner called from across the room.

"Right there, hon," she said and hurried off.

Ed tapped out an order, then switched the screen to news, silent mode. Most of the reports were of Earth politicians spouting off about how more money was needed for Martian security versus those who said they were spending too much on Mars already. Decker hadn't announced his plan for a moratorium on space and science funding, yet, but his opponents were lining up as if he had, arguing about "not giving in to terrorists." As Ed sat there, waiting for Jessica to show up, he realized the detectives from Manny's extensive library of old movies had an advantage on a stakeout. They could hide their faces behind a newspaper, back when that meant real paper. Ed tried to make do with a small fern in the window.

It was about 1945 hours when Ed spotted Juarez leaving the station. But Juarez made no side trips, no furtive glances. He didn't spot Ed behind the fern as he walked straight to his hotel.

About 45 minutes later, Jessica left the station with five students in tow, four male, one female. He waited while they went to the hotel for Jessica's gear she had stashed at the front desk. They quickly loaded up a cart, and one of the students drove it away. Jessica and the rest walked back toward Burroughs Street, and Ed panicked when he realized they'd walk right by his window. He quickly ducked beneath the table and watched as they passed.

"Lose something, hon?"

Ed looked up and saw Frances hovering over him with a coffee pot and an annoyed look at him for taking up her table for most of the evening.

"What? Uh, no," Ed said, straightening. "I – I'm just tightening my shoe."

"Yeah, that Velcro stuff can be tricky, huh? You sure you don't want anything else?"

"No, thank you, I'm fine. I was just leaving."

"No need to hurry. Why start now?"

Frances stepped aside to let Ed out of the booth. He stayed inside the front door of the diner to see if anyone followed Jessica and the students to Burroughs, and had nearly convinced himself of his foolishness when he saw someone, not Juarez, slip out of the shadows between buildings across the street. He was tall, slender, blond. He walked slowly at first, crossing the street at an angle.

As Ed stepped out of the diner, there was no sign of Jessica and the students, but the blond man was walking faster to where they must have turned the corner. Ed picked up his speed, too, but instead of turning on Burroughs, he just took a quick glance down the street. Jessica's group was at the next corner, and the blond man had slowed again, looking in a storefront window.

Ed walked along Sagan another block before turning down Welles. Jessica's new place was near the corner of Welles and Wells. Her apartment was on H.G. Ed was on Orson, a narrow street, most of the shops and small offices already closed. Ed ducked into a walkway and down an alley parallel to Orson. Where it came out on H.G., Ed found a spot where he could watch both streets and the apartment entrance as the students unloaded Jessica's gear from the cart and carried it in.

The alley stank from spoiled food in bins waiting for the auto-recyclers to make their pre-dawn rounds, and the muffled sounds of partying along Burroughs echoed past him. Ed peered around the corner to see if the blond man would reappear, or if Juarez would show up. But as he did ....

"Better red and dead!" a wall poster bellowed.

"Oh, shit." Ed ripped the poster from the wall and ducked back into the alley, crushing the electronic paper in hopes of silencing it.

"Will we change Mars simply because we can?" the poster went on, slightly garbled. "We despoiled one planet. Do we have to go for two?"

"Shut up already." Ed threw the poster into one of the trash bins, but it's muffled message continued. From the shadows, he looked out into the street to see if anyone noticed, so he wasn't ready for the hand that gripped him from the back and threw him against the wall.

"Now, be quiet," said the voice in his ear. "Step back slowly and lean against the wall, your hands high."

"Hey! Our voices will be heard," came from the crumpled poster in the bin. "And you can help stop the Blue Menace. Go to RedandAngry-dot-mars...."

"Enough already," said the unseen man, and Ed heard the sharp crackle of an electric stunner shot into the trash bin. The poster went abruptly silent.

The man turned his attention back to Ed and began to pat him down.

"I don't have a weapon," Ed said.

"Too bad. I guess I'll just have to run you in for tearing down that poster. Now turn around slowly."

"You're a cop?" Ed turned and saw the tall blond man holding a stun gun on him and flashing an I.D.

"OSAR investigations. You want to tell me what you're doing hiding in an alley?"

Ed quickly read the name on the holo badge. "Stan Olas?"

Puzzled, the man reached into a jacket pocket with his left hand, pulled out a small flashlight, and shined it on Ed's face. "Let's see some I.D."

As Ed pulled it out, Olas flashed the light on the I.D. and again on Ed's face. "Ed Ferald. I'm surprised you're here." Ed noticed the expression on Olas' face was not surprise but exasperation.

"I was worried about a friend of mine who's moving in across the street."

"Jessica Cantrell. Yeah, that's why I'm here." Olas switched off the flashlight. "Capt. Lenowitz asked me to keep watch on her tonight, to see if anyone followed Ms. Cantrell to her apartment."

"Did you see anyone?"

"Besides you? Possibly. The Captain told me to be on the lookout for a Juarez Santiano. I have a photo. I saw him leave the hotel by a side door soon after Ms. Cantrell arrived with her friends to pick up her luggage. I thought I might have seen him on Burroughs, a block beyond H.G. I wasn't certain. But then, just a while ago, I spotted a man that might have been Juarez walking down H.G. toward the apartment, but from the opposite direction. You didn't see him?"

"No."

Olas kept shifting his gaze as he spoke, checking out the streets and the alley. "Almost certainly he saw you, because he stopped.

I thought you two exchanged signals. Then he just turned round and went back. When he reached the corner of Bradbury, he turned toward Sagan and disappeared. But you were still here, an accomplice, I thought. A rather bungling accomplice. To what, I didn't know."

"I guess you and I were on the same watch, and I scared him off."

"Yes you did. Now why don't you go away while I stay here and see if he comes back."

Ed didn't want to annoy Olas any further and left without another word.

By the time he reached Viking Glen, fears of conspiracies and shadowy figures on the street had been replaced by exhaustion. Ed grimaced at the thought of getting up early in the morning. He checked out an electric cart and drove back to his place.

Ed had spent so much time that evening looking for suspicious people and peering into dark corners that he forgot to do the same as he approached his own house. But he froze when something moved in the shadows of the patio, and a voice came out of the gloom.

"Alone?"

It took a second to register. "Faizah?"

She leaned forward in her seat, bringing her face into a light thrown from a distance. "I wasn't sure you would be back tonight. But that's right, Hafiz told me Jessica has a roommate in her new place. What's the matter, you didn't trust her to move in here? Or was it that Jessica didn't trust you? Now that's an interesting turn."

The burst of fear when Ed first saw movement quickly turned to annoyance. "Why are you here? It must be well past midnight."

Faizah checked her watch. "Just halfway through null time. Only 2420."

"You were waiting for me?"

"I wasn't," Faizah said, nodding to her right, "but he was." Ed stepped forward and peered toward where she nodded. A body lay against the patio wall.

"Or maybe he didn't expect you back either," she said. "I'm not sure."

Ed looked intently at the body, but didn't step any closer. He turned back to Faizah.

"Is he dead?"

She smiled and leaned back into the shadow. Without changing the direction of her gaze, she sent a soft kick into the body's shins. The body groaned.

"No."

"What happened?"

"Your house alarm went off at Chubeck's, but no one else was around. It was about to relay to Public Safety when I shut it off so I could check it out myself. I took one of Roger's electric stunners, but I left Ariel back at the house so she didn't give me away. I found him trying to get through one of the windows."

"Who is he?"

"Let's roll him over and you'll find out. I think he's coming to." The man groaned as Ed and Faizah rolled him onto his back

"Charlie McKracken?" Ed said.

"That's right – the shipbuilder and supposed ally of Chubeck."

"And burglar."

Charlie brought his hand to his forehead to squeeze out the pain, and barely got his words out. "It's just a sideline."

Faizah bent low over his face. "Don't quit your day job."

"God, do you have something for the pain?"

"Ed, go inside and see what you've got. Just lay flat on your back, Mr. McKracken, and relax. The pain will ease."

"Call me Charlie."

"It's always nice to be on a first-name basis with your burglar." As Charlie lay there, Faizah noticed a black tube on the floor where he'd been lying face down seconds before. She picked it up and held it near her waist.

"What's that?" Ed asked as he came back with pain killers and water.

"A scanner. It detects memory devices, disks, microphones. OSAR searched my room with one like it yesterday."

"Charlie, what are you doing here?"

Charlie swallowed the pills before answering. "I was looking for something."

"Really? Aw hell, Faizah, let's just call the cops and be done with him."

"No – Ow! My head hurts – please, don't."

"Just lay there for 10 minutes. Ed, hold up on that call."

"What?" Ed already had his com in hand.

"Charlie here has a lot to lose if he gets arrested for trying to break into your place."

"Why do I care?"

"Aahh, not so loud," Charlie groaned.

Softer now. "Again, why do I care?"

"Charlie," Faizah said, "close your eyes and lay back. We'll get back to you in a minute. Just don't try to leave."

"As if I could."

"Ed, come inside. We can watch him from the window." Ed and Faizah went into Ed's living room. Faizah closed the door, but positioned herself by the front window to keep an eye on Charlie.

"OK, Faizah, why don't we just turn him in?"

"And then what?"

"And then OSAR arrests him and finds out what he was doing here."

"Are you certain?"

"They gotta arrest him."

"Even if they did, they don't have to do anything more than charge him with trespassing. It'll be bad for him and his business, but it won't do us any good."

"What makes you say that?"

"This." Faizah held the black scanner in front of Ed.

"The scanner? You said it was like the one OSAR used in your room. What of it?"

"Not like – this is the one OSAR used in my room."

"How can you be sure?"

"The latest version is extremely sensitive. I keep emergency memory chips in my hip that are supposed to be shielded against scanners, but this one picks it up."

"In your hip?"

"Yeah, see?" She waved the scanner across her body, and the readouts registered a contact.

"Lenowitz said you were hard wired."

"I'm not surprised he told you. I don't spread it around. It gives me an advantage. The thing is, we had a couple of these scanners at InterCorporate to test, but one of the agents using it said it had bugs, which delayed it going into production. OSAR had some on order to replace their old ones. The manufacturer must have sent them a Beta model, but sure as hell no one else on Mars has one."

"So how did Charlie get it?"

"That's what I want to find out."

Faizah opened the door and stepped outside. Ed realized there was nothing to do but follow Faizah's lead. Charlie was sitting up, still rubbing his head. "Starting to come around?" Faizah asked.

"Barely," Charlie said. "Why did you have to shoot me with that stun gun? Couldn't you have just yelled 'Freeze, business consultant!'?"

"I guess I'm not that kind of consultant."

"No, you're just the kind of consultant that stuns your client's business associates."

"I think she does that every time she walks into a room," Ed said.

"Really?" Faizah said, giving Ed a very raised eyebrow. "How charming of you to say so."

"I'd probably agree with you, Ed, but I'll have to wait until my eyes can focus. Right now my mind's too fogged to remember."

"Maybe you can remember why you were trying to break-in through Ed's window."

"Because the door was locked."

Faizah squatted next to Charlie and took hold of his shirt below the neckline. But instead of pulling it away, she pushed her grip against him while running a fingernail across his chest, slowly.

"Charlie, I can always stun you again if your answers don't please me, and while you're out, we'll call the cops. When you wake up, you'll have twice the headache, a felony charge for breaking-and-entering, and probably a lawsuit or two from 4th Orbit for corporate spying. By day's end, your reputation will be ruined, your business will be in shambles, and you'll be lucky if you end up sweeping the vestibule at St. Joe's. If you please me, I won't shoot you, and I won't call the cops. Now, why were you trying to break-in through Ed's window?"

"This guy said Ed's door wouldn't be locked. Now wait, don't shoot. Help me to a chair and I'll explain."

Faizah backed off while Ed helped Charlie to his feet and got him to a chair.

"What guy?" Ed asked.

"I don't know his name. Never saw him. He's the one who provided the scanner."

"You tried to break into my place on the word of some stranger?"

"I told you, I wasn't supposed to have to break in."

"Give me the gun, Faizah."

"Now hold on, Ed, this is starting to be intriguing. Charlie, why don't we go back to some point you would reasonably consider the beginning."

"I don't know how much I should tell you."

Faizah laid the stun gun on the table, the whine of its recharge rising. Her thumb caressed the discharge button. "Everything."

"All right, just shut that thing down. I guess it began last night. I had dinner downtown with Arthur Strand."

"Of Ares Manufacturing?" Faizah asked.

"Yeah. It turns out he had been approached by the same people at Astech who approached me."

"Astech approached you?"

"I told Ed about it the night of the dinner at Chubeck's. An Astech rep had told me Astech was interested in buying a stake in my company."

"When did the Astech rep approach you?"

"About a week ago, before Ed landed."

"So what happened last night?"

"Arthur told me Astech was checking his company's capacity to make equipment for a manufacturing operation on Ceres. It sounded like equipment to produce fusion drive components."

"What of it?"

"Arthur and I were talking that something didn't sound right about Astech. They were never interested in ship building before, except for some slow robot haulers. And with everything else that was happening, we weren't sure what we were getting ourselves into. Arthur seemed more upset about it than me."

"Why?"

"Someone convinced him Astech was into something shady, and it could backfire on Arthur if he got in too close with them."

"Did he convince you of the same thing?"

"I'm not sure I needed that much convincing. Astech has been getting pretty heavy handed out in the belt – the way they deal with independents, their dealings with me and other vendors. The Astech rep on Mars seemed reasonable, not like the weasel they have running the place on Ceres. The trouble began when Astech named him manager there. I wasn't anxious to give him a say in my company."

"So tell them no deal," Ed said.

"Astech doesn't take rejection well. Arthur thought we needed something on Astech to get them to back off."

"And you thought you'd find it here?" Ed asked.

"Arthur thought so, or maybe this other guy convinced him. He told Arthur that Astech was also a client of InterCorporate, and if Faizah had any info on them, she may have stashed it here."

"That's what the scanner's for?" Faizah said.

"Yeah, that's right."

"Did Arthur give it to you?"

"This afternoon, at the Wahoo! He wouldn't tell me anything more about the man who gave it to him. This other man did tell Arthur that Ed keeps his doors unlocked and that if we really wanted to get to the bottom of Astech, we should look in Ed's place for a Q-disk."

"What's a Q-disk?" Ed asked.

"A Quantum disk," Faizah said. "Ultra-high density, very small, almost impossible to detect electronically," she raised the scanner, "until now."

"The scanner was set to register only for Q-disks. Arthur said he was told that's where the information was stored."

"Did this mystery man tell Arthur what kind of information I stored there, or why I would stash the disk in Ed's place?"

"I don't think Arthur knew what the information was. But he did say you were seen coming over here yesterday morning shortly before OSAR searched your room and everything else at Chubeck's."

That surprised Ed. "Someone was watching us?"

"I guess."

"Never mind that," Faizah said. "What were you to do with the disk if you found one?"

"I was just supposed to take it. I'm meeting with Arthur back at the Wahoo! for lunch to give him back the scanner – and the disk if I found it."

Ed picked up the scanner. "How did you know I wasn't going to be here?"

"I didn't know for sure until tonight. I was supposed to have dinner in the village here and wait for a call. It took longer than I thought, but around 2230 I got the call. It must have been the guy who talked to Arthur. I couldn't recognize the voice. But he told me I was in the clear."

"You know, Charlie, I should take this scanner and bean you in the head with it. Why did you ever think to go through with this?"

"It seemed a good idea at the time last night, and I didn't take into account the number of beers I had. By this afternoon, it just had its own momentum. Even here, when I found the door locked, I don't know why I didn't just leave instead of trying to jimmy the window. I'm no burglar."

"That's obvious," Ed said.

"So what happens now?"

"You just leave," Faizah said. "Oh, if that's all right with you, Ed. It is your house."

"I'm glad somebody recognizes that. Yeah, Charlie, just go."

"What do I tell Arthur?"

Faizah looked at Ed, then they both answered in unison. "The truth."

"Face it, Charlie, you're probably just as bad a liar as you are a burglar," Ed said.

"What does Arthur tell his mystery man?" Charlie asked.

"I don't believe the truth would do, there," Faizah said. "At least not all of it. Have him say you found the door locked, and when you tried to get in through the window, you tripped off an alarm. Leave everything else out."

"Arthur could probably pull that off." Charlie got up, slowly, wobbling a bit before steadying himself. "I think I can make it back, now. But if you need Arthur to give that story, I'll need the scanner back."

"When are you meeting Arthur?" Ed asked.

"1230."

"I'll leave the scanner in a package for you at the bar in the Wahoo!," Ed said. "You can get there early to pick it up. How does the scanner indicate it found a Q-disk?"

"Here, push this test button," Charlie said, reaching over Ed's hand. The scanner let out a soft double beep, and a set of numbers flashed on the readout followed by a "Q". "I'm told someone with experience can tell what he has just by the numbers. Set for a specific search like now, it lets out a double beep when it gets a hit."

"OK, Charlie, take off."

Faizah and Ed didn't say anything as they watched Charlie head down the road, wavering a little, but mostly recovered. As Charlie walked out of sight, Ed entered his living room and began moving the sensor across shelves and around furniture.

Faizah followed him in. "You don't really believe I stashed a Q-disk in your house, do you?"

"No, of course not. You were sitting at the table yesterday morning, right?"

"Yes, at this end, you twit."

"Eh, nothing here. I'll check the bedroom."

"In your dreams. You know I wasn't in there."

Ed began a slow, methodical search around the bed. "My dreams have nothing to do with it. You could have shut down the alarm system from my Uncle's place and come in here anytime you wanted while I was gone. For that matter, you knew I was going to be gone the night of the Serling Heights blowout."

"How convenient," Faizah called from the living room. Ed continued his search across the room, but found nothing. When he came out, Faizah was standing by the table, her arms crossed, her face stern.

"But no," Ed said, "I knew you were not in my bedroom."

Her face softened, and her arms unfolded like a knot unraveling from released tension. "Jessica?"

"It makes more sense than it being you. Who knows where you would have recorded anything: a desk unit, your notebook, portable chips and disks – your hip? You're a walking hard drive. Yet someone knew there was specific information on a specific type of disk. That suggests to me something being carried by a courier. You don't fit that description."

"But Jessica does."

"Very well. She seems to have known Averink, even though she told Lenowitz earlier that she didn't. She reacted rather badly to Lenowitz executing his search warrants yesterday. If she did stash it here, maybe she was afraid if they searched my uncle's place, they'd be just as likely to search mine."

"Frankly, I'm surprised they didn't."

"So's Lenowitz."

"What?"

"When he was here that morning, he was waiting for a search warrant for my place, too. He told me Keritan decided against it."

"So someone else could search it instead?"

"That's the way it looks to me."

"So OSAR's part of this conspiracy, too."

"Or someone in OSAR."

"And that someone has access to that scanner."

"And can convince Keritan to pull back a search warrant. But why not search the place himself?" Ed asked.

"To avoid getting seen or caught. This way, McKracken didn't even know what was on the disk he was looking for." Faizah paused, and slightly cocked an eyebrow. "You know what's on the disk, right?"

"Averink's research."

"It never sounded right to me that no one ever found any of his plans," Faizah said. "I thought his research assistants lied about not having any of it."

"Even if they had a copy, it didn't seem logical that Averink didn't have his plans with him, that he only brought along his prototype component."

"No, he must have had his plans," she said. "It's possible he kept them with his prototype, but I thought it was more likely – if he was the target – that a murderer on board the *New Brunswick* found them."

"Unless Averink gave them to Jessica ahead of time," Ed said.

"Which may explain why she's been so desperate to get to Ceres. She probably promised to deliver it to Minglong, never contemplating she'd need another ship to get there. Sorry, Ed. She used you."

"I've been used worse."

"Here, give me the scanner," Faizah said, adjusting the settings. "We need to make a thorough search of your place, and I know how to use this rod."

CHAPTER 17

Manny

Faizah went over the house thoroughly, and Ed kept watch on her to make sure she was straight with everything the scanner detected. But it turned out the scanner only found the electronics that were supposed to be there.

It was late when they started, and early by the time they finished. Ed decided against going to bed since he still had to meet Jessica at the spaceport that morning. He grabbed a shower instead and caught an early train into Tiu City. A steady rain was falling when he arrived, and robotic street cleaners were the only movement and sound on the deserted streets. Ed checked his watch, saw he'd have another 15 minutes to wait before the rain stopped, and he didn't want to wait. Running didn't seem to offer much advantage, but at least he wouldn't have to endure the downpour as long. So he ran in the long, loping strides that Mars gravity allowed, reaching the 4th Orbit offices quickly.

Ed had access to the office safe with a hand scan and combination. He took out the bag Jessica had left, then pulled out the scanner from a pant leg pocket. Ed checked the settings, then moved the rod around the bag, surprised when the readings turned up nothing.

Ed rechecked the setting, pressed the test button to be sure the double beep sounded if it detected a Q-disk, then scanned the bag again. Still nothing.

He hesitated, then opened the bag and ran the scanner among its contents. Nothing.

Even when Ed began searching his own place during the night, he was certain he would find the Q-disk in Jessica's bag. Why else had she left it in the office safe?

He closed the bag and put it back in the safe. Ed hadn't told Faizah about the bag, and he didn't think he would tell Jessica about McKracken. He wasn't sure if he should tell Lenowitz about either one. OSAR was compromised. Lenowitz himself seemed to suggest that. Yet someone also had to know Ed usually kept his door unlocked when he was on planet. Lenowitz found that out when he helped himself to Ed's beer the night of Chubeck's dinner. Also, the captain knew Jessica had spent the night at Ed's place. Did Keritan call off the search warrant that morning, or did Lenowitz just pocket it?

A collision of conspiracies, Lenowitz called it. It seemed to Ed they were all colliding in his head. Or maybe it was just the lack of sleep. He checked his watch and saw the rain had a couple of minutes yet to go. He went into the office restroom to straighten himself out and dry off his hair. The sky was beginning to show its pre-dawn hues, and a few people were on the streets by the time Ed left the office to catch the mag-lev for the spaceport.

ooooooooooo

"Ed? Ed?"

His name barely registered, but a tug on his shoulder brought him awake. He knew instantly he was in his pilot's chair, but it took him a second to realize he was still on Mars and not in space. Ed looked behind him.

"Jessica? Aahh, good morning. Is it 8 already?"

"Not quite. Were you here all night?"

"No, I got here early and must have dozed off."

"Hafiz figured you'd be late. You might have been if I hadn't looked in here for you."

"Is the module broker here?"

"Not yet, but he should be here shortly."

Ed had just enough sleep for his body to know how much more it needed. He went to the sink in the cabin to splash some water on his face and force himself into being fully awake. It didn't work. The broker had arrived and was standing on the dock with Jessica by the time Ed climbed out of the *Zach*.

"Good morning. Ed. I hope this isn't too early for you. Will your systems engineer be joining us?"

"Hi, Greg. Yeah, Manny's making the run with us. He should be here any minute with Laura."

"You mean I get to meet Laura's great husband?" Jessica said "I'm not sure I'm prepared for that this morning. He must be one hunk of a man to have a woman like Laura so guarded over him."

"You haven't met Manny?" Greg said. "I suppose Ed has warned you about keeping your hands off him. Laura's a great person, but she's very protective of Manny when other women are around."

"I'll try to resist."

"Resist what?" Came Laura's voice from behind them.

"Laura," Ed quickly broke in. "Glad you could come so early."

"We did have to rush it a bit to be here on time. It is a rather beastly hour, but if Manny had to be here, the least I could do was tag along. Oh, yes, Jessica, you haven't met my husband, have you?"

Standing next to Laura was Manny, his head not quite reaching her shoulder. He had curly, unkempt hair and thick glasses, and a baggy work shirt hung over a thin – slight? – OK, scrawny frame. The pockets of his olive green cargo pants bulged, and the pant legs flopped over his shoes.

"Jessica, it's so wonderful to meet you," he said, taking her hand in both of his. "The pictures on the news didn't do you justice. Of course, you had just been rescued from a ship that blew up under you. No one could be expected to look good under those conditions, but you pulled it off well. And, ah... and, then on the news again this week at the Serling Heights blow out, helping the wounded, all those people with blood streaming over their faces and onto those ghastly coveralls. Red is definitely not your color."

"I'm, um, pleased to meet you, Manny," Jessica said, hesitantly.

"Manfred," he corrected, still holding her hand. "It sounds more like a name adults would use. The other is something you get called on a playground for a pick-up basketball game. Though I'm actually very good at the Mars game. Height is very overrated here. My specialty is the low game. I get these giants to jump, and with their hang time I go under them, score a lay-up and stop at the bench to call in a reservation for the post-game dinner before the other guys ever make it back down."

"Come on, Manny, we have work to do," Laura said, stepping between them to link her right arm into his, and delicately disposing of Jessica's hand with her left.

Greg led them into the crew module, but Jessica stayed behind for a moment and whispered to Ed.

"That's Laura's husband?"

"Not the hunk you were expecting, eh?"

"No."

"Don't let first impressions fool you. Manny is a very capable man, and he does two things very well. He's an excellent systems engineer, perhaps the best on Mars."

"What's the other thing?"

"You'll have to ask Laura for that."

"Never mind."

They took an hour to inspect the crew and passenger modules. Manny meticulously checked readouts and programming, and pulled off panels to eyeball life support mechanicals. Jessica efficiently went through stocks of supplies, emergency gear and passenger amenities. She then began inspecting every cabin to be certain they were ready for her passengers.

Ed began the inspection with the rest, making sure the crew module was to his liking. But as Manny and Jessica began to do their jobs in detail, Ed dropped behind. He assured himself the module maintenance records were in order and certified, did his own eyeball inspection of the exterior to be sure it matched the records, then waited for the others to be done.

"That crew you have is pretty thorough," Greg said as he climbed down into the crew module. "It's going to take them a while."

"That's why I picked them. Listen, Greg, can you tell them I'll be in the *Zach* when they're done?"

"Sure, go ahead."

Ed could have used the time to take another nap, but instead used a tablet to call up a copy of the audit report on Averink's research and tried to read through more of it in detail. It still seemed very convincing, but if it was true, then the bombings didn't make sense, at least the one on the *New Brunswick*. Ed very much wanted to leave the case in the hands of OSAR, and hell, even with the FBI if they'd just leave him alone. But the trip to Ceres would put him back in harm's way, if he was ever out of it – unless this audit report was true and Averink had reached a dead end.

That Averink himself ended up dead suggested the report was a phony, but from what Ed knew about fusion drives, the report seemed accurate. Sam Weller was probably the only physicist on Mars who could tell if it wasn't, but now he was too frightened to talk.

The more Ed read, the more his mind was locked in its circular logic, until he was interrupted by Manny climbing into the *Zach*.

"Did everything check out all right?" Ed asked, putting the audit report on the galley table.

"Oh, sure, if you don't mind fluid flows that read as if they were going through my uncle Ralph's clogged arteries, and variable pressure valves that give you Niagara or nothing. I tell you, I think the attention to detail drops with the gravity."

"I trust that's not a problem with you."

"Me? Oh, no. My mind's as sharp as a laser. I exercise my brain as much as Laura exercises my body, that is, makes me exercise my body. She's not just my wife. She's my personal trainer. she really keeps me on my toes, let me tell you, unless of course she wants me on her...."

"Manny, I get it. Did you give Greg your exceptions list?"

"Yeah, I talked to him on the dock. He said he can have everything fixed by Monday. You just need to certify the order." Manny placed the tablet on the table for Ed to sign, and picked up the audit report. "What's this?"

"It's an assessment of Tim Averink's research project."

"That guy who was killed on the *New Brunswick*? Can I take a look?"

"Do you know anything about fusion drive research?"

"Are you kidding? It's a hobby of mine."

"Fusion research is a hobby of yours?"

"It's that exercise the mind thing." Manny quickly punched up new pages to skim through it. "Boy somebody sure wanted to cut off Averink's funding. Who did the report?"

"I don't know who did it, but it was done for a group of investors."

"Well, somebody in that group didn't want the rest to know what they had."

"What do you mean?"

"This report's a phony."

"You've been looking at it for less than a minute, and already you can tell it's a phony? It seemed to be pretty convincing to everybody else."

"It's a well done fraud. Even engineers who work on magnetic fusion reactor design could miss it if they didn't know what to look for."

"And you do?"

"The tack Averink takes, I saw that right off. It was put aside in the '2040s as too far fetched, but there's been an underground movement to take a second look at it."

"Movement?"

"Very esoteric, like a conspiracy theory for theoretical physicists. I think an early paper Averink posted on the InterPlanet resurrected it. That's how I found it."

"So what are you looking for?"

"Stuff like this." Manny used his finger to draw a couple of circles on the tablet's screen, then showed it to Ed. "These two numbers, the values this comes up with. They're impossible."

"Why?"

"Why? Have you got three years? Have you been reading up on this between orbits?"

"Make it simple."

"Make it simple, he says." Manny paced the cabin, his hands clenched behind his head, struggling for a way to make Ed understand. "OK, try this. You have two glasses, same size, one full of water, the other empty. You pour some of the water into the empty glass."

"I was always lousy at word problems."

"This is kindergarten physics, Crayola fusion. You pour some of the water into the empty glass. You could have one glass a quarter full, the other three-quarters full, or both glasses half full. But you can't end up with both glasses three-quarters full. You have to end up with the same amount of water you started with."

Ed read over the equations on the tablet. The numbers still didn't make sense, but he caught the drift of Manny's explanation. "So these numbers are two glasses three-quarters full?"

"In a more convoluted, technical fashion, yes."

"If you're faking this report, how could you make such a bonehead mistake?"

"Someone could know a lot about the physics and still miss this."

"Could someone at Interplanetary Drive Systems have done this?"

"Possibly. They're pretty set in their ways over there, but if someone researched the theory Averink was following, they could have come up with enough to fake the report. If they went into that much effort, though, I would have thought they understood the theory enough so these numbers would stand out. Perhaps a graduate student or research assistant could have done the report and missed this."

"You're sure this isn't just a typo?"

"No, the report's conclusion that Averink's drive doesn't work depends on these numbers. Without these results, the audit report doesn't exist."

CHAPTER 18

Crossed Wires

While Ed left early for the spaceport, Faizah caught about three hours sleep, her body aching to have at least one morning to wake up leisurely. But not this morning. Ed had seemed content to let Charlie McKracken break the news to Arthur Strand about Charlie's failed break-in, but that wouldn't do. Faizah wanted the news to come from her, and see if surprise would bring any hints, maybe even an admission out of Strand on who gave him the upgraded scanner and pushed him to have Ed's place searched.

She arrived in Tiu City's industrial district around 1000 hrs. The streets whined and crackled from the sounds of the Saturdim morning shift, working overtime to fill orders on shipments to asteroid mines approaching Mars in their orbits. Open doorways gave glimpses of sparks from auto-welders and robot assemblers. In one of the bays, Faizah saw a group of worried foremen and one technician huddled around a robot, while a pair of men threw apparently misassembled parts into a scrap bin.

Faizah dodged around a street transport hauling a couple of trailer loads of parts. But as she turned the corner for Ares Manufacturing, emergency vehicle lights brought her to a sudden stop.

Public safety transports and an ambulance were parked haphazardly by a wide doorway into the plant, and she could see more emergency lights flashing inside. But nobody was rushing. Workers were filtering in and out of the plant, one of the public safety officers was talking into his radio, and another one was talking with a Mars News reporter. More officers and plant workers gathered inside near an assembly line. The ambulance crew was outside standing by their vehicle with an empty gurney. They had the look of waiting for a medical examiner.

Faizah didn't want to approach, but she spotted a man walking back from the scene, probably from another plant. She stopped him as he was about to walk by.

"Excuse me, what happened down there?"

"Don't know for sure. Sounds like a robot fried itself, and took a man with it."

"Do you know who?"

"Yeah, it was old man Strand himself. They say he always does a walk-through of the plant around 0930. A foreman there, a friend of mine, said Strand was walking by the robot when it happened."

Faizah stepped around so her back was turned toward the news crew in case they turned in her direction. "Exactly how does a robot fry itself?"

"I wish I knew. I have the same model in my plant, and I'm shutting them all down until someone can tell me how this happened and can assure me it won't happen again."

"How did it kill Mr. Strand?"

"No one seems to know for sure, at least from what my friend can find out. The robot turned the wrong way and they think it hit Strand. Whether it was the blow or electrocution that killed him, no one is saying. Sparks started flying from the robot and it burned out. I'm sorry, did you know him?"

"A business acquaintance."

"With everything else that's been happening, at least this just looks like an accident."

"One would hope."

oooooooooo

Ed reached the Wahoo! shortly after 1100, but before the lunch crowd showed up. He had the scanner wrapped in a black plastic bag with Charlie's name on it, and was about to hand it over to the bartender when a hand on his arm stopped him.

"Hold up with that."

"Faizah?"

"We need to talk."

"OK, but we don't want to be here when Strand shows up."

"He's not coming. Pardon me, could you turn up the sound on the news?"

The bartender grunted as he touched a button on the bar, and the sound of Jeff's report on MNN came over the speaker.

"... was doing what his co-workers said was Strand's normal routine of walking through the plant when a robot assembler malfunctioned and somehow struck the factory owner just as he passed it, apparently killing Strand instantly. Witnesses said sparks and flames were seen shooting out from the robot immediately afterward. The maker of the Maxi-Assembler 720 ...."

"They had this on all morning," the bartender said, reducing the sound a notch or two. "At least since I came to work. Haven't you heard it yet?"

"I haven't," Ed said. "Can we go upstairs?"

"It's closed."

"Perfect," Faizah said. "We'll take a couple of waters with us."

"Suit yourself."

Ed and Faizah took a table near the center of the upstairs balcony, out of sight from the street.

"I don't suppose there's any chance it was an accident," Ed said as he sat down.

"Hardly. It doesn't sound like an accident I've ever heard of. And Strand may have been the one man who could identify who took the scanner from OSAR."

"Did he even know it was from OSAR?"

"Probably not. Strand may not have even known the person was an OSAR staffer."

"It's a small world, with not many people on it."

"True. Then again, maybe Strand met with yet another middleman."

"I wouldn't think so. Let too many people in on the conspiracy and word gets out. It looks like someone was trying to reduce the number of people who knew anything – at least by one."

"Maybe more," Faizah said, taking a sip of water.

"You mean us?"

"We still have the scanner. When someone at OSAR realizes it's missing, it shouldn't be hard to figure out who had the opportunity to take it. Whoever did take it will want to get it back before then."

"Which surprises me the murderer didn't wait until Strand had the scanner back."

"He, or she, wouldn't have known that we would give it back. Clearly somebody spotted us with Charlie last night. Charlie didn't know enough to give the conspiracy away. But whoever gave Strand the scanner couldn't risk Strand identifying him, to Charlie or us. So he took care of Strand first, and worried about getting the scanner back later."

"But not much later. Maybe we should have tried to talk to Strand this morning."

"Actually, Ed, I was on my way there. I was a half-hour too late."

"Did he know you were coming?"

"No. I wanted to surprise him. Your uncle told me this morning that Strand usually had some time after his daily walk-through of his plant, always at 0930. Apparently his routine was well known."

"But Strand couldn't have been so punctual that someone could set that robot to go berserk on a timer when he walked by. Someone must have been inside the plant."

Faizah shook her head. "No, the machine was visible from the street through an open bay door. Most likely someone just watched from the street and waited to set it off until Strand passed by. Apparently from the people who saw it – and the news report had this, too – sparks and flames started shooting from the robot after it hit Strand. That was probably a controller on a self destruct, burning out itself and the rest of the robot's electronics to cover the murderer's tracks."

"The guy must have slipped in during the night. Probably went there straight from Viking Glen. So what do we do with the scanner, just hold on to it until someone tries to take it back?"

"I don't know what we should do with ... No, wait. Let's give it back."

"To whom?"

"OSAR. It's theirs. In fact, call Capt. Lenowitz right now and tell him you have it and to come get it."

"And when he asks how I got it?"

"Tell him the truth. OSAR can't ignore someone stealing their own equipment. They'll have to figure out who did it."

"The truth, eh? It might work," Ed said. "That's what we were going to have Charlie do." Ed took out his com and called Lenowitz, his direct number. He answered quickly.

"Captain Lenowitz."

"Captain, this is Ed Ferald."

"Ed, what can I do for you this morning?"

"It's the other way around, this time. I have something of yours."

"Of mine?"

"Of OSAR's really. The scanner for electronic devices you used to search my uncle's place the other day."

"I do not believe any of our scanners are missing."

"Check again."

"How do you know it is one of ours?"

"Faizah recognized it as a new model, not in full production yet. She figured OSAR would be the only group on Mars to have one."

"The thing is, Ed, I happen to be at the OSAR investigations headquarters downtown, ah, how do you say, vacating my drawers?"

"Cleaning out your desk?"

"Yes, that is it. Any way, I am looking right now at the locked rack where we keep those scanners, and all four of them are there."

"Are you sure one of them's not an old model?"

Lenowitz was slow to answer. "I do not believe so. Where did you find this scanner?"

"On a guy trying to break into my place last night to search it."

"Really? Did you have a chance to ask him where he got the scanner?"

"Yeah. From Arthur Strand."

Lenowitz took a moment. His tone turned serious. "Where are you now?"

"At the Wahoo! We convinced the bartender to let us into the balcony before they opened it."

"Are you visible from the street?"

"No."

"Good. Stay there. I'll be there in 10 minutes."

"They're going to open the balcony for the lunch crowd soon."

"Don't worry about that. Just order lunch and wait there." Lenowitz switched off. A waitress came up a couple of minutes later to take their order, but the rest of the balcony tables remained empty. It seemed better to order lunch than just sit there, and besides, Ed was starving. Faizah only nibbled at a salad by the time Lenowitz joined them.

"Sit down, Captain," Ed said. "I'm surprised we still have the place to ourselves."

"No surprise. I called ahead and had them close the balcony to everyone but us. I still pull some weight on Mars. Where is this scanner?"

"Here," Ed said, pulling it out of the bag. "Charlie McKracken was trying to break into my place through the window when Faizah stopped him."

"Through the window? You're locking your doors now?"

"So Charlie found out," Faizah said. "He isn't a very good burglar."

"What was he looking for?"

"A Q-disk," Faizah said, "with some information on Astech's plans to get into shipbuilding." She shrugged her shoulders. "At least that's what Strand told Charlie. Somebody convinced Strand there was something shady about recent business proposals Astech made to him and Charlie, and that I had information on it stored on a Q-disk."

"Do you?"

"No. I have plenty of information on Astech. Maybe some people would find it shady, but nothing I'm trying to hide on a Q-disk."

"So what is on the disk?"

"We surmise the results of Averink's research."

"You surmise?"

"We didn't know anything about the disk until Charlie told us," Ed said. "At least I didn't know anything about it, and who would know on what kind of chip, disk or hard drive Faizah would store anything?"

"Well, then, if it wasn't Faizah, then who ...," Lenowitz stopped. "Of course, Jessica."

"Yeah."

"We suspect Averink gave her the disk for safe keeping and asked her to take it to Ceres," Faizah said.

"That clears up some points, but not everything," Lenowitz said. "You said Strand gave the scanner to Charlie. How did Strand get it?"

"He told Charlie someone else gave it to him, but he wouldn't say who," Ed said. "Faizah was going to ask him about it this morning, but she was too late. We're guessing it was someone from your staff."

Lenowitz reached into a pocket and pulled out another scanner.

"This is the scanner we checked out to search Chubeck's place. Why do you say it is the one you have?"

Faizah reached over and took the scanner from Lenowitz. She turned it on and checked the readings. "This isn't the scanner you used at Chubeck's."

"Why do you say that?"

"You recall how the scanner picked up memory chips in my hip?"

"It is hard to forget. The discovery made the young man holding the scanner very nervous."

Faizah stood up and moved the scanner across her hip. "Those chips are shielded, and this model isn't sensitive enough to detect them. Now this other one is the scanner we took from Charlie last night."

"How did you two catch Charlie so easily?"

"She caught him," Ed said. "I don't know how easy it was, but as Faizah said, he's not a very good burglar. He should have stuck to climbing Martian mountains."

"No, he should not. We had to send a rescue team last week to pull him off the escarpment of Olympus Mons. Someone in his party had taken a wrong turn and they were running short of air. Charlie takes too many chances. He believes in his own reputation too much."

"You know, we are talking matters of life and death here," an irritated Faizah said, "or do I have to whack you upside the head with one of these rods to keep your attention?"

"I am sorry, Faizah. I did not mean to digress," Lenowitz said. "Please go on."

"Thank you. This scanner, the one we took from our amateur mountaineer and novice burglar, is the latest model, and the only one sensitive enough to pick up these shielded chips or the Q-disk Charlie was seeking." As Faizah waved it across her hip, the rod beeped and its numbers flashed. Faizah sat back down. "It's not on the market yet, but I know they were rushing through an order for OSAR on Mars. In fact, I was surprised the order made it on time, but this model is the only one you could have used at Chubeck's."

Lenowitz took the newer scanner from Faizah and examined it, casually. "The company that makes these scanners did ship our order on time, though just barely. But it never arrived."

"Don't tell me," Faizah said.

"I'm afraid so. It was a late shipment on the *New Brunswick*. It was in the beta cargo module, the same one that held Averink's fusion drive component. If we used a new model of scanner to search your belongings, Faizah, it wasn't from OSAR inventory. Someone made a switch beforehand without my knowledge, then switched it back."

"You're not saying that man who searched me – no more than a kid, really – is somehow involved in this?"

"No. He only handled the scanner for a few minutes, and simply followed instructions when he did use it."

"Who gave him the instructions?" Ed asked.

"The lead technician with me that day, a Lt. David Carstol. He is expert with these scanners, and would have known if he was using a newer model. He must have known."

"Even so, how did he get it?" Ed asked. "Did someone lift it off the cargo module before the explosion?"

"Perhaps, unless someone brought another scanner from the Moon."

"Faizah said these things aren't even on the market, yet. The one for OSAR was a special order."

"Yes, and generally OSAR does not publicize its special orders in equipment. It defeats the purpose if the wrong people find out about an upgrade in our devices. But you knew about that order, Faizah, and how this device works."

"As I already told Ed, InterCorporate Resources field tested two of these scanners for the manufacturer. The company was trying to work out some bugs we found in time to fill your order. You can take it up with the manufacturer if you think they shouldn't have told us that. As for me, I'm experienced with the older model, and I tried out the new one a couple months back, but that's all."

"Wait, are we going back to Faizah as prime suspect?" Ed said. "This is getting old. Why would she smuggle in a high tech scanner so you could search her stuff with it?"

"Actually, I was thinking the same thing," Faizah said.

"On the contrary," Lenowitz said. "I am finally convinced you are not a suspect."

"OK then, I guess I'm lost," Ed said, "though it seems I've been that way for a while now."

"Do not be hard on yourself. In fact, it is something you said to me early on that is only now making sense to me and helping me see how some of the pieces fall into place."

"Something I said? What?"

"It was when we were talking about how Faizah could not be both suspect and intended victim in the *New Brunswick* bombing. But whereas I insisted she must be one or the other, you suggested she could be neither. You said the message she received that it would be dangerous if she took the *New Brunswick* to Mars may not have been a threat at all, but a warning. The question I could not answer until now was who would warn her."

"So who would?"

"Oh my god," Faizah let out softly. "Someone from InterCorporate?"

"Precisely." Lenowitz said. "Someone who did not want to risk you being harmed, Faizah, but was callous about other people's lives. And apparently, someone who is familiar with the new scanner."

"Do you have a name?" Ed asked.

"No. But perhaps, Faizah, you can come up with one?"

"Not so fast. These are people I've known and worked with for years. I don't want to be too quick to label one of them a murderer."

"But what I suggest has a ring of truth, yes?"

"I'm afraid it does. But it's not the company itself. I'm sure of that"

"No, I agree, just as it is not OSAR but members of the organization that are also involved."

"More than one?" Faizah asked.

"At least two. David, certainly. But he could not have stopped the search warrant on Ed's place. That required someone with more authority."

"Keritan?" Ed said. "The timing was certainly convenient to replace you as head of investigations."

"Keritan is on my list," Lenowitz admitted. "But it took the head of OSAR's Mars base to reassign him."

"The vice admiral? That's going pretty high up the food chain."

"Perhaps Keritan persuaded the admiral, or maybe someone else engineered things. And it only had to be someone in the legal department to stop the search warrant. I am afraid I have no answers. It will take some delicate digging on my part to find them. Perhaps your part, Faizah, will be just as delicate?"

"I'm afraid so. Several possibilities among the InterCorporate staff come to mind. We have enough contracts with space companies, particularly large contracts with companies like Astech. Most likely someone on staff saw an opportunity and took it, or was bought off."

"I don't see why Astech would want to blow up Averink's work," Ed said. "It seems to me they'd rather keep that project alive if it really worked. My money's on Interplanetary Drive Systems being at the bottom of all this."

"Remember what I told you, Ed," Lenowitz said, "a collision of conspiracies. It appears we will need a conspiracy of our own if we are to solve this, and reach Ceres alive. I will see what I can uncover in the ranks of OSAR. Faizah, perhaps you can determine who among your colleagues is most likely to have turned free lance."

"And still care enough for me to avoid my getting killed?" Faizah said. "That will be an interesting list."

"So what do I do in this conspiracy," Ed said, "just pilot the ship?"

"No," Faizah said. "You have a friend who works for Astech. And didn't you say they were interested in having you be a pilot for them? I don't see Astech's motivation in this either, but its name keeps popping up too often to ignore. Maybe you can use the company's interest in you to learn something."

"Also, my friend," Lenowitz said, "you may have the most delicate job of all. You must find out from Jessica if she indeed has a Q-disk with Averink's plans, and recover that disk before someone else does."

Ed reached over and picked up the new model scanner. "Then I guess I better take this with me," he said, sticking it in his pocket.

CHAPTER 19

Art Critic

"An art show? Tonight?" Ed asked. "Actually, I wanted ...."

"C'mon. It's the campus gallery, and it's only a couple of blocks away on Orson," Jessica said, going into her bedroom to grab a jacket. "Is that all right?" she called back. "You didn't mention doing anything special tonight. You're not one of those space pilots who hates art, are you?"

"No, uh, not at all," Ed said, switching on the scanner but leaving it in his pants pocket. "I've been to that gallery quite a bit." He started to walk "casually" beside the living room bookshelves. "In fact, most spacers I know come to love art. Some even try their hand at it. Maybe it's seeing all that beauty out there and knowing it's all so deadly."

"You're not an artist yourself, are you?"

"Me? No. I like art, though. I ship enough of it back on the Lunar run. But I really need ...."

"Damn, you're on edge tonight," Jessica said as she re-entered the living room. "Why are you pacing so?"

"Pacing? No, I ... it's just that I need to talk with you tonight."

"Can't it wait? We'll have all night to talk."

Focus, Ed thought. But he didn't want to ask her about the Q-disk out in the street, and Jessica was already dragging him out the door.

"C'mon. Besides, I promised my roommate I'd be there tonight," she said as they reached the street.

"This can't be a showing of any of Chen's work, is it?"

"No, but some of Amy's students are showing their past work."

"OK. But these things are always too crowded to see the art anyway. We'll take some wine and cheese, look at a few paintings and get out of there."

"It won't be that bad. Let's not rush through the show. The gallery's just ahead. It's a gorgeous building, isn't it? Still, with all the adobe designs, I'm starting to miss steel and glass skyscrapers, and aluminum sided homes."

"You're kidding, right? You've only been here a week."

"Don't get me wrong, Tiu City's beautiful, and Serling Heights will be again. But I didn't expect it to be so – alien. The Moon really is an Earth outpost, but here, everything's almost familiar, yet it's just enough off to keep me unsettled. Arches are too tall, steps are too steep, days are too long."

"You have to remember, you're the alien here unless you adjust."

"It's going to take some getting used to, but I have two years before the next window to become a Martian."

"First off, that's one year by the Martian calendar."

"See what I mean?"

There was a decent-sized crowd by the time they arrived at the broad veranda that was the gallery's entrance. The building was four stories tall, housing faculty and student studios as well as the gallery beneath its stepped roof.

"I've never seen a gallery with so many balconies before," Jessica said.

"Someone told me the balconies are meant to extend display and studio workspace into the open."

"That's another thing."

"What?"

"Martians never seem to say 'outside,'" Jessica said. "Whenever they leave a building, it's always to 'go into the open.'"

"You should know why after the other night. Look up. We're not outside. All that steel and glass you say you miss from Earth is all around us on Mars, to protect us from the outside. Being outside means something much different here, and that barrier above us is a constant reminder. That's what we don't get used to."

"That and the pink sky."

"No, the sky kinda grows on you. But we do say 'inside,' so let's go in." Now that they were there, Ed wanted to get in and get out as quick as they could.

Sculptures and multi-media works were displayed just beyond the entrance. An interior gallery held the paintings, each with vivid colors and sharp lines.

"These paintings are so bright," Jessica said. "I guess I'm used to art shows on Earth where the colors are more subdued, or at least the tones are varied. Here, the colors are so vibrant, so ...."

"Childlike?" came from a voice behind them.

"Amy!" Jessica said. "See, I told you we would make it."

Amy Chen, her left arm still in a cast, smiled broadly at Jessica. Slim, streaks of gray in her black hair, and wearing a long deep blue dress, she appeared to Ed to be in her late-20s/Martian. She extended a hand to him.

"Ed, it's so nice to talk with you finally under circumstances that are neither dire nor solemn," she said, "or is that how space pilots feel about art openings?"

"Not at all," Ed said. "Really."

"Why do you say this work is childlike?" Jessica asked.

"Please, don't get me wrong. Some of the craftsmanship here is remarkable. It's the color selection, mainly. When people go to a children's art show on Earth, they're always struck by how bright the colors are. Children aren't experienced enough to use subtlety in color. On the other hand, adults tend to forget the vibrancy of the primaries. When I was back on Earth, the work I saw that came back from Mars or The Moon had that same quality. The focus on bright colors and sharp-edged super realism struck me as amateurish, inexperienced at least. I'm sorry, I didn't mean to give an art lecture."

"That's why the university brought you here, to give art lectures," Ed said. "And apparently to bring subtlety to Martian art."

"I admit, I did see the advancement of subtlety here as my mission."

"Well, good luck," Ed said. "Now let's see what the students are ...."

"You did see it that way," Jessica said. "No more?"

"That idea lasted only until I opened my eyes in Earth orbit," Amy said. "Mind you, that took a while. This is my first trip off Earth, and I had my eyes shut from 10 minutes before launch until final engine burnout. Even then, I kept them closed until the vertigo from weightlessness made me open my eyes to look for, what do you call it, a barf bag. But when I did, I looked out the window and saw Earth, and from that moment, I understood. I was speechless – and my friends would tell you that's unique in my life – and when I did start to talk again, it was only to babble on about how beautiful it was. Everything else I've seen in space since, and even under the Martian domes, convinces me the artists here aren't lacking subtlety or are locked in a super-realistic technique. They're naturalists. It's just that the natural reality out here is undiffused by miles of atmosphere, weather or contaminants. The colors you see are all in high contrast, and the natural backdrops are all stark. It's no wonder there's no such thing as a Martian impressionist."

"I see," Ed said. "Maybe we should get some cheese over at ...."

"So you're converting to the Martian style now?" Jessica asked.

"Not quite. The images are still too noble. I'd still like to see more grit in the portrayals. But come see for yourself. I drew some quick sketches on the *New Brunswick* and in Serling Heights after the blow out. I was staying there that night. They're in my studio on the third floor."

"I thought your work wasn't going to be on display tonight," Ed said.

"It wasn't supposed to be, but a few of the other artists were showing sketches and works in progress in their studios, so the gallery decided to include the studio space as an informal part of the show. The curator insisted I include my sketches. I don't feel they're anywhere near ready, of course, but people want to see what the new artist on the planet has going for her, so I guess it's only fair. Oh, Megan!" She turned to greet a woman just coming into the gallery. "How nice of you to come. I'm sorry I only have these rough ...."

"If her sketches are nowhere near ready, maybe we shouldn't embarrass her by seeing them," Ed said as Amy walked off.

"Stop it," Jessica said. "This isn't that terrible to endure. Let's go up," dragging Ed into an elevator.

"You know, Amy is kind of full of herself, isn't she?" Ed said as they reached the third floor.

"You have to get used to her. Get her away from talking about art, and she's really quite down to Earth, uh, Mars? How do you say that here?"

"I'm not sure we have an equivalent phrase," Ed said. "You wouldn't come to Mars at all if you were the type of person who's really 'down to Earth.' You know, there's almost as many people up here as there were downstairs, and it looks like most of them are trying to cram into Amy's studio. Can't she give us a private showing later?"

"I've only seen a couple of these. I'm eager to see the rest. There's been quite a bit of chatter on campus about Amy's arrival, or so the students tell me," Jessica said. "She's a pretty big deal in the art department."

"So I've been told," Ed said as they edged to the first of Amy's sketches.

Though not a formal display, her sketches were clipped to the walls precisely straight and at exacting heights, unlike the casual hangings in the studio next door. Ed and Jessica found themselves viewing Amy's sketches in reverse chronological order, going against the flow of the crowd.

The first grouping was of the aftermath of the Serling Heights blowout. For Mars, it was an alien scene of chaos beneath the dome; of scattered debris and haggard faces, breaths of frost coming out of their mouths, fog and mist hanging in the air. Most of the sketches were black and white, but Amy had added color to some, soft colors that diffused images and strayed beyond sketch lines, colors of confusion and fear in what had been an ordered world. Blurs of speed and urgency of the rescue workers contrasted with the stillness of battered residents in shock.

"Maybe we do have our first Martian impressionist," Ed said.

The Serling Heights scenes drew a crowd around them. A smaller crowd stopped around scenes inside the *New Brunswick*, mostly of injured passengers and their shipmates trying to help. He recognized some of the faces. George, the chief steward, with a badly bruised chin and a nasty blow to the back of his head, as hands – presumably Jessica's – tried to bandage it. Other sketches portrayed Jessica's face, grim and dirty, and Faizah's, determined but her eyes shifting to the right, as if trying to see what threat would come next.

There was one sketch of Juarez, still in his spacesuit but helmet off, floating in a hatchway. He looked exhausted. Apparently it was soon after he came back from clearing the wreckage, but before the *Zach* had them underway again.

Ed heard Jessica catch her breath. He looked over and saw her looking at a sketch done before the explosion, more detailed than the rest.

"That's Averink, isn't it?" he asked.

"Yes. He looks very troubled, doesn't he?"

"Was he like that all the time?"

"No. Most of the time, he seemed angry."

"Even on the Moon?"

Jessica turned to stroll down to the next set of drawings. Ed followed at her side.

"I really didn't know him on the Moon," she said. "I saw him a few times, but that's all."

"But you did …"

"No," she said, putting her hand on his chest. "Not here. Later." Jessica gently slipped her arm into his and led him to the last of the sketches, showing the *New Brunswick* before its launch.

Ed casually glanced at the sketch, then stopped and took a closer look.

"You're the first one to examine this sketch so intently," Amy said, stepping up behind Ed. "Most people seem more interested in my disaster drawings."

Ed was bent over the sketch now, his face inches from the printout. "When did you do this?"

"The night before we launched. The shipping foreman was kind enough to let me watch the preparations in the loading docks, though he didn't let me get too close. It's an interesting scene, with the men working on the scaffolding against the ship, and the play of lights and shadow. But there's too much emphasis on the mechanical, and not enough …."

"What were they doing?"

"What? I don't know. Loading cargo, I guess."

"Shifting cargo, it looks like," Jessica said. "I remember George telling me he had to make room for late shipments."

Ed reached over and unclipped the sketch from the wall hangers.

"Excuse me," Amy aid, "but this work, as uninteresting as it is to anyone but yourself, is on display."

"Where can we talk?" Ed said.

"We're talking now."

"Privately."

"All right, then, the balcony. You know, Jessica, I'm afraid your pilot friend has spent too much time in space."

Ed led them to the balcony, then closed the door behind them. Ed wasn't sure he could trust Jessica, but he saw no way to exclude her. Besides, Ed thought, she may be useful – or let something slip.

There was no light on the balcony, but the light from inside gave enough spill so they could see as he laid the sketch out on a table.

"You said this was the night before launch. About what time, do you think?"

"Seven, maybe a little later."

"That sounds about right," Jessica said. "George was shifting crates around, and transferring some to a cargo module before they sent it into orbit ahead of us."

"So this part here, two men carrying a crate halfway in the passenger's module cargo hatch. Were they bringing it in or taking it out?"

"Taking it out, most definitely," Amy said. "Is that important?"

"It may be if anyone can identify the shipping label on the end here. I can identify the other three crates in the picture, but this one I can't make out. The logo looks like a star burst."

"It's not precise. I was in a foreman's office. They wouldn't let me go out on the dock itself."

"Jessica, do you know if that starburst could be part of the logo for Averink's research company, Polaris? "

"It could be. I've seen it, and it has a starburst. In fact, Tim mentioned something about changing it, on board he mentioned it."

"Tim Averink?" Amy said.

"Yeah," Ed said. "Why?"

"This is his crate."

"You know that for sure?"

"Mr. Averink showed up while they were moving it. He argued with the steward about taking it off the ship. I didn't hear all of it, but I know he went with them to another dock and watched as they loaded the crate into the cargo module to be sure it wasn't left behind. The module was sent into orbit about an hour later. He was still very angry about it days afterward."

"Have you shown this sketch to anybody?" Ed asked.

"Maybe a hundred or so by now, before you took it off the wall."

"I mean, did you show it to anyone from OSAR?"

"The investigators? No. Of what interest would this be to them?"

"Maybe none. In fact, don't show it to the OSAR's investigations office. But can you send a copy to Capt. Lenowitz aboard the Grissom?"

"The captain gave me his address when he was investigating the case," Jessica said. "I'll give it to you at the apartment."

"I can upload a copy to him, but would you care to tell me what this is all about?"

"No," Ed said. "It's better that way. Just don't put this sketch back on display."

"Keep it, if you want. I can always print out another copy. I need to return to the guests." Amy left and closed the balcony door behind her. Jessica, however, looked at Ed even more puzzled, and angry, than Amy.

"Do you want to tell me what this is all about? I mean, sure, this is Averink's prototype component. So what? We already know it was moved to cargo module Beta."

"Why move it? All four of these crates are the same size, interchangeable. Averink's prototype was already stored in the luggage hold. The drill crate with the bomb, this one here. – I've shipped the drills before so I know their crates – the drill crate was supposed to be stored next to Averink's. Instead, they both and end up on opposite ends of the ship, the bomb where it will destroy the tug, the prototype in the cargo module I couldn't bring back."

"Why would someone make the plan that complex?" Jessica asked. "The prototype is as good as destroyed anyway."

"Someone wanted to destroy it. Someone else wanted to steal it. A collision of conspiracies, that's what Lenowitz called it. I see now what he means. Look, let's get out of here."

There was even more of a crowd in the studio when they went back in, and some students were moving tables and boxes to make more room. Amy was directing them.

"Leaving so soon?" Amy asked as they walked past. "You're certain you don't want to take any of my other sketches before you leave?"

"No, the one's more than enough." Just then, the scanner in Ed's pocket beeped twice.

"Is that your com?" Jessica asked.

"No, it's not, uh, never mind," Ed said as he took a step back and around Amy, trying to figure out what the scanner had picked up.

"Did you change your mind?" Amy asked, stepping up behind him.

"No, no. I thought I dropped something, that's all."

"Does this something levitate? You don't seem to be looking for it on the floor."

"What? No. It's just that …. Look, Amy, I'm sorry. I know I'm acting strangely. I'll just leave."

The apology did nothing to soften Amy's stony countenance. "I should warn you, they're a little more sensitive downstairs about patrons just taking the artwork whenever they feel like."

"It was just your artwork I was interested in."

"I'm flattered – I think."

Ed and Jessica didn't say anything to each other until they reached the open and started walking back to her apartment. "What was with you tonight?" she asked. "First there was that sketch, and then when those beeps went off, you just about jumped out of your skin. What was that?"

"It's a scanner for electronic devices. I have it in my pocket."

"What kind of devices?"

"The kind that are very hard to find, that most scanners don't pick up."

"Why do you have it?"

"We took it from a guy who tried to break into my place last night."

"We?"

"Faizah caught him."

Her hand, which had been holding his arm loosened. "She was there last night?"

"Not at first."

"But later."

"Yeah. She found a guy trying to break-in through the window and zapped him with a stunner."

"What was he looking for?"

"A Q-disk. I think it has Averink's plans on it."

"Why did he think you had it?"

"Because you spent the night there."

Ed tried to read the emotion in her eyes in the dim light. There was no surprise. No anger. They seemed – calculating.

"I think we'd better go inside," Jessica said, and the two were silent until they entered her apartment. "You think I have this Q-disk?" she said as she closed the door behind her.

"You told Lenowitz at the memorial service you didn't know Averink, but the morning after the Serling Heights blow-out, you were pretty quick to rise to his defense. You knew he graduated with honors, and just tonight when you looked at the sketch of him, you knew enough to recall he always seemed angry."

"You get to know things about your passengers, particularly on long trips."

"I think you knew that before you ever left Luna. I don't know what your relationship was, but I think it was enough for Averink to give you a Q-disk with his plans on it – for safe keeping."

"And what was I supposed to do with this Q-disk?"

"Take it to Ceres, and give it to Minglong."

"So that's it. You think I slept with you just so I could catch a ride to Ceres?"

"No, of course not. You caught a ride to Ceres because we needed a steward. You needed a job and proved yourself more than capable on the *New Brunswick*. I think you spent the night with me because we just went through hell together, twice, and we both ... well, we just did. But you are holding something back – about you and Averink. I need to know what it is."

Jessica turned away from him and said nothing for a moment, staring out a window for long seconds. "He didn't trust you, you know."

"Averink didn't trust me? I never met him."

"Not you directly, but 4th Orbit. He said not to trust anyone from there. He suspected your company was just as bad as Interplanetary Drive or Astech, that you all wanted his new drive."

"You know, it was my uncle who was paying for his trip to Ceres."

"It doesn't surprise me. Tim would have taken the passage, but not give up any secrets for it. Maybe that's why he seemed so nervous about 4th Orbit, afraid of what he'd have to give up for that ticket off the Moon."

"How long did you know him?"

"I didn't know him at all, really. I thought I did. He was a childhood friend – and later, he was more. But that was before he left for the Moon. We both grew up in Milwaukee. I looked him up when I started on the Earth-Lunar run, but he didn't have much time for anything but his work. Are you going to search my apartment?"

"I have to. There may be too many lives at stake." Ed took the scanner out of his pocket. "Unless you want to tell me where it is."

"Go ahead and search," she said angrily. "I don't have this Q-disk you're looking for." Jessica slowly paced the living room, her arms crossed, only occasionally glancing at Ed as he walked across the apartment, carefully.

"If you don't have the disk, why were you so desperate to get to Ceres?"

"Remember, I was desperate for a job. My passengers were still going to Ceres, and I was supposed to be going with them. It's just that now, you're the pilot."

Ed came up behind her and touched her shoulder with his right hand. "It's more than that."

"Tim said not to trust anyone, and 4th Orbit was one of one of the companies he put special emphasis on. Who's to say he's not right?"

"You are. You trusted me in space when I got you and your passengers back to Mars. You've trusted me on the planet, and you'll have to trust me to get you safely to Ceres and back."

"You're not showing me an awful lot of trust."

"Damn it, Jessica, there's a very good chance the *New Brunswick* and Serling Heights bomber will be on board the *Zach*, so maybe I'm not taking anyone's word at face value right now. But you had better believe me that keeping us safe may mean finding out as much as I can about what has happened, all the details."

Jessica stepped away, and Ed entered her bedroom. But the scanner registered nothing unusual. Jessica remained quiet until he came back into the living room.

"Tim did give me something to give to Minglong on Ceres, to give him personally. A book. A philosophy book."

"Do you have it here?"

"No, though I'm surprised you didn't find it. I'm sure you searched my duffel I left at the 4th Orbit office."

"I thought you didn't trust 4th Orbit."

"I said Tim didn't trust 4th Orbit. I'm still on the fence. There were some things I didn't want OSAR investigators rifling through, and the book was one of them. Did you find it?"

"OK, I did run the scanner around your duffel. It picked up your passport, and a few other things, but nothing like that."

"No, a book."

"This scanner's pretty sensitive. Even if the reader was off or it was just an insert chip, this scanner would have picked it up."

"Ed, A book! Like, with real pages, you know?"

"One of those?"

"We still use them on Earth."

"Yeah, my parents had some back at our home in Ontario. I can't remember ever turning one... that is, opening one. I didn't notice it in your duffel, but I wasn't looking for that. It must be old."

"Very old, mid-20th century. It must mean something special. It was a gift for Minglong. They apparently became very good friends, though they never met. Maybe that's why I feel so strongly about keeping my promise to bring it to Ceres."

"Why did Tim want you to take it there?"

"He said it was for safekeeping. It didn't make sense to me at the time. But the way Tim was, I think he knew his life was in danger. He gave it to me the night before we left the Moon, and insisted I give it to Minglong personally. The book didn't have anything to do with his research. Looking at it now, I think it's a goodbye gift."

"Maybe."

"Are you going to take a look at it?"

"I have to, though I doubt I'll learn anything from it."

"You never know. It must be a pretty good book."

CHAPTER 20

Above the Horizon

The Grissom hung in Martian orbit, it's three oblong crew compartments and extended passageway booms rotating around the ship's axis to give the crew artificial gravity. For the work crews at Phobos, the Grissom looked like a spinning, gleaming white wildflower drifting slowly above a desolate expanse of red desert – or it would have if the spacers ever thought about wildflowers. Mostly it looked like the next ship to refuel.

The booms met at a hub that connected them to the rest of the ship. Above it sat the bulging disk that was the command center, holding control, navigation, communication, everything needed to direct the ship across the solar system. Two taxis for transferring crew and supplies between the Grissom and asteroid mining stations were docked on the axis between command center and the hub. Below the taxis was an interorbital rescue tug capable of traveling short distances in the asteroid belt, or across the Solar System if need be when attached to a fusion drive, if one was available. They rarely were.

The Grissom carried its own permanent fusion drive, overpowered so it could push the ship at speeds comparable with passenger runs. It also carried chemical rocket engines to provide high-thrust boosts if needed on rescue missions.

"You know, Captain," said the Grissom's executive officer Alena Nikitin, "it seems most new commanding officers spend much of their time looking out this window. From the bridge, this offers the best view of the ship. Mostly I think they are excited about the responsibility, and worried about bringing this ship back in one piece. With you, it seems to be something different."

Lenowitz turned so he could see his first officer floating up behind him. "And what makes me so different, commander?"

"You are afraid of what you are leaving behind on Mars."

"You did not discern that by noticing how I look out the window."

"No. I see enough and I hear enough. Your last minute transfer to command was odd, but having the commanding officer and the executive officer both be from the East, that is unprecedented. Americans rarely give up that much power."

"Unless?"

"Unless someone wanted you off Mars very badly."

"Unless the Americans wanted me off Mars very badly," Lenowitz said. "You are wrong, by the way."

"Sir?"

"It is not what I am leaving behind on Mars that concerns me. It is what and who is going along with us to Ceres that has me worried."

"You do not think whoever is behind the bombings will try to get the *Zach*?" Nikitin said

"Or us?"

"It could not happen. They have doubled security inspections on everything being sent to the ship."

"Let's not depend on someone else's security, commander. I want you to put together teams – no one new to the Grissom – and search every inch on board, including personal gear. I do not want anything suspicious, so much as a match to come on board."

"I'll see to it, sir, but ...."

"Yes?"

"When you said no one new to the ship, I assume you do not include the investigative team you had transferred aboard. They are the investigators you worked with on Mars and trust the most, Dah?"

"Not everyone. I've worked with the new lawyer they are sending, but I did not request her."

"No one trusts lawyers. But I was thinking of Lt. David Carstol. By his file, he is an expert in scanning – chemical, electronic, whatever. We could definitely use his help."

"I am sure you could. But no, do not include Carstol or any of them on your search teams. In fact, Carstol and the rest are due to arrive soon, correct?"

"Within the hour."

"Scan and search everything of theirs before it comes on board."

"The shuttle pilot will raise hell. He will have to wait an extra orbit to return."

"Give him my sympathies."

"Yes sir."

"Commander, were you able to download the radar track of the Umi Explorer?"

"Yes sir. You can see it on this console." Nikitin punched in a command, and the track of the salvage ship came on display. "It rendezvoused with the fusion drive from the *New Brunswick* as planned."

Perhaps the message from Ed was another dead-end, Lenowitz thought as he drifted over to the console and studied the track. "No deviations from its flight path?"

"Deviations? What kind deviations?"

"Such as meeting up with the cargo modules first."

"The drive and the cargo modules have drifted hundreds of kilometers apart. It would have taken too much time to rendezvous with both."

"What's this small blip? It must be too intermittent to record a track."

"I do not know, Captain. We did not have a radar lock on the Umi through its whole flight. It could be debris from the fusion drive trailing behind, or perhaps even something from the cargo modules. It seems more in line with them."

"Could it be a tug?"

"Nyet, the Umi tug is too big. It is debris."

"Perhaps."

Nikitin pushed off to leave, but grabbed a handhold to stop herself. Her body swung around to face the captain again. "Is there something you are not telling me?"

"Many things. But begin the search first. We will have time to talk before we break orbit."

ooooooooooo

Chubeck had just come from the pastures, and though he left his boots outside, the earthy smells of the herd hung about him. Faizah had become used to the smells, even welcoming the organic aroma that overcame the metallic air of native soil.

He came over to her desk as she scanned records and images made during the latest Mars-Earth window. "Any luck?"

Faizah shook her head. "I studied the security recording from Mars Customs, but none of the cameras caught a clear face of the suspect, nothing of value anyway."

"No chance of recognizing him?"

"No one would recognize him. He's an Invisible."

"An Invisible?"

"Someone with no record: no eye scans, no fingerprints, no DNA samples on file. Mostly they come from Africa, South America or Asia."

"But usually the ones with no records don't have enough money to get to Mars, either," Chubeck said. "How'd he get here?"

"There's an underground market for them as couriers who must leave no trace, no hint of a connection to who hired them," Faizah explained. "Brokers even groom them for years for these types of jobs so they come off as educated and sophisticated. They make good money – for one assignment only. For that assignment, they get their eyes scanned, their samples taken, but their history is all fiction, and there is no record to contradict it. And once the assignment is done, they're paid well enough to disappear again, for good. If the pay's high enough, they even buy retina transplants so they don't have to live in seclusion."

Chubeck took a closer look at the image of the suspected bomber, the face half turned away from the camera. "So how did Interpol identify this man as having a fake passport?"

"His history didn't hold up under scrutiny."

"It had to be pretty good to get off Earth."

"That would have been a good trick, but not impossible to hack into the right databases and pull off."

"But not good enough to last?"

"It wasn't supposed to be." Faizah switched the screen view to a rundown of the man's record. "His history suggests a connection to the Earth Firsters, but it blanks out when you go back a fews years, so it would send off alarm bells if someone looked closer. This man isn't the bomber."

"What makes you say that?"

"As I said, they're used as couriers, smugglers. Sometimes as bombers, but nothing this sophisticated. Remember, the bomb was planted outside. He'd have to be trained in a vacuum suit. I doubt if that's a specialty the brokers of the Invisibles keep on hand."

"So why did he come to Mars?"

"To throw investigators off the trail. To give the FBI an out. The bureau identified an untraceable terrorist, so it can blame whomever it damn well pleases. His record was supposed to set off alarm bells."

"So who would have known how to contact these brokers, or know how to hack into the system to give this man a history to last just long enough?"

"The history comes with the service. As for contacting the brokers, I could have done that." Faizah looked over her shoulder at Chubeck and gave him a smile. "Don't tell Lenowitz, because there aren't that many out here who could."

"And so could your friend?"

"He'd know how, but let's be clear. Alan wanted to be my friend," Faizah said with clear distaste. "He wanted to be more. He kept insisting that with him handling the Astech account, he and I should work more closely together. Neither I nor InterCorporate saw it that way. The company wanted to keep an official distance between the two accounts per your concerns. I just wanted to keep my distance from Alan. But that doesn't mean he's behind sending the Invisible here. If this was set up on Earth, or even the Moon, there are many others who could have done it."

Chubeck stepped over to a stuffed chair and let himself fall into it in the slow motion afforded by Martian gravity. "How long would it have taken to make the arrangements?"

"Not long. Just a couple of weeks, maybe a month before the Invisible bought his ticket to leave Earth."

"How much money would it take?"

"That's something Alan couldn't pull off, not by himself. The tickets would be bad enough, but the fee for this Invisible would have to be pretty big. He had to stay in character for quite a while. And he had to stay very quiet when he got back."

"There's one way to assure that."

"Invisibles usually survive their assignments. It's bad business for the brokers if they don't. And it's not necessary. This guy doesn't have much to fear. He just took a trip to Mars and enjoyed himself. He doesn't have a clue to who paid his way, or why."

"Are you certain that's all he did? You're probably right, they don't keep trained vacuum suit workers on standby, but Netjackers are another story. I would think Invisibles would be perfect for that job."

Faizah turned back to her screen. "There is that," she said slowly. "This guy may have planted the freeze-out program, but he may not have even known what he was planting. He still would have to be pretty good to get in undetected, and I'm sure he couldn't have slipped into Serling Heights environmentals on his own."

"But Alan would have known how to do it, and maybe instruct this courier how to plant it."

Faizah stood up and walked to the window, looking out over the orchard, picking her words carefully. "The freeze-out, maybe. As Lenowitz would say, he has the capability. I doubt if Alan would have met with this man personally, but he could have arranged something. But the InterPlanet is just enough different from Earth's Internet that someone experienced would have been much better at it."

"You're sure Alan couldn't have hacked in himself from the Moon?"

"I couldn't, and I don't think he's any better than me. You just can't get around the time delays for inputs to reach Mars. Secure systems on Mars sense the delays in responses and shut the connection right down." Faizah paused. "Someone had to do it from here."

"Even so, Alan could have arranged, even wrote the script for someone else to enter."

"He had the opportunity, but I don't have a clue for a motive. Astech doesn't profit from all this. Ed's suspicions are probably right, that it was Juarez who planted the bombs, but I don't know his motive either."

"Are you suggesting this Alan and Juarez were working together?"

"Now we're venturing even more into the unknown. Juarez freelances for mining companies, several of them by his record, possibly including Astech. More than that, I can't say."

Chubeck slammed a fist on a small table, startling Faizah as he stood up and began to pace the floor, exhibiting a doubt that she never saw or heard in him before. "Damn it! There are too many unknowns, the risks too great. I'm canceling the Ceres flight."

"You can't. We'll never get to the bottom of this if we don't go to Ceres. No one will. And whatever is behind all this is already in play. I don't think the *Zach*'s a target. We can handle the risks."

"Really? Faizah, you, my nephew, and about 20 other people are heading off into space in two days with a suspected bomber on board, and this co-worker of yours is on the loose who apparently can manipulate computers to rather dangerous ends. They may be working together, or they may even be working at cross purposes. Someone, quite possibly from OSAR, convinced McKracken to break into Ed's house to look for a Q-disk which may have had Averink's plans on it, but the disk and plans are still missing, and poor Strand was probably killed over it. I don't know what it would take to make the risks any worse."

"I do," Faizah said softly.

Chubeck stopped pacing. "What?"

"I checked with the home office on Alan's whereabouts. He's traveling aboard the ship you just bought, the Halifax. He'll arrive at Ceres just about the time the *Zach* gets there."

ooooooooooo

People were just starting to arrive for the Sundim morning Mass at St. Joe's. Ed watched the people as they came in, recognized a few of them, but didn't spot who he was looking for.

"Ed," came a voice from behind him. "I don't see you here often enough. Or with all that's happened, are you looking for some extra assurance before your next flight?"

"An extra prayer for the *Zach* and all she carries wouldn't hurt, Fr. John," Ed said. "You're right, I don't get here often enough. But I'm looking for someone this morning."

"That's why most people come here."

"The person I'm looking for is on this plane of existence – George, the chief steward from the *New Brunswick*. I'm told when they released him from the hospital, he came here to recuperate."

"Yes, a very troubled young man. His physical wounds are bad enough, but the psychological blow of the tragedy has taken its toll. It'll take time before someone can talk to him about it and help him deal with it."

"I'm afraid that time is up. Where is he?"

Fr. John was taken aback by Ed's attitude. "I'm not sure I should tell you. He feels terrible guilt over the loss of life aboard the *New*

Brunswick. If you're going to talk to him about it, you could do more harm."

"Father, George may have reason to feel guilty. You may want to talk to him after I'm done, but I need to see him to make sure no one else loses his life, including me."

"Ed, he is seeking sanctuary from all that's happened."

"I'm seeking protection from what still could happen. What he knows could help me."

The priest turned away. "My mission is to help him. But I can't put you in harm's way if I can help it. George is in the flower garden on the other side of the church." Fr. John turned back to face Ed. "But I'll come with you."

"Suit yourself. Let's go."

The two walked to the other side and found George among the blooming plants and shrubs.

Ed felt himself immersed in the fragrances of rose, honeysuckle and lilac, peaceful scents that for once couldn't reduce his tension. George saw them coming, but made no move to meet them, waiting instead on a narrow red gravel path, turning his attention back to the flowers.

"George, Ed Ferald here would like to talk with you."

"I don't think I'd like to talk with him," George said as he bent over to sniff a lilac.

"I think you'd better," Ed said, and unrolled Chen's sketch of the Lunar loading dock.

George looked at the sketch, and slowly straightened up.

Fr. John touched Ed's arm. "Ed, I'm sorry, but if he doesn't ...."

"No, Father, it's all right," George said. "Don't you see? He's figured it out."

"Figured out what?" the priest asked.

"That George, here, was the one who placed the bomb aboard the *New Brunswick*," Ed said.

"Ed, you're going too far. I can't ...."

"I didn't know it was a bomb, Father." George said softly. "You have to believe me."

"Fr. John doesn't have to believe you," Ed said sternly. "He only has to offer counsel and forgiveness. You had better concentrate on convincing me. If you didn't know it was a bomb, why did you switch the crates around?"

"Because someone paid me to do it."

"Someone?"

"I don't know who he was. I only met him once, in a back hallway near the loading docks." George hesitated. "He stayed in the shadows. It's a little hazy."

"But you remember more than what you told OSAR investigators."

"Yeah. He approached me the night before launch. We had some late crates to load. Did Amy Chen do this? She was doing a lot of sketches on board."

"Let's get back to this guy who approached you," Ed said.

"He wanted me to keep these two crates from Astech together," George said, pointing out the crates in the drawing, "and to put them in the luggage hold."

"And you just did it for him?"

"No. He offered me money, a lot of money. I was badly in debt and he knew it. He offered to bail me out of trouble if I did what he asked, no questions."

"Didn't that make you suspicious?" Fr. John asked.

"Yeah, but I was really in debt and there didn't seem to be any way out of it until this guy came along. I just figured it was drugs, and they had some scam to get it on Mars, but only if it was in the luggage hold. Maybe they paid off the baggage handler here like he was paying me off. I didn't know it had anything to do with a bomb."

"Did he tell you which crate to move out?"

"He didn't have to. There was only one of that size in there. But he was insistent that crate go up to the cargo module. That poor kid, Averink, caught me and one of the crew moving his crate and gave me all sorts of hell for it. He thought I was going to leave it behind. He had to watch me as I loaded it onto the Beta cargo module. I think he kept watch on it until the robot launcher took it into orbit."

"Did the mystery man tell you to put the fourth crate, the one for the drill, into the tug?"

"You mean the crate with the bomb? There was no other place for it. The pilot gave me hell for putting it in there without telling him first. But it was too late to move it."

"Why didn't you tell any of this to OSAR investigators?"

"I was so far out of it, even when I reached Mars, that I couldn't tell how much was real. At first I remembered only bits and pieces. I still wake up thinking it's only a dream. I didn't even realize moving the crates around had anything to do with the bomb until Captain Lenowitz grilled me about the drill crate. ... No wait, that's not true."

"What?" Ed demanded, but George hesitated.

"I – I'm sorry, I'm getting very tired."

"Maybe I should take you back to your room," Fr. John said.

"Wait, Father, please," Ed said. "George, what were you going to say?"

"It's just a flash of a memory. It was just seconds after the explosion. I was near the bottom of the passenger module, and the blast had thrown me against the bulkhead and the walls. I was trying to find something when I saw Averink in his cabin."

"He was alive?"

"Yeah, I guess so. He had this shocked look on his face, maybe anger. He just said, 'You did this.'"

"Anything else?"

"No. Something hit me and I blacked out. When I woke up, Jessica had me strapped in a bunk, and I drifted off again. It was pretty much like that for days."

"You don't know what happened to Averink?"

"Only when someone told me he died. Must have been the same thing that hit me."

Ed turned away from George and the priest. "Or the same man," he muttered to himself.

CHAPTER 21

A Long Trip on a Short Fuse

"**P**hobos, *Cydonia Zach*," Laura transmitted. "Ready for fusion ignition."

"Roger, *Zach*," came the reply. "Have a good flight – and a safe one."

"Don't worry your soft little head about us, sweets. We'll be back at your rock before you know it. *Zach* out." The drive kicked in, and Laura and Ed sank slowly into their seats. As gravity took hold, a drawn out clatter of cascading objects hitting the deck sounded behind them from the crew compartment.

"Sorry," Manny called out.

"I'm not sure I want to see what all that was," Ed said to Laura.

"Don't worry. If there's something broke, he can fix it. And he usually doesn't break the vital stuff."

"That's reassuring, I think," Ed said as he unstrapped himself. "I'm going to see how our passengers are faring since we left Mars."

In the crew compartment, Manny was on his hands and knees, picking up meters, tools and other gadgets scattered across the floor.

"I-I-I left my tool box on the shelf, and the strap just gave way. Must be defective Velcro."

"I'm sure it was, Manny," Ed said, gingerly stepping around the fallen debris. He reached the ladder and climbed up through the crew module and into the baggage hold of the passenger module. Ed couldn't help but take yet one more look around the crates, duffels and boxes stuffed into the hold. Everything in the hold, all the carry on luggage in the passenger cabins, everything shipped in the cargo module including the two crates from Astech, had been searched. Ed used his captain's prerogative to oversee those searches and read the scanning reports. Nothing got through that wasn't legit.

But as sure as he was of that, Ed still took one more look around, then continued on toward the passenger decks.

There was a small elevator the rest of the way, but Ed took the steep stairway, so he cold walk through all five decks. Some of the passengers were heading for the observation deck on top. Others seemed to be content with staying in their rooms as their stomachs settled down.

"Making sure everything is ship-shape?" Faizah asked when she spotted him on the third deck.

"That's what a ship's captain is supposed to do."

"And how do you find your ship?"

"The ship is running true. The passengers seem to be holding their own."

"That shouldn't be too surprising. They appear to be an experienced lot."

"Experienced at what is the problem."

"True. But I think we're safe for now. Your ship's steward, however, seems a tad frosty."

"I think she's still a little burned about my wanting to search her apartment Saturdim night."

"I still don't buy her story. Do you really think the philosophy book was all Averink gave to her?"

"She had no reason to lie at that point."

"She didn't have enough of a reason to lie before. Did you learn anything from that book?"

"Only to be more accepting of people."

"You picked a helluva bad time to learn that lesson."

"Oh, excuse me," Charlie McKracken said as he stepped out of his cabin.

"Case in point," murmured Faizah.

"What's that?"

"Nothing, Charlie," Ed said. "You survived the launch in fine shape, eh?"

"Yes, quite well. Frankly, I'm glad to be off Mars," Charlie said. "I'm kinda surprised you let me ship out with you."

"I couldn't leave you stranded without calling in the cops," Ed said. "I still have my reasons not to do that. But if you give me any more reason on the flip side, the cops are only an hour behind."

"Oh, I wouldn't bother them," Faizah said. "Ed, here, has a stunner on board, and I can always use the practice."

"I think I'll head up to the observation deck."

Faizah gave him a wink. "'Bye, Charlie." As Charlie meekly climbed out of earshot, she turned to Ed. "You do have a stunner on board, right?"

"Oh, yeah," Ed said. "I wonder if it's charged, though?"

"Maybe when you head back down you can make sure. Listen, I need to fill you in on some things, but we can't talk here."

"Call me in 20 minutes, and I'll let you into the crew module."

"Fine. I'll just wait in my room and you can continue your captain's walk."

When Ed reached the observation deck, there were seven passengers there, including Charlie and Juarez. Jessica was there as well, making sure the food and beverage machines were working and the passengers were all settled in.

"Are all our passengers faring well, Jessica?" he asked her.

"There's one on deck four who isn't so hot. He's the geologist who's replacing the woman who died on the *New Brunswick*."

"Apparently his stomach isn't as anxious to reach the Belt as the rest of him."

"I don't think any part of him is anxious to be out here. I overheard him telling another Astech staffer he would have preferred to stay on Mars, but the company didn't give him much choice in the transfer."

"Listen, Jessica, I need ...."

"I have to keep making my rounds," she interrupted. "Is there anything you need right now?"

"No," Ed said. "No, go ahead."

Jessica turned and quickly went down the stairway. As she did, Juarez stepped up to the beverage dispenser nearby.

"Wow, I guess she doesn't have much time for you today," he said.

"Excuse me?"

"I'm sorry. I just meant she must be pretty busy as the only steward aboard."

"Yeah, she must be." Ed turned to leave when Juarez stopped him.

"You know, I didn't get a chance to buy you that drink I promised. Maybe later today?"

"Give me a couple of days," Ed said. "I'm still adjusting to the switch to Universal Time and going back to only 24 hours a day. I'll look you up."

"OK, but don't forget."

Ed wished he could. But he had to keep an eye on Juarez.

He stopped to talk to a couple of other passengers he knew as he walked back down. Ed passed Jessica, but they didn't speak as she carried some more medication into the geologist's room.

When he reached the bottom of the passenger module, Faizah was already there.

"I was just getting ready to call you," she said. "You want to unlock this hatch?"

"Sure, let me get to it."

"Any surprises up there?"

"Juarez still wants to buy me a drink," Ed said as he opened the hatch. "Go ahead, I'll close it after us."

"Are you going to take him up on it?"

"In a couple of days. We've got time." Ed closed the hatch and dropped down to the deck. "Here's good. Laura and Manny are down in the tug."

Faizah slid into a bench on one side of the mess table. Ed took the other side.

"You know, Ed, Juarez may be trying to find out how much you know."

"That's only fair. That's what I'm trying to do with him."

"Except if we're right, he kills people who know too much."

"The trick is finding out all of it before he can act."

Faizah poured a cup of water from a table-side spigot. "Well, he won't do anything before we reach Ceres."

"Being on a ship didn't stop him before."

"But we have, as you say in your native land, the cavalry ready to ride to our rescue an hour behind us."

"Actually, in my native land, we say mounties."

"What do you say on Mars?"

"We're on our own."

"That's comforting," Faizah said. "Tell me something. You believe Jessica when she said she never had the Q-disk?"

"As Lenowitz told me, she's a bad liar."

"Ed, our lives may be at stake if she's a better liar than you think. Her life may be at stake."

"I don't think so. It may be more important to find out why Averink was so insistent that Jessica give Minglong that book."

"Didn't Jessica say she thought the book was just a gift?"

"As I said, Jessica's a bad liar."

"Right, then. But you didn't find anything unusual about the book?"

"It's a very unusual book, 'Zen and the Art of Motorcycle Maintenance,' written in the second half of the 20th Century. But I don't see the connection with Averink. He never struck me as a Zen master."

"He grew up in Milwaukee where they still make Harleys," Faizah said. "They're far different now than they were back then. I know. In South Africa, a bikers club once or twice a year put aside their current bikes for a few vintage models. Smelly, noisy beasts, but I imagine people in Milwaukee still have a soft spot in their hearts for those bikes. Maybe something in the book got through to Averink. I heard of the book; it was a piece of pop-culture philosophy. I'm not sure I see the connection with Minglong, though. A Zen Franciscan?"

"No, that fits," Ed said. "Minglong picks and chooses from a variety of religions and philosophies for his own beliefs. Calling him a monk is more an honorary title, and he respects the traditions of the order. The monastery doesn't care because he brings in so much business through his fusion work, from small generators to drive units. Even IDS farms out specialty work to him."

"Unless Minglong and Averink were going to write a new version, 'Zen and the Art of Fusion Technology,' I still don't see that the book gets us anywhere."

"Neither do I, yet. When I went back to the office to look at it, I scanned it again just to be sure a disk wasn't embedded in the cover or something. But no. There was an inscription on the inside cover. 'Buddha is in the helium.' I don't know what that means."

"You didn't press the issue with Jessica?"

"She wasn't ready to tell me, so no. We have three weeks for her to defrost." He paused, unsure if he should go on. "There is ...."

"What?"

"How common are Q-disks?"

"They're fairly new, but they're the rage in security circles," Faizah said. "They're not only hard to detect, they're even harder to decode."

"Are they too new to be on Mars, except for the one we're looking for?"

"I don't know. They went on the market about a year – about 12 months ago, so they could have only reached the planet this window. We arrived at the end of the window, so yes, there could be other disks on the planet. Why?"

"Maybe nothing. The scanner went off in my pocket while I was in a crowd in the art gallery. It registered as a Q-disk, but I couldn't tell from where."

"There's not much reason for an artist to have one."

"Yeah, but an art show draws all sorts of people. It was probably an accountant with his company records taking work home for the weekend. So what did you want to tell me?"

"Have you taken a look at the passenger list for that new ship 4th Orbit bought?"

"The Halifax? No, why?"

Faizah switched on her tablet and slid it across the table to Ed. "There are some interesting names on it, many from Astech."

"That's not surprising. It makes two other stops in the Belt before it reaches Ceres, so there are a lot of crew transfers going on."

"One name will surprise you."

Ed took the tablet and scanned down the list. "Paul Cherault?"

"That's your friend, right – the one who shipped those two crates for Astech?"

"Yeah, but that doesn't mean he had anything to do with any plot. Someone could have just told him to do it."

"But it's curious he's coming to Ceres, and you didn't know about it."

"It says here he's booked all the way to Mars. Maybe he just wanted to surprise me. Friends do that, you know."

"Pardon me if I'm a little suspicious of convenient surprises lately," Faizah said. "Particularly since it turns out you're not the only one being surprised by a 'friend.'" She reached over and pointed to another name.

"Alan Thiegold?" Ed said. "That's the guy you said works on the Astech contract for InterCorporate."

"I don't know what role your friend played, but Alan is in it deep, I'm sure of it," Faizah said.

"Why do you say that?"

"You know that fake tourist to Mars, the one the FBI said planted the bomb? He's what security people call an 'Invisible,' someone with no record, no trace of a history. Someone who can easily disappear again."

"Sounds like a perfect candidate for a bomber."

"Except these people come from very poor countries. That's why they remain invisible. I can't imagine any of them ever trained to work in a vacuum suit on Mars."

"What does that have to do with Alan?"

"He'd know how to buy one, who to contact to make the arrangement. He'd know how to get the money, and this job had to be very expensive."

"And this invisible man's job was just to throw everybody off the track, have the FBI and Interpol looking for this fake tourist while the real bomber is on Mars?"

"It has to be," Faizah said.

"Even if Alan did know how, do you have anything to suggest he actually did arrange for this 'invisible' to fly to Mars?"

"Alan was back on Earth about two months before the window, for only about two weeks. He could have made the arrangements then."

"He could have been taking a vacation."

Faizah sat back in exasperation. "Yes, it's thin. But I'm told his reports back to InterCorporate have been erratic lately. He risked getting in hot water over it, but Astech staffers covered for him, so our Earth office dismissed it. And the staffer who seemed to cover for him most was Paul Cherault."

"Now that's really reaching," Ed said, angrily. "Paul wouldn't be involved in any bombing, even if this Alan guy is. And you haven't convinced me of that, either."

"But remember that warning I received about traveling on the *New Brunswick*. There are a number of people I know devious enough to try to pull this off. But not only did Alan have the best chance of succeeding, he was the only one who would care enough about me to be sure I wasn't on board."

"Oh?" said Ed, surprised. "Did you two have a thing?"

"He had a thing for me. Believe me, it wasn't mutual."

"Even so, Faizah, it's just as likely someone didn't want you on board because you might have gotten in the way, even stop Averink from being killed."

"You may be right, but Alan would have been the one who best knew I could have interfered with the plot. In my mind, it all still points to Alan."

"And to Paul?"

Faizah turned a shade sympathetic. "I don't know. But Paul seems to be working very closely to Alan these days."

"Why is Alan going to Ceres, anyway?"

"He's making a tour of Astech operations now as part of his contract. He, too, is booked all the way to Mars."

"There are plenty of Astech staffers on the Halifax – and the *Zach*, but that's normal for a Ceres run."

"Nobody on the *Zach* from Interplanetary Drive Systems?" Faizah asked.

"Actually, we do have a couple people from IDS aboard the *Zach*. They're going to recertify repair facilities."

"Great," she said. "All we need is a rep from the Mother Earth Defense Alliance, and someone from Decker's campaign, and we'll all be on that rock together."

As she spoke, the hatch above her opened, and Jessica stepped down into the crew compartment.

"Faizah," she said as she stepped onto the deck, "have you joined the crew now?"

"Ed and I needed to discuss some things in private. I'll be leaving now." But as she moved to stand up, Ed took her arm and stopped her.

"No, wait." he said. "Jessica, join us."

"I don't .... Why?"

"We still need to clear up some things about Averink."

"I already told you Tim didn't trust 4th Orbit."

"But he was willing to take its money," Faizah said, "even to the extent of paying his way off the Moon."

"That worked out well, didn't it?"

"OK," Ed interjected. "Averink was afraid 4th Orbit was just trying to expand its operations. He was right. I'm sure that's what my uncle had in mind. He's very American that way. But people who get caught up in 4th Orbit's expansions tend to do very well for themselves. My uncle doesn't kill people. Who else was Averink afraid of?"

Jessica didn't sit down, pacing slowly across the deck instead. "IDS, definitely. I don't know much. But one night a few months ago I was in Averink's apartment. Tim seemed very frustrated. He probably had too many beers, but he was complaining how IDS was ready to throw him all the money he wanted when the company thought he was working on an improvement to their design. But when IDS realized Tim's research would make the company's fusion drives obsolete, it was doing everything it could to stop him."

"Tim didn't give you any details on his research?" Faizah asked

"I wouldn't have understood it if he had. That night at Weller's restaurant was the first time I heard an explanation of what Tim's drive was supposed to be capable of."

"What about Astech?" Ed asked. "The other night you put them on the list of companies Averink didn't trust. Why?"

"Just that someone at Astech wanted to buy Tim out."

"Someone?" Faizah asked. "Not the company itself?"

"I'm not sure about that. Tim said it seemed very unofficial. The offer was firm, but the ties to Astech were unclear. That's what made Tim nervous. It was like someone was trying to break off from Astech and go off on his own, yet the money was coming from somewhere. Tim's research assistants were angry Tim didn't take the offer so the project could be completed. But Tim didn't want anything to do with it."

"When did that happen?" Faizah said.

"A few months back."

"Before the Earth-Mars window opened up?"

"Yeah, maybe two or three months before then."

"The timing's right," Ed said.

"For what?" Jessica asked.

"For a lot of these pieces to fall into place," Faizah said. "But not all of them. For instance, we still don't know what happened to the Q-disk that we suspect holds Averink's research."

"You mean the disk Ed was looking for?"

"I mean the one you said you didn't have."

"Ed believed me," Jessica said. "That isn't enough for you?"

"It will have to be," Ed said, firmly.

"I bow to your judgment," Faizah said.

"If you have no more suspicions, I'm on a short break, and I need to get some stuff out of my room. So if you'll excuse me."

"I should be heading back up myself," Faizah said. She stood up, a little too quickly, but grabbed a handrail and guided herself the rest of the way through the hatch. Jessica turned to enter her room, sliding the door shut behind her.

"This is going to be a long trip," Ed said to no one as the hatch above him locked in place.

Chapter 22

Don't Ask, Don't Die

Nearing the halfway point in the trip, passengers frequented the observation deck less often except for card games or group viewing of vids. It turned out Manny had an extensive selection of 20th century movies, and this evening a small group had turned out for "The Maltese Falcon." Ed had to admit, it was much better than the 100th anniversary remake – and made the mistake of admitting it to Manny.

Most of the deck had cleared by the time Manny was done explaining the finer points of the original. He finished only because it was time to take his shift in the pilot's chair.

On the opposite side of the deck from Ed, the geologist – by now well past his space sickness – and a female engineering tech, her anxiety growing at the approaching unknown, looked out at the stars. Both were nervously heading for their first long-term assignment in the Belt and cautiously seeking each other out for some comfort against the long, strange months ahead on Ceres.

The smell of popcorn still hung in the air, and the crumbs littered the floor. The auto-cleaners would take care of that in a couple of hours. Ed sipped a lemon-water to remove the last of the salt and butter from his taste as he looked out his side of the ship. Mars was only a brilliant red dot in the star field, barely in view toward the stern.

"Ed, you should try your ship's bloody Mary's," Juarez said too loudly, startling Ed as he came up from behind the pilot. "It's not like the ones they make at the Wahoo!, but it's pretty good."

"Juarez. I thought you left. Sorry, I have the morning shift in the pilot's seat," Ed answered, trying to calm his nerves from the sudden jolt. Maybe it wasn't a good idea to watch a movie about too many people telling too many lies about an object of which they know too little – and too many people dying because of it. "Besides the morning comes 40 minutes earlier aboard ship."

"So you'll be at the controls when we do the flip over. Are you nervous?"

Ed noticed the engineering tech glance over her shoulder at Juarez. "What for? It's a simple enough maneuver to turn off the drive, turn the ship around, and restart the drive to decelerate."

"Yeah, but it was just before the flip over when the *New Brunswick* bought it. I'm starting to feel a little déjà vu."

There was a rustling behind them as the geologist and the engineering tech headed for the stairwell. Juarez took a long sip from his drink, but didn't say anything more until they left. When he did, it was at a lower volume.

"He's been trying to work up the nerve to ask her to his room for the past hour. I thought I'd give him a little push."

"By scaring them?"

"No, by being obnoxious. They're already scared."

"Of what?"

"Of what they'll find on Ceres, and no matter what they find, having to endure it for well over a year, a Martian year at that."

"It doesn't scare you, Juarez."

"I've been there, and I know what I'm getting into. Ceres is the rock of opportunity. It's a great place."

"If you can get past it being a rock."

"Hey, Mars was just a cold, rusty desert. Look at it now."

"Mostly, it's still a cold, rusty desert."

"Yeah, but with a few bubbles of paradise."

"Almost one less bubble a couple of weeks back," Ed said

"True enough. I hope they find the bomber who did it, but he's probably disappeared on Earth by now."

"Maybe not."

"You think he's still on Mars? You don't buy the story about the Serling Heights bomb being planted weeks ago?"

"I know that's what the FBI said," Ed said.

"But you don't believe the FBI?"

"I don't know why I should start now. They first thought I blew up the *New Brunswick*."

Juarez laughed. "You're right. I didn't believe that either when I first heard it on the news. So you do think the bomber's still on Mars."

"He could be, but then a lot of the passengers on the *New Brunswick* were heading for Ceres."

Juarez's voice dropped to a conspiratorial whisper. "You think he's on board?"

"You're the one who said you're experiencing déjà vu."

"I take it you don't believe that Earth Firsters were behind the bombings: a little too convenient for you?"

Ed feared he was letting Juarez ask too many questions, and asked one of his own. "Do you think it was something else?"

"You mean as in Weller's story at the service about that researcher being a target for murder? That's crazy. If that's true, why do the blow out at Serling Heights?"

"For cover, or maybe other reasons. It may not be a coincidence the bomber picked the agridome that holds Weller's vineyards."

"You mean as a warning for him to shut up?"

"Could be."

"Maybe that's a warning you should take seriously," Juarez said, crunching down on a celery stick.

"What are you saying, Juarez?"

"Why are you so interested in who did the bombings?"

"Who says I am?"

"I hear things. You seem preoccupied with it – you and Faizah."

"I'd like to know if he's on my ship." Ed tried to sound officious. "There are a lot of people on board, and it's my responsibility to keep them safe."

Juarez's tone turned low, just above a sinister whisper. "If all you're interested in is the safety of you and your ship, your best bet is not to ask too many questions. You might not like the answers, and you may give someone reason to be interested in you. If you're right, and all that's happened is leading to Ceres, well, I know that rock, and the people on it. They know you, Ed, but they don't care that much about you – yet. Give them a reason, though, for them to think of you as a threat, and you won't be safe. The people you care about won't be safe."

"They're not safe now. I was in Serling Heights when it blew out. What's next?"

"What if it's over?" Juarez said. "You and Jessica were in Serling Heights, and Jessica was on board the *New Brunswick* when it blew. She's on board now. You don't want to put her at risk again. Maybe the people behind these bombings have already got what they needed, and you don't have to risk anything or anyone. You can just fly back to Mars, and leave the mystery to the FBI."

"Or unsolved."

"There are many unsolved mysteries out here. What's one more?"

"This one has so far killed eight people."

Juarez looked confused. "Eight? You mean seven, don't you? No one died in Serling Heights, at least not that I heard of, and ... wait, you don't mean Arthur Strand? You think he's part of this?"

"Suspicious timing, I guess," Ed said. "Even just the seven, I think we all want to know who the killer is."

"If you're right, somebody on board does know."

"Perhaps I have already asked one too many questions."

"Keep going and you'll ask it of one too many people," Juarez stood up to leave. "Just stick to flying your ship the rest of the way, and you'll make it back to Mars all right."

By the next morning, Ed was back in the pilot's seat, preparing for the flip over. Lenowitz was on a laser com link so their conversation couldn't be intercepted.

"He's right, you know," Lenowitz said. "You will ask your questions of one person too many."

"I'm sure I already have," Ed said, "though Juarez was the one asking most of the questions. I was doing my best to avoid him."

"A very difficult thing to do for such a long time on such a small ship."

"Even so, he seemed to be giving me the word that if I shut up now, I'll be safe."

"I am not sure I would want to trust my safety on the word of a suspected killer. But with all eyes turned toward the Earth Firsters, whoever is behind this will not want to shift attention back to Mars, or worse for them, Ceres."

"Have you found out anything more on Juarez?"

"He's had several contacts with Interplanetary Drive Systems, nothing specific with Astech. But he does seem to be around when misfortune strikes, particularly for their competitors or union organizers. He fits the pattern of a goon for hire."

"For both companies?"

"And others. Nothing this spectacular or blatant, however. Most of the events that have happened when he's been around have been written off as accidents – suspicious events, but officially accidents."

"So why not make it seem like an accident aboard the *New Brunswick*?"

"I do not know, and Ed, please don't ask Juarez."

"Roger that. Anything more on the Umi Explorer?"

"The crew reports they retrieved the fusion drive and nothing else. By the radar track, they could not have reached the cargo module unless they had a second tug. It does not appear they have one."

"You're not sure?"

"Ceres reports they only left with one tug, but the track showed a small, intermittent blip, which made me curious. But it seems unlikely."

"Maybe we'll find out more when we reach Ceres."

"You may have found out enough, Ed. Please be careful."

"I'll do my best. Out."

"Mind if I join you?" Jessica said from the hatchway.

"Hi. Sure, come on in."

Jessica eased into the co-pilot's seat. "I can't stay for long. I have to head back up before the flip over. I just need to catch my breath and composure."

"Why?"

"A run-in I had with Laura. The water recyclers went down, and Manny spent a long-time early this morning getting them back up. I was helping him out."

"And Laura took umbrage at that?"

"Manny's rather fun to work with, and maybe he's a little flirtatious."

"A little?"

"OK, a lot, and I flirt back, but I'm not interested."

"Laura didn't see it that way."

"She came up on us after he had the recyclers fixed. She misunderstood, and after Manny went back to the crew module, she laid into me, and that's when I said the wrong thing."

"What?"

"I told her I wasn't interested in Manny, and besides, what's so hot about him anyway?"

Ed grimaced. "And she told you, right?"

"Oh yeah, in detail."

"No wonder your face is so red."

"I mean, I never imagined ... that is, I guess that's why she gets so jealous."

"I know. The way Laura talks, no man holds a candle to Manny."

"Oh, you had your moments."

"Moments!?"

"I gotta run to make sure all the passengers are strapped in," Jessica said, getting out of her seat and slipping through the hatch. "See ya."

"Moments," Ed grumbled. "If Laura's so damned jealous over her husband, why does she keep bragging about him?"

∞∞∞∞∞∞∞

The flip over and deceleration went without a hitch, and in the 11 more days it took to reach Ceres, the routine was so rarely broken that it became oppressive for Ed. He was never so glad for a trip to be near its end.

"Ed, you look like hell," Faizah said as he walked by her cabin. "Shouldn't you be at the controls?"

"We've got some time before we cut the main drive and dock at Ceres. I thought I'd get some breakfast upstairs, give some of the passengers a send off. That sort of thing."

"How sporting of you. Did you happen to run into Juarez?"

"Thankfully, no. He made his point, and I don't think he wants to press it. But what's been hell is being locked in with a man you believe is a murderer and is capable of blowing up space ships, even if he's on it."

"There's no way. The inspection on loading was too keen, and he'd be found out if he tried it. But if you didn't see Juarez, how about Charlie?"

"I think Charlie's been avoiding me. Why?"

"Come in here and close the door."

Ed stepped in and slid the door shut behind him. "What's this about?" he asked as he pulled down a folding stool to sit on.

"It seems Charlie's been talking to Juarez," Faizah said. "Perhaps it started the other way around. Yes, I'm sure that's it."

"What do you mean?"

"Juarez had dinner with Charlie last night. I happened to see them. It started off friendly enough, but Charlie seemed to be getting rather nervous toward the end."

"You couldn't hear what they were talking about?"

"Not without getting too close and being obvious about it. But I went to see Charlie later. Juarez had been pumping him about Arthur Strand."

"What about Strand?"

"Juarez apparently is linking Strand with the other deaths, and was trying to find out what Charlie knew about it."

"Damn it. That's my fault. When he was trying to pump me, he did a good job of it. I let slip that I thought Strand's death was part of the bombings and other threats. He seemed surprised by that, but I thought he was just trying to cover up something."

"I don't believe so, Ed. Charlie got the impression Juarez was trying to figure out what Strand had to do with all this."

"Did Charlie tell him?"

"Apparently Juarez went to his room later and made some rather subtle but clearly ominous threats if Charlie didn't tell everything he knew."

"And so he did."

"Enough to suspect that all of Averink's work wasn't destroyed in the blast," Faizah said. "Juarez also asked a lot of questions about Astech and its interest in building fusion drives. It seems Juarez didn't know about that either."

"Well then, if Juarez wasn't working for Astech, he must have been acting for Interplanetary Drive Systems. Can't prove it, but that does seem pretty clear now. Only ...."

"What?"

"I may have given him enough reason to act again," Ed said.

"I don't know about that. Someone believes the Q-disk exists, but so far we have no evidence that it does."

"But if Juarez was the bomber of at least the *New Brunswick*, his job is to make sure Averink's work doesn't survive."

"Relax, Ed. He's not going to blow up the ship."

"Doesn't have to. He probably figures you, me or Jessica have the Q-disk. It's like a shell game."

"But in a shell game, the trick is not to have the pea under any of the shells."

"And you know how to beat the shell game."

"By eliminating two of the shells. Or in this case, you and me?"

"I'm sure the thought has at least crossed his mind."

"Great. And I'm supposed to be meeting with Astech execs on Ceres. I suppose that makes me target No. 1."

"I don't know, Faizah. I think the only sure bet for Juarez is to get rid of all three of us."

"Except none of us has the Q-disk," Faizah said. "At least Jessica claims she doesn't have it. I know I don't have it, and I'm pretty sure about you."

"Jessica doesn't have it, even if she has something she's not telling us. But right now, I don't care as much about the disk as keeping us alive. I'm not convinced the disk exists."

"Someone convinced Charlie to look for it."

"That's just it. If someone at Astech was so set on finding that disk, he would have searched the place himself and not convince Charlie to do it for him. Doing it by proxy was safer, but had less chance of success."

"The risk of exposure was too great?" Faizah asked.

"Or finding the disk was of secondary importance because they already had the plans."

"How?"

"I don't know," Ed said. "But if Astech does already have the plans, all they have to do is make sure a second set isn't lying around somewhere."

"Doesn't that go back to eliminating the shells?"

"Yeah, I'm afraid it does."

"Great. Maybe it's time you broke out your stunners?"

"I have two. I'll give you one after we dock."

"Without delay."

Ed left Faizah's cabin and hurried down to the tug. Laura was in the pilot's seat, but Manny was at the controls, anxiously awaiting the fusion drive's cutoff.

"He's all yours, Ed," Laura said as she got up to make room for Ed. "Keep a good watch on Manny. And Manny, please be careful not to dent up the ship – like last time."

That stopped Ed short. "Like last time?"

"What a kidder she is," Manny said. "Don't listen to her. Last time? Ha! Last time was smooth as silk. Well, OK, maybe a wrinkle or two. A gust of cosmic wind threw off my instrumentation, but it was only a bent strut, hardly noticeable. A good whack of a hammer, some touch-up paint – good as new."

"Yeah, well, I just had to get some of my struts replaced after the last trip. I'd hate to bend up the new ones."

"Don't worry. Take a nap if you want to. You won't feel a thing."

"I think I'll stay awake for this," Ed said, touching the control screen for the ship's com. "Ceres control, *Cydonia Zach*. Coming up on fusion drive cutoff."

"Roger, *Zach*. We'll be waiting for you."

The computer counted down: five beeps and then cutoff.

The gravity wasn't much before, but instantly, what there was of it was gone. The ship coasted slowly toward the asteroid.

"*Cydonia Zach*, Ceres. Continue in under thruster control. Break. Umi Explorer, hold station. We'll clear you after the *Zach* is in."

"The Umi Explorer's out there?" Ed asked.

"Yeah," Manny said. "Actually, it arrived ahead of us, but Ceres told it to wait because it's going to take awhile to detach *New Brunswick*'s wrecked drive. The drive is okay, but the front end of it is a mess."

"Our cameras can pick it up?"

"No, but I can tie in to the Ceres docking cameras." Manny touched a command. "There, on your screen."

The view showed the extra grappling arms of the salvage ship's extra long axis securely holding the fusion drive unit from the *New Brunswick*. "Look familiar?" Manny asked.

"Actually I never saw the drive unit after the explosion. The way my radar showed it cartwheeling, I wanted to stay as far away from it as I could."

"It must have taken some pretty good piloting to grab it and get it under control. Maybe that's why they took the extra taxi along, to help out."

"Taxi? What taxi?"

"Just forward of the New B.'s drive," Manny said, reaching over and pointing to a spot on the screen. "Zoom in the shot and you can see it better."

Ed selected a corner of the view and enlarged it. It took a second for the new image to refocus. "That's a long range taxi, isn't it?"

"Yeah. McKracken makes them here. Some of the mining ships use them to explore nearby asteroids without having to move the whole ship."

"How long can they last on their own?"

"Depends. Standard gear, about three or four days. Longer if they put on extra tanks. But the rocket they put on that taxi has a pretty high thrust, so they're usually not out that long. You don't want to go to Jupiter in one of those things, but there's enough power there to easily switch orbits and come back."

"Right. You'd better watch your rate of closure."

As Manny adjusted his thrusters, Ed switched on the laser link and connected with the Grissom. "Grissom, *Cydonia Zach*. Can you get me the captain on a secure line?"

There were some muffled voices, then the tone switched and Lenowitz's voice came over. "Ed, I am rather busy at the moment, as I imagine you should be. What is so urgent?"

"Can you pick up docking camera 7A from Ceres?"

"I imagine so. Just a minute, yes, I have it. The Umi Explorer and the salvaged drive from the *New Brunswick*. What of it?"

"Zoom in forward of the salvaged drive, and you'll see a taxi."

"Yes, Ed. I recognize the model. We have a modified version of it aboard the Grissom."

"Small enough to give only an intermittent radar image from Mars?"

"Yes, but they're very short range."

"Not this one. Manny tells me it's a long-range taxis capable of switching orbits, and they're made right here. Call up the specs on it."

"Hold a minute," Lenowitz answered. A minute later, he came back on. "You are correct. This upgraded model is definitely powerful enough to rendezvous with the cargo modules while the tug salvaged the fusion drive, but still not show up steady on the Grissom radar."

"And with enough cargo space to bring back at least one standard shipping crate – with Averink's prototype fusion drive component."

"I will find out. I will have a search warrant by the time we reach Ceres. Grissom out"

"What was that about?" Manny asked as he fired the rear thrusters. Ed felt himself sink softly back in his seat and quickly checked the readouts. Manny was right on the mark.

"The taxi you can see on the Umi Explorer, it isn't supposed to be there. We think it was ... Wait, where did it go?" The view on the camera was suddenly blocked by a mass of gray. The camera refocused until the image resolved into another drive unit and axis slowing to a stop.

"That's us," Manny said. "Our fusion drive must be blocking the view. Do you want to announce us, or should I?"

"Go ahead."

Ed could see part of the *Umi Explorer* on his own screens now, but not the part where the taxi docked. Out the opposite view, Ed looked out on the ragged globe of Ceres, dotted with the spindly structures of mining companies and servicing docks, their lights throwing sharp shadows on the gloomy rock.

Ed heard Manny's exchange with Ceres control, and saw the small tugs rise up from the surface to take away the *Zach*'s fusion drive. It wasn't long before the tugs latched and moved the drive to the servicing dock. Ed was ready to take over the controls, but Manny handled it smoothly, turning the tug tail first toward the asteroid and dropped the *Zach* and its modules slowly toward the surface. Ed felt the bump as it landed, a little more jarring then he would have liked, and Manny fired a burst of forward thrusters to hold the ship down.

"Not bad, Manny."

"Not bad? I-I was a master, I was so smooth, I ... I feel like I'm going to faint."

"Just sit here until they lock everything down, while I go ...." Just then, Ed glanced at the screen showing the image from camera 7A. The Umi Explorer was back in view, but the taxi was gone. Ed pounded the controls to reconnect the laser link to the Grissom, but no luck. He switched to broadcast, ship-to-ship.

"Grissom, *Cydonia Zach*."

"Go ahead, *Zach*."

"I need to speak to Capt. Lenowitz."

"I'm sorry, he's not available."

"It's urgent."

There was a pause from the Grissom. "This is first officer Nikitin."

"This is Ed Ferald. I need to talk to the captain immediately."

"Then your need will go unfulfilled. Is there anything else?"

"Tell him it's about the Umi Explorer."

"Hold on, please." A moment's silence. "I am on headset, what about the Umi?"

"Tell Lenowitz the taxi is gone."

"He is obtaining search warrant for the Umi and the taxi right now."

"What should I do?"

"Find it. The captain has briefed me on this case, but we can not reach the surface for at least 20 minutes. I will have the captain call you on your personal com. Grissom out."

"Ed, that taxi you're looking for?" Manny said. "I think this is it, heading for the public warehouses." He brought up a view of the taxi just as it reached the dock.

"Damn it." Ed flipped on the ship's intercom and punched in Faizah's room number.

"Faizah, are you still there? "

"Just getting ready to leave, why?"

"Drop your bags and come down to the crew module. And hurry."

"I'm on my way."

Ed switched off and rushed into the tug's crew cabin.

"What's in that taxi that's so important, anyway?" Manny asked.

"A whole lot of grief." Ed unlocked a small locker and took out the two stun guns. He hesitated for a second, then took out the scanner as well.

"Here now, what's this all about?" Laura asked. She had been sitting in the compartment during the landing, but stepped out of Ed's way when he came in.

"A bit too much to explain, Laura. You're licensed for a stunner, right?"

"Naturally."

"Here," he said, tossing one of the guns to her. "Keep watch on Jessica and tell her not to leave the ship."

"You want me to threaten her with this?"

"What? No. But things are happening, and you may need it to keep her, and you, safe."

"Oh, well all right then."

"It's about that bogus report, isn't it" Manny said, "and Averink's research. That drive component everybody said was lost. That's what's in the taxi, right? And you're going to go get it. Let me go with you. I can handle a stun gun."

"You've never fired a stunner in your life, love" Laura said.

"Well, no. But I'm a fast learner."

Ed entered a command to unlock the hatch above to let Faizah in. "Just stay here and make sure no one bothers with the ship. Down here, Faizah," he called up.

"I guess I'd better go on up and join Jessica," Laura said, waiting until Faizah dropped down before pulling herself up.

"Where are we going?" Faizah asked.

"The public warehouses, to find out where they're stashing Averink's component."

"What?"

"I'll explain on the way."

CHAPTER 23
Sailing Through Caves

There's gravity on Ceres, if you wait for it. Even though it's the largest asteroid in the Belt, with a diameter about the size of Texas, its gravity is only 3 percent of Earth's. In the maze of tunnels and work habitats that riddle the spheroid, a dropped tool takes an agonizingly slow time to reach the floor. A worker who tries to hurry through the tunnels can forget in which direction the floor lies as he pulls and pushes from handholds to footholds.

Ed was sailing through the passageways, but Faizah was falling behind.

"Ed, wait. I'm not as good at low-g as you are."

"No time!" Ed grabbed a handhold and swung himself around. "Meet me at Dock 23. That's where the taxi ended up. Here, take the gun," he said, softly tossing it to her. "I'm not as good with it as you are, and you may need to bail me out of trouble."

Ed didn't wait for her to catch the stunner, but turned and continued his half run, half flight down the tunnel. He knew Ceres enough to know where the public warehouses were, and there were plenty of maps Faizah could link into with her hardwire system to direct her. He didn't know what he was going to do when he reached Dock 23, but all he had to do was figure out where they were taking Averink's prototype.

Ed reached the warehouses and slowed his progress to loping hops as he moved down the docks: ... 19, 20, 21 – he grabbed a handhold, and his body swung around until his feet gently settled back on the floor. Two men at dock 23 were loading a crate onto a cart and strapping it down.

"Damn it, that's the one all right," Ed thought. "Now what?"

"Ed? What are you doing here?" Came a voice behind him. Ed easily recognized it – calm, perhaps concerned. "Your ship just landed."

Ed turned to face him. "Paul, why are you here?"

Paul Cherault flashed his smile. "You don't sound so surprised I'm on this rock."

"I knew you were going to be on Ceres. I saw the Halifax passenger list. What are you doing on this loading dock?"

"Here? Just to make sure that crate gets to where it's supposed to go."

"And where's that?"

"That's confidential, Ed. I'm sorry."

Ed grabbed Paul by his jacket lapels and shoved him against the wall, the force of the move lifting both of them off the floor.

"Where are they taking that crate?"

"Are you crazy? Put me down. What's gotten into you?"

Ed's feet landed back on the floor, but he still held Paul high against the wall. "That crate's from the *New Brunswick*, isn't it?"

"It's legitimate salvage."

"And how legitimate was the bombing?"

"We had nothing to do with that."

Ed's grip tightened. "We? Who's we?"

"That would include me, Mr. Ferald," said a voice from behind him. "Please, put Mr. Cherault down and turn around slowly. I do have a stunner if you wish to cause problems. I have worse, but an electric discharge raises fewer questions, not that they ask very many questions on Ceres."

Ed let go and turned while Paul sank slowly to the floor.

"Alan Thiegold, right?"

"Paul, see to the crate. I'll take care of Mr. Ferald."

"Wait a minute, he's my friend. I don't ...."

"You needn't worry, Paul," Thiegold said. "Nothing will happen to Mr. Ferald. In fact, this all ends here if he simply walks away. Now, hurry, take care of the crate while I convince your friend to make a wise choice."

Paul's face showed desperation, a sadness. "I will." He turned to Ed. "I'm sorry." He walked off gingerly toward the crate, where the men had finished strapping it down to the cart.

"And you're supposed to just let me walk away?" Ed asked.

Thiegold put the stunner in his pocket. "Why not? Of course Astech knew about Averink's work. I knew even more about it. We didn't want to see his theories die with him, unlike IDS."

"You didn't want to lose that chance for profit."

"That, too. But such attitudes are refreshing out here. In fact, your uncle is a major proponent of profit beyond Earth, unlike the corporations that want to pile up losses on their books to get as many tax breaks and subsidies as they can."

"Last I looked, Astech was one of those corporations."

"But now it will be given a chance to diversify. I had hoped we could talk you into being our chief pilot, or maybe work out a partnership with 4th Orbit, an arrangement that was better for everybody."

"At the cost of the lives you murdered?" Ed took a side step closer to the gate, continuing to draw Thiegold's attention.

"Me? No. I think you know that I did not plant a bomb aboard the *New Brunswick*, nor did anyone else from Astech, even your friend, Paul."

"No, you just arranged it so the bomb would go where it would do the most harm, and allow you to steal Averink's prototype." Ed saw Paul switch on the cart's electric motor, and guided by a recessed center rail that held the cart firmly to the floor, it went around a corner and out of sight.

"All that happened is Paul shipped a couple of crates late. There's nothing suspicious about those crates. In fact, you carried them aboard your ship from Mars, right? I've read the reports that the bomb was moved because of late shipments, but surely, that was an accident."

Ed saw a slight flash of bright blue from around the corner. No one else on the dock noticed.

"But you are keeping that crate you salvaged from the New B. secret. You haven't filed a salvage claim, and you sure were in a rush to get it off the Umi Explorer."

"We wouldn't want to invite any more mishaps, or wait around for complications from OSAR if we can avoid it. And it appears we can."

"Except for me."

"Do you expect me to kill you, or arrange for you to have an accident and be flushed out an airlock? How dramatic." Thiegold put an arm around Ed and guided him back to the passageway. "No, Ed – You don't mind if I call you Ed? Paul has told me so much about you – No, your death would cause still more complications, needless ones. I'm just going to walk away, and I suggest you do the same. If you do, 4th Orbit still has much to gain by our success. So do you. Think of what it means to fly through the Solar System in days instead of weeks or months. Or you can make your claims of conspiracy if anyone will listen, but you can't pin the bombings or murders on us, and we will succeed regardless. As for you, you'll be stuck with drives from IDS. That would be a pity."

"You expect me to forget about eight murders?"

"Eight? Ah, Arthur Strand. You don't believe that was an accident. Well, neither do I. Perhaps someone panicked. That whole episode was unnecessary. Tell you what. If you walk away, I'll see what I can do about bringing justice in the Strand case – swift justice."

"And justice for the other seven?"

"That is complicated."

"And you hate complications."

"See! You do understand. Perhaps, in time, justice will come even for those seven. But it would be a disservice to their memories if we did not press on."

"You're stealing Averink's drive in honor of the *New Brunswick's* dead?"

"Ah, put that way – no. But in time, think of all our futures when that drive is developed. My partners and I have the drive, and can stake a legal salvage claim to it if we wish to make it known. You really have no choice."

"I guess I don't," Ed said. He backed slowly away, and even when he turned, he kept Thiegold in the edge of his view. Thiegold himself turned and headed for the passageway where the cart had gone.

Ed turned a corner and picked up speed. He turned another corner, grabbed a handhold to pull himself to a stop, and flipped on his com.

"Faizah!"

"Ed, you all right?"

"Yeah, thanks for asking. Thiegold let me go."

"I figured he would. No percentage to do otherwise."

"You've got Averink's prototype?"

"Yes. Stuck the poor guy from the cart into a closet."

Ed winced. "Where are you taking it?"

"Minglong's. The only place I could think of."

"You know how to get there?"

"I looked it up. I'm five minutes away."

"Good, I'll meet you there."

Ed switched off his com. Lenowitz was going to try to contact him any minute, and Ed didn't want to take that call just then. Now that Faizah had Averink's component, Ed wanted some time to figure out what they could do with it, rather than just hand it over to OSAR as evidence and months of legal wrangling over who had legal right to it.

He moved on again, picking up his pace to put more distance between him and Thiegold. It wouldn't be long before Thiegold discovered the crate was missing – or Paul woke up.

Ed turned down a darker, longer tunnel. The St. Joseph mission was scattered throughout the asteroid, and Minglong's lab was part of it. Minglong stayed there most of the time, bent over stubborn drive components and maddening computer screens, or after-hours just in quiet meditation of his theories on the unseen building blocks of the universe – and his beliefs on their Builder.

As little as Ed went to church, he always made time to see Minglong when he was on Ceres. The conversations were always good, the topics varied and unpredictable. So as confusing as the maze of tunnels were, Ed readily knew how to get to Minglong's lab.

The lab's door was locked, highly unusual since walk-ins for business or friendship were always welcome. Ed tapped the intercom.

"Minglong, it's Ed."

A chime rang and the door slid open, closing and locking again after Ed stepped through. The lab, dug out of a crater wall, was a cavern with natural rock walls and roof sealed to keep the room airtight. The lab's freight airlock opened onto the crater floor.

The cart and crate were inside. Waiting for him were Minglong and Faizah – and Jessica and Manny.

"Jessica, what the hell are you doing here? I told Laura to keep you on the ship."

"Yeah," Manny said, "but you also said Laura couldn't use her gun to keep her there."

"She could have shown some initiative."

"I had to see Minglong," Jessica said. "I promised Tim."

"It couldn't wait? Never mind. We can't keep this crate here. Thiegold will know Averink was coming to see Minglong. He'll show up here as soon as he realizes we have Averink's prototype."

"Thiegold's probably on your heels," Faizah said. "He's liable to see us if we move the crate into the passageway again. We're better off trying to hide it in here."

"No," Minglong said. "Best to take it outside."

"But like Faizah said," Jessica objected, "Alan's liable to see it."

"No," Ed said. "Minglong means outside – on the asteroid surface. Do you have a suit that fits me?"

"I believe so," the monk said. "Come this way. Hurry."

Minglong's legs, covered by loose, brown coveralls that hid their bony, misshapen form, wouldn't have held his weight even on Mars. But in the subtle gravity of Ceres, they were enough, though he usually used his hands to propel himself forward. Ed followed him to a suit locker, and picked one from the three inside.

Faizah had disengaged the cart's rail guide, and she and Manny maneuvered it around the benches and lab gear toward the airlock.

"Maybe I should go with you," Manny said. "The weight's no problem, but it is big, and its mass makes it clumsy to handle. It nearly took out my knee bringing it in here."

"I'm afraid my space suits may be too big for you," Minglong said.

"Do you have one that will fit Faizah?" Ed asked.

"Probably," Minglong said.

"Good. We're better off if Faizah's not here when Thiegold shows up."

"Afraid I'll kill him?" Faizah said.

"The thought occurred to me. Even if you restrained yourself, it could be trouble. Alan will probably figure it was you who zapped Paul. If he finds you here, he'll know the crate's nearby."

"Oh, was that your friend?" Faizah said with a mocking sweetness. "I am sorry."

"Here, this suit should fit you," Minglong said, pulling out a rack with a space suit on it.

"Maybe I should stay here," Faizah said, "in case Alan tries anything."

Ed shook his head as he grabbed suit meant for him. "I don't think he will. He can't afford a murder on Ceres."

Manny dropped the crate. "Murder! Did you say murder?"

"It would cause too many complications," Ed said, "and Thiegold hates complications. Watch your toes."

"Simplicity, I always said that was a noble trait in criminals," Manny said, moving his foot before the slowly falling crate hit the floor.

"Quick, everything in the airlock," Ed said. "We'll put our suits on in there."

Manny shoved the crate the rest of the way into the airlock. Ed and Faizah grabbed their suits and stepped inside while Minglong closed the hatch behind them.

"You know, I still would have felt better if I stayed behind," Faizah said. "Alan is going to start feeling pretty desperate about now."

"Maybe. But Lenowitz and a squad from OSAR are going to be serving a search warrant on the Umi Explorer at about the same time. Once he hears that, he's not going to want to pull anything that makes too much noise. Ready?"

Faizah clicked her helmet shut and checked her readings. "Ready," came over the suit radio.

Ed cycled the atmosphere out of the airlock, and opened the hatch to the surface. An empty landing pad and scaffolding took up the middle of the crater floor. Five other freight airlocks opened onto the crater from other maintenance shops. Ed closed the hatch behind him, and the two of them pulled the crate to the side and out of sight from the lab's window ports.

"I'm guessing Alan already knew about the search warrant," Faizah said. "That's why he wanted Averink's crate off the ship so quickly."

"You think someone from the Grissom tipped him off – that lieutenant, what's his name, David something?"

"David Carstol. Maybe him, but I'm thinking it was one of the JAG officers. Lenowitz said one was added late to his crew, and an officer from the legal office would also have been in a position on Mars to quash the search warrant on your place."

"How far do these conspiracies spread?"

"Lenowitz can worry about his own crew, Ed. We have enough to worry about with Alan and keeping Averink's component safe."

"Don't forget, Juarez is out there someplace. I think just keeping us safe is going to be hard enough."

"So what now? We can't stay out here forever."

"Thiegold will reach the lab soon. Let's get to that airlock a couple doors down, 17A. It's a small shop. I know the guy who runs it. He'll let us in."

"If he's there."

"Let's move, but stay on the concrete pad. We don't want to give anyone footprints to follow."

"Ed. This is Minglong. Cut your radios. Once Thiegold doesn't find you in the lab, he might think to start scanning suit frequencies."

"Right."

The two carried – or more often guided – the crate along the aster-oid's surface, resisting the urge to go too fast so they didn't lose control of the prototype's mass. As they neared the airlock farther down the crater wall, a faded 17A painted on its door, Ed kept looking back to-ward Minglong's lab, half expecting to see Thiegold, or Paul, step out onto the surface to look for them. But no light from an open hatch spilled onto the crater surface.

When they reached 17A, Ed plugged into the intercom.

"Larry, this is Ed Ferald. I'm outside your airlock door. Let me in."

Faizah leaned over to touch her helmet with Ed's. Her muffled voice came through the contact. "What if no one's home?"

"Then we keep knocking on other doors until someone let's us in."

"Great. I'm starting to feel like a Jehovah's Witness."

Ed was about ready to unplug from the intercom and try another lab when the airlock opened. He and Faizah carried the prototype into the chamber and Ed cycled in the air. Once pressurized, Ed opened the inner hatch, and the two of them removed their helmets.

"Larry? Larry, where are you?"

Faizah took a step into the darkened lab. "No one's here?"

"Who let us in?" Ed said.

"Damn," Faizah said, and desperately tried to undo her spacesuit.

"Don't bother Faizah," came an unseen voice. "You should have put your stunner in an outside suit pocket where you could reach it. But it wouldn't have mattered."

Ed peered into the dark, trying to make out a figure. "Juarez."

Juarez stepped into the light near the hatch. He was holding a Smith & Wesson recoilless .44. "You two left the ship so quickly that I figured, Ed, you must not have taken my advice. I didn't get a chance to follow you, but I could follow Faizah. She nearly saw me when she zapped that other guy and grabbed the crate. Once I figured she was heading for Minglong's, I knew what this was about. That's Averink's prototype in the crate, isn't it?"

Faizah undid her gloves and let them drop gently to the floor. "How did you know we'd come here?"

"Simple. I got to Minglong's lab ahead of you, and I saw you in an awful hurry bringing that crate in. Then Ed rushes up a few minutes later. You were running from someone, and I figured your next step would be to go outside. I set my com to scan for suit frequencies, and pretty soon I picked you up. Ed, here, was kind enough to mention the airlock number."

"What happened to Larry?" Ed said.

"Luckily for him, he wasn't here. Breaking in was no big deal. And if we take care of our business quickly, Larry will stay lucky."

Ed felt a despairing knot in his stomach. "But our luck won't hold," he said.

"Ed, I'm afraid you pushed your luck too far."

"But you can't just shoot us," Faizah said. "Capt. Lenowitz would know it was you."

"And Capt. Lenowitz is just chomping at the bit to get this case back under his jurisdiction. You're right. If I could just shoot you, I would have done it already and been out of here."

"And now you're trying to figure how to deal with Ed and me and shift the blame on Astech," Faizah said.

"That's about right."

Faizah smiled. "Maybe I can help."

"What!?" Ed reeled to face Faizah. "You're going to help Juarez kill us?"

"No, deal with us. Deal is the operative word."

Juarez shook his head. "I don't see much of a deal that leaves you two alive."

"I don't see much chance for you if you leave both of us dead," Faizah said, coolly.

"Faizah, do you think he's going to worry about us after killing seven people?"

"No one was supposed to die on the *New Brunswick*." Juarez said. "I was only supposed to blow up the luggage hold and destroy what's in that crate."

"And that's why we can deal," Faizah said.

Ed felt that knot in his stomach tighten even more. "Wait a minute, Faizah. You said Juarez can't leave both of us dead?"

Juarez grinned. "You know Ed, I think I'd like to hear the lady out after all."

"Actually, Juarez, you're in trouble if either of us is dead," she said.

"That's not how I see it. You have too much on me."

"All we have on you is suspicions – or at least that was all until you blurted out that admission a moment ago."

"What admission?" Ed said.

"It doesn't matter," Faizah said. "We have no hard evidence. All you need is some assurance that we'll keep you out of it."

"I'm just supposed to take your word?"

"No."

"Then the only way to keep people quiet who have something on me is me to have something on them. Did you kill anybody lately?"

"Not yet."

"What are you saying?" Ed asked.

"I'd like to know, too," Juarez said, "This is getting interesting."

"Look, the one we really have to stop is Thiegold."

"Thiegold? Why him?" Juarez asked.

"You didn't know? He's the one who arranged to have your bomb moved so it would do enough damage to destroy the *New Brunswick* and send Averink's prototype off to where he could steal it. He's your real threat. He must have known you planted the bomb, or hired you?"

"That son of a ... And he's the one you're supposed to kill?"

"We'll have to make it look like self defense, but you'll know the truth. We can't turn you in without having you turn us in."

"But if Thiegold did what you said, OSAR won't mind him being dead," Juarez said. "You won't be murderers, you'll be heroes."

"Lenowitz won't press an investigation on us, but he can't tolerate vigilantes. If we try to get you arrested, how long do you think it'll take before your lawyer starts trying to use our involvement as part of your defense? If that happens, OSAR will have to investigate and prosecute."

"Even so, I'm bound to serve a lot more time than you will."

"Ok," Ed interrupted. "Now you're nitpicking. We're still all better off if we keep quiet about each other."

"Oh, now you like the idea," Juarez said.

"No, I think the idea stinks," Ed said. "But it's better than you killing us. Faizah's right, it's better for all of us."

"Maybe," Juarez said. "But it sounds like this Thiegold has a lot more people involved. How do we stop all of them from talking?"

"Killing us won't stop them either," Faizah said. "But there may not be that many people who know about you. And OSAR isn't going to be too anxious to look for them, either."

"Why not?"

"Politically, it's too sensitive," Faizah said. "The American administration will want to wrap it up after a few arrests. A widespread conspiracy would probably mean the administration gets kicked out of office, and the Americans are pulling OSAR's strings right now. OSAR isn't going to be looking for you unless you give it a reason to, such as killing us."

"I don't like it, but it makes sense. Even so, I still destroy Averink's prototype."

"Wait, you can't do that," Ed objected.

"No deal otherwise," Juarez said. "I have a contract to fulfill."

"It's all right, Ed," Faizah said. "This is the best we can do. We have no evidence Averink's prototype worked anyway."

"It's a deal, then," Juarez said. "First, Faizah, pull out your stunner, gently, and slide it over. After I make sure neither of you have any more weapons, you can tell me your plan on how we kill this guy Thiegold."

CHAPTER 24

Between a Rock and ... Other Rocks

"You don't really have a plan, do you?" Ed whispered to Faizah while Juarez checked a computer screen for Larry's schedule.

"Hey, I'm thinking."

"You're thinking?"

"We're still alive, aren't we? I got us that far."

"But do you really want to kill Thiegold?"

"I've had worse ideas."

"Cut the talk, you two," Juarez called out angrily, waving his gun at them for emphasis.

"Oh, we're just plotting," Ed said, "working out the details for Thiegold's murder, that sort of thing."

Juarez walked over to them seated on the floor by the airlock door. "Is that so? In that case, I want to hear your plan. Your friend, Larry, is on the other side of Ceres working on a miner's tug. He won't be back for hours. We'll have plenty of time for me to blow up the prototype and then discuss how we pull off this killing."

"You can't destroy Averink's prototype," Faizah said. "At least not right away."

"The hell I can't."

"No, Ed was right. We need it as bait. The prototype is the only thing we have to lure Thiegold in, and we just can't pretend to have it either. It has to be the real thing, in working order."

"You said you didn't think the thing worked," Juarez said.

"I don't know if it'll do what Averink claimed, but it must do something, even if it just flashes lights and registers on a meter."

"Is Thiegold going to live long enough to see more than the crate?"

"He may," Faizah said. "We don't want to tip him off too early."

"And exactly how do we lure him in?"

Ed snapped his fingers. "We make a deal."

"What?" Juarez said. "I think I've already made one deal too many here. No more deals."

"No, wait. Hear me out."

"This better be good."

"Oh, I'm certain it is," Faizah said, giving Ed a not quite reassuring look.

"It is. Really. At the loading dock, Thiegold mentioned something about a partnership with 4th Orbit."

"Why would he cut you in?" Juarez asked.

"We do a lot of shipping, not just on our own tugs. My uncle could generate a lot of business for Thiegold."

"I see what you're driving at, Ed," Faizah said. "I'm sure Thiegold was planning to hold all the strings, but he'd offer 4th Orbit enough to make sure Chubeck didn't cause trouble. It could have turned out profitable for both sides."

"How does that help us?" Juarez said. "Thiegold's not going to want to make a deal with you now."

"But now, he has to," Ed said. "We've got the prototype."

"And we tell him the only way this works is if it's a shared project," Faizah said. "It makes sense. If we just turn this over to OSAR, the prototype becomes evidence, and the rights to it become entangled in lawsuits from all the investors. But 4th Orbit trying to develop the drive alone with Thiegold still out there doesn't work either."

"It's starting to make too much sense," Juarez said. "How do I know you won't double cross me?"

"Because you have the gun," Faizah said.

"Remember that. I've had enough double crosses in this job."

"Really? You've had others?" Faizah asked.

"Never mind. How do we pull this off?"

"First," Ed said, "let's find out what's happening at Minglong's."

"You think I'm going to let you make a call?"

"Minglong's lab is the best place to meet with Thiegold," Ed said. "If he did send anyone over there to look for us, they're probably gone by now."

"How do you know?"

"I don't. That's why I need to call."

"Ok. Use the lab phone – on speaker."

Ed punched in Minglong's number on a wall set. The monk answered quickly.

"Minglong's."

"It's Ed. Do you have company?"

"Just from your ship. Some men showed up from Astech, and I blessed them. They seemed confused by that. They had a look around, but then a couple of officers from OSAR arrived, and the Astech men decided to leave."

"Are the OSAR officers still there?" Ed asked. Juarez raised his gun and clicked off the safety.

"They're out in the hallway, by the door, checking anyone who comes in," Minglong answered.

"Do you know them?"

"No, but I think one of them knows you. Tall, blond. Stan I think his name was."

"Stan Olas?"

"Yes, that's it."

"Good. He's all right."

"They're looking for you," Minglong said. "Lenowitz desperately wants to reach you, but your com must be off. He wants you to call him."

"Later. Let's leave OSAR out of this for now." Ed said. Juarez lowered his gun, but kept the safety off. Ed continued, trying to hold down his nervousness. "Listen, Minglong, you and the others stay put in your lab. It's safer. Tell Manny we can leave my ship unmanned for now. Just don't let anyone else in until we get there. We're going to come back to your lab through the airlock in maybe 40 minutes. Watch for us."

"Are you all right?"

"So far. But we're going to have to play it close to the edge to keep it that way."

Ed clicked off. Juarez looked like he was going to shoot him anyway.

"Are you crazy? You expect us to go back to that lab with OSAR at the door?"

"It's perfect," Ed said. "No, really. Thiegold can't send anyone busting through a guarded front door, and there's no way they can break in through the airlock. We only let in who we want to let in. And no one will pull anything with OSAR guards in the hallway."

"Aren't we supposed to pull something, like a murder?" Juarez said.

"Ok, there's that. We tell Thiegold he has to meet us at the lab, but he has to enter through the airlock, and take out the prototype the same way."

"He may want to make sure we have it before he arrives," Faizah said. "So we let one of his techs come in through the front door to inspect the crate. We know he can't bring in a gun that way because of the OSAR guards. The tech confirms we have the prototype, and Thiegold uses the airlock."

Juarez clicked his gun's safety back on.

"And then what?"

"Then what? Well, he comes in, and we … and – Faizah?"

Faizah gave Ed a smirk. "Oh, and you were doing so well, too," she said. "Well then, we could keep it simple and just shoot him when we open our side of the airlock."

"Do you think I'm going to give you my gun?"

"Ok, we open the hatch and you shoot him."

"Then you'd have something more on me."

"We'd still be accomplices," Ed said, but Faizah gave him an exasperated look. "Just trying to be helpful."

"Not helpful enough," Juarez snarled. "I'm swinging back to just shooting you two, blowing up the prototype and taking my chances with OSAR."

"Can we wait until Thiegold is in the airlock and removes his helmet," Faizah said, "then open the outside hatch?"

"Won't work," Juarez said. "We'd have to re-engineer the circuitry to overcome the safety locks when the airlock is pressurized. And there's an emergency button inside to stop depressurization."

"Wait a minute," Ed said. "Thiegold will come to listen to our offer, but what are the chances of his accepting it?"

"Pretty slim, I would think," Faizah said. "We could make it impossible."

"And Thiegold as much as admitted to me he was carrying a gun. What are the chances of his using it or waving it around when he says no deal?"

"Very good," she said, "if that's the word for it."

"But then it is a clear case of self defense. Juarez, all you have to do is hide in the lab – and there are plenty of places to hide – and when Thiegold pulls his gun, you shoot him. We tell OSAR your were our backup. We still can't turn you in without your lawyer making things way too complicated for us."

"But you still have to keep us alive," Faizah said, "because you need us to back up your story."

"What about Averink's prototype?"

"We throw it outside, and you dispose of it in your own expert way," Ed said. "You didn't bring the gun on board the *Zach*, so I'm guessing you have a place on Ceres to stash your equipment, like guns and explosives."

"Don't guess too much, but yeah, I have what I need."

"There you go," Ed said, checking the time. "Let's get going. I'm sure Larry has a suit that will fit you."

There were three spacesuits in the locker, and the largest one fit Juarez. He made Ed and Faizah stand against the airlock's outside hatch while he suited up. Juarez took the stunner he found on Faizah and the scanner he found on Ed and put them into a pocket on the suit's pant leg. The gun he held in the open. The gun was customized so he could still fire it despite the bulky gloves.

"Your radios stay off," Juarez warned. "If you try anything, I'll shoot both of you and destroy the prototype on the spot." He slammed his helmet shut, and Ed and Faizah sealed their own suits. They depressurized the airlock and stepped out onto the crater floor.

There were a couple of taxis on the far side of the crater, and two suited figures were hauling some equipment into another workshop. Even if the two looked up from their work, they wouldn't have seen anything strange about Ed and Faizah carrying the crate, or Juarez trailing behind. They were too far away to see the gun Juarez carried against his leg.

Minglong apparently did see them approach and opened the airlock door. Ed and Faizah carried the crate in, but a flash of blue light stopped them. Ed dropped his end of the crate and whirled in time to see Juarez falling to the ground, sparks still flying off his suit, and a fourth suited figure come up and kick the gun away. Ed switched on his radio.

"Laura, is that you?"

"Right you are, love. I wasn't sure I was going to be able to figure out who to zap, but him carrying the gun made it easy. Who is he?"

"Juarez, from the flight."

"Ow! I liked him. He used to let me win at cards, or else he was lousy at the game."

"Let's drag him in and get the door closed, quickly."

"I have his gun," Faizah said, brushing dust off the weapon.

"Make sure you get the stunner out of his pocket, and fast," Ed said. "The suit would have protected him from much of the charge. He's already coming around."

Juarez's arm flailed at Faizah when she tried to open his pant leg pocket, but he stopped when he saw her point his gun at his face plate. "That's better," she said, digging out the stunner and the scanner. Juarez couldn't get to his feet, but Ed helped him crawl into the airlock. Laura closed the outer door behind them.

"We'd better get his helmet off him as soon as there's air," Laura said. "His suit systems look fried from that charge." As air rushed in, they opened Juarez's face plate then removed his helmet. He gasped painfully.

"I'm ... I'm surprised you kept me alive."

"The issue's still in doubt," Faizah said, still pointing the gun at him. "We don't need to kill you, but no one will shed a tear if we do."

The inner hatch opened to the lab, with Minglong standing by the door controls. "Everyone is all right?"

"Juarez here isn't doing so hot," Ed said, "but yeah, the rest of us are fine, thanks to Laura here."

"I knew it!" Manny said. "Didn't I tell you Ed was sending me a message? 'Leave the ship unmanned,' he said."

"Nicely done, Manny." Ed said, slapping him on the shoulder.

"A real hero," Laura said, and stepped over Juarez to give Manny a hug.

"Me? No, you! You could have been killed."

"We still can be," Ed said. "This isn't over yet. Let's get Juarez inside the lab and close the hatch."

"Should I call in the OSAR guards?" Minglong asked.

"No, I don't want to bring OSAR in just yet."

"I thought you said Stan Olas was OK?" Jessica said. She stayed near the front counter while the others took off their spacesuits.

"I think Stan's OK," Ed said, flipping on a security camera for the hallway. "But I don't know this other guy. We know there are other people in OSAR involved in this in some way, so let's take this one step at a time."

The lab phone chimed, and Minglong answered. Then he handed the handset to Ed.

"It's for you. It's Thiegold."

Ed took the receiver. "It didn't take you long to call."

"Ed, you knew I'd have someone watching."

"It saves me from contacting you."

"Oh, now you want to deal?"

"Now I have something to deal with."

"Perhaps you have," Thiegold said. "I'm sending someone over to inspect the items."

"Just one person, through the front door, unarmed."

"He's an engineer. I wouldn't trust him with a gun. When I receive his assurance, I'll arrive through the airlock. Acceptable?"

"It'll do," Ed said and switched off. "Thiegold's sending someone over here to inspect the prototype, to make sure we have what we say we have. Then he's coming here himself."

"When you say one step at a time, you mean big ones," Faizah said. "What's your plan?"

"Plan? Why start now?"

"That's what I thought."

Jessica didn't take it as calmly. "You're not just going to let Thiegold walk in here?"

"If we call in the law now," Ed said, "Thiegold just denies any involvement. Who do we have to contradict him?"

"How about Juarez?" Faizah said.

Her suggestion took Ed by surprise. "Juarez? He wasn't in on Thiegold's plot to steal the prototype."

"No, but Thiegold was in on Juarez's plot to plant the bomb on the *New Brunswick* in the first place." Faizah leveled the gun at Juarez, still on the floor but sitting up against a wall. "In fact, you brought him in on it, didn't you, Juarez?"

Juarez shook his head and smiled, menacingly. "Look, if you're going to call in OSAR on this, do me a favor and call my lawyer, too. If you're just going to shoot me, do it. Nothing I say is going to stop you."

"Wait for it," she said. "One way or the other, you're through."

"Juarez brought in Thiegold?" Ed said. "Why?"

"He knew how to set the bomb, but to get it on board he needed Thiegold to come up with a shipping order that couldn't be traced," Faizah said. "They worked together before. Juarez always seemed to be around when someone needed a goon, particularly IDS and Astech. Except when I checked, his connection to Astech always seemed hidden a little better. I asked Lenowitz and he found the same thing. Juarez wasn't smart enough to cover his tracks so well, but Thiegold was. Alan is an expert at rigging computer records."

Juarez's attitude didn't budge. "I didn't need Thiegold. What makes you think I brought him in on this?"

"You said it," she said. "Someone double crossed you. No one was supposed to die, remember? Were you just supposed to threaten Averink to keep quiet after the explosion, was that it? But when the bomb destroyed the tug and killed its crew, you were in too deep. There was only one way to keep Averink quiet then."

"Instead of blowing up the prototype," Ed said, "Thiegold arranges to steal it without anyone knowing, and uses your bomb as cover. Thiegold set you up, Juarez, and because of him, you'll face seven counts of murder."

"I'll take my chances."

"Laura, keep watch on him. Manny, Minglong, why don't you take a look inside that crate. We may not have Averink's prototype for long, but maybe you can get some ideas on what he was doing. Faizah, let's duck into Minglong's chapel for a minute. We need to talk."

Ed took out the scanner from his pants pocket before entering the small room Minglong used for prayer and meditation. It had been a safe-room when this was one of the original living quarters on Ceres. Ed closed the hatch. "How do you check for bugs with this thing?"

"Here, let me," Faizah said. "You put it on a broad setting, and it picks up any signals being sent without having to get close to a mike." She clicked it on and watched the readings. "It's clear," she said, handing the scanner back.

"Good. Lenowitz may have had Olas plant a bug in the lab when he first showed up, or one of Thiegold's men. I don't want to take any chances on anyone hearing this."

"You want to know how we play this," Faizah said.

Ed turned and said nothing for a few seconds, trying to come to grips with some lousy options. He had been in the chapel before, more like a grotto of dark stone with a small, gray altar, lit by synthetic candles. There were several pictures on the walls, including what looked to Ed to be a new relief sculpture of Joseph of Cupertino, like the ones the mission sold on Mars and in the Emporium. But instead of the monk floating against the blackness of space, he was floating above a diffused painting of Mars and its rose-hued sky. Ed wondered if the patron saint of spacefarers covered situations like this, then turned back to Faizah. "Lenowitz is probably on his way, but if we get a chance, do we make a deal with Thiegold?"

"You want to make a deal with a murderer?"

"You were ready to make a deal before."

"I was lying."

"Yeah, I know," Ed said. "So was I. But Juarez was right, an arrangement with Thiegold is starting to make too much sense. If he gets arrested and the whole case blows up, Averink's drive will be locked away in legal haggling for years. If it ever does see the light of day, it's liable to be under IDS control. They'd have won."

"But the alternative is letting Thiegold win."

"For now. But he'll start producing the Averink drive, and that opens up the Solar System in a way that hasn't been done before. We have some leverage. Can't we use it to our advantage and make Thiegold share control of the drive?"

Faizah shook her head. "That leverage could be our death warrant. Even if we could get Alan to agree to some deal now, if he thinks we can prove his involvement in the bombings, he'll find a way to kill us. He's in too deep."

"But we just can't let him walk away with the drive."

"We can call in the law right now and no one gets the drive."

Ed shook his head. "That's what I'm worried about."

"Maybe we'll get lucky and find that Q-disk with the plans."

Jessica's voice interrupted them on the intercom. "The engineer Thiegold sent is here."

As Faizah and Ed stepped out of the chapel, they saw the engineer, with a haggard face, receding hairline, and long, thin fingers, already at the work table where Manny and Minglong had set Averink's prototype.

It didn't look like much to Ed – an unfathomable assortment of tubes around a tank and coils. What part it played in a fusion drive, he didn't know. But Manny and Minglong had taken great interest in it, and the engineer was eager to join in. After a few minutes, the engineer picked up his com.

"Mr. Thiegold. They have the unit. I recognize it as the one we picked up. And the other package is here too, in decent shape." He switched off. "Thiegold will be right here," he said, then added excitedly, "You know, this is the first chance I've had to really take a good look at this. There wasn't room in the taxi to take it out of its crate."

"Engineers. You gotta love 'em," Laura said.

Faizah went to the airlock controls to wait for Thiegold. As she did, Jessica came up to Ed, her anxiety clear to see on her face and hear in her voice. "You have to call in OSAR now before Thiegold arrives."

"We can't. We have to play this out. OSAR is right outside the door. If things get too tense, just scream and they'll come busting in."

"That may be too late."

"Too late for what? He can't shoot us here, and we can search him when he arrives."

"That's not what I mean."

"Then what?"

"He's here," Faizah called out. Jessica said nothing.

"Let him in," Ed said, "and keep your gun on him until I can search him."

The inner hatch slid open, but Thiegold didn't step inside. He took off his helmet, but made no motion to remove the rest of his suit. "I can't stay long, in case Capt. Lenowitz was watching just as I was." He moved to unzip a pocket.

"Easy," Faizah said.

"Ah, of course. Ed, will you be so kind as to unzip my pocket and pull out the device in there. There is no gun, but you can search me if you wish."

Ed stepped into the airlock to search him. With Thiegold's suit sealed, Ed couldn't verify he didn't have a weapon inside it, but there was no way Thiegold could get to it. He had nothing else in the outside pockets except the device, an electronic scanner.

"I believe you know what this is for," Thiegold said, and set it on the same setting that Faizah used on Ed's earlier. "Good, there are no bugs in here. I don't need to go in any farther. Ed, I think we should talk. Faizah, please, join us in the airlock, and close the hatch."

"Throw your helmet in the lab, first," Ed said.

Thiegold smiled. "Of course." He tossed his helmet in, and Ed shut the hatch after Faizah entered.

"So you have Averink's component, but you realize the situation is much too tenuous. Your only hope is to make a deal," Thiegold said. "What is your offer?"

"Understand, we can always just call in the cops," Ed said.

"That's my plan A," Faizah said.

"But you don't want to do that," Thiegold said, "because the Averink drive would be buried. And you are in more critical need of it now than ever. With the Serling Heights blow out/freeze out, Mars faces a severe food production shortage, and the new agridome is nowhere near ready to take up the slack. And certainly Chubeck's plan to endorse Sen. Decker's moratorium and go it alone in space has been dealt a fatal blow. If Decker wins now, you will all be forced to return to Earth."

"But Averink's drive saves all that," Ed said.

"Not all of it. Chubeck must give up his independence movement, and his endorsement of Decker."

"We won't agree to that," Ed said.

"You'll have to," Thiegold said calmly, but with a threat unmistakably there below the surface. "The senator must not be elected. But with enough cooperation, and a renewed commitment from Earth, the Averink Drive can be up and running in a year – excuse me, an Earth year, shortly before the election, I think. I'm told the food reserves on Mars can hold out that long."

"So Serling Heights was part of your plan all along?" Faizah said.

"My plan? No. But it is elegant how it all turned out, isn't it?"

Faizah gave him a disgusted look. "Right."

"I don't know, Alan," Ed said. "It's all right if I call you Alan, isn't it? It seems to me that we have enough on you that you just can't walk away having it all."

"On me? I don't think so. If OSAR starts questioning me intensely, I can show them how it was Faizah who entered the program to drop the temperature in Serling Heights, triggering the explosion."

"Damn, that's what I was afraid of," Faizah said.

Ed turned to Faizah, incredulous. "That's what you were afraid of? What, you committed electronic sabotage by mistake?"

"A big mistake," she said. "I entered in a surveillance program on a company in Mars that Astech deals with. Alan asked me to do it when we were still on the Moon, and I slipped it onto the 'net when I reached Mars – before I thought Alan was involved in any of this. I didn't know it was encrypted to hack into Serling Heights' temperature controls."

"I asked you?" Alan said. "Do you have any evidence to suggest I asked you to hack into the InterPlanet on Mars?"

"I see where you're going with this," Ed said.

"I can go further."

"You didn't ask me to do anything."

"No, not you, Ed. But you don't want to push me. Besides, the FBI has always put you on its suspect list. If they find out Faizah hacked in the temperature coding at Serling Heights, it's not much of a leap to connect you with her for the crime."

"There's still Juarez," Ed said. "He knows your involvement with the *New Brunswick* bombing. And he will be arrested."

"Arrested, probably. Charged, we'll see. If you throw enough money and lawyers at a problem, it's amazing what you can fix. And there are people on Earth ready to give me enough of both as long as I have the Averink drive. You can't stop me. You can make it harder for me. You already have. But I'm willing to forget that and even cut in 4th Orbit for a good portion of the business if you stay quiet. Well, a portion anyway. That's the deal."

Thiegold stepped to the controls and punched open the inner door. Inside, Juarez was standing, flexing his muscles to shake off the effect of the electric shock.

"Juarez, I hope you haven't said anything," Thiegold said, stepping into the lab and picking up his helmet. "As a friend, I will get you legal help if you're arrested. I have plenty of resources to get you off. And these people aren't likely to turn you in anyway."

"Just shut up if I know what's good for me, right?"

"Precisely. Now if someone will please take Averink's crate ... ," but Thiegold spotted the prototype on a workbench with Minglong, Manny, and his own engineer huddled around it. "What's this? I only wanted you to verify it was here, not take it out and dissect it," he said angrily and turned to Ed. "I warn you, I will prosecute for industrial sabotage if you've stolen any of its design."

Thiegold turned back to the men at the workbench. "Now pack the prototype back up and put it in the airlock," he demanded

Ed just spread his arms in defeat. "Do as the man says."

"Wait," Jessica cried. "You're just going to let him take Tim's work?"

Thiegold smiled and brushed a hair back from Jessica's forehead. "There's not much anyone can do about it, Jessica – least of all, you."

She slapped his hand away. "You can't let him take it. I can't"

"Oh, let him have it," Manny said, stepping dejectedly around the table. "It's a worthless piece of junk anyway."

"What?" Ed said. Everyone turned to the workbench.

"It's bogus," Manny continued. "All bells, no whistle."

"That can't be," Thiegold said. "You're lying."

"No, it's the truth, Mr. Thiegold," the engineer said, looking as glum as Manny.

"Then they must have replaced the real prototype with a phony."

"No, this is the one we found in that drifting cargo module. Everything's the same, even the markings on top. I just never got a good look inside to see what it was all about."

"Face it," Manny said. "That report you had doctored up to make it look like Averink was a fraud – the numbers were all wrong, but the conclusion was right. He scammed you."

"That – that can't be."

"I'm afraid it is so," Minglong said. "I am as distressed as you are, though for more sincere reasons." He reached into the equipment and snapped off a pipe. "This is just a standard pump component with a few extra pipes and heating elements to make it look like something more. But once we had it out of the crate, it only took a few minutes to realize what it really was."

"Or wasn't," Manny said.

Thiegold's knees seemed ready to buckle, and the pallor of his face matched the asteroid's surface. "Are you certain?"

"Mr. Thiegold," the engineer said, "you could add more g's to your velocity with a suit thruster than you could with this."

"Oh it added g's all right," Manny said, "right into some bank account Averink had stashed somewhere."

"I ... I think I'd better be leaving now," the engineer said and slinked out the front door. Juarez stood up to follow him.

"Where are you going?" Thiegold demanded.

"I'm outta here."

"Those OSAR guards will arrest you."

"Then I'll find a lawyer and we start making deals."

"You can't," Thiegold said. "If you stay quiet, I can protect you."

Faizah took a step closer to Thiegold and gave him a triumphant smile. "You're going to use all those resources you're supposed to have from your friends on Earth?"

"Without Averink's drive, you ain't got squat," Ed joined in. "You're not going to get any high priced lawyers to get you out of this."

"I have a cousin who works here in the Public Defender's office," Manny said. "I can get you his number."

"Shut up!" Thiegold snarled.

"No, they're making sense," Juarez said. "I ain't the smartest guy off Earth, but I can see when we're screwed, and we're screwed. It's every man for himself now."

Thiegold said nothing, taking a slow step back. Then suddenly he whirled and swung his helmet around so it knocked the gun Faizah was still holding out of her grasp. Thiegold dove for the weapon. Laura raised her stunner, but Faizah stopped her as Thiegold came up, waving the gun at the group, then pointing it at Juarez. "You're coming with me."

"So you can shoot me when we get out there?"

"I don't have to shoot you. We can work this out." Thiegold couldn't hide the edge of desperation in his voice. "I still have plenty on them so they won't talk. But you have to come with me now."

"My suit's fried after she zapped me."

"Minglong has spares. Use one of his."

"Just the top is fried," Faizah said. "The pants are OK."

"Great," Juarez said sarcastically. "Then find me a new top out of his locker."

"Hurry," Thiegold said, the gun wavering, but always coming back to center on Juarez. Deliberately, Juarez put on the suit, sealed it, and entered the airlock.

"Against the outside door," Thiegold ordered, then entered after him, punching in a command on the control panel by the inner hatch.

The hatch clanged shut as Thiegold clumsily put his helmet on while still holding the gun on Juarez.

Ed stepped up next to Faizah near the airlock, watching a camera image of the two men inside. "When Juarez was still talking about destroying the prototype," he said quietly, "I got the impression he had some explosives and a detonator on him to do the job. Did you happen to find it when you searched him?"

"Oh, is that what that was?" Faizah said, innocently.

Thiegold began cycling out the atmosphere. Ed and Faizah stepped backward.

"You left it in the suit's pants pocket, didn't you?" Ed asked.

"Yep."

"Does Juarez know it's still there?"

"Oh, he knows."

For an instant they looked at each other, then wheeled around.

"Quick," Ed yelled, "everyone into the chapel."

Faizah grabbed Minglong, Laura grabbed Manny, Ed shoved Jessica toward the chapel as they all dove through the hatch.

Ed just reached the chapel hatch when an explosion ripped through the airlock and tore through the inner seal. As Ed got through, Laura and Faizah slammed the hatch shut and sealed it. An alarm in the lab blared, but became tinny as the air screamed to escape. In about a minute, everything was silent. A glaring red light shown above the chapel hatch.

"Laura," Ed said, "Call OSAR and tell them we're all right." He stopped and looked around. "Everyone is all right?"

"If you call being slammed to the floor all right," Manny said. "What was that explosion?"

"Juarez keeping up his part of a deal," Faizah said.

"Some deal."

Laura was on the com link fast. "OSAR? Great. We have an emergency .... Yeah, I'd say it's a big emergency .... Yes, but .... Listen you twit, that explosion is what I'm calling about. That was us. Well, not us exactly .... Yeah, we're all right. We're locked up in Minglong's safe room. I don't know about a couple guys who were in the airlock .... Terrif." She clicked off the lab com and turned to Ed. "An OSAR lieutenant said they'll get to us soon.

"Good," Ed said, and turned to face Jessica. She was sitting on the floor, her arms wrapped around her knees, rocking slowly. "Jessica, we don't have much time. It won't take OSAR long to seal the airlock door. But there are no microphones in here, we already checked. I need you to come clean. What did you do for Thiegold?"

"What?" Jessica said . "What are you saying?"

"It's what Thiegold said when you protested him taking the prototype – that none of us could stop him, 'least of all you.' What did he have on you, Jessica?"

"Nothing."

"Nothing?"

"I'm telling you the truth."

"Stop it." Ed raised his hands in exasperation and paced the floor. "I don't know if I've ever heard the truth from you. Lenowitz said you're a bad liar, but you keep practicing. You said you didn't know we were coming to Ceres until we hired you, but the other passengers already told you the *Zach* was taking them here. You told Lenowitz you didn't know Averink, but in fact you were lovers. And why was everyone on Mars looking for Averink's plans on a Q-disk?"

"I told you I don't have that Q-disk."

"How did they know to even look for it unless someone told them, someone close enough to Averink to know he was using a Q-disk?"

"We weren't that close anymore."

Ed extended a hand to help her up from the floor. "You loved him."

"He loved his work."

"Yet you followed him to the Moon, and you were ready to follow him to Mars."

"Yeah, I guess I was." Jessica took his hand and stood up, gently to not bounce too high in Ceres gravity. Yet just as her face seemed ready to soften, Jessica turned angry again. "But even Mars wasn't far enough. He had to come to this damned rock halfway to Jupiter – to work with a monk. I finally got the message."

"And you wanted to strike back."

"What does it matter? I've just been trying to forget ever since I got to Mars, but things kept bringing me back, you kept bringing me back into it. Well, the real bombers just blew themselves up. It's over. It's finally over."

"No, it's not over," Ed said. "Thiegold's dead, I'm certain. Juarez may have dodged the blast, but even if he's alive and talks, he doesn't know enough. Someone will take the fall. Juarez for sure. They may even try to pin it on Faizah and me if we can't convince them otherwise. But that's where the trail ends, and the people who want to hold on to power out here will still have it. I'm not going to take the fall for them, and I'm not going to take the fall for you."

"For me?"

"One more lie, Jessica. You said you found Tim dead after the blast, but he was alive when you saw him. George saw him alive seconds after the blast. George said Tim looked angry and said, 'So you did this.' But Tim didn't say it to George. He said it to you. You were in his cabin."

"What's he doing?" Laura whispered to Manny.

"The final scene of the Maltese Falcon," Manny answered, "when Sam Spade turns in the dame."

"So Jessica is Mary Astor?"

"Yeah, but Ed's no Bogart."

"Oh, I don't know," Faizah said.

They tried to keep it quiet, but Jessica heard them. She just smiled faintly at their remarks. "Is that what you're going to do, Ed – turn me in?"

"Just the truth. Then we'll see what happens."

"Maybe they should arrest me. I started all this."

"How?"

Jessica didn't answer at first, as if gathering resolve. Then she started, slowly.

"Tim started planning to leave months ago, soon after that report came out slamming his work. I was just beginning to think we could restart something between us when Tim tells me he's going even farther away. I was irrelevant. I hated his work. I hated that I loved him. The night he told me, I walked out and ended up at a Lunar bar, ready to pick up some guy, any guy, just to spite Tim."

"And the guy turned out to be Thiegold," Ed said.

"Yeah, except after a couple of drinks, I began telling the whole story. Suddenly Alan wasn't interested in me as much as finding out more about Tim's plans. He planted the idea of revenge that night, and I grabbed hold of it."

Faizah gasped. "You wanted to kill Averink?"

"No! Not that." Jessica's voice flashed with anger, but she became subdued again before continuing. "I wanted to destroy his work. Maybe I thought that was worse. Thiegold kept meeting with me, urging me to give him more details. I didn't know everything Thiegold was planning, very little, actually. I didn't really know what Tim was doing. I had no idea the prototype was a fake. But when I had the opportunity to join the flight to Mars as crew, Alan urged me to take it. And you're right, Tim did tell me he put his plans on a Q-disk. I saw him do it, and erase or destroy all other copies except for the prototype."

"Did Thiegold ask you to get the Q-disk?" Ed asked.

"He asked me to try. Alan said he didn't think he could break the code on the disk without the key, but if I could get the disk, the job would be complete. Tim would have nothing left of his work. He would be ruined. Somehow, I came to believe that's what I wanted."

"Alan made you believe it," Faizah said. "He was good at that."

"What happened to the disk?" Ed asked.

"I don't know," Jessica said firmly. "And that is the truth."

"But Alan showed you how to use a scanner to find it – this scanner," Ed said holding up the one from his pocket. "We thought it was Alan's, but he still had his back in the airlock. But only you and George had access to the cargo module during the flight, and Thiegold told you to take one from OSAR's shipment."

Jessica nodded. "The second day out while Tim was at lunch, I found the disk in his room, but Alan said I wasn't supposed to take it until just before the halfway point in the trip."

"Just before the flip over maneuver."

"Right. Alan didn't tell me why. But when I looked for the disk again, it wasn't there. I don't know what happened to it."

"Alan didn't believe you," Faizah said. "He thought you kept the disk. That's why they were looking for it on Mars."

"I thought you had it," Jessica said. "After we had the injured taken care of, we started talking and you mentioned you worked for InterCorporate, as did Alan. I thought you came on board to find the disk."

"And that's why you were upset when Lenowitz showed up with his search warrant that day," Ed said. "If he found the disk, you were afraid it could lead back to you."

"I didn't know what to think," Jessica said. "It all went so wrong. I was scared."

"Did Averink find you the second time you looked for his disk?" Faizah asked.

"Yes. I told him I was there for housekeeping stuff. But I was still in his cabin when the *New Brunswick* blew up. I didn't know what the explosion was. But Tim – it wasn't anger so much as he looked betrayed. I was just scared. The ship kept shaking badly after the explosion. I got out of his room, but I didn't see George, not until later when I went back to that deck and found him in an empty cabin. Then I found Tim. With all the shaking, I still thought it was an accident. I wanted to believe it was an accident."

"Juarez insists nobody was supposed to die," Ed said. "But he was the one who knocked out George and dragged him inside a cabin. He must have hid there until you left. Juarez probably realized already the tug crew was dead, and when he heard Tim blame you for what happened, he couldn't risk leaving Tim alive. The trail would too easily lead back to him. So he killed Tim, and dumped whatever looked like Tim's records outside when he went EVA for me. He thought he had it all. What did you do with the OSAR scanner?"

"I just left it on the ship. That's what Alan told me to do."

"And someone from OSAR, Carstol probably, picked it up after landing," Ed said.

"It doesn't really matter what happened to the disk," Faizah said. "Without the key, it's worthless. They can be set so one wrong attempt and the information is erased. That must have been why Alan was more determined to get the prototype instead of the disk."

"But Jessica brought the key," Ed said.

"You mean, like a password? No, Tim gave me nothing like that. Just that book."

"A book he was insistent you deliver personally to Minglong, a de-livery you were determined to make – out of guilt, love, fate – the reason doesn't matter. The book probably doesn't mean much to most people. But it means something to you, Minglong, right?"

"It meant more to Tim," Minglong said. "It was the only thing that touched him that let him put aside his work for a time."

"I'll say," Jessica said.

"I'm sorry. I don't mean to offer up more pain. I think Tim iden-tified with the author, and was thrilled by his linking of the mystical with the mechanical. He saw the same when he studied the heart of a fusion drive. It was because of that perspective that he made a break-through, one too startling to explain over the InterPlanet."

"Is there some phrase, some, I don't know, saying that he would use as a key to unlock the disk?" Ed asked.

"In a message he sent before he left the Moon, Tim said he would pose two questions to me, and the answer would unlock wonders. I don't have the questions."

"And that would be on the missing disk," Ed said, "as a prompt."

"Maybe Juarez got lucky and threw out the disk with anything else he found in Averink's cabin," Manny said.

"Then there's nothing left from Tim except some words of philosophy," Jessica said. "You shouldn't turn me in, Ed. You should just push me out an airlock."

"The only airlock around here is out of order right now," Ed said. "Besides, Thiegold used you. Maybe you can do some good if you tell Lenowitz what you know."

There was a clanging at the hatch door, and in seconds it opened. An OSAR officer, wearing a space suit but without a helmet, was on the other side. "You can come out now," he said. "The temporary seal on the airlock door should hold for a few days until you get it fixed."

"It is going to take more than a few days to untangle this mess," Lenowitz said, walking up from behind the officer. "I trust you all had time while waiting for your rescue to get your stories straight?"

"Mine's straight," Ed said. "How about yours, Faizah?"

"As straight as it's going to get."

"Good. Manny?"

"Mine could use a little work. The part where I decipher your secret message and come to your rescue."

"This is a criminal investigation, not public relations," Lenowitz said. "I do not suppose anyone – besides Manny – will volunteer to be interviewed first?"

"That would be me," Jessica said. "You'll want to talk to me."

Lenowitz's tone softened. "Yes, I imagine I will. Olas, take her to headquarters. Take another man with you. We don't know who else is still out there."

"Are Thiegold and Juarez dead?" Faizah asked.

"Thiegold, yes. Juarez tried to slip away," Lenowitz said. "He tried to get to a mining tug getting ready to depart. Juarez may have prearranged it as his getaway. But we spotted him and pulled him in instead."

Lenowitz walked over to the workbench and the equipment saved from the *New Brunswick*. "What is this?"

"The stuff dreams are made of," Ed said.

"Averink's prototype?"

"Yeah, but it doesn't work. It's a phony."

"So he was a fraud after all, the final conspirator. Unfortunately he fooled the wrong people, people who were willing to do anything to believe him. Ed, Faizah, I'll be sending someone for you. Do not leave until OSAR personnel arrive to escort you. An investigator will be here to talk to the rest of you."

Lenowitz left, and Minglong turned to re-enter the chapel. "Someone should say a prayer for Thiegold."

"It's a little late for him," Manny said. "Jessica's the one you should be praying for."

"True. Thiegold took advantage of her anger, and her love, for Tim," Minglong said. "It is a pity that Q-disk is lost. It would ease her mind to know Tim's work at least survived."

"I'm not so sure it's lost," Ed said, stepping into the chapel.

"You don't think Jaurez threw it out with the rest of the records in found in Averink's room?" Faizah asked.

"Remember, Jessica said the scanner didn't pick up any sign of the disk when she searched Averink's room just before the explosion."

"Averink hid it somewhere else?" asked Manny.

"Maybe," Ed said. "Minglong, the relief on the wall of St. Joe of Cupertino. It's new, isn't it?"

"It just arrived. It came on your ship."

"Quick delivery."

"A cargo handler spotted the address and dropped it off before taking a load of packages to receiving. It came just before Faizah arrived."

"Who sent it?"

Minglong shrugged his shoulders. "Don't know. We get anonymous gifts regularly. People are grateful."

"This relief is a new line. The monastery sells these on Mars, and the Wayfarer delivered a shipment to Moon for Marta to sell in the Emporium. Except those have a black background of space, not an impressionistic landscape of Mars."

"So, you're an art critic now?" Manny said.

"I learned enough to know there's only one impressionist artist on Mars, and she was on the *New Brunswick*."

"Amy Chen?" Faizah said. "What of it?"

"Amy must have spent some time with Averink. She did a very detailed sketch of him on the trip from the Moon. It really captured his soul, as the art critics would say."

"So she paints a pretty picture. So what?" Laura asked.

"Maybe Averink had two gifts for Minglong. Perhaps he bought this on the Moon, but asked Amy to customize it, say as a price for sitting for his sketch."

"Did Jessica ever mention it?" Faizah said. "She's her roommate after all."

"No, but maybe Averink asked Amy to keep it to herself, and send it anonymously, to make sure the book and the artwork were kept separate."

Manny looked puzzled. "Why?"

"Faizah, about how big is a Q-disk?" Ed asked, taking out the scanner and changing the settings.

"It varies. About 5 to 8 centimeters."

"Say, about the size of Joe's halo?" Ed said, moving the scanner across the relief. It beeped – twice. He examined the halo carefully, then picked at it, prying loose a thin coat of plaster on its back, and the small disk it disguised.

Minglong stepped up and took the disk from Ed, brushing away the particles. "It is a Q-disk. The surface is virtually impervious, so the plaster wouldn't have hurt it."

"Is there someplace out of sight of the OSAR staff where you can read this?"

"I have an alcove I call my study, but I don't know if the officers will let us all go there."

"They're still working on the airlock," Laura said. "I'll keep 'em occupied."

Laura sauntered over toward the airlock, drawing the officers attention, while Minglong and Ed walked over to the study on the far side of the lab. Manny and Faizah followed a couple of minutes behind.

Minglong was already slipping the disk into a reader when Manny stepped up behind him. "Now if you can only figure out the answer," he said.

"I already know the answer," the monk said.

"How? The disk hasn't popped the question yet."

"When Ed found the disk in St. Joseph's halo, I knew," Minglong said. "It was an intersection of beliefs, a convergence of philosophies. Watch."

A question appeared on the small screen. "Where resides the Buddha?"

Minglong answered out loud. "As comfortably in the circuits of a digital computer or the gears of a cycle transmission as he does at the top of a mountain or in the petals of a flower."

"And the will?" read a new question.

"The will is what man has as his unique possession," Minglong said. With that, the disk's program began to boot up.

The monk turned to Ed. "The first phrase occurs near the start of 'Zen and the Art of Motorcycle Maintenance.' It's what convinced Tim to keep reading when he first picked it up in a small bookstore back on Earth."

"The second answer is what you read at the memorial service," Faizah said.

"From the sayings of St. Joseph, yes," Minglong said. "I think Tim at times felt his will was all he had."

"I don't think this is any scam," Manny said as diagrams began appearing on screen. "This looks a lot more complex than would have fit in any crate, but I bet it's the real deal."

"Patience," Minglong said. "You know, Manny, Zen would do you a world of good, and it will take time to figure this out."

CHAPTER 25

Leaving Ceres

The cargo loading was nearly complete for the return to Mars, but Ed was still juggling passengers with the Halifax with less than a day to go.

"The Halifax is full up. I can't transfer any more of my passengers over there," Ed told Lenowitz on the Ceres loading dock. "If you arrest anyone else that I have to take back to Mars, I'm going to have to lease another passenger module. The trip is going to take a helluva lot longer that way."

"This is the last," Lenowitz said. "Anyone else who turns up will have to stay here."

"Frankly, I don't see why they don't all stay here. If they're going to spend time in prison, they deserve to spend it on Ceres."

"There is that pesky thing about having the trials first."

"They have a court here."

"The treaty governments seems more comfortable to have the trials on Mars," Lenowitz said. "Otherwise, It seems too much like frontier justice."

"Mars is still a frontier."

"But Ceres is a barren outpost. No, it is better if the trials are on Mars."

"At least they can't take 'em back to Earth."

"True. Then it would turn into media justice, and that is no justice at all."

"Will Jessica's name get dragged through all this?"

"I do not know. Manny's cousin, he is a good lawyer. I may have been willing to grant her immunity anyway, but he made it easy for me to do. Her information was invaluable for new leads and to confirm the ones we had. But she only knew Thiegold, and with him dead, she may not need to be called to testify in any of the other cases."

"No one else knew about her?"

"Carstol did, but he is willing to deal. It was he who rigged the robot that killed Arthur Strand. He is desperate to avoid a life sentence. The story Jessica told, do you believe her?"

"Compared to what?" Ed said. "It may be as close to the truth as you're going to get."

"You do not think she intended to have Averink killed?"

"As she told me, she may have been trying to do worse by destroying his work. Or she may have been looking to simply have a good cry and fall in love with someone else when she had the misfortune to run into Thiegold."

"Perhaps she did fall in love – with you."

Ed hesitated, and let his gaze stray. "No, she was just trying to forget."

Lenowitz shrugged. "Pity. Will she continue to fly with you and 4th Orbit after this trip?"

"No. She decided to take a job offer she has on Mars. I think she wants to stay out of spaceships for a while."

"So she is starting a new life and moving out of yours."

"You never know; it's a small world," Ed said, wistfully. "But yeah, probably." He made his voice brighten as he turned back to Lenowitz. "At least you're out of my life until the Grissom returns to Mars."

"Not so," Lenowitz said. "Check your passenger list for OSAR personnel escorting the prisoners. You'll see a change."

"Don't tell me," Ed said, taking out his tablet and calling up the list. "You're going back to Mars. How come?"

"The scandal has rocked OSAR very badly. There are special hearings in the EU, the Asian consortium, and the U.S. In fact, Sen. Decker's committee requested I be returned to Mars to head up criminal investigations and, as you say, to clean house."

"But you lose your command. Will they give you the White or the Chaffee when they come back around?"

"No, the appointment will last at least a year, probably longer. They may give me the Grissom again when Nikitin brings her back. Alena will make a good captain. She deserves command."

"At least that will give you plenty of time to get things back in order."

"True," Lenowitz said. "And perhaps, when the trials are over, we will find time to sit on your veranda late at night drinking your beer, with Ariel lying between us, and you will tell me what really happened."

"In time."

"We have plenty of that on Mars. Ah, it appears Faizah is looking for you."

Ed turned and saw her wave to him near the entrance to the dock. "I better see what she wants."

"And I have to see to the transfer of command on the Grissom," Lenowitz said, and walked off to another exit while Ed joined Faizah.

"How is our dear OSAR captain?" Faizah asked. "Is he feeling vindicated?"

"I would think so. He's getting back command of criminal investigations on Mars. He's coming back with us."

"Oh great. Now he'll have the whole trip to grill me."

"C'mon, Faizah, he likes you."

"Sure he does. I'm his favorite unindicted co-conspirator."

"Actually, I'm surprised you didn't know already. Sen. Decker's committee apparently asked that Lenowitz be reinstated."

"That makes sense, but I didn't have anything to do with it." Faizah said, and motioned Ed to join her in an unoccupied office. She made a quick check for bugs with the scanner they still hadn't returned to OSAR, and satisfied herself it was clear. "Maybe Chubeck made the suggestion to him directly, or maybe the senator realized that was a way to embarrass the administration even further."

"Is my uncle still going to endorse Decker?"

"He'll decide when we get back," she said. "He believes he can still make Decker's moratorium work to our advantage, even with the food shortages, provided the Averink drive can be ready in 12 months."

"Minglong and Manny said it will be ready."

"That's putting a lot of faith on a monk and a neurotic."

"I have a lot of faith in Minglong," Ed said. "And while there aren't many things Manny's good at, there are a few things at which he's great."

"Yeah, I heard about one of those things."

"He's also great at fusion drives. It's a hobby of his."

"You're trying to raise my confidence, right?"

"My uncle's confident."

"That he is. We finished the arrangements this afternoon to fund the project, and quietly pay off the remnants of Polaris."

"The researchers?"

"Partly. They finally did show up on Earth. But apparently Averink didn't fill them in on all the details of the work, though the FBI's talking to one of them about that bogus report attempting to prove Averink's work was a fraud. The rights to his research, however, are held by Averink's estate. Don't know the benefactor, but the lawyer worked out a good deal."

"Not such a great deal for me. I had to scramble to get another pilot and engineer for the flight back."

"Eventually it'll be a good deal for a lot of people," Faizah said. "If Minglong and Manny can figure it out, Laura will test fly the Averink drive out of here a short time after the U.S. election."

"I'm surprised my uncle could come up with the money."

"I said we arranged funding. I didn't say it was all his. I've been meeting with Astech officials all day yesterday and today."

"Astech's funding it?"

"Indirectly, and they don't know it. Astech officials here – and everywhere else – were looking for cover after Thiegold's connection became known. Chubeck offered to provide Astech some of that cover, as long as Astech made a substantial contribution to the rebuilding at Serling Heights – and agreed to cover 4th Orbit's, um, damages."

"Damages? That sounds more like ...."

"What, we're playing charades now?"

"Never mind."

"Good. Astech's still scrambling with damage control, though, trying to isolate their top officers from the plot. They fired your friend Paul this afternoon."

"Paul? He wasn't charged with anything. Paul just shipped some crates."

"He did cover for Alan. Maybe he didn't know all that was going on, but Astech fired him for 'improper contact with a company consultant.'"

"I'd better check with him, see if he's still coming to Mars on the Halifax. Maybe I can let him stay at my place when he gets there."

"I'm not so sure you should do that," Faizah said. "Keep your distance until things settle down."

"Should I keep my distance from you? After all, your fellow employee devised this plot."

"I almost wish you could keep your distance," Faizah said. "I've lost track of how many investigations have been aimed at InterCorporate since this broke. My boss suggested I quit the company in protest and reveal its secrets. He even suggested a couple secrets I could use that would sound sensational but not really do too much damage. But whatever I do with InterCorporate, Chubeck insists I'm with him for the duration, now."

"With him?"

Faizah smiled. "With 4th Orbit. I'll be finding my own place when we get back. But so long as you're stuck with your uncle, you're stuck with me."

"That I can handle. But I'm not turning my back on Paul."

"Just don't embrace him too publicly, at least for a while."

"That makes sense, at least until we see how all this is playing out back home on Mars."

Faizah stepped toward the door to leave, but stop and turned back to Ed. "Do you think Lenowitz knows we have the Q-disk?"

"He knows," Ed said. "He's just not asking the right questions so he doesn't find out officially."

"It's too bad we couldn't tell Jessica we had the disk. Maybe she would feel better to know Tim's work wasn't destroyed."

"What makes you so sure she doesn't know?" Ed asked. "You don't think she was actually telling the truth back in the chapel, do you?"

www.ingramcontent.com/pod-product-compliance
Lightning Source LLC
Chambersburg PA
CBHW050017180626
46810CB00002B/463